The Christmas Eve Daughter

Book 2
The Christmas Eve Series

A Time Travel Novel by

Elyse Douglas

Copyright

The Christmas Eve Daughter
Copyright © 2018 by Elyse Douglas
All rights reserved

This is a work of fiction. Names, characters, places and incidents are either the product of the author's imagination or are used fictitiously. Any resemblance to actual persons, living or dead, events, or locales is entirely coincidental. The copying, reproduction and distribution of this book via any means, without permission of the author, is illegal and punishable by law.

ISBN-13: 978-1724734174
ISBN-10: 1724734172

Quotes

You may delay, but time will not.
—*Benjamin Franklin*

Love is space and time measured by the heart.
—*Marcel Proust*

The bottom line is that time travel is allowed by the laws of physics.
—*Brian Greene*

The Christmas Eve Series

The Christmas Eve Letter
The Christmas Eve Daughter
The Christmas Eve Secret

For Delia, and all her dancing dreams.

The Christmas Eve Daughter

CHAPTER 1

Eve Sharland and Patrick Gantly stared at each other, their bodies tense, their minds reeling. Standing in the renovated kitchen of their Upper West Side New York City apartment, the chilly silence gathered around them, shutting off ambient sounds: a distant police siren, and the chopping blades of a helicopter passing over. The silence lengthened, became stretched taut, and felt like a threat.

"I don't believe it, Patrick," Eve said, once she'd finished reading the article. She knew it was about to rupture their lives—their loving and wonderful lives. She sat on the stool for long minutes staring hard. Finally, her attention returned to the laptop and the article before her. She read sections of it again, feeling a dread, like a cold liquid slowly filling her body.

She heaved out a sigh, stood up and turned to face a worried Patrick, his arms crossed against his wide chest. The open laptop lay on the counter, its screen seemingly alive, pulsing out an alarm.

An hour earlier, while waiting for Eve to get home from work, Patrick had sat on a kitchen stool sipping a mug of coffee, munching a New York bagel and surfing his own name on the internet. He'd done it often in the past, looking for Gantlys in the U.S., finding some in Chicago, Minnesota, and Canada. Of course, he'd also found Gantlys in New York, but he'd never approached them through email or letter. How would he have explained who he was and where he'd come from? "Hello there," he might say, "I'm a relative of yours from 1885."

No, he wasn't ready for that. Even nearly two years after his arrival in this wondrous 21st-century world from his now alien world of 1885, he was still finding it difficult to adjust. Although he loved modern technology, he also found it intrusive, demanding and, at times, downright bullying. It robbed people of their innate need for peace and privacy.

The restless sounds of the modern-day streets still jarred him, and the casual mode of dress he thought weird and at times vulgar. He constantly struggled with the loose, edgy mainstream language that was batted around ceaselessly, peppered with needless and repetitive profanity. He did not, in any way, consider himself to be a prude. After all, in 1885 he had been a New York City Detective-Sergeant. He'd known violence, death, poverty, and a brutality that people in 2018 would never see or experience. But he found that this modern-day communication-obsessive society was filled with rudeness and disrespect, and the harsh jargon was an insult to his ears.

Eve had helped him make the difficult transition from an 1885 gentleman to a 2018 guy, but it was often a battle for him to let go of his old ways and his more formal style of speech, which that Eve's friends and parents thought archaic and a little humorous. In many ways, Patrick admired New Yorkers in 1885 for their formalities, courtesies, and mode of dress. They were less vulgar, at least on the surface, and the manners of his time far surpassed the near lack of manners of 2018. To Patrick, it seemed that everyone had a chip on their shoulder and was ready to lash out at anybody who didn't agree with their beliefs, no matter what they were.

Sometimes Eve would say "Patrick, you have to live the time you're in. You can't be an 1885 man living in 2018. It will pull you apart."

And she was right. Patrick knew that, and he also knew that he loved Eve with all his being, in any time or place. She was his pulsating heart, his wife and tender lover; his best friend, who had saved his life. Her time travel back to 1885, their meeting then, and their time travel together back to 2016, were the best things that had ever happened to him, and he wouldn't let anything get in the way of that.

But that afternoon, while Patrick had searched for Gantlys, he'd clicked on a link that landed him on a page he'd never seen before and could have never anticipated. As he nosed closer to the screen, eyes widening, reading the article and studying the grainy black-and-white photo of the young woman looking back at him, he was shaken to the core. He began to tremble, and sweat beads popped out on his forehead.

It was unbelievable. Impossible. How could it have happened? The more he read, the more he knew it was not impossible. The more he realized, without a doubt, that what the article said was, in fact, the truth. The whole, painful, shocking and devastating truth.

It was an earthquake that shook down inner towers and crumbled the walls of past and present. It was a catastrophe. What had he done?

While waiting for Eve to arrive home, Patrick had paced the apartment and then taken Georgy Boy, their half-beagle, half-springer spaniel, for a walk in Riverside Park, hoping a change of scenery would help him untangle his gnarled thoughts.

But as soon as Eve had opened the door, she'd noticed his troubled expression. She'd knelt to rub Georgy Boy's ears, allowing him to lap at her cheek, all the while gathering herself, finally glancing up at Patrick and asking him what had happened. Still shaken, he'd asked her to go into the kitchen and read the article he'd pulled up on the laptop.

She'd done so, hesitating before she eased down onto the kitchen stool, her eyes reluctantly lowering as she began to read. Minutes later, she was still, her face slowly drained of color. The words came alive, and they had a terrible, immediate impact.

The article was an old one. It was an interview of an actress, dancer, and singer who had performed in the first Ziegfeld Follies back in 1907. The article held a secret about Patrick that would utterly change their lives, and Patrick wondered if their marriage would survive it.

The Theatre Magazine, December 27, 1914
Naughty Parts in Naughty Plays
Remembering Maggie Lott Gantly

Some women are born to it, some can achieve it, but it is never acquired by practice or through tireless publicity. It is that ineffable something that cannot be defined by words, cannot be touched and, once held, can never be lost. Of course, I am referring to the innocent magnetism of Maggie Lott Gantly, the original naughty girl. In Miss Gantly's most famous role as Henrietta in **The Silk Lady***, she is frivolous, discreet, conventional and very smart, even if she is not always attracted to the right kind of man. This, of course, is what brought New York theatre audiences to the theatre time and time again, if Maggie Lott Gantly's name was on the marquee.*

Maggie Lott Gantly was the quintessential naughty actress, whose real life often mirrored her stage roles. On stage, you marveled at her pretty, diamond-shaped face, those baby doe almond eyes and the luscious brown curls of hair. Miss Gantly could deliver a naughty line that somehow never went beyond her peach-colored, pouty lips. She could stand willowy and tall, with a hip poised, suggesting a naughty invitation, even while speaking a series of naughty lines that sounded like she was reciting a nursery rhyme.

In the role of Eve, in the successful and hilarious **Up in Eve's Room***, Miss Gantly lost her garter during a 13th-century ball, and King Edward III of England found it near his fashionable shoe. After he retrieved and examined it with much lusty delight, Eve strolled up* *to the king, bobbing a bow, staring at the monarch with Biblical innocence, saying, "Your Majesty, pray you return this most cherished article to me. I fear some rascal is out to do me mischief. I am most distressed and in need of exceptional human warmth and comfort. I believe you, your Majesty, to be the most exceptional human man I have ever seen."*

At that, the infatuated and outraged King turned to the gathering, holding high the garter and, in a booming voice, he shouted, "Shamed be he who evil thinks of it. I shall punish the rascal and rescue the lady."

The audience would shout with laughter at Miss Gantly's all-so-innocent manner and girlish manipulations.

Men on and off the stage realized that Miss Gantly was a dangerous provocateur when it came to love and lovers. The gossip columns in the newspapers attested to that, but theatre audiences loved her as if she had descended from Mount Olympus, ready to bless each one with her incomparable, mythical essence.

Two nights ago, on December 24, 1914, her twenty-ninth birthday, Maggie Lott Gantly was found dead in her Fifth Avenue St. Regis bedroom.

She was murdered in the vilest and cruelest of ways, stabbed to death repeatedly and viciously by her gentleman companion, Big Jim Clancy, a known New York gambler and saloon owner. He was found at the scene, knife in hand, "weeping like a child." He readily confessed to the murder saying, "My dearest Maggie, my dearest girl, is all mine now, and no other man shall ever touch her cheek or kiss those lips."

Some years before, Miss Gantly had fallen on hard times, a result of excessive alcohol consumption, and the taking of narcotics and sleeping capsules. More recently, however, she had seemed to have made a comeback, having overcome her addictions.

Her relationship with Big Jim made all the New York papers, and it was well documented to be a volatile one. People in the theatre world blamed Miss Gantly's decline on Big Jim and his easy access to alcohol and narcotics.

Miss Gantly had always defended him, claiming he was "true" to her, even though it was widely known that she often played the naughty lady with men of influence and status in this town.

Maggie Lott Gantly was born in lower Manhattan on December 24th, 1885. Her mother, a shop girl at the Arnold Constable & Company located at Broadway at East 19th Street, died from complications a few days after her child's birth.

According to an interview with Maggie in 1905, she stated that she was delivered at home by her Aunt Augusta, who was a midwife, who then took Maggie to live with her aunt and husband in Bushwick, Brooklyn.

In that same interview, Miss Gantly insinuated that as she grew to be a young woman, advances of an unseemly nature were made in the home by her stepfather. Maggie Gantly left that home at 16 and never returned.

She began to sing and dance in vaudeville theatres in Brooklyn and New York until finally being discovered by Cornelius Luther and then by Florence Ziegfeld. She appeared in the first Ziegfeld Follies Premier on the roof of Jardin de Paris in 1907, and her fame quickly spread from there.

It was reported that Mr. Ziegfeld was quite smitten with Miss Gantly, calling her 'a bright spark in an often-dark world.'

In a 1909 interview, Miss Gantly was asked if she knew the identity of her father. She was reflective and emotional as she spoke about him. "He was a Detective Sergeant in the police department. He was the personal bodyguard of Albert Harringshaw, you know, and he was shot in the line of duty defending Mr. Harringshaw at his famous ball in 1885. The papers reported that my father died from his wound and was called a hero. There were even songs written about him. I sang one of those songs in my vaudeville act in 1900. It was entitled **Duty to Rich and Poor***."*

Miss Gantly continued speaking fondly of her father. "I am not angry with my father, even though he refused to see my mother when she was carrying me. According to my aunt, one of the policemen in the precinct ordered my mother to leave when she attempted to leave a note for Patrick. He ripped it up. He said that the child was not Patrick Gantly's and that she should never try to contact him again.

I believe my father would have eventually acknowledged and loved me, had he lived. He seemed like a good man. I don't know why he didn't want to see my mother. Well, that happens in life, doesn't it? Whenever I enquired about him, other detectives said he was a man of character, well respected and liked. They said he was an honest man."

Then Miss Gantly smiled, proudly. "I took his middle name, you know. Lott. Yes, his full name was Patrick Lott Gantly."

Then Miss Gantly smiled, a little sadly. "I think he would have been proud of me. I'm sure he's looking down from heaven right now, the proudest father of them all."

There will be a private service held today at St. Paul's Chapel. Maggie Lott Gantly will attain her final rest at Green-Wood Cemetery in Brooklyn.

Eve's eyes slowly lifted from the laptop article. She stared uneasily, feeling a rising nausea. Patrick was downcast, his eyes searching the walls. The couple remained silent, breathing in and breathing out, as if hoping the air could provide some answers.

CHAPTER 2

"Why didn't you tell me you had a daughter?"
"I didn't know, Eve. I swear I didn't."
"How could you not know?"
"Because I didn't."
"You must have slept with the woman."
Patrick turned away, a hand massaging his forehead. He had a headache.
"Yes, Eve, I had relations with Pauline."
"You mean sex?"
"Yes…if you want to put it so crudely."
"Why didn't you tell me? After all we've been through together, Patrick, why?"
"Because it was only one time—it was before I met you…and a gentleman in 1885 did not speak of such things."
"Well, they certainly speak of them in 2018."

He arched an eyebrow, lowering his cool eyes on her. "Have you told me about all your previous relationships with men, Eve? Not that I want to know."

Eve looked down and away. "No... I haven't. Okay, point taken."

"I was lonely. Pauline reminded me of my wife... Her voice, her walk, I don't know, there was just something about her that was reminiscent of Emma. After Emma and my child died, I was very depressed. I slept little and I seemed to be walking in a fog for weeks and months."

"Where did you meet Pauline?"

Patrick shoved his hands into his jeans pockets, looking down at the floor. When he spoke, his voice was nearly at a whisper.

"Pauline and I met quite by accident at a street vendor's cart. It was a fellow I knew, John Weaver. He sold raw oysters. I'm sure you remember those carts"

"Yes, I remember them. I was scared to death to eat from them."

"John had good oysters, and I often got a tin of stew for lunch."

"We're dancing around this, Patrick. Let's just get on with it."

"So, I met Pauline there, ordering oysters. We talked, casually. One thing led to another and we decided to meet the next day for dinner. Afterward, we walked for a time and then...well."

He shook his head and turned away embarrassed.

"Okay, whatever. It's fine, Patrick. I don't need to know everything. I just wish you had told me."

"I was ashamed. It was a night of weakness on my part. It was a night of weakness for both of us. She'd lost her husband from a fall in a construction accident only a few months before. We had those spousal deaths in common. We tried to comfort each other. It should not have happened, but it did. We were both lonely and …"

Patrick lifted a hand and then dropped it. After a heavy silence, Patrick leaned back against the refrigerator and stared down at the floor. "It all seems like a dream now. Like I dreamed it long ago. Like I watched it on that huge TV that dominates our living room."

"Did you ever see Pauline again?"

"I tried. I went to the store where she worked. She wouldn't see me."

"Why?"

Patrick shrugged. "I don't know. I tried a number of times. I even waited for her after work one night. I walked with her for a few blocks. She told me she was sorry for what had happened. She told me she was a good Irish girl from a good Catholic family and that I had deceived and debased her. She told me she never wanted to see me again, and that I should never try to see her again. She said nothing about being in the family way."

"You mean pregnant?"

"Yes. Maybe she didn't know then. I don't know, but I swear to you that I never knew."

Patrick lifted his eyes on Eve. "I didn't force myself on her. You must believe me about that. We… well, we… It just happened. It was a mutual choice. I did not deceive or debase her. I would not do that."

Eve's stare was direct, but warm. "I know that, Patrick. I know what kind of man you are."

"I am not a saint, Eve. My life back in 1885 could be hard and brutal, and sometimes deadly. After Emma's death, after I lost both my wife and my child, that's how I saw life...as cold and brutal. I became bitter for a time. I was not always the best of policemen then, nor the best of men. Until I met you."

Patrick let out a heavy sigh. "But I won't make excuses for what I did. I was sober and clear when I was with Pauline, but I did not know that she was with child. If I had known, so help me I would have married her and helped her raise our child with all my breath and love, with all the support I could give. I would have died protecting Maggie. Please believe me, Eve, I did not know. It breaks my heart to think that Pauline tried to get in touch with me but was turned away."

"Why would the policeman at the desk do such a thing? I don't understand."

Patrick pulled a hand from his pocket and made a vague gesture. "It was a different time, Eve. It is distasteful to say, but that kind of thing happened often. It was very much a man's world, as I'm sure you recall. Men always protected other men. I'm sure the other policeman was just trying to protect one of his own."

"And no one ever told you about Pauline... that she was pregnant with your child?"

She held his eyes to get his reaction.

"You doubt me, Eve? The policeman who took Pauline's note probably didn't even know who I was, and he didn't care. If she had written again pleading for help, some other policeman would have written her back to say that I was not the father of her child, and that if she ever wrote again, she would be tracked down and jailed. Those kinds of responses were routine.

Pregnant women were often turned away with a threat. They would have thought her a prostitute. You see, Eve, desperate women did this kind of thing all too frequently. Some were genuine, and some were not."

Eve stared ahead, remembering the raging poverty in the tenements between East 14th and East 23rd Streets, and the thousands of homeless kids wearing rags, living on the streets and sleeping in the hay barges on the East River.

Patrick continued. "Women had so few choices back then. Pauline was lucky she had relatives to help her out and take Maggie after she died."

"Thank the merciful God for that," Patrick said. "Although it sounds like Maggie's uncle was not much of a father to her." He clenched his fists. "It was such a violent world back then. Children were not cared for the way they are now. How many times did I pass an alleyway to see dirty and poorly dressed Bootblacks and Newsboys shooting craps with their hard-earned money? I knew within a few years they'd be in the police books, soon to wind up in the criminal courts."

"It broke my heart to see those starved, desperate children living on the streets."

"And at the other end were the corrupt political leaders, and the head of the New York City Police Detective Department, our friend Inspector Byrnes, who was chasing us when we escaped to the future. Have you forgotten those things, Eve? Have you forgotten what the world was like in 1885?"

Eve saw a vacant, weary look in Patrick's eyes, and it moved her. Her eyes grew tender. "Of course, I haven't forgotten. I'm just trying to understand."

He lifted his eyes to her. "I would not have turned away from a woman carrying my child, Eve." Patrick hung his head. "I did not know, Eve. Do you doubt me?"

Eve softened, pained by the hard, sad reality. "No, Patrick... No, I don't doubt you, and I don't mean to judge you or make you feel any worse than you already do. I'm just in shock, that's all."

"As am I, Eve. To think that that girl, that famous actress, was my daughter, and that she did not have her real father, and that she died so violently, with no parents, with no one to protect and defend her...Well, how can I bear it? Had I known, I would not have left her. I would not have left 1885."

Eve's blue eyes darkened. "I'm not so sure I like the sound of that."

Patrick, a tall, broad, handsome man with dark blue eyes and stylish black curly hair, stared back at his pretty, strong-willed wife and smiled. He went to her, placed his big hands on her shoulders and gently drew her into him, kissing her hair, holding her close.

"So, we would have lived our lives together in 1885, Eve. I would not have left you either."

"You'd been shot, Patrick. You would have died had we not returned so you could be treated with antibiotics."

"I know, Eve. I know. If it hadn't been for you and your love for me, I would be dead in so many ways."

Patrick held her at arm's length, taking a good, loving look at her. "You are beautiful, you know."

"So you tell me, Mr. Detective."

"Former detective. I am now a student, thanks to your father's influence and the FBI giving me a modern identity. I made my final selection this morning. I start school next Monday."

"Yes, I was thinking about that today," Eve said. "Why did you choose Forensic Psychology and not, say, Police Studies, since you want to be a modern detective?"

"Because I will be learning to employ an empirical approach to understanding human behavior, especially your behavior," he concluded with a wink.

"Oh, I find that very sexy, Mr. Detective. Am I so inscrutable?"

Patrick drew her back to him, focusing on her lips. "Oh, yes, Miss Kennedy, from 1885. You are indeed inscrutable, and deliciously desirable."

He kissed her, his tongue flirting with her lips, slowly parting them. They fell into a long, warm kiss.

As they broke, and just before he moved in for another kiss, Patrick whispered.

"Shall we wander toward the bedroom, so we can become man and wife once more?"

Afterward, they ate pizza in bed, with Georgy Boy curled up on the floor beside them. Eve turned to Patrick.

"I didn't even know your middle name was Lott."

Patrick made a face. "Sometimes when you leave the past, you want to leave certain things behind, at least all the things you didn't like. I never liked the name, Lott. It was my mother's maiden name. My grandfather was British, from Kent. It always reminded me of *The Book of Genesis,* and how Lot's wife was turned into a pillar of salt after she looked back at Sodom."

Eve looked up at the ceiling thinking. "You know, the more I think of it, the more I find it very touching that Maggie used your middle name. She had a lovely name, didn't she? Maggie Lott Gantly."

"Yes… it is a lovely name and ever since I read that article, I feel Maggie's presence around me, vaguely and wildly, almost as if she's calling out to me from some hidden world."

Eve's eyes came to his. She loved his eyes, now filled with so much sorrow.

"Patrick, I know what you're thinking, but you can't go back."

Patrick looked away, tossed his half-eaten piece of pizza in the open delivery box that lay between them, reached for a paper napkin and blotted his lips. His head slipped to one side as he went into thought, and he shut his eyes and massaged them.

"It seems so long ago…that time I came from. It seems like another lifetime—someone else's lifetime, not mine."

"And it was another lifetime, Patrick. This is where your life is now. It's where our life is."

Patrick opened his eyes and turned to her. "And yet, we still have the lantern."

Eve felt her throat tighten, but she didn't answer him.

"Don't you see, Eve? It's as if I've stumbled about in darkness and now I've found a secret door, a door that opens into a past I didn't know was there—a past where I have a daughter."

Eve dropped her mostly eaten slice of pizza in the box on top of Patrick's. As she chewed and swallowed, she felt a rush of heat; a rush of dread. She leaned right for her glass of red wine. She sipped it, tamping down a mounting discomfort.

"Patrick… I can imagine how you feel, but we can't go back. We just can't."

"You said you believed the lantern still held power."

"I don't know what it holds. I should have thrown the damn thing into the Hudson River months ago."

"Why didn't you?"

"I don't know why, but I will. I'll throw the thing away tonight."

Patrick looked at her. "Okay, Eve. All right. Let's not talk about it anymore tonight. Let's watch a movie and forget all about it."

Eve felt a storm building her chest. "But you won't forget about it, Patrick. I know you. Once something grabs you, it grabs you. You will never let go of this."

Patrick threw back the sheet, stood up and slipped into his royal blue robe. He turned to Eve.

"What would you do, Eve? What would you do if there was even the slightest possibility that you could save your child from a terrible fate—a fate that could have been avoided if only you had been there to stop it, to change it, to make it right? What would you do?"

Eve pulled the sheet up to her chin, covering her bare breasts. "What's done is done, Patrick. It's all in the past."

"You're ducking the question, Eve."

She trained her focus on him. "We just barely made it out of 1885, Patrick. You almost died. I was almost a sex slave to the wealthy, overbearing and odious Albert Harringshaw."

"It will be different this time."

"Patrick, we don't even know if the lantern will work. If it does work, we don't know where we will end up. We could both die or end up in the middle of the ocean. We just don't know. We could wind up right back where we started from, not knowing each other, and either playing out the whole crazy drama again, or never finding each other and playing out some other drama, some other fate. It's just too much to ask. I just don't want us to take that chance."

"Not *we*, Eve. Me. You're not going."

Eve sat up, her face flushing with anger. "Oh? And who suddenly made you the king of this marriage. What are you, Mr. Patriarch Man from 1885? You don't tell me what to do, Patrick. If I want to go, I'm going, and that's the end of it. Not that I'm saying that I *do* want to go. And what are you grinning at?" she snapped.

"You… I sometimes forget how stubborn you are."

"Don't change the subject." Eve dropped her arms to her side, shook her head and looked away. "I know how you feel, Patrick, I do, but it all happened a long time ago. It's over. All those people are dead and gone. We have a life here, now, in 2018, not in 1885."

"Again, Eve, if things were reversed, what would you do? If you had just learned what I learned, don't tell me you wouldn't want to go back. Can you sit there and say, No, Patrick, it all happened so long ago, and all those people are dead and gone? It just doesn't matter to me. I can forget the fact that a child I didn't know was mine, died a tragic death because I wasn't there for her?"

It was a cold and impossible moment. Eve struggled to come up with a logical argument. "I don't know, Patrick. Look, we've been married almost two years. We were going to start our own family. We are moving on with our lives. Do you want to jeopardize all that? If we are killed trying to go back to 1885, what about the child *we* never had? What about our family that will never be, and what about the love we feel for each other here and now? What if that is somehow destroyed?"

The stressful energy in the room awoke Georgy Boy and he got up, giving himself a big shake. He turned his watery brown eyes on Eve.

Patrick nodded. "All right, Eve. All right. You're right. I can't deny any of what you say. We do have a good life."

He ran a hand through his thick hair, inhaled a deep breath and let out a sigh.

"We should sleep on this, Eve. It's been a shock to both of us. Let's just let it go for now. I'll just let it go."

Eve tossed off the sheet, swung her feet to the cool wood floor and went to him, wrapping him with her arms, resting her head against his shoulder. She loved the solid feel of him—and that warm feeling of safety and ever-new love. She breathed him in, and her heart thrummed and swelled with contentment.

"I don't want to lose us, Patrick. I don't want to lose what we have. It's so rare, and we nearly lost it once."

Patrick held her close, as the air circulating around them held a sudden restless uncertainty.

"As my old grandmother used to say, Eve 'A good laugh and a long sleep are the two best cures for anything.'"

"Okay, so what did your grandfather used to say, because I know you always follow up a quote from your grandmother with one from your grandfather."

"Ah, yes, Eve, so good of you to notice that. Well, let me see now. Old grandad would say, with a very thick Irish brogue, of course, 'A man in love is incomplete until he has married—and then he is finished.'"

Eve pushed back, playfully slapping Patrick's shoulder.

He cowered, pointing at her, laughing. "See what I mean? I'm finished."

CHAPTER 3

It was the third night in a row that Patrick had awakened her with a screaming nightmare. Eve jerked up straight and switched on the light, gently shaking him. He sat up, his eyes wide with terror, face pallid and slick with sweat, the sheets tangled around him.

"It's okay, Patrick," Eve said, soothingly. "It's okay now."

He swallowed, mouth twitching, big scared eyes fixed ahead as if he were peering into another world.

"Maggie came to me again, Eve, calling for me, begging me to come for her."

"It was only a dream, Patrick."

"No, Eve. It was real. I saw her clearly, her almond brown eyes, her thick glossy curls. Her complexion the color of cream, her pink mouth tight with stress, her face filled with fear."

Eve tossed back the covers. "I'll get you some water."

He clamped a firm hand on her arm to stop her. "No, Eve. Stay. Please stay..."

Eve sat back, covering herself. She reached over and stroked his damp hair. "It's okay, my darling. Lie back down. All this will pass."

Patrick lay back, struggling to settle his staggered breathing, while Eve stroked his brow.

"I went to the Cathedral of St. John the Devine yesterday, Eve. I sat in the glory of that edifice and begged God to forgive me for what I'd done."

"Patrick, you didn't do it on purpose. You're a human being. We have all done things we wish we hadn't. Don't beat yourself up over this. It happened over a hundred years ago."

He didn't seem to hear her. "How do you name the unnamable pain, Eve? The unnamable sadness I feel over Maggie?"

Her eyes darted around the room, seeking some kind of answer. "...I don't know, Patrick. We just have to give it more time."

Outside came a rumble of thunder, and rain began beating against the bedroom windows. Georgy Boy crouched and wiggled himself under the bed, already spooked by Patrick's screaming nightmare.

Patrick turned toward the window, and when he spoke, his low voice sounded far away.

"It's November. I used to love October and November when I was a boy. The change of wind from humid and warm, to cool and crisp. The leaves gradually changing their colors. I loved the smell of burning leaves, all the earthy smells. The smell of the horses' stalls, the pungent smells of the food push carts. I miss those smells. Sometimes I miss my time, and I feel displaced."

While Patrick talked, Eve's worried mind wandered. She had refused to think about the lantern during the past few days. She'd refused to let it gain power over her as it once had. But now, she had to think about it. She had to consider it. She had to at least tiptoe toward the possibility of lighting it again.

Why hadn't she tossed it into the Hudson River? She could have many times. Why hadn't she just thrown it away?

Something pacing in the hidden recesses of her mind had stopped her. If she allowed that pacing animal to speak, she could understand its words.

"You might need it someday, Eve. It has great power, and no one else in the entire world has any idea what it has done and what it can do. No one knows its power—except you, your friend Joni, and Patrick."

So there it sat, in the back corner of her closet, hiding like some live thing, asleep, hibernating, waiting for the inevitable day when it would once again awaken and work its mysterious magic.

Eve recalled the first time she saw it, sitting on a shelf in that Pennsylvania antique shop. She had stepped gingerly toward it, feeling its allure, its strange attraction. The lantern lay innocently next to an old heavy typewriter, both relics from the long past. Why she'd been drawn to it, she didn't know. It was handsome and wonderfully old, about twelve inches high and made of iron, with a tarnished green/brown patina. There were four glass windowpanes with wire guards, and an anchor design on each side of the roof.

She had loved the sturdy feel of it and the pleasing design. Where had it come from? Who had owned it? How did it wind up in Granny Gilbert's little broken-down antique shop?

When Eve had slid one of the panes open to look inside, she'd seen something blocking the wick. To her surprise, she found an envelope wedged behind the pane. Intrigued, she tugged at the edge of the envelope and, with a little effort, it slid out, a cream-colored envelope, glazed with dust and soot.

When she turned it over to see the addressee, a shiver ran up her spine. It was addressed to her, Evelyn Sharland. The postmark circle read New York, New York Main Post Office, December 24, 1885, 3 p.m.

Eve had not opened the letter in the shop. Shaken, she'd purchased the lantern and the letter, and returned home. In the quiet of her apartment, she'd opened and read it. Her heart raced when she realized it had been written by a distraught man in 1885, confessing his love for a woman who was poor, while he was the wealthy John Harringshaw, heir to the fortune of a famous New York society family.

He was full of despair because he hadn't asked Evelyn to marry him and now it was too late. She was dying. Eve read that it had been the lantern that had connected the two: she, Evelyn Sharland, a distant relation to Eve, had come to the man's rescue when his carriage had overturned in a blinding snowstorm. As she clambered into the overturned carriage, it was the lantern's warm glow that first revealed John Harringshaw's handsome and frightened face.

It was that lantern that, with Eve's help, would be the conduit—the object that would bind the two lovers together through the rolling years. Following the instructions in the letter, Eve had lit the lantern, and the magic flame had sent her bursting through a boundary that separated the present from the past. She had landed in 1885, New York.

During her time travel adventure, she had met Detective Sergeant Patrick Gantly and they had fallen in love. Patrick had also been instrumental in helping her save Evelyn's life, and bringing Evelyn and John Harringshaw together so they could marry and live a happy life together.

But all had not gone well for Patrick. As a detective, he had been assigned to protect Albert Harringshaw, John's notorious brother. During the famous and celebrated Harringshaw ball of 1885, Patrick had been shot and mortally wounded by Albert's former mistress, who was trying to kill him. When Patrick was close to death, Eve stole him from the hospital, lit the lantern and returned them both to 2016 so Patrick's life could be saved by modern medicine.

A short time after Eve and Patrick returned to 2016, a letter arrived from John Harringshaw, dated 1930. In it, he thanked Eve for bringing him and Evelyn together. To show his gratitude, he had set up a trust for Eve, which she would receive in 2016. At the modern rates, the trust turned out to be worth over five million dollars.

Free from the past, Eve and Patrick fell deeply in love and were married in February 2017. Eve had the life of her dreams: a man she admired and loved; a profession she loved, as a nurse practitioner; and plenty of money to live as they pleased. She did not want to lose this wonderful life to return to an uncertain past where she could very possibly lose everything.

But after reading the article about Maggie, the daughter Patrick never knew he had, Patrick was tormented and unhappy. Old memories were dragging him into the past. What was she going to do?

Patrick left the bed, stepped to the window, peeled back the curtain and peered out into the darkness. As Eve took him in, she marveled at his muscled frame, his taut stomach, his wide chest and the forest of black hair covering his chest. How much she loved him!

"I feel like a ghost sometimes," Patrick said, staring out the window into the black, rainy night. A ghost roaming lost in a black night like this. I feel like a man who doesn't belong anywhere, and who wanders in a fog. When I read that article about Maggie… when I felt that sharp urge to go get her, I thought: I will be a man of flesh again. I will have something from my time that I can bring back and it will help make me whole and complete again."

Eve breathed in her anxiety, her eyes staring hard at her twisting hands.

"I hear Maggie's plea all the time, Eve. I hear her pleading call to me, her father, to come save her. Don't you see? We can bring her back to this time and give her all the love and support she never had in the past. It is my duty as her father to do that. How can I live this good life with you here, knowing full well that my daughter Maggie perished in a fog of drugs and alcohol, left to die at the hands of some low-life villain? She deserves better, Eve. My mind is aflame with torture and guilt."

Eve wanted to hold fast to the present, to Patrick, to the miracle of their marriage and to their hope for future happiness, and yet she knew now that the only way to keep Patrick was to let him go.

With a weary resignation, she knew they'd have to try to return to his time, 1885, to retrieve his baby daughter, Maggie, and bring her to this time. It was a terrible risk. It was an awful decision to have to make.

"Patrick…" she said softly, mustering the courage to say the words that stuck in her throat. "Let's go back and get Maggie."

Patrick shot her a look, his face stricken.

And then Eve saw a flash of hope in his eyes. He backed away from the window and straightened to his full six-foot-three inches height, looking newly energized, and gloriously sexy.

"Come here, Patrick," Eve said, in a low, caressing voice.

CHAPTER 4

Sunday morning came with a late autumn sun, a clear blue sky, and chilly air that trembled and scattered yellow leaves. While Patrick slept, Eve took Georgy Boy for a walk in Riverside Park. She was meeting her friend, Joni Kosarin, so she could tell her about Patrick's dilemma and their shaky decision to use the lantern to return to the past.

Joni was the only person alive who knew about Eve and Patrick and their time travel adventure. She was an actress, dancer and singer, who often worked out of town in regional theatre. When she was not performing, she supplemented her income working in sales at a camera rental house, renting cameras and lenses to Indie filmmakers and companies like *Netflix* and *Hulu* for their movie production streaming service.

Joni was tall, with a jet-black Cleopatra hairstyle, snow white skin and dark blue eyes that looked out into the world with both wonder and suspicion.

She came striding toward Eve and Georgy Boy with a broad smile, her red purse swinging. She wore skinny jeans, a black leather jacket, gold sneakers and big sunglasses. She was clutching two paper cups of Starbucks coffee, with a bag of cinnamon donuts tucked under an arm.

"Hello, dahling," she said in her affected style of talking, like a theatre actress diva from the 1920s. Georgy Boy's tail went into full wag when he spotted her, and he strained on his leash. Joni had cared for him when Eve had vanished into 1885, and so Georgy Boy loved her. She gave Eve a peck on either cheek, handed Eve her coffee and the bag of donuts, and then stooped to stroke Georgy Boys' head, her lips puckered as she baby-talked him.

They found a bench and sat. Georgy Boy crouched at Eve's feet, his eyes alert, searching for squirrels, his tail flicking.

The girls sipped their coffees and nibbled the donuts, as if small measured bites meant they were consuming fewer calories. They talked about their work and a few mutual friends, presenting their faces to the dazzling sun.

Finally, Joni rolled her head toward Eve. "Do I really want to know what you're about to tell me? I heard the tension in your voice when you texted."

"How can you hear a text, Joni?" Eve asked.

"When you're tense, Eve, you text words like 'Need your advice' and 'You're not going to believe this.'"

"Well, you're not going to believe this," Eve said, with a little shake of her head.

Joni turned away, leaned her head back and shut her eyes. "Don't tell me Patrick wants to join the FBI and work with your father."

"No, nothing like that. You know how suspicious Dad already is about Patrick and my flimsy excuse about why I can't remember what happened to me for all those months."

"Well, I don't blame him. I told you that was a stupid excuse. You should have just told him the truth."

"Yeah, right, Joni. Like he'd believe me."

"And if he did, he'd want to show the lantern to the FBI."

"Which brings me to why I need to talk to you," Eve said.

Joni's eyes popped open. "Oh, no... Don't tell me."

Eve produced her phone, logged in and found the article about Maggie Lott Gantly.

"I'm not going to say anything until you read this," Eve said.

Joni made a sour face as she reluctantly took the phone. She twisted away from the sun, using her body to block the sunlight so she could read.

Eve watched leaves sail and drift while she mindlessly finished a donut and sipped coffee, feeling wound up and edgy.

Eve knew Joni had finished the article when she heard her say, "Oh, my God."

Eve looked at her friend. "Patrick wants to go back."

Joni focused on Eve, giving her a keen appraisal. She handed Eve's phone back to her and then rose to her feet. Georgy Boy got up, looking at Joni, who toed the ground with her metallic gold sneakers.

"You can't do it, Eve."

"Then I lose Patrick. He's determined to light the lantern, go back, find Maggie as a baby, and bring her back here."

Joni's mouth firmed up. "Do you know what I think about that lantern? It's like a ticking, unstable bomb about to go off. It's too dangerous. I thought you were going to toss the thing."

Eve tried to settle the thoughts that swarmed in her head. "I didn't, Joni. I wish I had, but I didn't."

"Well, toss it now. The woman died in 1914. It's over. You and Patrick have it all, Eve: you love each other, you have a job you love, and you have mucho money…"

Eve's voice was low, and she avoided Joni's stare.

"Will you take care of Georgy Boy for me? Will you look after things while we're away?"

"Away? You sound like you're going on a vacation to the Caribbean or something. Are you crazy, Eve? Are you completely out of your friggin' mind?"

"We've planned it out. When we get there, Patrick will look up his police buddies, and he'll find out where Maggie is in Bushwick, Brooklyn. We'll move in fast, grab her and run for it."

"And how will you get back? As I recall from the last time, the lantern in this time didn't follow you back in that time, remember? After you had vanished, the police gave me the lantern to hold on to, along with your cell phone and your purse. They were sure you had meant to hide for a time. You had to go search for the lantern in 1885 to return home, remember?"

"Yes, Patrick and I thought about that."

Joni lifted her hands and cocked her head, as if to say, "Yeah. So?"

Eve shot up. "I don't know, Joni. We may not land in the same place or even in the same year. I just don't know. We may get stuck and I may have to live out the rest of life back there. I just don't know. I've tried to talk Patrick out of doing this, but he has nightmares. He wakes up screaming. He's not eating. He feels guilty."

"I gather you didn't know about any of this? I mean, Patrick didn't tell you?"

"No... Patrick keeps going to the Cathedral and asking for forgiveness. Joni, in many ways, Patrick is still a 19th-century man. And I think, in many ways, he misses his time."

Joni scratched her head. "Okay, Eve. Let's walk and talk."

They passed parents pushing kids in strollers, and Eve pushed away thoughts of her and Patrick starting a family. Joggers puffed by; bicyclers slowed and weaved along the edge of the wide carriage path, and dog walkers smiled when they saw Georgy Boy, who barked at the dog cluster.

"Eve, what if you end up back where you started from? What if you have to do the whole thing over again? What if you don't meet Patrick or..."

Eve cut her off. "...I know, Joni. I know. I've thought about it ever since Patrick brought it up. If we make it back to 1885, all we can hope for is that somehow the lantern is smart enough to at least drop us where we were when we left last December."

"Oh, that's great," Joni said. "So then Patrick is dying from a gunshot wound and there are no antibiotics back there, so he'll die."

Eve stopped short and shut her eyes, obviously struggling with emotion.

Joni went to her. "Okay, I'll stop with all the scary questions. Yes, if you really want to go through with this thing, I'll take care of Georgy Boy and look after things for you. Whatever you need. I guess if I was married to Patrick Gantly, I'd do it too. I mean, let's face it, Eve, Patrick is the hunkiest and sexiest man either of us has ever known. You know how jealous of you I am."

"You have Rick."

"True, true, and Rick is good looking."

"Yes, he is. And he loves you, and he makes good money."

"Yes… But Patrick Gantly he isn't. Let's face it, Eve, there's just something about Patrick's old-world charisma that doesn't exist today."

They started walking again.

"Okay, so when are you two going?"

"Saturday afternoon, November 24th. I need to give some notice, and we need to arrange some things. I'll transfer money into your account for expenses, and I'll give you extra for helping us."

"You don't have to do that, Eve."

"Yes, I do."

"What are you going to tell your parents?"

Eve sucked in a breath. "Listen to this. I'm going to tell them that we're going to the Amazon for a few weeks, to live like the natives. We won't have cell phones; no way to stay in touch."

"And you expect your father to believe that?"

"No, but it's the best I've got... so far."

When Joni turned her eyes on Eve, Eve avoided looking at her.

"Eve, you could still throw the lantern in the river, or even better, you could take a hammer to it."

"And then I'd lose Patrick. I love him too much to see him in so much pain. I keep hoping that when we light the thing, it won't work. I keep hoping that it has no power, or that the power is all used up."

"Have you thought about where the other lantern might be? The lantern that remained in 1885 and got you back home. Do you have any idea where it might have ended up?"

"Yes... You remember that two men helped me get Patrick out of the hospital, into a hospital ambulance, and then out to Central Park. I'll never forget their names: Daniel Fallow and Jacob Jackson. In the letter that John Harringshaw wrote in 1930, he said that after we vanished, a lantern was found on a park bench in Central Park. But then it disappeared, and no one knew what happened to it. I keep thinking and hoping that either Daniel or Jacob took the lantern. I mean, who else would have taken it, if not them? I'm hoping I can find them and persuade them to let me use it once more. It's a long shot, but it's all I've got."

Joni shook her head. "What if you can't find them?"

"Then we'll be stuck in 1885."

Joni shook her head again. "The whole thing just blows my mind, Eve. It's just so weird and hard to believe. I have a good imagination and I've got to tell you, I can't imagine what it must be like to time travel like that."

A pigeon with one hopeful eye turned up and watched them, as a flock of sparrows skimmed overhead and landed in the trees, screeching.

Eve shrugged loosely. "It's another world back there, Joni. It's scary, wonderful and so foreign from this world. The people are different, the smells, the manners, the speech, the food… everything. It's like being on another planet."

Joni thought about that. "Part of me wishes I could go with you."

"Don't even think about it."

"You know what intrigues me, Eve? That Patrick's daughter was a well-known actress and performed with the Ziegfeld Follies. That is just so awesome. Do you know anything about the Ziegfeld Follies?"

"Not much."

"If you were an actress, dancer, or singer back then, you definitely wanted to get into the Ziegfeld Follies. They were massive, lavish revues—kind of like the later Broadway shows and the higher-class Vaudeville variety shows. You remember the musical *Funny Girl* with Barbara Streisand?"

"Yeah… I saw it a long time ago."

"Well, it was based on Fanny Brice's life. She was one of the top entertainers for the Follies, like Eddie Cantor, Josephine Baker and Ann Pennington. Anyway, Patrick's daughter must have been a real talent to be performing in the Ziegfeld Follies, and from her picture, she was a hot beauty."

Joni finally finished her coffee and tossed it into a garbage can. The two moved on for a time, before Eve turned to view a sliver of the Hudson River, glittering in the sunlight.

"Joni... Will you come with us to the park and take the lantern and my cell phone and my purse back home with you, after we're gone? They didn't travel with me the last time and I'm sure they won't this time either. I'm planning on wearing a security belt this time, though, and I hope and pray all the things I put in it will travel."

Eve's words hung in the air, waiting.

Joni zipped up her jacket. "The whole thing freaks me out."

"Will you, Joni? I can't ask anyone else, and I can't leave them in the park."

"Yeah, sure. But if you two do vanish, I'm probably going to faint."

Eve drew in a breath, trying not to sound scared. "To be perfectly honest, I don't think we'll make it back, Joni. There are just too many unknowns. It's going to be almost impossible to find that lantern in 1885. And without it, we're not going anywhere."

Joni stopped; Eve did the same. Joni stared at Eve, tears suddenly springing to her eyes. "Don't say that, Eve. You'll find a way. I know you will."

"If we can't get back, I'll write you a letter and take it to a law firm. I'll have them put it away until December 2018, and have it delivered to you, just as John Harringshaw did for me. In that letter, I'll let you know what happened to us. I'm also making sure that if anything does happen, you'll get some money."

"I don't want your money, Eve. Just come back. I want you back in time for your 31st birthday on December 17th."

Eve fixed Joni with a solemn gaze. "We're leaving on Saturday afternoon, Joni, November 24th. I'll call you that morning."

Joni drew in a worried breath.

"I'll be with Patrick, Joni. That's all that matters."

From the corner of Eve's eye, she saw a splash of red. She turned to watch a cardinal fly by, riding the currents of the wind, dipping, banking and sailing off toward the Hudson River.

CHAPTER 5

Eve enjoyed her work as a nurse practitioner, working part-time in a doctor's office on the Upper West Side, and part-time at a Women's Free Clinic in Lower Manhattan. Just as she had before her time travel to 1885, she now worked with doctors giving routine GYN exams, Pap smears, and HPV testing. She also counseled women on family health, emergency contraception and STD testing and treatment.

Eve was sad to be leaving her work. She loved her profession, the doctors, and many of the patients, and she truly believed she was making a difference in the world.

For all these reasons, Patrick insisted she remain in the present and allow him to travel alone to 1885.

"It is too dangerous for you to go back there, Eve," Patrick had said during one heated exchange. "I know that time well, and I have connections, and I can move faster and more efficiently if you're not with me."

"And what would have happened the last time if I wasn't there, Patrick? You'd be dead."

"It will be different this time."

"We don't know how it will be. I'm going. We're married, and we're in this together."

"But Eve…"

She'd thrown up the flat of her hand, face hard and determined. "I'm going, Patrick. End of story."

Patrick searched online and found a costume shop on West 44th Street, where he purchased the period clothes they'd need for 1885. Some of the garments were made of polyester, which means they did not look particularly authentic, but they'd serve their purpose until he could find more suitable clothes in 1885.

They'd also need money, and Patrick had a solution. When he left 1885, he had about sixty dollars in a savings account at the Seaboard National Bank of the City of New York. That should suffice. Based on his research, sixty dollars in 1885 was worth about fifteen hundred dollars in 2018. That would be enough to get them by. Patrick did not intend to hang around 1885 any longer than necessary.

But if the lantern didn't travel with them to the past, and if they couldn't find the original lantern in 1885, then they would have to grab Maggie and run for it. They'd book passage on a clipper ship bound for San Francisco. No one would dare follow them there, but the trip would be expensive and dangerous, especially as the ship navigated around Cape Horn.

The fare was about two hundred dollars each in 1885, but if they survived the trip, they'd be safe to live in San Francisco, as long as they left before the April 1906 earthquake which devastated the city and killed hundreds. Being aware of that was one advantage to knowing the future. They would plan to be long gone before then.

The Tuesday before they planned to leave, Patrick suggested they drive to the antique shop in Pennsylvania, where Eve first saw the lantern with the Christmas Eve letter stuffed inside. Ever since his arrival to 2016 New York, he'd wanted to visit the shop where Eve's adventure had started.

Eve hesitated; she'd have to take a day off from work and the thought of returning there somehow unnerved her. But when Patrick said again how much it would mean to him, she agreed to drive him. Patrick still didn't have a driver's license, since he'd received his legal identity papers from Eve's FBI father only two months before.

They left early the next morning, on a day that was nearly an exact duplicate of the day she'd traveled there the year before. Under a crystal blue November sky, they drove along a quiet, two-lane Pennsylvania road that threaded its way past bare-limbed trees, gurgling streams and graceful farmland, spotted with grazing cattle, dairy farms and old weatherworn barns.

As they rattled across a wooden bridge leading to the town of Combs End, Eve felt herself tense up.

"Are you all right?" Patrick asked, noticing Eve's sudden stress.

She sighed. "This just brings back weird memories."

And then she saw it—the old antique shop. She craned her neck. "There it is," she pointed.

Patrick removed his sunglasses for a better look. He saw a sun-bleached, sad looking little shop, nestled under stately elms and maples, with quiet homes behind. On the right, there was a large RV partially hidden behind a row of manicured hedges.

The car turned right, tires popping across the gravel lot, and came to a stop. Eve killed the engine and she and Patrick sat staring at the place. They saw a faded sign in the filmy, 12-pane vintage farmhouse windows:

CLOSED
FOR SALE OR LEASE
CALL NUMBER BELOW FOR DETAILS

Eve climbed out into the crisp cool air, with Patrick behind her. In silence, they walked to the windows, shaded their eyes, and peered in. In the dim shadows, they saw a wide empty room—just a shell where dust danced in spears of sunlight. A crow fluttered down to the peaked roof and glanced about, as a motor scooter growled off in the distance.

Patrick drew back. "It's not quite what I'd pictured."

Eve pressed her nose against the glass, remembering the first time she'd come, feeling once again the shock and turbulent emotions she'd experienced when she first discovered her name written on the old envelope.

"The room was filled with wonderful old things...a fun little shop. And the woman who ran it, Granny Gilbert, was a character right out of a Hollywood movie."

Patrick stuffed his hands into his denim coat pockets and stared, trying to imagine Eve finding the lantern. And then his thoughts drifted like the hawk circling overhead against the brilliant blue, cloudless sky.

"How do you think it works?" he asked, as Eve drew back from the window.

"You mean the lantern?"

"Yes... How could something like that draw you back in time?"

"I don't know, Patrick. I consider myself a scientist, and the whole time travel thing makes no sense to me, except that I experienced it. I traveled back in time to 1885 and met you. And, here you are."

Wearing white sneakers, Patrick kicked at the gravel. "I've been reading about wormholes, black holes, parallel universes and string theory," Patrick said.

"Oh, wow, Patrick. That's a black hole in itself. All that stuff just blows my mind. I can't get my head around any of it."

"It is all so strange and fantastic, Eve. I've had difficulty understanding Einstein and quantum mechanics, but I keep thinking that if space-time bends, much like a fabric, and then somehow inflicts gravity, perhaps the lantern is an energy doorway or a conduit, a kind of tool, like a pair of scissors, that tears a hole into space-time and allows us to travel, to slip inside, so to speak, and time travel. But if there are parallel universes, then which universe are we traveling to or from?"

Eve zipped up her brown leather jacket, stepped over to Patrick and took his hand.

"Welcome to the 21st century, where there are so many theories and opinions about everything that your head explodes if you think about them too much."

He shook his head. "This time is so mind-bending to me, Eve. There are always so many things coming at you all the time: all those electronic devices, and things flying in the sky, and there are so many cars and people, and so much local and world news. How can we get out from under it all and understand what is truly going on around us?"

"I have no idea. I guess you just adjust to it. I mean we have to adjust to it, don't we? And you adapt. I don't think a human being can ever understand it all."

"But we must try, Eve. We must."

Eve looked up. "Look at the hawk," she said pointing. "He can fly and glide all over this land, and yet he will never know how vast the entire Earth truly is, or what lives in the oceans or how deep they are, or that an airplane is flying above him, right over there. In many ways, I think we're like that hawk. We lack a broader vision—a greater perspective."

Patrick kissed her nose. "Well... my love, I just hope that lantern takes me back, so I can save my Maggie."

Eve fixed him with a sharp eye. "Takes *us* back, remember? You and me, married and together, always."

"Yes, of course. Takes *us* back."

"Well, the lantern brought us together, and whatever energy or consciousness or intelligence that was, it did a good thing, didn't it?"

He smiled warmly at her. "Yes," he said, pulling her into an embrace and kissing her hair. "By the grace of all goodness, the God of all things did indeed bring us together."

As Saturday approached, Eve grew quiet and Patrick moody. They'd seen to all the practical details, and all that was left was to pull the lantern from the back closet and ensure it was in good shape.

On Friday night, Eve found the closet light switch, brushed aside a rack of summer clothes and reached down for the lantern. She was again surprised by the weight of it, and by its handsome style. Patrick stood behind her waiting, impatience making him edgy.

"How does it look? Is it all right?"

Eve brought it out into the light and held it up. They stared at it with fear and awe.

"Well, it looks harmless enough," Patrick said. "Does it have enough oil? How's the wick?"

Eve handed it to him. Reluctantly, he took it from her and walked into the kitchen and set it down on the table. He checked the oil lamp font and saw that it was at about five-eighths capacity, up to the side filler. He examined the four glass windowpanes with wire guards, and the anchor design on each side of the roof. The wick was also in good shape. To him, it looked like any number of lanterns he'd seen during his life back in the 19th century.

Eve ambled in, her arms crossed tightly against her chest, her face drawn, eyes tired.

Patrick ventured a look at her. "I guess I can't test this thing to make sure it lights."

Eve shook her head. "I wouldn't advise it."

"All right then. We should both get some sleep. Tomorrow is the day."

Eve looked directly at him. "We're going to need a lot of luck, Patrick."

Patrick stepped to her, pulling her into his arms. He dropped a kiss to her forehead.

"It's going to be all right, Eve. We'll move in quick, get Maggie and get out. I've been thinking about it, and I bet you that Danial or Jacob will have the other lantern. I'm sure of it. I'll find them. I was a detective, you know?"

Eve's eyes lowered. "Yes, I know…"

On Saturday morning, Eve went to the Women's Clinic to see a few favorite patients, knowing she might be away for a long time, or even indefinitely.

Patrick took Georgy Boy for a short walk and then left the apartment, ambling up Broadway through Columbia University, crossing the campus, and then strolling south on Amsterdam Avenue to the entrance to the Cathedral of St. John the Divine.

Inside the quiet and cavernous cathedral, he sat staring at the grand altar, lost in prayer and contemplation. He felt at home in this large, Gothic structure, whose cornerstone had been placed on December 27, 1892, only seven years after 1885, the year he'd time traveled.

Again, he prayed for God's and Pauline's forgiveness. He prayed for Maggie's soul, and begged God to allow him the opportunity to right the wrong he had committed.

Finally, he asked God to protect Eve, the woman he loved with all his heart, and then he prayed that she'd forgive him for what he was about to do.

Patrick had decided to take the lantern to the park without her, light it and time travel back in time by himself. He couldn't, in good conscience, risk Eve's life for a wrong he had committed; risk her life in the off-chance that they could survive the travel, much less save Maggie's life and return safely to 2018. No, he loved Eve too much for that. He knew the chances were slim-to-none that things would go as planned. There were no assurances. There were no guarantees. He would not risk Eve's life because of his sins.

He left the Cathedral, taking long determined strides. Back at the apartment, he dressed in his 1885 dark suit, high collar shirt and blue tie. He slipped into his overcoat, slapped on his black bowler hat, checked himself in the mirror and nodded in solemn resignation.

He took the note he'd written earlier that day and left it on the table.

Dearest Eve:

Please forgive me for what I am about to do. But in all good conscience, I cannot risk your dear and precious life on this tenuous and improbable venture. We both know that my chances of successfully accomplishing what I am setting out to do are dubious, and yet, it is what I must strive to do with all my heart. You mean too much to me, my love, for me to jeopardize your life, your work and your long fruitful years of life ahead, for this personal and impossible journey.

So, forgive me for leaving you behind. With a heart that swells with love for you, rest assured I will return just as soon as God allows it. If I do not return, it is because I have failed, and can find no practical way to get back to you. Please do not try to follow me, Eve. It will just make things more difficult for the both of us, and chances are we'll be lost to each other for all time.

My dearest Eve, thank you for your warm love and support, and I will always love you, through all eternity.

Your devoted and loving husband,
Patrick

Patrick grabbed the lantern, bent to stroke and say goodbye to Georgy Boy, and then stood up, giving a last glance around the apartment before leaving.

Outside, the sun slid in and out of gray moving clouds. It was a chilly day, only 41 degrees, with a sharp wind. Patrick glanced down at his watch as he walked toward Broadway. It was three-thirty in the afternoon.

Patrick removed his hat to look less conspicuous, and at Broadway and 107th, he hailed a yellow cab.

Once inside, Patrick closed the door and sat back, as the red-turbaned driver with a snow-white beard swiveled around. "Where to, sir?"

"Central Park and East 66th Street."

Now that it was time to go, Patrick was ready. A fire had been set in him and there was no turning back.

CHAPTER 6

Eve arrived home at a little after four, concerned that Patrick had not responded to any of her texts or calls. While Georgy Boy swam around her heels, she called to Patrick. When there was no answer, she grew even more concerned. She passed through the living room, searched the empty bedroom and entered the kitchen. Her eyes fell on the note, and she froze.

She snatched it up and, with a racing heart, read it. Disbelief surged, then hurt and angry tears. She slung the note away, cursing. How could he do this to her? She had trusted him. He had told her he wouldn't go without her. He had lied, and he had never lied to her before.

Then came the hot panic—life without Patrick. For a few paralyzing minutes, Eve struggled to think. How long ago had he left?

Eve sprang into action, unbuttoning her shirt and flinging it away. She reached for her jeans' zipper, tugged it down, dropped the jeans and kicked them away.

Minutes later, she was struggling into her security belt, her corset and her royal blue, two-piece bustle dress, with buttons up the front. Its low waist and low bust, supported by the corset, were already uncomfortable. She dressed the best she could, smoothing out the folds, drapes and pleats, twisting and adjusting the bulky, restricting thing.

Next, she pulled on her high button-up boots and then stumbled over to the mirror. She looked harried, her eyes bloodshot from tears, and her hair was all wrong for 1885. There was no time to style it. She had to run for a taxi and get to Central Park. If she was lucky, Patrick hadn't had enough time to light the lantern.

As she flopped down on the bed to call Joni, Georgy Boy whined for attention. She patted his head, absently, waiting anxiously for Joni to pick up.

"Come on, Joni. Come on… Pick up. Pick up the phone!"

"Eve?"

Eve spoke rapidly. "Joni, can you come to the park now?"

"Now?"

"Yes. Patrick left without me."

Silence.

"Joni… Please, can you come?"

Joni sighed into the phone. "Yes, Eve. I'm leaving now. Should be there in twenty-five minutes or so."

With no time to spare, Eve swung into her long burgundy Victorian coat, snatched her purse and cellphone, and boiled out of the apartment, turning abruptly to whisper a goodbye to Georgy Boy.

She hailed a green cab on Broadway, swung in and gave him her destination, asking him to drive as fast as possible. The young driver, wearing a Yankee's baseball cap, accepted the challenge with a sharp nod. The cab jumped away from the curb and gathered speed, swerving out into slow traffic.

At East 66th Street, Eve paid the driver and exited, glancing about, unaware that her costume was drawing curious glances, even from New Yorkers, who'd seen it all and then some.

Just as she had done nearly two years ago, she entered Central Park, walking briskly west under a gray sky, against a pushing wind, oblivious to the steady stream of people entering and leaving the park.

Eve pressed on toward the beautiful Bethesda Terrace and the Central Park Mall that runs through the middle of the Park from 66th to 72nd Streets. She half walked, half ran, craning her neck, searching for Patrick, soon arriving at her destination—*The Poet's Walk*, at the southern end of The Mall. She rushed past the four statues of renowned writers, Fitz-Greene Halleck, Robert Burns, Sir Walter Scott and William Shakespeare.

Of course, Patrick knew where to go, and which bench to find. It was the same bench Eve had sat on when she first time traveled to 1885, and where she and Patrick had returned in December 2016.

The wind came in bursts; the sky threatened rain, and as tourists and joggers drifted by, many glanced skyward, their expressions darkening as they began making their way to the nearest park exits.

When Eve saw Patrick sitting dejectedly on the bench, she stopped short, hands on her hips, breath coming fast, relieved, but fighting back anger.

He sat hunched, hands folded in his lap, his face rigid and sad, the lantern standing beside him, unlit. What a picture they were, he in his 19th-century clothes, and the old lantern looking alien and forlorn. Both looked out of place and time.

Eve gathered herself and marched forward, stopping directly in front of the bench and Patrick, her steely eyes fixed on him. It took a moment before he lifted his somber gaze to see her.

She crossed her arms, shaking her head, her face pinched with accusation.

"How dare you do this to me," she said, her voice quivering with emotion.

He looked at her with a tender sadness. "I couldn't let you risk your life, Eve. I just couldn't do it."

"That is *my* decision, not yours. Sometimes you still think like a man from 1885."

He sat up, his face filling with conviction. "I *am* a man from 1885, Eve. That's who I am, and that is the time that made me and shaped me. I cannot change in a few short months, nor will I change being the man that I am. If I did, I would not be the man you loved and married."

Patrick stood, gazing hotly down at her. "I have had to adjust to this time, Eve, and it has not always been easy. It's not a culture that is comfortable to me or, frankly, one that is especially appealing. But I have worked to fit into it—to bend myself to it. However, in many ways, I cannot bend, and I cannot change, and I will not completely change who I am. I did not want you to come with me because I love you, and I need to protect you from harm. That is what a man does when he is in love with a woman. At least, that's what a man does in my time."

They glared at each other as the wind circled them and as a light mist began to fall. Passing eyes threw darting glances over shoulders at the strangely dressed couple who seemed to be having a domestic argument. Or were they acting out a scene, practicing for some play to be performed?

Eve slowly uncrossed her arms, some of her anger melting away.

"Well, okay then, Detective Sergeant Gantly, I guess you told me. Now I will tell you. I don't care what time you're in or what has made you who you are. I love you, and since I married you, Mr. Detective, that means we stay together for better or worse, in sickness and in health, for richer or poorer, in whatever century we find ourselves, and we stay married and together until death do us part. Now, what do you have to say about that?"

Patrick looked at his wife, pointedly. He straightened his shoulders.

"Well, as my old dear Da used to say, 'May you have the hindsight to know where you've been, the foresight to know where you are going, and the insight to know when you have gone too far.'"

Eve cocked her head to the right, a little bright twinkle in her eye. "Is that an apology, Detective Sergeant Gantly?"

He lifted an eyebrow. "No, it's an insight."

Eve rolled her eyes. "Okay, whatever. It's getting cold out here, and it's going to rain."

Eve's eyes strayed to the lantern. "Why didn't you light it?"

"I tried."

Eve shot him a look, gently alarmed. "You did try?"

He nodded. "Yes…"

"And it wouldn't light?"

He shook his head. "It lit, but nothing happened. I sat here with the lighted lantern, with people staring at me like I was some kind of madman, and nothing whatsoever happened. I finally stopped trying."

Eve wasn't sure if she was relieved or disappointed. Maybe, a little of both. She turned in a circle, thinking.

Patrick continued. "As I sat here, I began to think that maybe this was a sign. Maybe I shouldn't try to go back. Maybe I should leave everything as it is, and leave Maggie in her eternal rest, if that's what she is doing. Maybe this is what the fates are trying to tell me."

Eve stood stiffly, already feeling chilled to the bone. "Maggie may be at rest, but you never will be, Patrick, unless we go. Therefore, I won't be at rest, nor will our marriage be at rest, nor our future life together. You will always be haunted by this. For purely selfish reasons, my dear Detective Gantly, we are going to try again."

His eyes widened a little. He turned to the lantern. "But it doesn't work. Nothing happened."

Eve pinched the coat collar tighter around her neck. "Patrick, I found the lantern in the antique shop. I found the John Harringshaw letter. It's possible that the lantern will work only for me."

Patrick's expression turned hopeful. "Do you think so?"

She shrugged. "Only one way to find out."

Just then, Joni appeared, walking briskly toward them, wearing a blue ski cap and brown raincoat. She drew up to them and stopped, swinging her curious gaze first to Eve and then to Patrick.

"So, what's up? What's going on?"

"We're ready to go, Joni."

Joni looked up at the darkening sky, the clouds shrouding the distant Manhattan towers and lowering over the tops of trees. "Well, you've picked one dark, moody and rainy day for it. It feels like the opening of a horror movie."

Patrick looked to Eve, waiting. He ran a hand along his jawline, and Eve saw that his hand was shaking.

Now that it was time, Eve felt a hard lump in her throat that she couldn't swallow away. Her stomach growled, and the chilly air made her shiver.

She inhaled and blew it out, audibly. "Okay, let's go."

Eve sat down, and as Patrick eased down next to her, she placed the lantern between them. He handed her the box of kitchen matches.

"I hope the genie in this thing doesn't have a black sense of humor," Patrick said.

Eve took the matches, her eyes examining his handsome face. She saw the grim set of his mouth.

He jerked a nod. "Let's do it, Eve, and let us both whisper a prayer for our safety and for Maggie's rescue."

Eve managed a tight smile, then she looked up at Joni, who stood stiff and worried.

"I wish I could say I felt good about this," Joni said.

"Thanks for your help, Joni. See you soon."

"I hope so... Hurry back."

Eve slid open the matchbox, drew out one single match and, with her other hand, sheltered it from the falling mist. She opened one glass pane and struck the match, cupping the trembling flame in her hand to protect it. She hesitated, whispered a little prayer and lit the white wick. It seemed to reach out and snatch the flame and hold it. All three watched in tense wonder as the lantern filled with warm, golden light.

Eve gently closed the glass frame. The trio waited, eyes not straying from the buttery, steady spear of light that was swelling out into a cone, slowly wrapping itself around Eve and Patrick in an egg-shaped golden light.

Joni stepped closer, hypnotized by the flame. Eve held up her hand.

"Step back, Joni. Go back ten or fifteen feet. Step out of the light and don't look at it."

Joni backed up and turned away, feeling the first drops of rain.

And they waited.

"It's not working," Patrick said, in a weary voice.

"Stare at the flame, Patrick. Don't pull your eyes from the flame."

Eve heard the soft moan of wind as it stirred across her face. The world suddenly seemed to be melting—the trees, the sky, Joni—as if rain were striking a newly painted landscape, and colored streams ran down the canvas, washing it in a rich golden orb of light.

Eve tried to stand, but her legs were buttery soft, and they gave out. She dropped back down onto the bench. She forced her head to turn toward Patrick but, to her shock, he wasn't there. He was gone. Had he changed his mind? Had he bolted away and left her to go on her own?

Voices traveled to her on the breeze, but she couldn't make out any words, only murmurs. Images drifted by, but with no definite shapes or forms.

Eve heard gongs. They rattled the air and echoed, and the sky fractured, clouds rolled, crumbled and fell about her like large pieces of ice and snow.

And then a powerful cone of blue light encircled her, sucked her up and spun her around like a top until she was dizzy and nearly lost consciousness. Eve called out to Patrick, searching for him in all directions.

In a whooshing sound, she was tossed and thrown helplessly toward a universe of spinning stars and planets, their shapes and sizes distorted. Several clock faces whizzed by, the hour or minute hands spinning wildly.

She reached out to one as it sailed by and she caught it. It was pliable and plastic, and as she grabbed the large, black hour hand, it snapped off and the clock disintegrated and melted away in her hands.

Eve swallowed hard when she saw a massive oak door appearing in the distance, swiftly rushing toward her, closing the distance. Eve struggled to move away from it, as a blue swirling cloud overtook her. With her limbs flailing, working, she strained to avoid a certain collision.

The collision was imminent. At the last moment, she shut her eyes and waited for impact. When nothing happened, she squinted a look. She gulped in air when she saw the gigantic door, towering 50 feet high, motionless before her. Its glossy veneer shimmered and glowed. A doorknob, just large enough for her hand, jutted out, as if daring her to grab for it, and open the door.

Eve shrank away, waiting, watching. Should she open it? Surrounding her were swirling stars and shining planets, shooting stars. She watched in terrified wonder as a large yellow moon pulled the sky open, as if it were a massive theater curtain.

Carefully, Eve mustered courage. She reached for the golden knob, turned it gently and tugged it toward her. Despite its mammoth size, the door moved easily, and it opened.

Eve ventured a look inside. She saw stunning, flowing ribbons of reds and gold, like Christmas ribbon dropped from hundreds of unwrapped packages. She swallowed, gathered her courage and placed one foot inside, into the empty bottomless space.

Some force shoved her forward, and she plunged down helplessly through smoky red and blue clouds, hearing the distant cry of birds and the persistent bong of church bells.

CHAPTER 7

Eve's eyes popped open, breath coming fast. Her head was spinning, body pulsing, and the high, shrill ringing in her ears sounded like the overtones of a violin.

For a time, she was paralyzed, unable to move a limb. Was Patrick there beside her? Her eyes shifted from right to left. No, Patrick was not there. Her purse was not there. Patrick... where was Patrick?

She fought panic. Minutes later, to her relief, the feeling in her legs and arms began to return. Her neck, though stiff, swiveled slowly left and then right as she sought to confirm that Patrick was not seated next to her. Her heart kicked at her chest.

She recognized the feelings. She'd experienced the same dizzy, disoriented sensations the last time she'd arrived in 1885. As her surroundings slowly took shape, she saw bare trees, heavy clouds, and vague pointillistic images passing; it was as if she were peering through a beaded-up windowpane. She blinked, shut her eyes for a moment, reopened them and focused. Something was wrong. Her throat tightened. The world gradually took on definite moving shapes, and she noticed that the passing people gazed back at her strangely.

An attractive woman in her early 20s drifted by, dressed in a sailor-style jacket and an ankle-length narrow skirt with a slightly raised waistline. She wore buttoned-up black and tan two-tone boots, and carried herself in an airy, stately manner, looking at Eve as if she were something to be avoided.

Two other women soon passed, wearing long, narrow skirts that impeded their stride. Eve had seen these skirts in old photographs on *Pinterest*. They were called hobble skirts because they forced women to walk with small steps.

Eve shifted her weight, still too disoriented to stand. Another woman approached, wearing a narrow skirt, a jacket with slightly sloping shoulders and a very attractive dark green velvet hat. She was joined by several other women, all dressed similarly, all wearing hats with feathers, bows, flowers or lace. Most of the hats had high crowns and small brims. Some of the hats were simple, some elegant. All the women wore gloves, mostly white, but a few were brown or green.

Eve instantly knew she had time traveled, from the way people were dressed, the way they held themselves, and how they walked. Modern women had a more carefree walk, their posture was more relaxed, their dress more casual. Fashion in the past was all about status and wealth. Okay, so she knew she had time traveled, but to what past?

Eve sat still, as if the wrong move would be fatal. Her body was sore and bruised, her mind a mass of scrambled thoughts. Men strolled by wearing dark suits, ties and a variety of crown hats, some a rich shade of dark brown, others a subdued green. They puffed on cigars; they had bushy mustaches and trimmed beards.

No, this was not 1885 fashion. Her dress, coat and shoes were all wrong. She stood out. She was blatantly conspicuous. No wonder people were staring at her.

Straining her tight muscles, she turned left and right, again searching for Patrick. He wasn't there. How could that be? They had left 2018 at the same time and from the same place. What had gone wrong? She was completely alone and, of course, the lantern was nowhere to be found.

Her heart sank. Where had the lantern dropped her this time? And where had it sent Patrick? Her worst fears had been realized. She was marooned in some past time without Patrick, and without any way to get back to her time. No doubt he was in some other time, perhaps sitting on the same bench thinking the same thoughts.

With great effort, she shoved her fears aside and struggled to rise to her feet. She pushed up and managed to stand, but her legs were wobbly. The persistent stares from the passing crowds didn't help ease her ragged nerves and self-consciousness. She wanted to shout, "Stop staring at me!" But she didn't. Her mouth felt syrupy, and her breath foul. Her lips felt glued together.

A young woman in her middle twenties glided by, her posture and poise "finishing school" perfect. She offered Eve an aloof passing glance. But then something stopped her in mid-stride, and she glanced back with a look of mild interest. Her lovely dark eyes expanded on Eve, the aloof expression slowly melting into curiosity. The woman turned about, taking hesitant steps toward Eve, being sure not to get too close, in case Eve was some demented thing.

Eve stood precariously, her aching muscles complaining. She had to work hard to stand up without bobbing and weaving like a drunken woman, although in fact, she did feel a little high and fuzzy, as if she'd drunk a vodka martini.

The woman ventured over a little closer. She was well dressed in a blue and gold three-piece skirt, closed at the side, with a smart matching tunic jacket. She wore a brightly colored turban over mounds of thick black hair, with a single feather and a brooch clasped to one side.

She had a small, pretty face with peaches-and-cream complexion. The luminous color of her cheeks added a look of vitality; her button of a mouth seemed prim, and her glowing hazel eyes twinkled with intelligence. In the weak sunlight, her eyes seemed to change from brown to green.

"I hope you'll pardon me," the young woman said, in a breathy soprano, with a slightly affected accent that Eve couldn't place. "You appear rather troubled and pallid. Are you quite all right?"

The language was formal. The words slow, round and well-formed. No modern slang, slurring or fast-talking New York accent.

Eve hoped the woman didn't think she was drunk. She suddenly noticed that the sun was out, bathing this lovely creature before her in a kind of angelic light.

Eve straightened as best she could, swallowed, and tried to find her voice. She opened her mouth to speak, but nothing came out.

The young woman's face filled with concern. "Oh my, I'm afraid you don't look at all well. Can I be of assistance to you in any way?"

Eve nodded and managed to say, "...Thank you."

Eve caught the woman examining her hair. She'd recently had it cut and styled in a 2018 messy wavy bob, just above the shoulder. It must have looked like a disaster to this well dressed, perfectly composed creature from... what year?

The woman extended her suede gloved hand. "I am Irene Wilkes Casterbury."

With a gloveless hand, and feeling grossly out of place and self-conscious, Eve took Irene's delicate hand. Eve decided to use her entire name. It was the only thing she felt certain about. The only thing that would help give her definition in this whatever time and place.

"I'm Mrs. Evelyn Sharland Gantly."

Irene's smile was sincere. "What a lovely name."

As they lowered their hands to their sides, Irene's eyes played across Eve's dress.

"Are you in the theatre, Mrs. Gantly? Are you involved in theatricals?"

Eve's brain went to work, although many words were standing on the periphery of her mind, just out of her reach.

"Well, actually, I was. I mean, well, my husband and I were practicing for an amateur theatrical."

"Is your husband close by?" Irene asked, her eyes searching the area.

Eve smiled, weakly, her stomach churning, legs feeling rubbery again.

"Well, yes, he is. Somewhere. Yes, he's around," she said uneasily.

Irene was puzzled.

Eve wanted to ask the obvious question: what was the date? Where in time had the lantern dropped her? From the fashion, Eve knew it had to be after 1885 and probably after 1900. But she was still too blunted and weak from the travel to speculate further, and she didn't want this friendly woman to think she was crazy.

"Is it Miss or Mrs. Casterbury?" Eve asked.

Irene offered a hint of a smile, and for the first time, Eve saw a bit of mischief in Irene's eyes.

"I am Miss Casterbury. And allow me to be bold when I say that I hope to stay that way for quite some time, no matter what my Mummy wishes. Perhaps I'll stay unmarried for my entire life, and just have men in my life who truly appeal to me, in various ways." She lowered her chin a bit, as if delivering a secret. "Well, you know…"

Eve felt her legs about to give way. "Miss Casterbury, I hope you won't think me rude if I sit for a moment."

"Not at all, Mrs. Gantly. Please do. Can I be of assistance in any way?"

Eve lowered herself on the bench, shutting her eyes. Her head began to ache, as white spots swam about in chaotic motion.

"I believe you are ill, Mrs. Gantly."

Eve fought overwhelming waves of exhaustion, just as she had the last time she'd been carried backward in time.

"I am so sorry, Miss Casterbury. I'm not quite myself."

"Do you have the strength to make it out of the park, Mrs. Gantly? I'll find us a cab and take you home. You can recover there."

Eve didn't want to leave in case Patrick appeared, but she was afraid she'd pass out and wind up in some hospital or police station. She struggled to decide.

Eve's eyes fluttered open. The world was spinning. "I don't want to be a burden, Miss Casterbury, but perhaps I do need to find a place to rest."

Miss Casterbury was eager to help. She took Eve's left arm and helped her stand.

"Can you walk, Mrs. Gantly, or should I ask for male assistance?"

"No, I can walk."

They started off, and it was slow-going at first, until Eve inhaled a few deep breaths that helped revive her. Soon she was walking on her own as they ambled down a winding dirt path, a cool breeze washing over them. Eve slowly became aware that the soft light of day was fading, and that many of the trees were bare. It was cold, but not frigid. Was it winter? But what year?

"Are you feeling better, Mrs. Gantly?" Irene asked.

"Yes, thank you," she answered, as they were about to exit the park on Fifth Avenue. And then it was strikingly evident to Eve that she was in a very different time and a very different universe.

This New York City was as different from 1885 as it was from 2018. She saw limestone mansions, Queen Anne Style houses with turrets and wrought iron balconies, and churches with rising spires. There was the clopping of horse hooves pulling hansom cabs, but also double-decker motor buses and the murmur of automobile motors, their exhausts puffing white smoke—and all were mixed in a collage of motion.

As crowds drifted by, everyone, men and women, wore hats and stylish coats, the men in dark tailored suits, the women in long dresses. Again, Eve felt conspicuous with no hat or gloves or purse, her long winter coat looking grossly out of style. Eve heard the hollering of newsboys as they waved about the latest editions. With compassion, she noticed their old, dusty pants, worn shoes, frayed coats, and tweed newsboy caps. Was she the only one passing them who observed their tired, hard faces, as they awkwardly assumed the roles and mannerisms of manhood? No doubt some were the sole breadwinners of their families; and if they had no family, they were forced to live and survive on the streets.

To Eve, this was a city in transition—horse-drawn carriages and streetcars mixed in with bouncing black automobiles that looked blocky and clumsy as they chugged along the streets.

Eve stopped, taking it all in, jarred by the sounds, look and smell of this strange but beautiful world. As if in a trance, she gazed numbly, feeling as though she'd been dropped in from another planet. And indeed, in many ways, she had.

Without thinking, and lost in wonder, Eve whispered, "What year is this?"

Irene stopped and faced Eve, staring at her in a new way. "What year, Mrs. Gantly? Surely you know the year we are living in?"

Eve snapped out of her daydream. "Oh, well, yes... I mean. Well, it's just that I don't quite feel myself today."

Eve glanced back over her shoulder, fear and dread arising. What had happened to Patrick? If she walked away now, would she lose him forever? But her legs were weak, her head spinning, and she wasn't thinking clearly. She had to find a place to rest.

She fought to keep herself from sinking, fighting a despair that caught in her throat, tightening it. Had Patrick remained in 2018? Had the lantern not affected him? Had he been sent to another time—perhaps 1885—while she'd been sent here? Was he in danger? As she stood there struggling to breathe, she wished again that she had talked Patrick out of using the lantern.

She was completely alone. She had no money. Nowhere to go. She needed somewhere to spend the night, so she could rest, and think, and plan a course of action. Out of utter desperation and fatigue, she turned her meek eyes on Irene.

"Miss Casterbury...I don't know what has happened to my husband. I'm very concerned."

Irene seemed to gain some strength from this. "I'm sure you will find him at your residence, Mrs. Gantly. He must surely be waiting for you there."

Eve held the young woman's questioning eyes. "Miss Casterbury, we... that is, my husband and I are from out of town. We just arrived."

Eve lowered her eyes. "Miss Casterbury, I'm afraid I have to ask you for further help."

Irene was quiet, but Eve could almost see her mind working.

"Miss Casterbury, frankly, I have nowhere to go and I have no money to pay for lodgings. May I please further impose on your generosity by asking if I may stay with you for one night? I promise I will be out and on my way by early morning. If I were not so desperate, I would not ask. I know this is bold, coming from someone you don't know, but I promise you that after tomorrow morning, I will leave and never bother you again. I need just one good night's sleep, and I will be restored, ready to meet my challenging situation."

Irene averted her gaze, her spine very erect. She stood in a perplexed reflection, while Eve watched a flock of birds tumble out of the trees and scatter across the lawn toward another line of trees.

When Irene finally spoke, her voice was soft and kind. "Mrs. Gantly, I must admit that when I first saw you sitting on that bench, I was taken by your rather unusual dress and manner, and by the fact that you seemed very much alone, and highly vulnerable. Mrs. Gantly, I trust you will not think me rude, but I respectfully suggest that you have no husband, or if you do, he has undoubtedly abandoned you and that is why you are in desperate straits and in need of immediate help."

Irene's chin lifted with her firm decision. "Well, I will help you, Mrs. Gantly, or whatever your name truly is. I will offer every assistance I can until you are able to thrive on your own."

Eve opened her mouth to speak, but Irene carried on, a sudden look of evangelistic fervor in her eyes.

"Mrs. Gantly, in March of last year, I marched down Pennsylvania Avenue in Washington, D.C., in the Women's Suffrage Procession, along with thousands of other women. Where you there by any chance?"

Eve shook her head. "No, but I read about it. Please tell me what it was like."

"As you know, it was the first suffragist parade in Washington, and it was scheduled on the day before President Wilson's inauguration. I went with a delegation from New York City. We marched in a spirit of protest against the present political organization of society, which excludes women from voting and from holding political office. We also marched to show the entire world that American women are intelligent and autonomous individuals, who deserve their own political identities. We further marched to show that we are not afraid of the men who think they hold power over us. They do not, Mrs. Gantly. We hold our own spark of the divine within us and we are, therefore, equals to men in every way."

Eve was taken back by Irene's sudden burst of zeal and passion. But when she'd heard Irene mention President Wilson, her mind went to work, straining to remember when Woodrow Wilson was President of the United States. She wasn't entirely sure, having not been particularly gifted in American History. Was it in the early 1900s? 1920s?

Irene inhaled a righteous breath and lifted her head in defiance. "Of course, you won't be a bother, Mrs. Gantly, and, you can be completely honest with me about your husband, or whatever beast of a man it was who abandoned you. If he has deserted you, please feel fully confident in confiding in me. And please call me Irene. All my friends call me Irene."

Eve nodded in compliance, gently reeling from Irene's rambling speech.

"All right, Irene, then you must call me Eve. And, Irene, please know that I am very grateful for your help."

Irene nodded. "Think nothing of it, Eve. Let us be good friends, and let us find ourselves a taxi, and I will take you home."

As they started forward, Eve again glanced back, feeling her breaking heart. Would she ever see Patrick again?

.

CHAPTER 8

As the taxi pulled up to the granite mansion on 48th Street and 5th Avenue, Eve's jaw nearly dropped. In Eve's time, a building such as this would have been a museum holding great works of art, or a library, or a foreign embassy. From her 2018 memory, the building was no longer there, replaced by towering luxury apartments and upscale retail stores.

"Is this your home?" Eve asked, as Irene reached to pay the driver.

"Yes, Eve. It is the Casterbury Mansion."

The ladies exited the taxi and Eve paused, gazing up at the mansion in awe, overcome by its size and rich classical style.

"My father was Silas Morton Casterbury. He died last year, poor Daddy, of a heart attack," Irene said, with a tinge of sadness in her voice.

Irene looked at Eve for confirmation. "I'm sure you've heard of him, even if you are from out of town."

Actually, Eve had only a vague recollection of the name Casterbury. Perhaps she'd met a Casterbury in 1885, during her last time travel adventure, when she'd attended the Harringshaw ball.

"Yes…" Eve said, not wanting to alienate herself from her hostess. "Yes, of course. I'm so sorry that he passed away."

"He was a stern man, Eve. A good daddy in many ways, but austere and awfully concerned with business. I seldom saw him, even as a little girl. Well, that's all past now, isn't it? He was chairman of the Carnegie Steel Company, and he also financed the construction of the Pennsylvania Railroad. I tell you this now, Eve, so that you will know that my family is quite wealthy and socially connected to similar families in New York, Boston, and Chicago. In the press, I have been singled out as one of the richest daughters in all of America, not that I have been haughty or proud by such praise. But I want you to know, Eve, that I intend to be useful in this world. I spend much of my time performing charitable work, as well as working with the women's suffrage movement."

They entered through double wrought iron gates and walked along a pea-gravel walkway lined with maturing pin oaks and red maples, passing a dormant fountain and manicured gardens, finally arriving at the front cement stairs.

A tall, silver-haired butler swung the door open as the ladies approached. Irene nodded to him.

"Good afternoon, Miss Casterbury," the butler said, with a courtly bow.

When the heavy oak door enclosed them inside, Eve found herself in a towering and grand one-story entrance pavilion, with rich oriental rugs and an enormous glistening chandelier.

"Good afternoon, Charles," Irene said, formally. "It is a lovely autumn day, but I fear the wind is picking up and it has chilled us. Will you please inform Mrs. McMurphy that Mrs. Gantly and I will require tea and sandwiches in the library? Also, let Mrs. McMurphy know that Mrs. Gantly will be staying with us for a fortnight or more. She should prepare the West guest room for her."

Eve nearly spoke up to say she'd only stay the one night, but she refrained. Anyway, until she could sort things out, maybe she'd be forced to stay longer.

"Also, please let Mrs. Dolan know we will have a guest for dinner."

"Very good, Miss Casterbury. It will be done," Charles said.

Tall windows permitted an abundance of light, and Eve heard the soothing sound of flowing water in the distance. It was coming from somewhere beyond the wide marble staircase, with its broad mahogany banister, that no doubt led to elegant upper rooms.

"This way," Irene said, leading the way along a marble-lined hall to the garden court. Entering the court, Eve's eyes expanded on soaring Ionic white marble columns, and a large circular fountain crowned by a golden angel with broad open wings. This was obviously the source of the water sounds. Graceful streams arched into daylight, as the fountain spilled over the basin into an elliptically shaped pool below, where goldfish slithered and drifted lazily.

Eve's head swiveled about as she took in the astonishing spaces, with so much to look at.

"This is amazing," she said.

Irene gave her a quick tour of the downstairs, including two dressing rooms, a three-story great hall, a ballroom, music room, dining room, family dining room, library, art gallery, and red and gold anteroom.

They settled in deep burgundy leather chairs in the expansive cherrywood library, with warm amber lighting. They were surrounded by three tiers of floor-to-ceiling bookshelves, with balconies and ladders, and original landscape paintings by Samuel Palmer, Francis Towne, and Copley Fielding.

When Eve asked about the striking marble fireplace that gleamed out old world comfort and privilege, Irene proudly stated that it was originally made in Belfast from three different types of imported European marbles: rouge royal, maxy black and tinos green.

"Well, it is nearly five in the afternoon," Irene declared. "A little late for tea, but I always say, better late than never."

A young, freckled-faced, red-haired under-butler named Mason soon arrived, carrying a silver tea set. He lowered it on a coffee table and then poured the gold-rimmed rose enameled cups half full, leaving room for milk. Eve stared hungrily at the finger sandwiches, artfully arranged on the rose enameled plates, resting on lace doilies. She wanted to snatch one of the white, thinly sliced and buttered sandwiches, but she refrained, feeling her mouth water.

After pouring the tea, Mason dutifully informed her that the sandwiches included cucumber, ham with mustard, smoked salmon and fruit jam.

He lifted the tray and offered it first to Eve, who politely reached for just two, one with smoked salmon and one with fruit jam. Mason then leaned and offered the sandwiches to Irene, who declined.

"Eve, my dear Mummy doesn't approve of my lifestyle, so she probably won't be more than just civil to you at dinner tonight. But then, Mummy doesn't approve of most things going on these days. She says I should have been married by now and, of course, she wants me to marry Winston Capshaw Morgan, who is so very rich, but he is 44 years old, and I am only twenty-eight. I have managed to delay that marriage. But for how long? Well, we'll have to see, won't we? Anyway, Mummy thinks that the old ways are the best days. She doesn't think women should vote and that they have no business in politics. Of course, she adopted most of her strong and inflexible opinions from Daddy."

Irene looked Eve over, with new interest. "We'll have to find a suitable dinner gown for you tonight. Mummy will never understand your mode of dress. She insists we dress up on Saturday nights. My brother will be in white tie, of course."

Eve looked up. "Brother?"

"Yes, my brother, Addison. He joined Daddy's firm when he graduated from Harvard, but Andrew Carnegie, one of Daddy's business partners, took him under his wing. Well, Addison soon had the right contacts to start his own businesses, so he has left Mr. Carnegie and is managing the family interests with great success, at least that is what he tells us. You will find him rather taciturn for a young man of thirty-three. I, of course, am five years his junior and he often treats me as if I were a silly child. Well, anyway, do not expect much conversation from him."

Eve nodded, suddenly dreading the dinner to come.

Irene rambled on about her own charitable works at The Society for the Relief of Half-Orphan and Destitute Children.

"I assure you, Mrs. Gantly, that I feel more like a good Christian engaged in that work than I have ever felt attending the Episcopal Church, but do not mention such things to my dear Mummy. You'll have her reaching for her smelling salts."

Eve knew what was coming. Irene was a curious, self-possessed, and well-educated woman. She would certainly press Eve on her history, and Eve had barely had enough time to come up with a plausible story and background.

Finally, Irene turned her enquiring gaze on Eve. "And where do you come from, Eve, and do you have family in New York?"

Eve munched on her sandwich and took time to sip her tea before turning toward the fire, hoping for inspiration. "I was born in Ohio... and no, I'm sorry to say, I have no family in New York."

Irene cleared her throat and took a swallow of her tea. "And will you return to Ohio now that..." she paused, considering her next words. "Well, now that your husband is missing?"

Eve spoke carefully. "Frankly, Irene, I don't know. I have much to think about."

Irene nodded and then touched her smooth white cheek with elegant care.

"I do hope, Eve, that you have the confidence to trust in me. I can be a good and helpful friend."

Eve liked Irene, but she was young, self-assured and most likely a gossip. Eve had no doubt that she had quickly become another charity case for Irene, and a mysterious one at that. With all her free time, energy and money, Irene would undoubtedly work to pry open all of Eve' secrets. Eve sensed, if not danger, then a possible threat.

After tea, Irene escorted Eve up the broad staircase, down a long, richly carpeted hallway to the spacious and richly decorated second-floor guest room. To Eve's astonishment, it was a private master suite, with its own bath and dressing room, a pink boudoir, a private sitting room and a wide canopied bed.

"I trust you'll be comfortable, Eve," Irene said.

Eve gawked at the room, nearly overcome. "It's magnificent, Irene."

"Grandmother Casterbury lived here for a time, but, poor thing, she began to hear voices and believed she was being visited by various Biblical figures, including Jesus. Mummy didn't mind her speaking to Jesus so much, but she was not so fond of Grandmother speaking to Pontius Pilate. Mummy suggested that Daddy take her to Europe to consult with Sigmund Freud, but Daddy would not hear of it. We had to have her committed to a sanatorium outside Boston."

Eve could only stare at her hostess.

"Now, Eve, why don't you rest and freshen up? I'll have my lady's maid, Mary, come by with two of my dresses. You may choose one for dinner. I'll drop by at 7 p.m. and escort you to the dining room."

Irene fluttered over and planted a soft kiss on Eve's right cheek. "You rest now, my new dear friend, and everything will soon be much better."

And then Irene was gone, with just a whiff of her vanilla and rose perfume left hanging in the air.

For a time, Eve didn't move from the center of the room. She had nearly forgotten that suspended feeling of being out of time and place—that numbing, nauseating sense of not feeling quite anchored in your skin, as if her atoms had been tossed and scattered like confetti into the wind.

Eve wandered to the bed, sat, and then dropped back, overcome by a crashing exhaustion. As she dropped into sleep, she was tormented by dreams of Patrick—of him wandering lost on damp, dark, winding cobbled streets, passing under smudges of yellow lamplight, glancing back over his shoulder fearfully, as if he were being followed.

Lady's maid, Mary Foster, awakened Eve with a light tap on the door. Eve wriggled out of sleep, shooting up, lost for moments until her eyes focused and she gradually reoriented herself. She pushed up, went to the door and opened it.

Mary held two dresses and bobbed a bow. Eve invited her in.

"Hello, Mrs. Gantly. I'm Miss Casterbury's lady's maid, Mary. She has sent me with these two dinner gowns for you to look at and choose one for this evening's dinner."

Mary wore a black uniform with a crisp, white apron pinned to her bodice and a little white cap on her head. She was a thin girl, with a pretty face, curly brown hair and gray/green eyes. She was attentive and carefully talkative, and she spoke with a charming Irish lilt.

Holding the gowns high, she crossed the room to the spacious closet and hung them. Eve observed that Mary had kept her eyes low, her shoulders forward, as if in apology. But Eve felt Mary's restrained curiosity.

No doubt, Irene had filled her in on how she'd found Eve in the park, and about her strange hair and clothes. Mary surely longed to stare at Eve's old dress and strange hairstyle. Eve's antique coat lay across the burgundy settee and she observed Mary's eyes steal a look at it.

Eve decided she had to know once and for all what time she was living in, no matter what Mary thought of her. From her time in 1885, Eve was aware that the lady's maid was often mistrusted and perhaps even disliked by the lower servants. They felt she was conceited or that she might even gossip to her mistress about them. Lady's maids had privileges that others did not have. This, in turn often made the lady's maid feel isolated, as if she didn't quite fit into either world.

So, Eve decided to ask Mary about the date and the year.

"Mary, I have not been feeling well, as of late. What I mean to say is that I am feeling slightly disoriented."

"I'm sorry to hear that, Mrs. Gantly. Can I order you some chamomile tea?"

"No... No, thanks. It's just that... well, don't think me a bit mad, Mary, but what is the exact date today?"

Mary stared, then blinked, then stared down at the thick burgundy and gold carpet, her hands clasped before her.

"Mrs. Gantly, it is Saturday, November the 28th, 1914."

Eve stared hard, with half-hooded eyes, then she turned from Mary, as one thought chased another. It's not that Eve was completely surprised, but finally learning the truth still had an impact.

Eve's mind spun into action. Maggie Lott Gantly would not be a baby, of course, but a full-grown woman, about twenty-nine years old. Unless someone or something stopped the course of fate, she would be murdered on December 24th, only a few weeks away. Eve's and Patrick's burning reason for returning to the past was to rescue a baby, not a grown woman, weeks before she was about to be killed. Eve wanted to drop to the floor and cry. Everything had gone wrong.

Okay, so what was plan B? Patrick's plan to return to 1885 to pluck Maggie away from her aunt was shattered. And where was Patrick? Was he still in 2018, somewhere in 1914, or was he somewhere else entirely, perhaps in 1885? Had he even survived the time travel?

"Are you sure you wouldn't like some tea, Mrs. Gantly?" Mary asked. "You look quite pale."

Eve shut her eyes and massaged her forehead. "No, thank you, Mary. I'm just not quite myself today, that's all. I'll be fine… It's just that…"

And then Eve's voice trailed off and Mary stood in silence, waiting.

But Eve wasn't fine. She felt the burn of panic fill her chest. She had no idea what she was going to do.

CHAPTER 9

Eve went into survival mode. The practical machinery of her mind began to take over. The nurse in her shoved away the fears, the judgments, and the wild extravagant emotions. She reawakened her practiced and developed skills and fell into the meditation of a problem solver.

Eve opened her eyes. Mary Foster was still standing by, waiting, her eyes shifting.

"I'm sorry Mary. Will you excuse me for a moment, while I freshen up in the bathroom?"

Minutes later, Eve returned to the patient Mary, whom Eve noticed was not standing in the same place as she was when Eve excused herself. She had probably searched the room for clues.

The water Eve had splashed on her face had helped. The time alone, staring at herself in the mirror, helped her regain her center.

Eve smiled pleasantly. "Well, I guess I'd better get dressed for dinner, Mary."

Mary nodded, moving toward her to help her undress. Eve suddenly remembered her security belt. She spotted a screen on the far side of the room and quickly moved toward it. "You must tell me where you come from," Eve said, hoping to distract Mary with conversation. She slipped behind the screen. "You have a beautiful Irish accent."

"Yes, Ma'am. I'm from Kenmare, south of County Kerry. Perhaps you have heard of Kenmare lace, Mrs. Gantly?"

"I'm afraid I haven't," Eve said.

"In the 1860s, a lace-working industry was established at a convent there, and Kenmare lace is now known worldwide. My grandmother worked there for a time."

As Mary spoke, Eve quickly removed her old dress, slipped out of her security belt and hid it under the skirt of an upholstered chair. Eve had not yet examined the contents to see if anything survived the time travel. She'd have to do that after dinner.

With just her corset and underwear on, Eve slipped in front of the screen. Mary examined her and then suggested a newer corset that would provide the long, smooth hipline needed for the extravagant dresses Irene had offered. How Eve hated wearing a corset! It cut off her air and blood supply and—there was no denying it—it made her feel bound and trapped.

After Mary removed the old corset, she placed the new one on Eve but kept it loose. Then she led Eve to the ornate dresser, where she held the chair for Eve to sit behind a tall, gilded mirror, complete with carved cupids and maidens.

Eve breathed in. It was time for a 1914 hairstyle.

"Miss Gantly, normally I would curl your hair using curling tongs, but I'm afraid we have no time for that. Miss Casterbury suggested I do a more simple but graceful hairstyle for this evening."

Eve grinned to herself. Irene was definitely in charge, vigilantly aware that Eve's modern hairstyle was not appropriate for this time. No doubt Irene's mother would be scrutinizing every detail and eccentric aspect of Irene's new-found friend.

"Yes, Mary, whatever style you choose, I'm sure will be the right one."

Mary went to work, backcombing, going for a pompadour style using back hair Tournure Frames, false curls, switches, and frizzle. All the back hair was pulled together into a flat coil and then drawn onto the crown of the head. Eve was impressed by Mary's nimble fingers, speed, and skill. When Mary was finished, Eve stared back at a woman she hardly knew.

"You have lovely thick hair, Mrs. Gantly."

Mary stepped back, appraising her work with some pride, moving her head from right to left in smiling approval. "Mrs. Gantly, you look positively regal."

"Thank you, Mary. You are an artist."

Mary blushed with pleasure. "Thank you, Mum."

With no time to spare, Mary applied makeup, or what there was of it. It was a light powder only, no lip rouge or lipstick or blush.

Eve pursed her lips in thought. "I suppose you don't use rouge or blush?" Eve asked.

Mary held Eve's stare. "Oh, no, Mrs. Gantly. Mrs. Katherine Casterbury would never allow rouge or blush in her presence. She still doesn't even use the telephone to speak with friends outside the house. She sends invitations. Mrs. Casterbury likes the old ways."

Eve nodded with a tight smile. "Of course, Mary."

Eve stood up, so Mary could tighten the dreaded corset. Eve's natural waist was 24 inches. She knew from her past time travel experience that the wished-for waist size was probably 18 inches. Eve told Mary that she would be happy with 20 inches, which Mary achieved by tugging and tightening the waist cords, cutting the four inches off Eve's natural waist size.

As Mary worked, Eve placed her hands on her hips and sucked in her stomach.

Eve chose a lavish emerald green gown that must have cost thousands. Eve had seen gowns like it in old movies or on T.V. shows such as *Downton Abbey*. It was made of ribbed silk and blue chiffon, trimmed with dark blue/green beading and silver lace that caught the light and glittered. It came complete with a peacock fan.

After Mary finished buttoning it, she helped Eve into the deep plush leather shoes with beaded, single button straps across the insteps, and 3-inch, Louis XV-style French spool heels.

Staring at herself in the mirror, Eve had to admit that she looked regally statuesque, and she only wished Patrick could see her. What fun they would have had "playing man and wife," as he would say, with Eve dressed in this elaborate ensemble. She sighed away her longing for him when she heard the ticking gold clock bong seven times.

"It is time, Mrs. Gantly. Miss Casterbury should be coming by shortly."

Eve turned to Mary with a warm smile. "Thank you, Mary. You are nothing short of a miracle worker."

Mary bobbed another bow and then, staring down, she chanced a question. "May I ask if your husband is from Ireland, Mrs. Gantly?"

A smile lit up Eve's face. "My husband's father was from Limerick and his mother from Parteen, a village in County Clare."

Mary's eyes danced with recognition. "I've been to Parteen. When I was a girl, my sister married a man from there. So, was your husband born in Ireland, Mrs. Gantly?"

"No, Mary. Patrick Gantly was born here, in New York."

"Perhaps I will have the chance to meet him."

Eve's smile faded. "Perhaps, Mary. I hope so."

Eve swiftly changed the subject. "Mary, what kind of people are the Casterburys? I'm not suggesting you gossip, it's just that I have never met Mrs. Casterbury or Addison Casterbury."

Mary lowered her chin, folding her hands humbly before her. "They are fine people, Mrs. Gantly. Fine and respectable people. I am very fortunate to be employed in this house."

Eve read between the lines. Mary was not going to be candid in any way. She couldn't afford to be.

The knock on the door stopped their conversation. Mary scurried over to open it and Irene swept into the room as if propelled by an ethereal summer breeze. She glowed in her long, silk burgundy gown, bedecked with glittering jewels. Her glossy black hair was piled high on top of her head in a loose bun, with soft wispy ringlets surrounding her face, trailing down the nape of her neck. Irene's was a naturally pretty face, showing light makeup, no rouge or lipstick.

Her pleased round eyes immediately fell on Eve's hair, dress and figure. "Well, you are changed, Mrs. Gantly. You are remarkably and wonderfully changed."

Eve nodded toward Mary. "Mary is a wonder worker."

Mary stood demurely, her eyes cast down.

Irene looked at Mary with approval. "Yes, Mary is a fine lady's maid and has been for the last three years. Now, shall we make our way to dinner, Mrs. Gantly?"

The ladies left the room and started down the seemingly infinite hallway, passing massive decorative vases blooming with fragrant, fresh flowers. Irene's expression turned serious.

"Eve, my Mummy is very English. For practical reasons, I have created the story of how we met. I think it will be best if we both are united in this. It will simply not do for me to tell her I found you on a park bench in Central Park, looking rather like a lost waif."

Eve felt the stirring of nerves. Lying was not one of her better talents. She was more of a tell-it-like-it-is girl.

Irene continued. "I will tell Mummy that you and I were introduced at The Society for the Relief of Half-Orphan and Destitute Children. That will placate and satisfy her."

"But what if she asks me direct questions about the type of work I do there?"

"Oh, just say that you are very much interested in their mental welfare. That will be the end of it. She is not comfortable with any sentence or question that has the words mental or mind in it. It reminds her of poor grandmother and that dreadful man, Pontius Pilate."

"What about your brother?"

"As I said, Addison will say little, so do not feel insulted, Eve. Most likely he will not even look your way except to be stiffly polite. You see, Addison is always stiffly polite. It seems that his mind is always set on some business issue or problem, following in our father's shadow."

Irene led the way left across polished parquet floors through a breathtaking, museum-like room. Eve began to think they would never arrive at the dining room. How could anyone live in a house like this? They passed elaborate wooden tables holding baroque style golden clocks and jewelry boxes, porcelains, ornate vases, and bronze and marble statues. Masterwork oil paintings hung on fabric-covered burgundy walls. In the center of one wall was a massive, white marble fireplace.

Irene gave the room a once-over, distractedly, having seen it all since childhood.

She turned to Eve. "Normally, Eve, we would proceed into the drawing room for pre-dinner drinks, but because Mummy has a social engagement later on, we are going directly to the dining room."

They advanced down yet another lavish hallway, decorated with exotic flowers and pedestals holding carved busts of poets and statesmen.

"Is he married?" Eve asked. "I mean your brother, Addison."

"He is engaged to Miss Katherine Griswold, and although the wedding is to take place in June of next year, Addison seldom speaks about it and I dare say he seldom speaks about, or spends much time in the company of, Miss Griswold. I don't know how she feels about that. Of course, her family is not as wealthy as ours, so I have surmised that Mr. and Mrs. Griswold are quietly anxious for the wedding day. I fear that Miss Griswold has no interest in suffrage matters and, therefore, we prefer to keep a distance from each other."

Irene stopped short, snagged Eve's arm, and drew her off to the side under a winding staircase. The dining room was ahead, visible as a shaft of amber light spilling out of an open door.

"Do not think of me as a gossip, Eve, but I do believe that my brother often visits the Lobster Palace restaurants, knows people in the Bohemian enclaves of Greenwich Village, and frequents the theaters dotting Broadway, where there are a variety of entertainments– and…" Irene lowered her voice, "women."

Eve stared, not finding the proper words, not finding any words. What should she say? Anything? Nothing? Eve found it all frightening and fascinating, but also baffling. Was Irene a more modern woman than most in her time? She had no idea.

Eve's palms were sweaty, her heart raced, and she was perspiring under that damned corset and heavy gown.

Irene didn't seem to notice Eve's silence. Again, Irene was lost in her own ideas and convictions, her eyes glazed over by personal thought that came spilling from her mouth.

"It's a man's world now, Eve, but we women are going to change all that. Yes, we are. When we get the right to vote, we will show those men what moxie we are made of. I dare say, after we get the right to vote, it won't be long before we vote in a woman president."

Eve swung her hesitant gaze toward Irene. There were so many things she wanted to say about the future. But of course, she couldn't.

Irene's eyes burned with a beguiling conviction. Eve was touched by her ripe vitality and boldness.

And then Eve had a thought. A wild speculative thought. Could Irene help her locate Maggie Lott Gantly? If they found Maggie, would Irene accompany Eve to meet Maggie? There was strength in numbers.

Irene returned to the present. "Listen to me go on, Eve. You must think me a regular Susan B. Anthony. Let us go into dinner. I am sure they are waiting for us."

How Eve dreaded going into that dining room and facing those people—those refined, highly educated, highly formal and highly wealthy people living in the world of 1914, a world she knew so little about. She already felt like a little sparrow amidst exotic songbirds.

Where was Patrick? What had happened to him? Would she ever know? With every passing minute, her heart ached for him.

Eve took in a sharp breath, straightened her shoulders, and plastered on a pleasant smile.

She followed Irene inside.

CHAPTER 10

The dining room was a resplendent and majestic space, with Tiffany lamps on side tables, two three-tiered chandeliers overhead, rich mahogany woodwork and a great fireplace and mantel of white marble, where two butlers stood at attention, wearing black tuxedos, white ties, tailcoats, and white gloves.

Eve swallowed away nerves.

The richly adorned dining room table dominated the room, with chairs enough for twenty guests. A fringed white tablecloth held a centerpiece of flourishing exotic flowers and golden candelabras, the white tapered candles adding a serene glow. There were cut crystal glasses, silver cutlery, white napkins, and Chinese rose medallion porcelain plates.

Irene led an overwhelmed Eve toward the table and began her introductions.

"Mummy, this is my lovely new friend, Mrs. Evelyn Sharland Gantly."

Katherine Casterbury was seated at the far end of the table, looking very much like a queen, dressed in a purple and violet gown, her neck and hands bedecked in jewels that Eve could only speculate were worth thousands.

She was not the matronly woman Eve had imagined. When she bowed her head, ever so slightly, Eve thought she appeared youthful, perhaps in her early 50s. Her features were well-defined and regal, and her silver-gray hair was combed neatly, sculpted into a kind of bun on top of her head. Her gaze was steely, her diamond-shaped face thin, her nose sharp, her mouth tight, but her overall demeanor one of polished sophistication, caution, and intelligence.

"I'm so happy you have come to dine with us, Mrs. Gantly," Mrs. Casterbury said in a thoroughly British accent, every word perfectly and beautifully pronounced, as if she were quoting Shakespeare.

Eve involuntarily bowed, clearing her throat before responding. "Thank you, Mrs. Casterbury, for your kind invitation and generosity."

"Not at all, my dear Mrs. Gantly. I look forward to learning more about you. My daughter is not often forthcoming in allowing me to meet her friends."

Addison Casterbury had properly risen to his feet when Irene and Eve had entered, and he was waiting patiently, hands clasped behind his back. In his early thirties, wearing white tie and tails, he was tall, with a tight build, a clean jawline and fine broad shoulders. His dark, wavy hair was swept straight back, adding a stylish flair, but a stiff formality. There was an upper-class severity about him, with his sharp upturned nose and dark gray eyes that took in the world with an ironic slant, the mark of being his father's only son, and the sole heir to a vast fortune.

To Eve's surprise, Addison left his chair and approached her, reaching for her hand. She offered it and he kissed it gently, in a courtly way. And then he fixed her with his penetrating eyes. Eve was sure she saw a twinkle of ardent attraction in them, and that unsettled her. Did she imagine it?

"I am so happy to make your acquaintance, Mrs. Gantly," he said, with superior, practiced protocol. Eve couldn't place the accent. It sounded stiff and affected, not sincere.

"And I am very happy to meet you, Mr. Casterbury. Thank you for allowing me to join you for dinner."

"It is all my pleasure, Mrs. Gantly."

Eve noticed he didn't say "our pleasure."

In a swift side glance, Eve saw Irene staring at her brother curiously.

The under-butler, Mason, appeared, and he ushered Eve to her chair and held it, while the second butler did the same for Irene.

Mrs. Casterbury sat at the head of the table, her son to her left. Irene sat to her mother's right, and Eve was placed next to Irene. The younger butler went to work pouring white wine, starting with Mrs. Casterbury, then Eve, Irene, and finally Addison. When Eve stared down at her place setting, she felt a hot catch of breath. What were all the knives and forks for? There were three glasses. She would have to approach each course slowly, and furtively watch Irene. Yes, she'd take her cue from Irene. Whatever Irene reached for, Eve would do the same.

After the soup was delivered and eating commenced, Mrs. Casterbury turned her attention on Eve.

"How have you found the weather today, Mrs. Gantly?"

Eve thought she saw Irene gently roll her eyes.

Holding her soup spoon over the turtle soup, Eve sat erect, chin tilted up, hoping to embody a woman of 1914 and not 2018.

"It was quite windy, Mrs. Casterbury," and then Eve thought of a better word. "Blustery for most of the afternoon. The leaves have nearly all fallen from the trees. But overall, the weather was most pleasant."

"I'm glad to hear it," Mrs. Casterbury said. "Although many of our friends despair of the coming of winter, I find all the seasons stimulating and necessary for good health."

"Right you are, Mother," Addison said, his eyes straying toward Eve.

Eve felt Addison's eyes, and Irene noticed as well, again with a rising interest.

Mrs. Casterbury continued discussing the weather for a time, finally shifting the conversation toward art and the charitable works she was involved in.

"You know, Mrs. Gantly, in 1912, our children's charity mailed cards to many of the City's wealthiest residents, asking for donations to help fund a precious commodity. Of course, that precious commodity is the children of our City. Don't you agree?"

"Yes," Eve answered, unsure if the question was rhetorical. Mrs. Casterbury nodded her approval and then continued.

"Over a thousand little white hearses passed through the streets of New York City in the summer of 1912.

Did you know, Mrs. Gantly, that one-eighth of the 123,400 babies delivered in 1912 died before they were twelve months old?"

Eve answered again, sincerely. "No, I didn't know that."

"One of the causes of this appalling infant mortality rate was a lack of access to clean, fresh milk among New York's poorest families. Well, our charity was responsible for raising thousands of dollars that went solely toward providing clean milk to the poor, and I am proud to say that for the first time in many years, the infant mortality rate in this City has finally fallen."

"Well done, Mother," Addison said.

"That is wonderful news, Mummy," Irene said.

Mrs. Casterbury continued deliberating about other charitable works, while the butlers worked the table, serving on the left side and taking away used plates from the right, always in a quiet manner, without disturbing the guests or interrupting conversations.

"And now this dreadful war in Europe is turning all our ready energies to supporting the war effort. I do hope that this war will not be a long one."

"Mother," Addison said, a glass of red wine poised at his lips, his expression that of a man about to profess a profound truth to the ignorant masses. "I am afraid that at the start of every war, many well-meaning but poorly informed people believe it will be a short one. I do not believe it. There are too many European alliances and too many pompous hotheads over there."

Mrs. Casterbury shook her sorrowful head. "It is a pity, Addison. Such a pity. My dear sister in London is simply fraught with despair over it."

Irene spoke up. "Let us not become morose, Mother. We do have a guest."

"Quite right," Addison tossed. "Quite right you are, Irene."

Eve lowered her head, carefully tasting the main course, mutton cutlets. Mrs. Casterbury leveled her eyes on Eve.

"Mrs. Gantly, will we be meeting your husband in the near future?"

Eve shot Irene a glance.

"Mrs. Gantly's husband is away on business," Irene interjected.

Mrs. Casterbury turned her cool eyes on her daughter. "And what business would that be, Mrs. Gantly?" Mrs. Casterbury continued, not removing her reproachful eyes from her daughter.

Irene stared back at her mother, as if in a challenge. It was easy to see that this mother and daughter relationship was not an easy one.

Eve's mind was thrashing about, struggling to come up with an answer, when once again, Irene came to the rescue.

"Mrs. Gantly's husband works for the government, Mummy."

Addison turned a sharp eye toward Eve, lighting up. "The government? What specific branch of the government does Mr. Gantly work in, Mrs. Gantly? We have several steel contracts with the government. Perhaps I know him."

Eve opened her mouth to speak, but Irene was ready with the answer. "I do think it is rude of us to continue with these incessant, personal questions pointed at Mrs.

Gantly. She must feel as if she is being cross-examined on the witness stand."

Addison glared at his sister. "I hope and trust that Mrs. Gantly does not believe us to be rude in any way. On the contrary, we are delighted to have Mrs. Gantly in our company and we simply have the polite inclination to know Mrs. Gantly a little bit better."

Irene glared back at her brother. "Mrs. Gantly's husband is in Washington, D.C. on government business of a somewhat sensitive nature and, as such, I invited Mrs. Gantly to stay with us for a few days until his return."

Mrs. Casterbury spoke up. "And, of course, that was a kind and proper thing to do, Irene. But when Mr. Gantly does return, I do hope, Mrs. Gantly, that you will feel comfortably inclined to introduce your husband to us."

Eve managed a smile. "Yes, Mrs. Casterbury, I would like that very much."

Mrs. Casterbury's icy stare fixed on her daughter, who obviously felt the coldness, but refused to look up from her mutton cutlets.

Mrs. Casterbury spoke in the sweetest of voices, with no hint of animosity.

"Perhaps it would be unobjectionable, Irene, if you were to tell your brother and me where you and Mrs. Gantly met?"

Irene chewed slowly, eyes focused ahead. It was obvious to Eve that Irene enjoyed tantalizing her mother and brother with her rebellious spirit. There was more to Irene than met the eye, and Eve wondered what behind-the-scenes mysteries this young woman was hiding. Mrs. Casterbury surely speculated that Irene's life was filled with shadowy secrets, which, in turn, almost certainly made Eve suspect in the woman's eyes.

As the chilly silence stretched out, and as James, the head Butler, now poured red wine, Eve felt dribbles of sweat running down her chest and back. How she wished she could escape upstairs, yank off the gown and corset, and dash around that large suite stark naked and free. The dinner couldn't end soon enough.

"Mother," Irene said, with an imperious lift of her head. "Eve and I met at The Society for the Relief of Half-Orphan and Destitute Children."

Mrs. Casterbury's eyes drifted toward Eve. "How fortunate for those poor children to have your good counsel and practical Christian help, Mrs. Gantly. Have you been involved with the society for a long period of time?"

Once again, Irene had the ready answer. "No, Mother, not long."

Mrs. Casterbury could barely hide her mounting irritation. "I am confidently sure, Irene, that Mrs. Gantly has the ability and ready vocabulary to answer for herself."

The tension in the room grew electric, and as if the mother and daughter skirmish weren't enough, Eve kept noticing Addison's eyes stealing furtive glances her way. Didn't Irene say he would hardly notice her? And no, Eve was not imagining it.

"If I may interject, ladies," Addison said, with a slight sniff. "I would like to offer a toast to our most mysterious and lovely guest, Mrs. Gantly."

He held his wine glass high as he met Eve's nervous eyes. "Further, Mrs. Gantly, I would like to add the hope, and indeed the wish, that you will feel comfortable staying at the Casterbury Mansion for as long as you wish."

The darting glance Irene shot her brother was filled with surprise and suspicion.

Mrs. Casterbury, too, seemed to be shaken off-balance for a few brief seconds by her son's interest and declaration. She recovered swiftly, with a sweet, practiced smile.

"Why, yes, Addison. How rude of me not to have toasted our guest from the outset of dinner. Of course, Mrs. Gantly, you are welcome to stay as long as you may wish to stay."

Eve's cheeks grew hot with embarrassment. It was obvious to all that this short statement from the aloof and withholding Addison was unusual and telling. It was certainly a flirtation.

After the toast, the table fell into a confused silence, and by the time the candied fruit and port arrived, the conversation had fallen back into the prosaic talk of weather, women's fashion and art.

After Mrs. Casterbury excused herself, Addison arose and bowed to Eve. With his coy eyes gleaming, he said, "I hope we will see you again, Mrs. Gantly. If you have need of anything while you are our guest, I hope you will not hesitate to let me know."

Irene snapped, "If Mrs. Gantly needs anything, Addison, I will ensure that she gets it."

Addison's easy stare remained on Eve. "As you say, sister dear," he said, his voice dripping with sweet disdain.

Irene led Eve into the drawing room for coffee. As they sat near the crackling fireplace, Irene lifted her troubled head, looking directly at Eve.

"Do you find my brother attractive, Eve?"

Eve set her coffee cup down on the pedestal table beside her, her eyes filling with annoyance. "Irene, I am a married woman who is very much in love with my husband, and I have no interest, whatsoever, in your brother."

Irene's expression didn't change. "It's curious, isn't it? I have never seen Addison so blatantly taken by a woman. Do not mistake me, Eve, you are very lovely, but tonight, my brother has revealed a part of himself that I simply find disturbing. If I were you, Eve, I would avoid him."

Eve sat up straight. "Irene, I don't plan to stay here. I plan to leave in the morning."

Irene appeared wounded. "I hope that is not true, Eve. I feel as if we could become…well, kind of sisters. We could confide in each other as we are doing right this very moment. We could gossip, and you could tell me truly who and where your husband is and," Irene lowered her voice to a whisper. "…I could share with you my own true love, that no one must ever know about."

Eve shut her eyes for a moment of escape. She had to flee this place and the sooner the better. If she didn't, she feared she'd be pulled into a family disaster.

Two hours later, Eve lay in the luxurious bed under a warm comforter. Although she was exhausted, her eyes were wide open, staring into the darkness. When they filled with tears, she turned over on her side and shut them.

Where was Patrick? How she missed their home, and their sweet, passionate and loving life.

CHAPTER 11

On Sunday, Eve awoke early, just as the sun leaked in from under the cream and burgundy pleated draperies. She sat up, feeling lethargic and slightly depressed. As she scanned the room, she awakened again to the fact that she was living in 1914, and she was without Patrick. While she was in this negative frame of mind, she could not make an appearance. She'd have to rest, gather her wits about her and start again on Monday morning. She would make excuses to Irene.

When she dropped back into the pillow, she fell immediately into a deep sleep.

On Monday, November 30th, she awoke rested and surprisingly alert, ready to solve problems. It was clear she had to take some action. She and Patrick had tried to plan meticulously for all possible contingencies, just in case something like this happened, in case they were separated or sent to different times. They had spent nights brainstorming all the things that could go wrong.

Tossing off the quilt and swinging her feet to the soft, deep carpet, Eve walked to the closet and opened the door. The gown she'd worn on her journey to 1914 now stared back at her and seemed almost alive, as if to say, "I've been waiting for you."

Eve nodded. "Yes, I know," she said out loud. "You're a costume from 2018, pretending to be from 1885, and I'm a woman from 2018, trapped, pretending to be a woman living in 1914, who has no idea where Patrick is or how I'm going to get back home."

Eve reached, touching the pleated side of the dress, feeling for it—feeling for the hidden pocket that had been sewn into the dress. Eve knew it was there. She'd felt it yesterday. Thank God the ring had time-traveled with her.

It was an antique English 18k gold ruby and diamond 5-stone ring that she and Patrick had found on *eBay* and paid over three thousand dollars for. The historical currency calculator revealed that in 1900-1915, the ring would be worth somewhere between sixty and seventy thousand dollars. That would be enough to keep them financially secure for a long time, if they lived moderately.

It was an advantage knowing you were about to embark on a trip to the past, giving you time to plan and strategize, unlike the first time she'd time traveled to 1885, unprepared, confused, with no idea what she was going to do.

Eve and Patrick had researched possible historical periods that they might find themselves in: 1885, 1910, 1920, even further back to 1850. They had learned that in the early 1900s, the average income for men was between $500 and $600 a year. For women, that number had to be cut in half.

There was no federal minimum wage in 1910. Only a few states were experimenting with it, and then it was only for women and children.

Eve figured that purchasing a house in 1914 would probably cost a little over $3,000, so she could live well with seventy thousand dollars.

Eve removed the gown from the hanger and carried it to the bed, laying it down. She located the pocket, and with a fingernail, she dug into the loosely sewn seam until she sliced open the pocket. As she reached in and drew out the ring, Eve sighed with relief. Smiling, she held it up into the light, staring at the pink-red rubies and diamonds that danced with fire.

Now all she had to do was borrow an outfit and a little money from Irene, and make her way down to Nassau Street, where the jewelry district and some pawn shops were located.

Mary Foster arrived promptly at 8:30, holding a striking brown pleated day dress, with lace collar and cuffs. Mary had also brought gloves, shoes, undergarments, and a purse.

"Miss Casterbury asked me to bring these to you, Mrs. Gantly. She's confident they will fit, as you are both about the same size. She also requested that you join her in the breakfast room at 9:30."

As Mary crossed the room to hang the dress in the closet, Eve thanked her and asked her where the breakfast room was. Mary said that Mason, the under-butler, would come by at 9:30 to usher her to the breakfast room.

Mason opened the door to the breakfast room and Eve entered, the lovely fitting dress brushing below her ankles. Again, Eve was taken by the extraordinary size of the room, with its gilded framed landscapes of hunting scenes and 18th-century portraits hanging on English walnut walls. An opulence of light streamed in through tall windows, partially covered by pleated, royal blue draperies. The generous stone fireplace caught Eve's attention for several moments. It was flanked on either side by marble Corinthian columns, which added to its regal quality.

Irene sat at one end of a magnificent oak table, covered by a white linen tablecloth and a bouquet of fresh flowers. She was scanning the morning paper and sipping coffee from a bone china teacup. She arose when Eve entered.

"Oh, there you are, Eve. I've been waiting for you. I do hope you rested yesterday and are feeling well today."

"Yes, thank you. I'm feeling much better."

"How utterly charming you look in that dress. I am so happy to see that we are indeed the same size, aren't we, just like real sisters?"

"It's so generous of you to share your wardrobe with me."

"Think nothing of it. Please sit down next to me here." Irene patted the chair to her right. "I have so many things I want to discuss with you. Oh, are you hungry? I'm afraid we are having an informal breakfast this morning. Mummy is having breakfast in her room. On the sideboard, you'll find fruit, ham, bacon and eggs with muffins and butter. And the coffee urn is brimming with fresh coffee."

Charles stood by, waiting for Eve's order.

After Eve was seated and began to eat, Irene turned to her with enthusiasm. "Now, first of all, I have made some plans for us. I hope you will agree with them."

"What are your plans?" Eve asked, bracing herself.

"Have you thought… Well, no, that's not the right word, is it? Have you had any further thoughts about where your husband might be?"

Eve looked down at her scrambled eggs. "Yes, I have. I simply don't know."

Irene jerked a nod. "All right then. I believe, quite firmly, that we should contact the police."

"Oh, no. No, Irene."

"Well, do you think they could help find him? I mean to say, well, your husband could have become injured or run into ruffians. He may be in grave danger."

"No… I mean…He's a big man. He can take care of himself."

Eve laid her fork aside, paused and then reached for her coffee cup. She had anticipated that Irene, who was very precocious and curious, would ask the question. Eve had formulated the answer. Better tell part of the truth than all lie. Isn't that what Patrick had told her?

"Irene, my husband and I had a kind of argument. As a result, he left me. I don't know where he went."

Irene's face fell into sadness, although Eve saw a glint of excitement in the woman's eyes. Eve suspected Irene loved adventure and intrigue.

"I am so sorry, Eve. So very sorry. Well, we shall have to find him, won't we?" And then, as an afterthought, Irene stopped, considering an idea.

"Or maybe not. Do you still have feelings for him, or is that too personal a question? Mummy and Addison would say so, but I believe that you and I can be open and honest with each other."

Eve hid her dubious expression. The last thing she could be with this woman was open and honest.

"I love my husband very much, Irene."

Irene straightened her shoulders. "Well then, it is settled. We shall have to search for him. You will stay here with us while we do our investigations, and this will be our base of operations. From here, we will launch forth and begin our search. Now, where do you think we should begin?"

Eve sat back in the chair, lowering her voice so that Charles couldn't hear. Eve wondered how these people could be so candid and bold, when a butler or servant could hear every word they said.

"Irene... You have been so good and generous to me, but I can't stay here. I must move on."

Irene's eyes searched Eve's face. "But where will you go? In the park yesterday, you said you had nowhere to go and no money to pay for lodgings. Was that a lie?"

"No, it was not a lie. This morning, after I'd slept, my mind cleared. I realized that I have a piece of jewelry that I can sell. From that, I'll be able to stay in a boarding house or a hotel."

Irene sat back and crossed her arms tightly across her chest. She stared at Eve with a new suspicion.

"Eve, you are not telling me the truth. I feel it so keenly. You are holding something back, and I don't know why. Are you in some kind of trouble?"

"No, no..."

"Well, then, where are you from, Eve? Do you live here in the City? Are you from out of town? Why were you sitting on that bench alone, confused and shivering, wearing that old coat and dress from, I don't know, thirty years ago? I have been honest and forthright with you, Eve. I have offered you our home and given you clothes from my own wardrobe, something I have never done before, with any woman."

Eve felt trapped. Her face grew hot.

Irene was waiting, tapping her foot.

Eve decided to deflect the questions. She decided to appeal to Irene's sense of rebelliousness and need for adventure. She decided to begin asking the questions. Go on the offensive, Patrick also said.

"Do you know who Maggie Lott Gantly is?" Eve asked.

Irene blinked. Her lips lost some of their firm determination. She stared at Eve with a new interest.

"I know of her. Why do you ask?"

"Have you ever seen her perform?"

"I may have. Why?"

"I would like to meet her."

Eve saw the barest hint of a smile form on Irene's pink lips. "And you think I would know that kind of woman? An actress, who is kept by a man, but not married to him? I have heard that she has been seen with many men, at least until this last one. Do you think I would know such a woman?"

"I don't know. Do you?"

The corners of Irene's mouth lifted. "I read the newspapers, Eve, something I'm told that women have no business doing. What for, the men like to say? You know what else I read? The newspaper *Votes for Women*. Maggie Lott Gantly gave an interview in that newspaper only a few months ago."

Eve inclined her head forward. "What did she say?"

"What else? She said that women should have the right to vote. She said that women are every bit the match for a man in all things. She said, it was all right to have a man and a relationship with one, but women should also have their own lives, just like men have theirs. She said, men have their own money and so should women. Men have mistresses…"

Irene paused, lowering her voice to a near whisper, considering her words carefully. "Maggie Lott Gantly said that women may choose to have other men acquaintances."

Irene waited for Eve to respond. She didn't, so Irene continued.

"And do you know what I did after I read that article? I went to the theatre to see Maggie Lott Gantly."

Eve stared into Irene's kittenish face. Eve could see a ripe rebellious spirit in this young woman.

"I went in secret, of course, because my Mummy and Addison would have been struck with apoplexy if they knew."

Eve decided to pry. "And did you go alone?"

Irene dropped her eyes and scratched at the linen tablecloth with a polished fingernail. "Maybe I did, and maybe I didn't. If you can have secrets, Eve, surely I can have mine."

Eve nodded. "So, did you meet Miss Gantly?"

Irene adjusted herself in her chair, looking up above the fireplace, toward the massive oil painting of an 18th-century man dressed in a red hunting jacket, white breeches, and glossy black boots, comfortably seated astride a magnificent white horse.

She lowered her voice again to a conspiratorial whisper. "Some months ago, I went to the Garrick Theatre to see Maggie Lott Gantly star in the play *Girl on a Swing*, with William Walker, who played her sweetheart in a most thrilling manner. Anyway, after the performance, I went backstage to meet Miss Gantly, to tell her how happy I was that she supported the woman's suffrage movement."

Eve stared, eagerly. "So, you met her? What happened?"

Irene turned darkly serious. "In person, I found Miss Gantly to be quite dreamy and confused, Eve. Her eyes were vacant, her speech wandering. I was astonished how well she had performed on stage, while in the flesh, backstage, she was obviously under the terrible influence of narcotics, or alcohol, or both. I had never before seen the dramatic and frightening effect these stimulants can have on a person. And just as I was about to ask if she needed any assistance, a brute of a man cruelly seized her arm and yanked her away. He looked at me with such venomous eyes, and then made a rude and crude remark. It really disturbed me. The man I was with was startled as well, and…"

Irene stopped abruptly, having said more than she had intended to.

"You were with a man?" Eve asked, intrigued.

Irene shifted in her chair. "Well, never mind about that."

Irene leveled her eyes on Eve again, trying once more to take control of the conversation. "So, who are you, Eve? And why do you want to see Maggie Lott Gantly? Is she related to you? Your husband's sister perhaps? A cousin?"

Again, Eve felt she had trapped herself. She produced a sweet, worried smile. "I am sure you are aware of how complicated and difficult family members can sometimes be, Irene. I am involved in many family struggles at this time, and I am not at liberty to speak about them."

This had the result Eve had hoped for. Irene's face first melted into instant compassion, and then into a righteous resolve.

"Well, don't you have a care, Eve. Whatever difficulties and obstacles you are currently facing, we can surmount them together and, with a good steely resolve, we will conquer them. And yes, I know about family complications and difficulty. Addison is a constant source of disappointment and irritation to me. I know that he gambles, cavorts with women in shadowy places and drinks copious amounts of whiskey, while boldly and stiffly denying his every misdemeanor. I fear he will be the ruin of our family. So, not to worry, my new friend, Eve. I understand your plight, and we will stand firmly together, shoulder to shoulder."

Eve could see it was going to be a challenge breaking away from this young woman. She had all the grit, determination and courage of a hungry lioness.

"I don't want to involve you in my personal problems, Irene. That wouldn't be fair."

"Poppycock, Eve. I will be your champion."

Eve almost burst out laughing at the expression "Poppycock," but she didn't. She also struggled not to show distress. Instead, she looked at Irene with a smile. "You are so kind, Irene. But now I must travel downtown to sell my ring."

Before Irene could jump in, Eve said, with a timid hope, "Will you accompany me?"

Irene shot up. "Of course, Eve, but I must protest at your selling any of your jewelry. It's absolutely crass and unthinkable."

Eve had to stand up to this strong woman. "I must do it. And I'm going to do it."

Irene lifted an eyebrow. "Well, if you are that determined, then I suppose you must. All right then, let me find a proper coat and hat for you and we will be away. You stay here, and I will return in a jiffy."

After Irene swept out of the room, Eve remained alone, with Charles standing by, his eyes staring ahead, his expression bland.

A few minutes later, as Eve was draining the last of her coffee, Charles drifted over. Eve looked up at him with a pleasant smile, expecting the butler to ask if she needed anything. Instead, he cleared his throat and said, "Pardon me, Mrs. Gantly."

She watched as he retrieved a sealed note-sized envelope from his inside coat pocket and placed it on a silver tray. He presented it to her, with an enigmatic smile.

"What is this?" Eve asked.

Her full name was written on the face of it in a florid style: *Mrs. Evelyn Gantly.*

"I was instructed to present this to you, madam."

Eve stared at it. "Instructed by whom?"

The strained smile remained on Charles' lips, but he said nothing.

Reluctantly, Eve took it. Charles immediately backed away.

"Do you require anything else, Mrs. Gantly?"

Eve glanced up, distracted. "...No, Charles. Thank you."

He retreated from the room. Alone now, Eve ran a finger under the flap and opened it. With a quick breath and an impossible hope that the note might be from Patrick, she drew out the note, shook it and began to read. Immediately, her heart sank.

My Dear Mrs. Gantly:
Perhaps you will not think this too bold or improper of me? I pray that the following will not, in any way, diminish me in your lovely eyes.

Will you do me the honor of having lunch with me on your next convenient day? I would very much enjoy the opportunity of getting to know you better. Additionally, I understand that you are currently involved in some personal and financial difficulties. Allow me to put forth the fortunate fact that I am both a respected man of business, as well as a man of means, who can offer you support in many ways and at many levels. You simply have to ask, and I will be your grateful and humble servant.

I would only ask that, whatever your decision in this rather delicate circumstance, you keep this note and the above invitation secret and only between the two of us, so that it is not misunderstood or misconstrued by others.

Rest assured that Charles is available, at all times, to attend to your reply in this matter.

With respect and warm regards, and with anxious anticipation, I am your waiting servant,

Addison Reed Casterbury

CHAPTER 12

They traveled downtown in the Casterbury's luxurious blue limousine, which boasted of class and smelled of expensive leather. William, the stern chauffer, was sitting erected and alert, dressed in a dark suit and smart black cloth hat with a vinyl bill.

As they approached 42nd Street, they sputtered past a tangle of wagons and cars, where adults and kids were swarming a curb, craning their necks, gawking at something that neither Eve nor Irene could see.

"It reminds me of the terrible day in April 1912 when we learned the Titanic sank," Irene said. "There were crowds of anxious people everywhere. Though Mummy forbade it, I had William drive me downtown to the White Star Line at the line's Bowling Green Office. We had friends on that ship, and I had to know what happened to them. Do you know, Eve, that Mummy and I had contemplated traveling to England with the intent of booking passage on the Titanic's maiden voyage? I shiver at the thought. If Mummy had not come down with a bad cough, we would have boarded the Titanic and probably perished, along with so many other poor souls."

Eve was only half listening. Her thoughts were swirling around the daring and flirtatious note that Addison had sent her. Once alone in the breakfast room, she had torn the thing up and tossed it into the fireplace. As the fire spat and popped, she had watched the pieces curl, turn brown and burst into flames. She could only hope that that would be the end of it, and she'd never have to see Addison again.

They left the limo on Nassau Street to travel on foot. The area was teeming with pushcarts, food vendors, bootblacks, crowds of people, and the earthy smells of horse manure and car exhaust. There were countless pawn dealer shops, jewelry stores, rag dealers and novelty shops.

Irene walked nervously, afraid to touch or brush against anyone or anything. She was obviously put off by the pulsing energy, the aggressive people, and the crass materiality.

Eve's eyes were alive to the world around her, fascinated by the look and feel of the place, especially by the groups swimming about with animated hands and talk. Brownstones and large federal buildings rose up, with zigzagging fire escapes and American flags snapping in the wind.

Eve decided to take charge. She saw an attractive storefront below a brownstone with the sign **West's Jewelers** above the doorway. It was a good place to start.

Eve led the way forward, with a complaining and haughty Irene behind.

"I don't like this area, Eve. It is not a decent place for women to be. Look how these men look at us. It's positively disgusting. Wall Street is filled with beastly men searching for loose women."

"Don't look at them," Eve said, pushing through a green door and entering the dimly lighted space. Several male heads lifted, some with surprise, some with curiosity and some with pleasure.

It was a long narrow room with a few tables in the center, and display cases and shelves along the walls. All the glass cases were crammed with jewelry of all kinds, some elaborate and expensive, some cheap or exotic.

Irene's eyes widened as she took in the spectacle, her near expert jewelry eye zeroing in on diamonds, emeralds, gold bands and pearl necklaces.

Eve swiftly scanned the faces of the men: two were young, one was middle-aged, and the one who stood behind a glass case was probably in his early sixties. He was a small man, dressed all in black, wearing a yarmulke, a long gray beard, and wire-rimmed spectacles. Eve was taken by his dark, warm, intelligent eyes and gentle smile. She went to him.

"Good morning," Eve said.

"Yes, a good morning, madam. May I help you?"

His accent was slight, his voice soft.

Eve reached into her purse and produced the ring, holding it up. "I want to sell this. Have I come to the right place?"

Irene slid in next to Eve, feeling an imperious need to take over. Eve took a step forward to take charge, as the other men looked on with keen and amused interest.

"Of course you have come to the right place, madam," the merchant said. He indicated with a shaky hand. "Please, let us step this way and I will have a closer look at the lovely ring."

Eve and Irene followed the merchant to a glass countertop, where he shambled behind it—obviously, his official office.

He smiled graciously. "May I examine the ring, madam?"

Eve gave a weak smile and handed it over.

The merchant's eyes twinkled with interest as he took the ring and held it up into the light. He nodded, his expression now serious, as he gave the ring a first appraisal. As he leaned in for a closer look, an eyebrow lifted. Eve wondered what that meant.

Next, the merchant reached to his left for a magnifying loupe. Both women watched, rapt, as the merchant held the loupe up to his face so that the first knuckle on his thumb was firmly pressed against his cheek and the glass was positioned directly over his left eye.

He began to hum, a low, almost inaudible hum, a tuneless hum. Eve wished she and Patrick had had the ring appraised before their time travel trip—and they had intended to—but then time ran out and Patrick had been anxious to go. What if the *eBay* ring wasn't worth seventy thousand dollars or even fifty thousand by 1914's rates.

With his other hand, the merchant moved the ring to within one-half inch of the lens. He held the loupe steady, as he studied and hummed.

Finally, he lowered the loupe, his gaze calm, his smile fatherly.

"May I ask where you purchased this ring?"

Eve thought fast. "It was a gift."

He nodded.

Eve spoke up abruptly, as if to plead her case. "I was told that it was worth about seventy thousand dollars."

The merchant didn't bat an eye, and his expression didn't change.

"It is a curious ring, madam. The ruby has inclusions; a dark spot inside the stone."

Eve's shoulders sank. "Oh... so that's not good then?"

"Not so bad. Most real stones have flaws, so the ruby is a natural one. I do, however, see clouds and twinning wisps in the diamonds."

The merchant held Eve in his inquisitive gaze. "But what I find most curious is that the cut quality of the stone—that is, the facets, alignment, and proportions—show wear. The entire ring itself shows years of wear, and yet from the cut and style of the ring, I'd say that it has only recently been fashioned. Can you tell me the age of the ring, madam?"

Eve stammered. "Well... let's see. My grandmother gave it to me. She said it had been in the family for a while."

The merchant's eyes lowered on the glass countertop, avoiding Eve's eyes. "You will forgive me, madam, but I don't believe that this ring is so very old, and yet as I said, it is curious that it reveals years of wear... Years of gracing the hand of some fortunate woman."

There was a brief silence while Eve's mind locked up, and Irene's gaze swung from the merchant to Eve, as she tried to decipher what was truly being implied.

The merchant nodded a little. "Well, I suppose there are many such mysteries in this world."

"Where did you get the ring, Eve?" Irene asked.

Eve grew defensive. "As I said, from my grandmother."

The merchant sought to placate his client. "Your grandmother, or perhaps the man who gave it to her, obviously had good taste in jewelry. Yes, I can see that."

And then the merchant pursed his lips in thought. "It is interesting that I have seen a similar ring to this only recently. Its artistic style was first created in 1912."

He held the ring up into the light once more, stroking his beard with his free hand. "Yes, this is not an old ring, and yet," he raised his eyes and lifted his shoulders. "…and yet this is an old ring. Isn't it curious?"

Irene spoke up. "Then its worth should be substantial."

The merchant's pleasant expression remained, but his voice deepened. "Although the ring does have value, I'd say that the apparent age of this fascinating piece diminishes its value considerably. The ring is an antique, but it should not be so, and I have no explanation for that. Perhaps you do, madam?"

Eve blundered on. "But you said the ruby is genuine, and the diamonds…" Eve sputtered, excitedly.

The merchant decided to end the speculation. "I can offer you fifty-nine dollars and ninety-nine cents for the ring, madam."

Eve felt a tremor of disbelief and distress. "Fifty-nine dollars?"

The merchant nodded with a gentle smile. "A fine piece. A curious piece. A wondrous piece. A good price, madam."

Eve struggled to do the math conversion in her head. She and Patrick had practiced conversions in their heads as a game, often over dinner. She shut her eyes and fought to control her spinning mind. The best she could come up with was fifty-four dollars had the buying power of about one thousand three hundred dollars in 2018. Not at all the seventy thousand dollars she was hoping for.

She shook her head. "No, no, that's impossible. I know the ring is worth more than that."

"Of course it is," Irene chimed in, seized by auction fever. "It is a beautiful ruby. A one of a kind. Sir, that is not a fair price for a one-of-a-kind ring."

Eve shot her a look. She didn't want her overplaying the scene.

The merchant's smile grew tired. "My final price is ninety-five dollars. I am sure, madam, you will not find a better price in all of New York. I am confident of that."

Eve thought fast. It would give her a little over two thousand dollars. Not seventy, but not bad. Should she take it? Just as she opened her mouth, Irene spoke up again.

"We'll go somewhere else. Thank you, sir."

The merchant nodded, still staring longingly at the ring. "In all honesty, madams, I have offered you a competitive price. Please do take the ring to others, but I believe in the end you will return to me, finding that my price is a fair one. You see, I find this ring extremely fascinating. I have seen much jewelry and many stones in my forty-five years in business, but I say to you, truly, that this ring appears to have come from another world or perhaps another time. My price is fair, and just to show you how much I am taken by this ring, I'll offer you one hundred and thirty dollars, and that is my absolute last offer."

Eve and Irene exchanged glances.

CHAPTER 13

The rest of Monday morning was spent at a bank, where Eve tried to open a bank account. When she presented the check from West's Jewelers for $130, about $3,300 in 2018 currency, the bank manager stiffly informed Eve that since she had no permanent address nor husband nor father to cosign the account, her request would have to be denied.

Frustrated and incensed by the obvious discrimination, Eve told the manager he was "an ignorant jerk," to which Irene, in solidarity, gave a firm nod and a bit of a snort, and then the women marched out.

Back in the limo, Irene turned to Eve. "Well done back there, Eve. Well done. Now you see why we must march for women's rights. But don't have a worry about setting up an account. I will talk to Addison about it. He will be more than happy to accompany you to the bank and co-sign the account. You will have available funds post haste."

Eve turned, alarmed. "Oh, no, I don't want to get Addison involved in this. I mean, I don't want to bother him. I know he is a very busy man."

"He won't mind a feather, Eve. Actually, I think he was somewhat taken with you. I've not heard him talk so much over dinner in months. But I wouldn't flirt with him, if I were you, even though I'm told women find him attractive. But you know how men can be."

"I didn't flirt with him, Irene," Eve said, forcefully. "I didn't even look at him."

Irene turned, her eyes enlarging. "Eve, it is quite all right. I understand. We women have to play the man's game to get what we want. Let's face it, attractive women always have the advantage in this man's world, if we play our given role just right. The trick is not to let them know we are beating them at their own game. Women are stronger, wiser, more well-rounded and much more intelligent. So it is all right if you find Addison attractive, as long as you play the cupid game just right."

Eve turned away, rolled her eyes and gazed out the window at the carriages and cars; at the newsboys and crowds; and at the green canvas awnings covering the windows of buildings.

"Now we will go to lunch," Irene declared.

She leaned forward so William could hear. "William, take us to Café Martin, Fifth Avenue and 26th Street."

"Very good, Miss Casterbury."

As Irene eased back, Eve's thoughts circled and returned to Patrick, as they always did. Eve played and replayed the events of their time travel from the time she and Patrick first sat on the bench, with the lantern between them, until the time she'd first seen Irene.

Why hadn't she and Patrick traveled to 1914 together? They had traveled together the last time, when they went from 1885 to 2016. What was the difference? Had they held hands? Had they touched? Was that it? In 1885, when Patrick was near death from a gunshot wound, she had wrapped him with her arms and held on to him tightly. Was that the difference? She had meant to take his hand. They had planned to join hands, but she couldn't recall whether they had or not.

Eve let out a low, troubled sigh. Had she lost her Patrick forever?

They ate an elegant lunch at a popular restaurant for the rich, but Eve's mind was distracted and flooded with confusion. As she pushed grilled lamb chops and peas around with her fork, she studied the plumes, feathers, and crepe on the ladies' elaborate hats. She tried to eavesdrop on the gentle murmur of conversation at a nearby table, and she watched tuxedoed waiters pouring reds into wine glasses. And then she gazed with humor and amazement at Irene, who was cutting into smoked ox tongue, forking delicate pieces into her mouth and chewing with energetic vigor.

When Irene's startled eyes lifted, and she stopped eating in mid-chew, Eve followed Irene's gaze. She saw a tall, broad, meaty man with football shoulders and a blunt sour face being ushered across the room by the aloof, sharp-chinned tuxedo-dressed maître d'. Trailing behind the big man was a young, strikingly attractive woman, wearing a long, muted-blue dress with cream lace and short sleeves, and long, soft-gray gloves, fastened with a row of buttons. Her lavish broad-rim hat was topped dramatically with ostrich plumes, and a long pin was pushed through the hat to anchor it to her brown curls and opulent hairstyle.

Eve was captivated by the woman's sensual body; she moved with a regal quality and voluptuous grace. There was a shell-like transparency to her skin, and her luminous red cheeks heightened her beauty and radiance.

"That's Maggie Lott Gantly," Irene said, at a whisper, "And that brute of a man with her is the same man who yanked her away from me the night I met Miss Gantly backstage at the theatre."

As the big man and Maggie sat in a private booth, all eyes in the room ventured coy glances, while mouths made little whispers.

Eve felt a shiver. There was something strange, unnerving and unnatural about the moment. But then, of course, it was unnatural. She was seeing Patrick's daughter in the flesh, as she had been in the past, and Patrick was nowhere around. Only a few short days ago, Eve didn't even know this woman existed. But there she was, and Eve couldn't help but stare. Unless Eve could find some way to stop it, Maggie would be murdered by the man who sat next to her, undoubtedly Big Jim Clancy.

Without Patrick, what was Eve supposed to do? What could she do? She felt an unexpected and irrational spike of irritation. She hadn't wanted to time travel again. She didn't want to be here, and she was angry at Patrick for suggesting it and angry at herself for agreeing to it. They'd had a perfect, loving life in 2018. How dare he risk that? Why had she listened to him? She should have refused to use the lantern again, no matter how good and noble the reason was.

For the second time in almost two years, her life was in jeopardy. She was trapped in 1914, alone and scared, and her marriage with Patrick was probably over. She would most likely never see him again. Had coming back to save Maggie Gantly been worth all that?

Eve's eyes narrowed on Maggie. If only Patrick had never found that article on his laptop.

"Is everything all right, Eve?" Irene said, concerned. "Your face has flushed red. Your eyes are burning."

Eve inhaled a breath to cool her churning mind and emotions. She wasn't ready to talk to Irene. She turned away.

There it was, the nagging and panicky thought: how in the world would she ever get back to her own time? At least the last time around she knew that if she found Evelyn Sharland's lantern, it would most likely send her back home. At least she had some hope of returning. This time, she had no idea where the lantern from 1885 was.

What had John Harringshaw's Christmas Eve letter of 1930 said? Eve had memorized most of it. In the letter, he'd spoken about the lantern.

All that was ever found was a lantern on a park bench in Central Park, but then even that promptly disappeared and it has never been found or accounted for. As I recall, one of the ambulance drivers who worked at the hospital admitted that he and another employee had driven you out to the park and deposited you and Detective Sergeant Gantly on a park bench. This ambu-

lance driver was questioned relentlessly, but nothing ever came of it. He simply stated that you and Detective Sergeant Gantly vanished into the night.

Irene spoke up. Eve flinched at the sound, startled. Her eyes flipped open. "What?"

"I said, are you ill?" Irene asked.

"No, no... Not that. I guess I'm just..."

Irene finished Eve's sentence in a sugary sweet voice that further irritated Eve. "You are missing your husband, aren't you, Eve?"

Eve fought the urge to tell Irene to shut up. Instead, her attention turned again to Maggie. She favored her father—the same sensual lips, high cheekbones, and self-assured look out of her almond eyes, although Eve thought Maggie's eyes were a bit glassy and unfocused. It was unnerving how much she favored Patrick, and it was clear that she was his daughter.

Eve studied the man with the menacing eyes, Big Jim Clancy. His thick, tawny hair was combed back tightly from his forehead, and it gleamed with pomade. His chipped green eyes were fixed in a challenge as he glared out into the faces of the fascinated diners. Big Jim's eyes were prowling with superiority, opportunity, and advantage.

How did Maggie manage to hook up with him? Eve thought.

Irene returned to her smoked tongue, but Eve slid her plate aside, mind working, body alert.

"I have to meet her," Eve said, abruptly.

Irene looked up with a knowing grin. "Based on our breakfast conversation, Eve, I was certain that you would want to. How serendipitous that Miss Gantly just happened to show up here for lunch. Well, maybe not so serendipitous. I've read that she often lunches here. That's why I decided to bring you."

Eve stared at Irene with new respect and new annoyance. This girl was just too much.

"Is she starring in a play now?" Eve asked.

"Yes, as a matter of fact, she is starring in *Rose Pepper* at The Harris Theatre. It is supposed to be quite good, and Miss Gantly is said to be both suggestive and funny."

"Can you get tickets for tomorrow night's performance?"

Irene studied Eve closely. "Eve, you are impulsive, and I must confess that I find it a thrilling trait, and going to tomorrow night's performance is an exciting idea. The problem with tomorrow night is that Mummy will want me to accompany her to one of her charitable events."

Irene made a sour face, her voice low with distaste. "I hear there will be opera scenes performed from *Lucia di Lammermoor*. If I am subjected to that mad scene once more, I believe I shall go mad."

"Can you make an excuse? Perhaps you can tell her that I need assistance?" Eve said, hopeful.

Irene placed a thoughtful finger at her cheek. "Yes, well, since you must now stay with us until Addison can accompany you to the bank, I believe that might just do the trick. I'll tell Mummy that I want you to meet some of our friends or something… No, even better than that, I'll tell her we must attend some sort of event at The Society for the Relief of Half-Orphan and Destitute Children. Yes, that should do splendidly."

Eve maneuvered a side glance toward Maggie. "I'd like to meet her backstage after the play."

"Well, that should be interesting," Irene said in a girlish, sweet tone.

Eve looked at her, carefully. Irene's smile held secrets.

"You know, Eve, I will have to bring my gentleman. I want you to meet him. And anyway, two women attending the theatre must be accompanied by a gentleman."

Eve saw a devious twinkle in Irene's eye. *The sooner I can escape from this girl the better,* she thought.

CHAPTER 14

On Tuesday evening, December 1st, Eve and Irene traveled down Broadway toward The Harris Theatre at 254 West 42nd Street. Eve was glued to the window like a little girl at Disney World, viewing the scintillating world of 1914 drift by in a magic of dazzling iridescence.

As the limousine passed the streetcars on 46th Street, Eve was enthralled by the lights of Times Square. Although it was nothing like the frantic blast of light and blazing neon color in 2018 Times Square, where Eve felt as though she was caught in a video game, this Times Square was still alive with exuberance and possibility.

The electric billboard signs seemed to sing out the lights of Fisk Tires, Squibb's Dental Cream, Maxwell House Coffee and Chevrolet. There were the dazzling theatre lights of the Palace Theater, the Columbia Theatre, and the Astor Theater, its flashing yellow and white running lights blazing out THE BROADWAY MELODY.

The chauffeured car bounced over streetcar tracks, motoring through a zone of excitement, elegance and class, where New Yorkers were richly dressed for a night at the theatre or dinner and dancing at a nightclub. No one was in casual attire as they were in Eve's time. There were no shorts, jeans, sneakers or t-shirts. No sweatshirts or sandals or ball caps, ski caps or LL Bean jackets. This world was all about high society style and class—a fashionable world that glimmered like diamonds. It was a thrill to experience this great city in the past, so shimmery and full of the high life.

As the car approached The Harris Theatre, Eve felt a touch of fear and apprehension. She peered out to see the bold theatre marquee:

MAGGIE LOTT GANTLY

in the smash hit

ROSE PEPPER!

Eve swallowed. She was about to meet Maggie Gantly, Patrick's daughter, and it felt surreal, dreamlike and just weird.

Minutes later, William held the door while Eve and Irene exited the limo, and then he watched attentively as they walked to the theatre entrance to wait for Irene's gentleman.

Fifteen minutes before curtain, Duncan had still not appeared, and Irene was a nervous wreck. The rebellious, determined suffragette was suddenly replaced by a hand-twisting, anxiety-ridden woman, who paced back and forth like a high school girl on a first date, sure she was being stood up.

"It is such an intimate affair," Irene said, looking at Eve with big, worried eyes. "My family can never know about Duncan. You must never tell anyone. Please tell me I can trust you, and that you will not, not ever, tell my secret."

Eve thought Irene was as dramatic as anyone she was likely to see on the theatre stage.

"Of course I won't tell. Anyway, I'm sure he'll be here soon."

Eve had worries of her own about seeing Maggie. She also began to pace.

Irene strained her neck, searching the busy sidewalks. "I have not shared him with any of my other friends. You are the first. They would not understand him. They would not understand my affection for him. But I can trust you, can't I? Please say, yes, Eve?"

"Yes, Irene. I said I won't tell anyone."

"He's so pitiable in a way. Boyishly good and handsome, though. He's a painter, and he is so very sensitive and so talented—but of course he has no money. But he has so much talent. You must come with me to Greenwich Village to see his paintings. I'm sure you'll see how talented he is," Irene said.

She glanced left and right, searching the elegantly dressed theatre patrons who streamed into the theater, the women bedecked with blossoming hats, long luxurious gowns and woolen coats, the men in tuxedos and long cashmere coats and top hats.

Eve was wearing another of Irene's gowns, a velvety burgundy dress trimmed in white lace, with a long-tailored coat. It was surely the most expensive dress and coat Eve had ever worn. Her hat was crowned with colorful silk ribbons, and the long suede gloves added an extravagant look.

Irene kept rattling on, nerves and apprehension beating away at her. "He has no money, Eve, but I make sure he has the money he needs for his studio and his paints. He's from a good Boston family, you know. It's just that they lost their money in bad investments and unfortunate speculation. They have even had to sell many of their rare paintings—works of art that had been in the family for generations. It's such a sad story, really, Eve, but you'll see what a dear boy Duncan is. What a special friend he is to me."

"Relax, Irene. You're making me nervous," Eve said, seeing an usher staring at them with stiff entreaty. "It's getting cold out here, Irene."

"Oh, Eve, I'm despairing now. I am afraid Duncan has had a change of mind and he is not coming. Did I say that he is so very sensitive? He sees the world as such an unhappy place, and I fear he tends more toward the melancholy than the cheerful. I believe his mother has some Russian blood in her, poor thing. But I'm good for him that way, Eve. I am his muse, you know, and I help keep his spirits up. Oh, my, where is he? The curtain will rise in ten minutes."

And then Irene's face lit up like Christmas.

Eve turned to see a lumbering young man approach, picking his way through the crowds, dressed in an ill-fitted dark suit, a lopsided bowtie, mussed black hair and a long cape, flapping in the wind. He lifted a tentative hand and waved back to Irene with a sagging frown. Was he happy to see her?

Duncan Beaumont was not at all what Eve had expected. He was tall, thin, nervous and shy. Irene hurried to him, she more breathless than he. Duncan's features were delicate, his eyes startled, his face indeed boyish, but as white as a sheet. As a nurse, Eve thought his thin frame and pale skin seemed sickly for a man in his mid-twenties. She wondered if the man had a poor diet, or maybe he drank too much. Perhaps he had a virus. His eyes were vague and foggy as he stared off into the distance, as if *Never, Never Land* might be close by. Maybe the guy just needed some iron supplements. He just didn't appear healthy, and Eve wondered if Irene was aware of his condition.

Irene seized Duncan's hand and tugged him toward Eve, flushed with excitement and pride.

"This is Mr. Duncan Beaumont, Eve. Duncan, this is my new and very good and trusted friend, Mrs. Eve Gantly."

Duncan's smile was strained, his eyes still holding that faraway look. He lifted a narrow, bony hand.

"So good to meet you, Mrs. Gantly."

Eve took his cold, clammy hand. "And it is very good to meet you, Mr. Beaumont."

Irene turned sharply toward the theatre doors. They were the last ones outside.

"Let's get inside and check our coats, before the curtain rises," Irene said, nearly dragging Duncan along.

Eve watched them enter the lobby and whispered under her breath. *"Well, opposites do attract."*

As she entered the theater, Eve now realized that Irene was out to save the world. That was rarely a good thing. One was always disappointed by the outcome. The world had its own way of being, as Eve knew all too well, and maybe you could help it, but save it? But then, isn't that what she and Patrick had set out to do? Try to save one person from her fate?

Inside, the theatre was lavish with frescoes, ornate moldings and elaborate chandeliers. It was a fantasy palace detached from the world outside and more beautiful than any theatre Eve had ever seen in her time. The auditorium had a loosely styled "Spanish-Moorish" motif, carpeted in royal blue, with wall panels of brocaded satin. As she sat, Eve calculated that the theatre held about a thousand patrons, and every seat was full. She sat in an aisle seat next to Irene, who sat next to Duncan. As the lights came down and the theatre fell into darkness, Eve stole a glance toward Duncan. His eyes were closed, and Irene was whispering something in his ear.

The maroon curtain rose to reveal an extravagantly decorated drawing room with a love seat, floor plants and French doors that opened onto a flowering garden.

A lone woman dressed in a long, flowing, white gown and a dramatic blue plumed hat, was gazing out above the audience, as if up into the sky. This was Maggie Lott Gantly.

The audience applauded the star, welcoming an actress they knew and had seen many times before. Eve studied her. On stage, Maggie had allure, sensuality and poise. The blue and gold lights that bathed her made her appear angelic and otherworldly. She was a striking beauty, and Eve only wished Patrick was here to see her. He would have beamed with pride.

When Maggie spoke, her voice was a lilting, resonate contralto, clear and warmly sexy.

"My dear friends, I have recently discovered that my quixotic gentleman friend has many secrets. How do I know? He told me so, one gloomy, rainy day. I suppose he wanted to cheer my mood. He said lovingly, and somewhat fatuously, that I am his most auspicious, capricious, and adored of all his secrets. He said I am his favorite secret, his most delicious secret, and his dearest girl, without a flaw. It did have the efficacious consequence of cheering my mood. Well, it would cheer any lady's mood, would it not?"

Maggie held up a finger, cocking her head coquettishly to the right. She grinned, mischievously.

"Of course, my dearest friends, I have many secrets as well, and being Rose Pepper, the guileless girl from Brooklyn, I will now tell you one of my little secrets."

She leaned toward the audience, cupped a hand to her mouth and lowered her voice to a conspiratorial whisper.

"Whenever my rich gentleman leans in for a little kiss, I sneak this dainty little hand," she raised a white-gloved hand and wiggled her fingers, "into his pocket and carefully and swiftly draw out several folded greenbacks. My gentleman loves his little girl and her kisses, and I love his greenbacks. Oh, he is never the wiser, although I fear he is very much the poorer. Ha Ha! But I? Well, I am always the wiser and the richer, am I not?"

The audience burst into laughter. Just then, a short, middle-aged man entered stage left, looking very much like a millionaire right out of the board game Monopoly. His dark suit helped set off his impressive white mustache, bushy eyebrows, and large bold eyes. He peered at a gold watch through a monocle over his right eye. When he finally snapped the watch lid shut, he dropped it back into his pocket and glanced around as if he were looking for someone.

Rose Pepper again leaned toward the audience, grinning with satisfaction, whispering, "There's my gentleman now, Lord love him. Let's see now..." She raised a hand and began to tick items off on gloved fingers.

"I need a new dress, a new hat, some shiny, glimmering diamonds and...let me see. Yes! I need a new little doggie. Don't you just love kisses? Don't you just love diamonds? Don't you just love little white doggies that go Bow Wow! NOW, when I leave you here, promise me that you will not tell him my secret. It is just between the two of us, as indeed everything you will soon witness must also be a secret between just you...and me."

When her gentleman turned and spotted Maggie, the monocle dropped from his eye, as he robustly exclaimed with boyish eagerness, "Miss Pepper! Miss Rose Pepper! There you are! Come to me, my dear girl. Your naughty boy needs a little kissy wissy."

Maggie pivoted and frolicked over to her gentleman for a kiss. As she leaned in toward him and puckered her lips, her left leg hitched back, theatrically, and she slipped her right hand adroitly into his pants pocket. Seconds later, she carefully removed a hand full of greenbacks. As the kiss lingered, Rose Pepper held up the greenbacks for the audience to see. There was a roar of laughter.

The play continued with the same general theme: a supposedly innocent gold-digger fooling a clueless old man, who at the end of the play did not notice Rose sneaking off with a handsome young man, waving greenbacks high above her head.

Eve didn't think it was a particularly good play, but the audience snickered and applauded, and Maggie was a good actress and comedian. Even Irene laughed, turning to Eve several times to say, "Isn't Miss Gantly a darling actress? She is so full of pep."

Whenever Eve ventured a glance toward Duncan, he seemed bored and tired. His head bobbed several times, as if he were fighting sleep. Eve was concerned. Toward the end of the play, he was slumped and listless. Irene didn't seem to notice. She was fully involved in the naughty comedy.

By the play's conclusion, Eve had decided how she would approach Maggie. From what Irene had told her about Big Jim Clancy, she knew she wouldn't have much time with the actress, so she decided to be blunt and honest.

After the final curtain call, Irene turned to Eve. "You go ahead backstage. I'm going to stay with Duncan. He is quite dispirited. I must try and cheer him."

Eve hesitated because she was concerned about Duncan. Then she decided to go, feeling this might be her only chance to meet Maggie, and Maggie was the sole reason Eve had risked her life to come to this time.

Eve got up and started down the aisle toward the stage. It was just at that moment that she suddenly had the odd feeling that Patrick was somewhere close by, watching her. The sensation was so strong that she felt the hair on the back of her neck stand up. She stopped and glanced about, blinking, expectant, but didn't see him anywhere in the departing crowd.

Eve sucked in a breath and marched forward.

CHAPTER 15

A thin, gray-haired theatre usher stopped Eve from entering the house door that led backstage. He was a weary, stooped-shouldered man, dressed in a loose-fitting navy-blue jacket with brass buttons, a white shirt and drooping bow tie.

"You cannot enter here, madam. The public is not allowed."

"But I want to see Miss Gantly, to congratulate her on her performance."

"She's not seeing anyone tonight. If you wish, you can wait outside the stage door. She might exit the theatre that way. Maybe not. Sometimes she waits until everyone has left."

Eve thought fast. "But I'm a relation, sir."

His gray eyebrows lifted a little. "A relation? Well, does Miss Gantly know you're here?"

"No…"

The experienced usher looked doubtful, especially as other theater patrons were lining up behind Eve.

"I'm sorry, but..."

Eve charged on. "Well, you see, it is a surprise. I know she'll want to see me. I'm sure of it."

The man scratched his patchy gray hair, twisting up his mouth in thought. He leaned, addressing the five people that were standing behind Eve. "I am very sorry, ladies and gentlemen, but Miss Gantly will not be seeing anyone backstage tonight. If you wish, you can wait for her to exit the stage door outside."

Disappointed, the little crowd mumbled and moved away.

"As I said, madam, I have strict instructions not to let..."

Eve cut him off. "...My name is Eve Gantly, sir. Maggie Lott Gantly and I are related, and if you ask her, I am sure she will want to see me. Tell her that I am a friend of her father."

His eyebrows lifted again. He was dubious and conflicted. He sighed. "Please wait here. I'll ask the stage manager."

Eve waited, turning around to see Irene link arms with Duncan and help him up the aisle toward the exit doors. There was definitely something wrong with that man, Eve thought. He should see a doctor. Eve would recommend it when she rejoined them.

The usher reappeared, his face softer. "This way. I will escort you. Please watch your step."

Backstage, Eve stepped over cables and around boxes and a row of stage lights. She looked left to see a circular, wrought-iron staircase leading up to rows of theater lights above. On stage, a man was sweeping the stage carpet, and a sturdy woman was removing the fresh flowers.

Near the rear of the theatre, the usher indicated toward a partially opened door. On it was printed in embossed gold letters MISS MAGGIE LOTT GANTLY.

"She is waiting for you, madam."

Eve thanked him and approached the door gingerly, licking her dry lips and straightening her shoulders, hoping to look confident. She was a mass of nerves as she knocked lightly. She heard a low, female voice from inside.

"Come in…"

Eve gently nudged the door open and stepped into a much smaller room than Eve had expected. On the left was a rack of gowns, to the right a sagging old couch. The room was filled with fresh flowers, mostly roses and lilies. Eve also caught a whiff of makeup.

Maggie was seated in an upright chair, facing a vanity makeup mirror surrounded by light bulbs. She was dressed in a skimpy, pink lace dressing gown that revealed the creamy tops of her ample breasts. Her hair was pulled back from her face, twisted up and tied with a red silk scarf, and she was applying cold cream to remove her stage makeup. Maggie looked at Eve through the mirror. It was a bland stare, with no real interest or curiosity.

That puzzled Eve.

"Welcome to my little prison," she said, reaching for a clean cloth to wipe the makeup from her forehead.

Maggie continued. "Everyone thinks theatre dressing rooms are exotic places, filled with glory and wonder—a place of romance and status. Well, look at this place. It's a dingy cell carved into the wings of this sooty brick building, with a dirty bathroom. I call all dressing rooms glorified prison cells."

Eve remained quiet while Maggie rubbed off the makeup.

"Would you like some Champagne?" Maggie asked. "It's in a bucket over there near the couch. The ice is mostly melted, but it should still be chilled enough."

"No, thank you," Eve said.

"Would you mind pouring me a glass then? There are two flutes around here someplace. One might be a bit soiled. I drank two glasses during intermission, and I don't remember where I put the glass. Oh, yes, there it is," Maggie said, pointing at the couch. "It has fallen like a good soldier to the back of the couch. Rest in peace, my good soldier Champagne glass."

Eve found a clean crystal Champagne flute on the end of the makeup table, grabbed the neck of the Champagne from its silver wine bucket and drew it out. The ice had melted. Eve poured a foaming glass full. When she handed the glass to Maggie, Maggie didn't take it. She took Eve in fully, and Eve felt the weight of her stare.

Maggie turned a little and rested back in her chair. "Well, aren't you quite the attractive girlie girl? Keep that glass for yourself. Pour mine in the dead soldier glass. I'll resurrect him like Lazarus."

Eve obeyed, pouring the Champagne and delivering it to Maggie's poised, waiting hand.

"I don't like to drink alone," Maggie said. "Of course I will, as a last resort, but I don't like to."

Maggie appraised Eve again. "Sit down on the couch and relax. We don't have a lot of time. My gentleman friend will be here soon. He doesn't like me to have visitors. Truth be told, he doesn't like me to do much of anything. He's funny that way, except that he doesn't have a good sense of humor, and that in itself is kind of funny. But I suppose funny is not the right word to describe any part of him."

Maggie lifted her glass. "A toast to whoever you are and whatever it is that you want."

Their glasses chimed. Maggie drank half of hers and set the glass down. "All right, Miss, or is it Mrs.?"

"It's Mrs. Gantly."

Maggie's eyes widened. "Oh, so you are standing by your creative theatrical story. Well brava, Mrs. Gantly, but let me stop this before it goes any further. I cannot help your career. Yes, you are pretty and yes, the rich men will like you, and yes, from the looks of you, you probably can act a little, but I am just not the one to help you. Not now. Maybe a few years ago I could have helped you, but not anymore. Frankly, I have grown weary of this whole circus. I'd like to run away to the West—maybe to California—or even further north. Maybe to Canada. I hear Canada is a lovely and a friendly country. I could use a place like that. Well, anyway, I congratulate you on your originality. A friend of my father? Very good, Mrs. Gantly... Is it truly Mrs. Gantly?"

Maggie faced her mirror again and went back to work, removing makeup.

Eve stiffened. "Yes, I am Mrs. Patrick Sharland Gantly. And I am a friend of your father. Now I know we don't have much time here today, but I would like to meet with you somewhere in private soon, so we can talk. It's very important that we talk."

Maggie laid her cloth aside and sat still for a moment. When she turned, she stared at Eve carefully. "You are quite serious, aren't you? Or are you perhaps a little bit balmy?"

"I am not," Eve said.

"Are you an actress?"

"No... I'm a nurse."

Maggie's eyes shifted. Her expression changed from doubt to suspicion. "How do you know my father? And who is your husband, and where is your husband?"

"I'll tell you everything you want to know, but not here and not now. As you said, your gentleman friend will be here at any moment. I don't think he'll want me here. Can we meet somewhere in private, and soon? Possibly in the next day or so?"

Maggie kept her wary eyes on Eve. "I do not know, Mrs. Gantly. I simply do not know. There is something about you that disturbs me...yes, and that troubles me. I don't like trouble, at least not that kind of trouble. A nurse you said? You're a nurse?"

"Yes..."

"Where?"

"I am not currently employed."

"Where are you from?"

"Originally, Ohio. I live here now. In New York."

"Where?"

"I have just arrived. I'm living with friends temporarily."

"What friends?"

Eve hesitated. She was about to speak when the large shadow of a man appeared in the doorway, blocking the outside light. The room turned suddenly cold.

Maggie sat back, unperturbed, looking at Big Jim through the mirror.

"Hello, Big Jimmy. How are the tables tonight?"

His quick, suspicious, green eyes glanced about. They settled on Eve. Eve swallowed as she slowly lifted her timid eyes on him. He was a big man, clearly as tall as Patrick, with a barrel chest, a paunchy belligerent stomach and menacing, challenging eyes that seemed to take in everything. His tweed suit was too tight for him and his bowler cap was pulled tightly over his head.

He glared at Maggie. "Who is this woman?"

"A new friend. An admirer."

"I said nobody comes back to see you tonight," he said in a slight Irish accent. "I told you, and I told everybody to tell you that."

"She was very kind and complimentary. I can always use new friends, Big Jimmy."

Big Jim lowered his half-hooded eyes on Eve. "Go now. Leave the glass and go."

"Don't be rude, Big Jimmy."

"You shut up!" he barked. To Eve, he jerked his thumb toward the door. "You, go. Get out!"

Eve arose with as much calm dignity as she could muster. She held Maggie's eyes.

"It was a real pleasure to meet you and to see you perform, Miss Gantly. I hope to see you again."

"Perhaps we can meet for tea some afternoon," Maggie said. "The St. Regis has a lovely tea."

"I hope we can," Eve said.

Big Jim stepped out of the doorway to let Eve pass, staring at her with stormy eyes.

"What is your name?" Big Jim asked as she passed him and moved out into the hallway.

"Eve Sharland."

He grunted something insulting under his breath.

Outside the theatre, Eve searched the street and saw William, the chauffeur, wave at her. She slipped on her coat against the quick, chilly wind and started for the car. He held the door for her and she slipped inside.

When the door closed, Eve saw Duncan's head resting on Irene's shoulder.

"Is he all right, Irene?"

Irene's face was pinched in concern. "No, Eve. I am very worried. I want him to go see a doctor, but he refuses. What should I do?"

"No doctor," Duncan said, in a low, muffled voice. "No doctors."

Eve struggled to shake her encounter with Maggie and the toxic energy of Big Jim. "Can you take him to your home?" Eve asked.

When Eve saw the terror in Irene's face, she knew the answer. "All right, let's go to his place."

Irene's mind seemed to lock up. "Why, Eve?"

"I'll examine him."

"What? You will do what?"

"I am a nurse, Irene."

Irene couldn't find any words.

Eve leaned forward. "William, please take us to Greenwich Village."

She turned to Duncan. "Duncan, where do you live?"

CHAPTER 16

Duncan's railroad style apartment was just off Christopher Street. William helped Duncan up the four flights of stairs to the two narrow rooms and eased him down on the rumpled single bed.

Irene turned a stern eye on William. "You cannot mention this to Mummy or to Addison, William. This entire night must remain the deepest secret. Do I have your word?"

William's eyes shifted; his nose seemed more pointed. He snapped his hands behind his back and stood at attention. "Yes, Miss Casterbury. You have my word. Shall I wait for you downstairs?"

Irene was tentative. "No... Well, Yes..."

Irene looked to Eve for help.

"Yes, William. Please wait for us in the car. We won't be long."

"Very good, Miss Casterbury."

And then he slipped silently away, like a shadow, leaving Duncan on the bed in a fetal position, Irene anxious and scared, and Eve shedding her coat, glancing about the apartment for clues as to medicine, bottles or pills. She wasn't sure what she was looking for.

She saw a painting easel and canvasses propped carelessly against the base of the walls, showing various abstract paintings, one looking much like a stormy sea or the inside of a hurricane. Another painting was of steel gray streets and distorted faces that were vague, lonely and peering out of a yellow, smoky fog.

On a rickety-looking kitchen table was a dirty plate and a glass half-filled with some brown liquid. Whiskey? Next to that was a wooden painter's palette, with six round wells, four rectangular wells, and one thumb hole.

"What should we do, Eve?" Irene said, her lashes batting with wide-eyed innocence and vulnerability.

Eve spotted a squat clear bottle with a silver label lying on Duncan's bedside table. She went to it and scooped it up. It was empty. She read the printed label:

BAYER PHARMACEUTICAL PRODUCTS
ELBERFELD HEROIN

Eve's eyes enlarged on the label. "What? Heroin?" She looked at Duncan, whose eyes were still tightly closed.

She held up the bottle. "Duncan, have you been taking this? Duncan. Wake up!"

His eyes fluttered open. "What?"

Eve held the bottle up. "Have you been taking this?"

He squinted at the bottle. "Yes..." he said, weakly. "A doctor down the street prescribed it. He said it would help my cough."

Eve thought of the opioid crisis in 2018. And then she thought of the famous quote *The more things change, the more they stay the same.*

Irene saw the alarm on Eve's face.

"Eve, what is it?"

Eve ignored her. "What kind of cough? How long have you been sick, Duncan?"

"I don't know."

"He's been coughing for a while," Irene said. "I sent him to a doctor."

Eve sat down on the edge of the bed and placed a hand on Duncan's forehead. He was burning up and shivering.

"Eve! That is unseemly," Irene said, as she clapped a hand over her mouth. "We should not even be in Duncan's room. Please stand up and away from Duncan's bed."

Eve shot her a look. "Duncan is very sick. We must get him to a hospital. Where is the nearest hospital around here?"

Irene stammered. "I don't know... I have no idea."

"Gouverneur Hospital on Water Street," Duncan said, weakly.

Eve shot to her feet. She knew about Gouverneur Hospital. She'd worked there as a nurse when she had time traveled to 1885. Was it still there, twenty-eight years later? Eve recalled the neighborhood. Not the best. The riverfront neighborhood of Water Street and Gouveneur's Slip was among the seediest in New York City in the 1880s, with nearby brothels, saloons and gambling dens. Stabbings, shootings, and beatings were common, and she'd seen it all working there as a nurse. It was the same hospital she'd taken Patrick to after he'd been shot at the Harringshaw ball.

"Are you sure it's on Water Street, Duncan?" Eve asked.

In a coughing, raspy voice he said, "Yes... I've been there."

Eve turned to a still-startled Irene. "Help me get him up and out of here, Irene."

Irene turned to the door. "I should call William."

"We can do it. Come on, help me. I'm betting Duncan has pneumonia."

Irene gasped.

"Now, Irene. Help me."

As the car approached the hospital, Eve saw that it was not the same hospital it had been 1885. It was newer and larger, four-stories now, built of red brick and trimmed in terra cotta. There were rounded balconies on each floor to provide privacy and protection from the direct midday heat. What a change for the better, Eve thought.

William helped lift Duncan from the car, wrapping an arm around Duncan's shoulder and walking him into the hospital. As they entered the narrow reception area, Eve and Irene drew attention. Many downcast eyes lifted in sudden surprise and fastened on to them. A white-haired man sitting in a wheelchair, with two trousered stumps for legs, stared up with misty drugged eyes.

Dressed richly as they were, and being assisted by a smartly dressed chauffeur, Eve and company looked very out of place in this hospital for the poor, like a royal family entering a neighborhood bar.

It was Eve who took charge and spoke to the helpful nurse at reception. Irene stepped over to assure payment for any services performed.

Within minutes, a male orderly appeared with a wheelchair and William lowered Duncan into it. Irene continued filling out the paperwork, as Eve followed the wheelchair down a long, gray-tiled hallway, past the Charity Department, continuing through two swinging doors, parted by a waiting nurse. Duncan's head had fallen to his chest, and Eve was worried. As they passed the Children's Ward, a sign on the door read QUARANTINED.

"Why are they quarantined?" Eve asked the young, athletic orderly, whose eyes were fixed ahead.

"Measles, whooping-cough and pneumonia. Infectious diseases spread quickly in the hospital."

He glanced at her, and Eve felt the young man's judgment of her: her clothes, the stylish hat and coat. He believed her to be part of the fortunate upper-class, of course.

"Maybe you don't know, Miss, but the Lower East Side is filled with tenements crammed with poor immigrant families."

Eve ignored his judgmental gaze as they pressed on.

Eve waited outside in the hallway while Duncan was wheeled inside a room. She was told that he would be undressed, placed in a cotton hospital gown and put to bed.

It wasn't long before a short, serious, middle-aged male doctor and a weary-looking nurse appeared. Eve was sure that the doctor's swift appearance had much to do with Irene, her class and her money.

When Eve explained Duncan's symptoms and the medication he was taking, the doctor averted his uninterested eyes, and the nurse simply turned away and went inside. Moments later, the doctor muttered a thank you, turned and left Eve alone in the hallway.

Eve returned to reception to find Irene pacing, worried and anxious. Six poor souls, waiting to be admitted, were staring at Irene, some with dry, weary interest, others with curiosity and awe. They were dressed shabbily, clothes soiled, shoulders hunched, tired faces fearful. Eve had forgotten about the variety of foul odors of this time. Clothes were not washed frequently, and bathing was not as common as it was in the 21st century. She wanted to step outside for a gasp of fresh air and, at the same time, she wished she had something to offer them besides a kind look: money, or medication from her time.

Irene rushed to Eve as she approached. "How is poor Duncan?"

"I don't know. The doctor is with him."

"Oh my, I cannot stay here, but I am so worried about Duncan. What am I to do?"

This once strong and forceful Irene was now a near basket case. It was obvious that she was head-over-heels in love with Duncan.

Irene lowered her voice, glancing about dismally. "Look at this place, Eve. The neighborhood is frightening, and this hospital is so, well, near the river. I wish I could have Dr. Winslow, our family physician, treat Duncan, but I dare not. Mummy will find out about Duncan and she will faint dead away, and make such a scene, demanding that I never see Duncan again. She will stop the flow of my funds. I must get home right away, or Mummy will be all frantic nerves. She may even call the detectives. It's getting so late."

"Okay, why don't you let William take you home."

"But what will you do?"

"I'll stay with Duncan until I learn something. Can you send William back to pick me up in a couple of hours?"

"Well, yes, of course, but what will I tell Mummy?"

"You can make something up. You're good at that."

Irene gazed sorrowfully down the long, dimly lit corridor where Duncan had gone. "I am so very worried about Duncan, Eve. You are such a dear to stay here with him, in case he needs someone. I knew you would be a true and trusted friend the moment I first saw you, looking so forlorn sitting on that Central Park bench."

"Go now, Irene. I'll drop by your room tonight when I return."

Irene lowered her head in defeat. "I am such a foolish girl to fall for such a lost soul. But what can I do? Dear Duncan has touched my heart like no other man has, or indeed ever could."

Irene kissed Eve on either cheek, and then she swept out of the hospital as if borne on a fortunate current of wind.

CHAPTER 17

Eve stood in the quiet reception room because all the chairs were occupied. One old wrinkled and stooped man pushed up with effort and graciously indicated toward his chair, but Eve shook her head, "No, but you are a true gentleman. Thank you, sir. Please sit down."

She wandered to the glass entrance doors and stood watching needle-fine rain wash the world, feeling as though she was in a border city, hovering between two countries, trapped, lost and utterly alone.

Two hours later, a new night duty nurse replaced the old. Eve approached the starched-faced woman with crooked teeth and flat gray eyes. Eve knew this type: she was just waiting to be offended. Undaunted, Eve stepped toward her and politely asked about Duncan. She was curtly told that she would be updated when the doctor saw fit to update her, and not before. The nurse finished her declaration with the jerk of a nod, as if to say, "Take that."

Not to be rebuffed, Eve asked another question. "Does Dr. Ann Long still work here?" Dr. Long was the head of the hospital when Eve worked as a nurse at the old hospital in 1885.

The nurse didn't look up from the newspaper she was reading. "No," she replied, flatly.

Eve pressed on, taking a long shot. She wanted to know if the two men who had helped steal Patrick's wounded body from the hospital back in 1885 were still employed. They would have witnessed her and Patrick lighting the lantern, disappearing and returning to 2016. If she could find those men, perhaps one would know where the lantern was.

"Then perhaps you know of two gentlemen who used to work here: Daniel Fallow and Jacob Jackson."

The nurse lifted her cold eyes, clearly annoyed. "I have never heard of them. Now, do you have any further questions, or can I return to my work?"

Eve flashed her a broad, media smile. "No, thank you, nurse. You have been so pleasant and helpful. I'm sure your patients love you, as I can see that you are truly a blessing to your profession."

With that, Eve reversed and walked away, leaving the nurse to fume and mumble curses under her foul breath.

Minutes later, when the front door opened, and Addison stepped in, Eve froze, eyes going wide with disbelief. A breath caught in her throat. She steadied herself with effort and stepped back. Addison approached, removing his hat. Little beads of rain clung to the shoulders of his black cashmere overcoat and hat.

He pushed a hand through his wavy hair and gave Eve a little bow. Again, all eyes swung to this wealthy out-of-place gentleman. The little group picked up the scent of a possible scandal that they would surely be able to follow in one of the eleven Manhattan and Brooklyn daily papers. Even the starched-faced nurse lifted her head in sudden interest, her hard expression softening as she took in the young handsome gentleman.

"My dear Mrs. Gantly," Addison said. "I must apologize for the ghastly way you have been treated. I am simply livid at my sister for leaving you in this..." he glanced about with a shake of his disapproving head. "... in this disreputable part of town."

Eve opened her mouth to speak, but Addison continued on. "I am here to personally escort you home and out of this stain of a place. I would have come sooner, but it took me an inordinate amount of time to pry the truth from Irene. She is a silly goose, I'm afraid, who is always entangling herself in situations from which I must rescue her. I told her that there will come a day when I will refuse to rescue her. I told her sternly that she will be quite on her own."

He offered his arm and Eve looked at it. She then turned back toward the nurse, who stared back, eyes watchful, jaw set.

Eve raised her eyes to Addison. "Mr. Casterbury, I'm sure Irene told you why I remained here."

"Yes, of course, and I can assure you, Mrs. Gantly, that it is not of the least consequence."

"I beg your pardon?" Eve said.

"Whoever that young man is has nothing to do with you or the Casterbury family, and I would not want the Casterbury name to appear in any of the morning papers. Irene has a talent for regularly doing the most scandalous things, and I must step in and stop it. Irene told me that she has already paid funds to help the man, and I think we can leave it at that. The doctors will no doubt restore him to health."

Eve kept her voice low but firm. "Mr. Casterbury, Mr. Beaumont is quite ill. I would like to wait to talk to the doctor before I leave."

Addison stared at her, as if trying to understand. "Is this Mr. Beaumont a friend or a relative, Mrs. Gantly?"

"No, he isn't. I just met him tonight, but…"

He cut her off. "…Then I don't understand. Why do you feel responsible? Why are you remaining here in this unsavory edifice, in the depths of the night, to learn of his condition? I can assure you, Mrs. Gantly, that Irene has a penchant for getting involved in lost causes, picking up every stray cat or dog, and trying to save them. I have warned her of such things many times, but alas, to no avail. I fear that someday her wayward tendencies will get her into real trouble."

Eve was about to ask if she was also a lost cause but thought better of it. After all, he was the man who would be able to help her open a bank account.

"Mr. Casterbury, Mr. Beaumont is a man, sir, and a very sick one."

"And he is none of our concern, Mrs. Gantly."

Eve was about to tell him to leave when he glanced past Eve's shoulder toward the reception nurse.

"However, Mrs. Gantly, if it will please you, I will inquire about Mr. Beaumont's condition."

He inhaled an impatient breath and marched to the reception desk with a posture and expression indicating that he was the lord of the manor.

"Nurse, will you please find the doctor in charge of Mr. Beaumont and tell him that Mr. Addison Casterbury would like to speak with him about Mr. Beaumont's current condition, and I would like to speak with him now."

To Eve's surprise and irritation, the woman's face melted into angelic worship.

"Of course, Mr. Casterbury. I will find Dr. McGrath right away," she said, snatching up the phone to find the doctor.

Eve shook her head, turning away in disgust.

It was a miracle. In less than three minutes, Dr. McGrath came striding down the hallway toward them. He was the same short, serious middle-aged male doctor Eve had met earlier. The same doctor who had basically discounted anything she had to say.

Now, he was all smiles and cordiality. Eve started toward both men, but Addison passed her a cool, halting glance, and she came to full stop.

That's right, Eve thought. This is a man's world, and she is not invited.

She watched with half-hooded eyes as the men spoke in confidential tones, gesturing and nodding agreement and smug satisfaction.

Minutes later, Addison shook Dr. McGrath's hand, bid him farewell and started back to Eve. With straight-back aplomb, he leveled his eyes on her.

"Dr. McGrath assures me that Mr. Beaumont is receiving the best of care."

"What is his diagnosis?" Eve asked.

"Mrs. Gantly, you do not need to concern yourself with that."

Eve hated this man's patronizing attitude, but again, she held her tongue. She would blast him later, once she had her money.

"I would be grateful to know, sir. Is it pneumonia?"

He stared at her, again showing impatience. "Yes, Dr. McGrath informed me that Mr. Beaumont has pneumonia. May we please leave this place now, Mrs. Gantly? Tomorrow will be a particularly busy day for me, and I must have my rest. I will be speaking at two events tomorrow at the Hotel Astor, where I will be offering a few enthusiastic words for *The American Women's War Relief*, and some inspiring words for a most worthy cause for children, the *Santa Claus Association*."

Eve watched him pull on his leather gloves, the gleam of pride all about him.

"You see, Mrs. Gantly, I hope to run for Manhattan Borough President at the next election. After that, who knows? Perhaps I will seek the office of the Mayor and become the next young Mayor, just as John Purroy Mitchel has done. I've been told I'd make a good Mayor. And then conceivably I could run for Governor of New York. And why not?"

Eve's smile was contrived. "Why not indeed, Mr. Casterbury."

The limousine drove away from the hospital in a rumble of gears and motored uptown in the rain. Addison sat on the far right and Eve on the left. Neither spoke for a time, Eve feeling drained and sleepy and Addison sitting erect and distant.

Finally, Addison cleared his throat and turned toward her.

"Mrs. Gantly, where did you say you are from?"

"Ohio..."

"Ah, yes, Ohio. Are you from a small town in Ohio?"

"Somewhat."

"I see. You have family there?"

"Yes."

"And why did you come to New York?"

"To see friends."

"And your husband? Did he also come to see friends?"

Eve hesitated. She had to stop this questioning. She'd learned from her last time travel adventure in 1885 that the fewer people knew about her the better.

"These are personal questions, Mr. Casterbury."

"Pardon me, Mrs. Gantly. It's just that... well, if you will permit me to say so, I perceive in you something of the unusual."

Eve looked away. "Well, since you already said it, Mr. Casterbury, I suppose I will permit it."

He stiffened at her remark, not used to be addressed so frankly by a woman. He cleared his throat again.

"Like my father, Mrs. Gantly, I pride myself on being an observant man. If I may say so, I see in you something that does not quite fit with—how shall I say it—the overall portrait of you. You are like a painting, a fortunate work of art, hanging in an exquisite gallery. When one passes and observes that painting, one is caught by mystery, grace and allure."

Eve's mind worked to find a way to change the subject. "You flatter me too much, Mr. Casterbury."

"Shall I be bold, Mrs. Gantly?"

"Perhaps you should not," Eve responded.

"Then I shall modify my words and my observations, Mrs. Gantly. I find it fascinating that you appear in our home quite suddenly, accompanying my sister, who is notorious for finding intrigue. You are a woman, apparently, without a home or lodgings, which suggests a lack of funds. You say you are married and yet, your husband is curiously absent. And he does not appear to be out searching for you."

Eve turned to stare out the window, willing Addison to stop talking. He didn't. What he said next chilled and paralyzed her.

"Mrs. Gantly, since you have come under our roof and have thusly been put in our charge, I feel personally responsible for you. Irene confessed to me that you have obviously fallen on hard times, reduced to selling a quality family heirloom so that you can subsist. I cannot allow you to do that, Mrs. Gantly."

Eve whirled to protest. "It was not a family…"

He held up a hand to stop her. "I will be happy to accompany you to the same merchant who bought the ring and buy it back from him at whatever the cost."

Eve became flustered. "Thank you for your kind offer, sir, but I don't want to buy it back. I want to go to the bank and open an account. Irene suggested you might be willing to accompany me there."

"It is my feeling, Mrs. Gantly, that you need some protection. I do not believe you have ever visited New York, and I can assure you, without protection, it can be a vicious and dangerous place."

Eve was too astonished to speak.

Addison set his chin. "Therefore, Mrs. Gantly, do not worry about funds. While you wait or search for your husband, I will see to it that you are given all the necessary funds to purchase all the practical necessities of life, and you will live well in Casterbury Mansion. You will dwell in the comfort and safety of our home and, of course, you can come and go as you wish."

Eve stared, dumbly.

"May I also be so bold as to ask you to dine out with me, perhaps tomorrow night? Afterward, I would enjoy showing you some of the more cultural parts of our lovely city. I'm sure your husband will not mind our innocent little excursion, Mrs. Gantly, because, frankly, I do not believe you have a husband."

Eve felt some of the life drain from her body.

CHAPTER 18

Early Thursday morning, December 3rd, Eve crept out of the Casterbury Mansion alone, found a cab and told the driver to take her to the St. Regis Hotel, which was only a few blocks away on Fifth Avenue and 55th Street. Fortunately, Irene usually slept late, and Addison had already left for his Wall Street office.

Eve forced herself to formulate goals, keep her mind busy, and keep her emotions in check. It was the only way she could deflect her mind from Patrick, and Addison's goal of keeping her caged in the Casterbury Mansion.

She had to push away any despair about Patrick and what had happened to him. There was absolutely nothing she could do to search for him.

Eve also had to face the fact that unless, by some miracle, she could locate the lantern that had been left behind in 1885, she would have to live out the rest of her life in this time.

Eve had two goals, and both were risky. Her primary goal was to get out of that house and away from Irene and Addison Casterbury as fast as she possibly could. Addison had made it abundantly clear that he wanted a relationship with her, and she was having none of it. He had the kingdom, the power and the money to get whatever he wanted, and he was no doubt used to getting his way one way or the other.

Eve knew what his plan would be. He would set her up in a gorgeous brownstone with lavish furnishings and give her a generous allowance, and then he'd drop in at his convenience for her "favors." She'd had a similar offer back in 1885, and she wasn't about to get herself tangled up in that vicious web again.

Even if she never saw Patrick again, and that thought sickened her, Addison Casterbury, despite his wealth, political ambitions and royal good looks, did not attract her in the least. Eve sensed cold calculations going on behind his dark gray eyes; a man who weighed everything by value, ownership and control. Undoubtedly, most women found him irresistible—and Eve was certain that he found himself irresistible, and in turn, he was baffled at her hesitancy to fall for him. No, she would never fall for him. But there was still a dark cloud hanging over her head: how could she avoid his dinner invitation?

On Wednesday, Eve had used a headache as a reason not to emerge from her room to see Irene or meet Addison for dinner. That morning, she'd sent a note to both Irene and Addison with her apologies that she was ill and would, therefore, need to spend the day and evening alone to recover.

But true to his word, Addison had sent money in a private envelope, through Mary. Eve wanted to refuse it, but she had no choice. She needed it to escape the man.

On Wednesday evening, she devised a plan, and now she was ready to implement it.

In the taxi, Eve opened her purse to ensure that the check for the pawned ring was there. It was. Her first goal was to visit Maggie Gantly. When she'd spoken to Maggie backstage at the theatre on Saturday night, Eve had seen the interest in Maggie's eyes. And when Big Jim Clancy entered the room, Eve had also seen fear rise in those same beautiful eyes. It was clear that Maggie feared the man, and she saw no way out of the relationship, short of risking violence on herself. Big Jim was a violent man. In a few weeks, just before Christmas, if Eve couldn't get Maggie away from Big Jim, he'd kill her.

The eighteen-story, lavishly Beaux-Arts styled St. Regis Hotel loomed ahead. Eve had read in the Sunday paper that the hotel was cited as "offensive" in a report of the City's Heights of Building Commission, because of its Fifth Avenue location.

The hotel still stood in 2018, but this 1914 building loomed tall and imposing against the shorter, less impressive architecture of this time. The St. Regis Hotel was definitely a standout.

Eve paid the taxi driver and swung out. She advanced toward the front doors in the cold December chill, and a tall, uniformed doorman was ready with an opened door. Inside, Eve felt expanded as she took in the marble floors, the Louis XV furniture from France, the Waterford crystal chandeliers, the ornamental ceilings and the antique tapestries and oriental rugs.

As she strolled toward the brown-marble lobby desk, she looked left to see two beautiful, fifteen-foot burnished bronze entrance doors parted to reveal an inner spacious library.

At the lobby desk, a stiff but smiling clerk wearing a dapper dark suit addressed her. His face was shiny and pleasant, his manner formal.

"Could you please call Miss Maggie Gantly, sir?"

"Is she expecting you, madam?"

Eve lied. "Yes, she is."

"May I ask your name, madam?"

"Eve Gantly."

He blinked, the name catching him off guard. He quickly recovered.

"Yes, Mrs. Gantly. One moment."

He reached for a clunky black telephone while Eve waited nervously, watching the parade of guests going and coming, the women bedecked in jewels, wearing colorful dresses with tunics and tucked waists, made of silks, cotton and lace. The hats with plumes were ever on display, and Eve was reminded of an article she had read in 2018. It discussed the cost of looking fashionable at the turn of the 20th century. It stated that by the early 1900s, the commercial plume trade had decimated many bird species to the point of near extinction, inspiring early environmentalists—many of them women and New Yorkers—to champion the protection of endangered birds.

The hotel clerk's voice brought her back to the present.

"Mrs. Gantly, Miss Maggie Gantly asks that you give her the courtesy of twenty minutes before visiting."

"Yes, of course," Eve said.

After all, it was only a little after nine o'clock in the morning and Maggie worked in the theatre.

Twenty minutes later, Eve tapped on Maggie Gantly's fourth-floor apartment door. When it opened, Maggie stood in a modest pink chiffon dress that Eve would have called a Maxi dress, with sheer long sleeves. Maggie's hair was twisted up and piled on her head, with loose tendrils dripping from either side of her face.

Maggie stood staring, her soft hazel eyes intensely serious, inspecting Eve up and down.

"I should have told the hotel clerk to throw you out," Maggie said in a low voice, still rusty with sleep.

"Why didn't you?" Eve countered.

"I don't know."

Maggie shrugged. "Maybe because there's something about you that scares me a little, and that interests me a little. Notice I said a little and not a lot."

"I'll take a little."

Maggie didn't move. "At first I thought you might be goopy. Now, I am not so sure."

"Goopy?" Eve asked, not understanding.

"Stupid. Okay, I saw you weren't so goopy, but then I thought maybe you were a hawkshaw."

"I don't know that word either."

Maggie narrowed her eyes on her. "Where have you been living, among the high rollers? A hawkshaw is a kind of detective. Big Jim has his ways of tracking me. He uses hawkshaws. But then I saw the way he looked at you. He'd never seen you before. He didn't like you. Maybe that's why I did like you. But I've got to be careful with Big Jim. So maybe now you've got to be careful with Big Jim, too."

Eve held her gaze. She could see Maggie still wasn't certain whether she should let Eve in or not.

"Yes, well, Big Jim is, well, big, and not so friendly," Eve pattered on, hoping Maggie would finally invite her in.

Maggie laughed. "Not so friendly? Ha! I like that one. Do you think Big Jim is pug-ugly?"

"Not so ugly. Scary."

Maggie's face fell into apprehension. "Yes, well, I thought he was keen at first. I don't know. Who remembers these things? Men come, and men go, like evening breezes. Like bubbles in a glass of Champagne. So, why are you here, whoever you are, and what do you want from me?"

"Can I please come in?" Eve said, glancing about the empty corridor.

"I don't know."

"Because I don't want to tell you who I am and why I came while standing out here in the hallway. I'm sure you can understand that. Maybe there's a hawkshaw lurking around somewhere."

Maggie took a breath, shrugged, and reluctantly stood aside, hanging her head in resignation. Eve entered.

The room was immense, with white marble floors, rich oriental rugs and a black and gold marble fireplace, with an immense gilded mirror above. Eve loved the glistening chandelier, the burgundy Victorian furniture, and the view of Fifth Avenue from the bank of windows. Shoulder-high palms and ferns filled the corners of the room. Large vases of fresh flowers sat on the tables, filling the room with their fragrances. Eve could only wonder how much a suite like this would cost in her time.

"Have a seat, Mrs. Gantly," Maggie said. "Biddy is around here someplace. She's not used to me being up so early. She's probably passed out in a bedroom, or maybe the bathroom. It's big in there and the bathtub is nice. I found her asleep in there once."

Maggie turned and bellowed. "Biddy!"

"Biddy is seventeen years old, from Dublin. She is a good worker, but a bit batty about the lads. I think she has two. One at the theatre. That's why you didn't see her the other night. She confessed she was with him."

Maggie called again. "Biddy!"

A few moments later, a thin, sleepy-faced girl scampered in, wearing a white-apron and white-cap, a bit askew. Her eyes darted about, seeing Eve. She bobbed a bow.

"Were you dreaming about him?" Maggie said, with a warm grin.

"Sorry, Mum... I was... I was cleaning the back bathroom."

"Sure you were, Biddy. Polishing the tub with your round apple-bottom you mean. Would you please bring some tea, bread and butter? And bring a bottle of Champagne. I need something that bubbles and makes me happy."

Maggie turned to Eve. "Do you like things that bubble, Mrs. Gantly?"

At the name Gantly, Biddy's startled eyes swung to Eve.

"Why not, Miss Gantly. I think we're both going to need it."

Maggie's eyes changed, and she suddenly looked uncomfortable.

"I dare say that is true, Mrs. Gantly."

CHAPTER 19

Maggie languished on a burgundy velvet sofa, staring across at Eve, who had settled in a pink satin parlor chair. Each continued to size the other up, letting the silence gather between them. They ignored the silver tray of buttered bread and tea, but sipped Champagne from long-stemmed coupe glasses.

"At the theatre on Tuesday night, Mrs. Gantly, you said you were a friend of my father. Were you lying?"

Eve took a long sip, measuring her response. "No…"

Maggie tilted her head a little to the right, her elegant eyebrows lifting as if to say, is that all? She took a drink. "And…? Can you please elaborate?"

Eve glanced about. "Is anyone around?"

"If you're referring to Big Jim, no. Sometimes he comes by, sometimes not. Anyway, he leaves early. He has many businesses. Now, about my father. Unless you are communicating with a ghost, then I assume you are speaking—how should I say—metaphorically?"

"Your father did not die in 1885, Miss Gantly."

"Oh, for pity sake, just call me Maggie."

"All right then, call me Eve."

Maggie tapped a foot. "And how do you know he didn't die in 1885? Who are you really? And stop being evasive. Either you have something to say or you don't, and if you don't, you are wasting my sleeping time, and I have a performance tonight."

Eve stared into her glass, watching the bubbles rise and play. "Maggie, I have come to take you away from here. You're in danger."

Eve didn't shift under Maggie's hard, thoughtful gaze. "Despite what you may think, Maggie, I am your friend."

Maggie slowly got up, fixing Eve with a frosty stare. "I don't know you, and you are certainly not my friend. You need to go now."

Eve set her glass down on a lace doily. She set her lips firmly and clasped her hands in her lap, thinking carefully. She lowered her voice.

"Maggie, between the two of us, we can get you away from New York and Big Jim. I saw the fear in your eyes the other night. You're scared to death of him. You feel trapped. As part of the Gantly family, I want to help you. I want to get you away from here, so you can start a new life."

Maggie gave Eve an empty smile. "What part of the Gantly family are you from? I've certainly never heard of you."

The Champagne made Eve a bit bold. "As I said, your father did not die in 1885. He escaped New York and lived in another place."

Maggie drained her glass, her hands restless, eyes moving. "What place? Where?"

"Ohio," Eve lied. "I'm from Ohio."

"What happened to my father? Why didn't he come? He'd be in his sixties now. Is he still alive?"

Eve had tried to plan for this conversation, and she had even rehearsed various versions of it, but she had no way of knowing which way it would go or how Maggie would respond. Eve would have to lie more than she wanted to, but there was no other way. Eve hoped that if things worked out, and if she could convince Maggie to escape Big Jim, perhaps Eve could tell her the truth later.

Eve continued. "No, he's not alive, but his dying wish was for me to come to New York and help you. He read the newspaper articles about you. He was worried and feared for your life with Big Jim."

Maggie marched to the golden wine bucket, yanked out the Champagne bottle and poured herself another glass. She did not offer to fill Eve's.

Maggie's eyes turned stormy. "Why didn't he ever come to see me? Tell me that? If he loved me so much, why didn't he come even once to see me for all these past twenty-eight years?"

Eve had anticipated Maggie's question. "Because he was poor and sick, and he didn't want you to think that he came seeking money. He was ashamed of himself, but very proud of you, Maggie."

Maggie's eyes teared up and she drank half of her glass. "I bet. When did he die?"

"A short time ago. He wanted me to come see you. It was his last wish."

Maggie's voice turned harsh. "Are you his daughter?"

"No, Maggie. I was his wife."

Maggie began to tremble, her face white. The glass shook in her hand, and she swayed unsteadily for a few seconds, as if she might faint.

Eve shot up, concerned.

Maggie blinked, inhaled a sharp breath and then pulled herself to her full height.

"Are you all right, Maggie?"

Maggie drank the remaining Champagne down in a gulp. "No, I am not all right. I'm angry. I'm confused. And I'm…"

She stopped, her now-flaming eyes burning at Eve. "I'm not sure I believe you or trust you. I wish I'd never met you. Get out of here and don't ever come back!"

Eve lowered her head, gathered her coat and started for the door. Maggie's choking emotional voice stopped her.

"No, stop. Don't leave. Don't go."

Maggie's head dropped. Her body quaked, and the tears began to flow. She held up a hand, and Eve didn't know what the gesture meant. Instinctively, Eve went to Maggie and stood next to her as her shoulders sank and the tears came pumping out, her body a spasm of anguish. Eve reached for her and drew her in with a gentle hug. They remained for long minutes as Eve allowed Maggie's emotion to wear itself out.

"Why didn't he come to see me?" Maggie finally managed to say, her voice tight in her throat. Why?"

Eve stayed silent. The conversation hadn't gone the way she had planned or hoped. She thought that if Patrick had been there, he would have said all the right things. She had probably said all the wrong things. She'd fumbled the whole thing. How could she convince Maggie to leave New York and Big Jim?

Minutes later, Maggie broke away and went to the windows, lost in thought, staring down at Fifth Avenue. In the silence, Eve could hear the drone of traffic, feel the thrum of her soft heartbeat, and see the sunlight fall in yellow planks on the marble floor.

"I suppose I have to believe you," Maggie said, in a low, sad voice. "But you are so young. Maybe thirty years old. He was in his sixties."

"He was a good man, Maggie. I still love him."

And now it was Eve's turn to fight tears. The truth was, Patrick *was* gone. Perhaps he *was* dead.

Maggie slowly turned, seeing the emotion in Eve's eyes. She smiled weakly.

"So, you came to save me?"

"We were both coming to save you, but Patrick..." Her voiced dropped into silence.

"Did he speak about me often?"

Eve nodded. "He didn't know about you for a time. When he found out what had happened to you, he spoke of nothing else. That's why I came. That's why I'm here."

Maggie turned back to the window, shading her eyes from the morning sun.

"I can't leave Big Jim. No matter where I went, he would find me. You don't know him. He wouldn't stop until he found me and killed me."

Maggie turned to face Eve. "He will kill you too, Eve. I can't let that happen. Big Jim will be watching you, you know. He is very perceptive and smart, like a cunning animal. He's a violent man. He's killed men with his bare hands, and he likes it. He probably has someone watching you. I am sure he knows you are here right now. That's why I was hesitant to let you in."

Eve shivered.

"You should leave town and go back to Ohio, Eve. You've done your duty. You can go now."

"No, Maggie. If we act fast, we can escape. Patrick used to say, 'Act fast. Attack before the other guy attacks. The sooner the better.'"

"Didn't you just hear me, Eve?"

"Yes, but Patrick wanted to get you out of danger, and that's what I'm going to do, if you'll let me."

Maggie's gaze slid down. "I admire your spirit, Eve, but it won't work. This is New York City, not some small town in Ohio."

"Are you too scared to even try?"

Maggie bristled. "I'm not a little ole' scared rabbit, Eve."

"Then let's try. Let's do it."

Eve watched possibility cross Maggie's eyes. Then they changed and grew distant, and Eve couldn't decipher their meaning.

Maggie grinned, but it was sad. "Maybe I deserve to be trapped like a bird by a brute man like Big Jim. Do you know what kind of a woman I have been? The kind of woman I am?"

"Come on, Maggie. Stop the self-pity. None of us are angels. None of us are as bad as we think we are or as good as we want to be. Maggie, please let me help you get away from here."

Maggie still hovered on the edge of indecision. "And go where? To Ohio?"

"Out west, I think. We'll be hard to track and find out there."

"West. Where out west?"

"San Francisco, or maybe further south near Mexico. There is a lovely town called San Diego. Have you heard of it?"

Maggie showed the start of excitement. "No, but I have wanted to travel to San Francisco. There are many theatres there."

"If we move fast, I believe we can escape."

Maggie's face lighted with sudden possibility. "Do you really think so?"

Eve moved toward her. "Yes, I do, but we have to do it quickly."

Eve's voice turned urgent. "But first, I need you to do me a favor. Do you have connections with a bank here in New York?"

"Yes, of course."

"I have a check I need to cash. Can you arrange it?"

"Yes… You can sign it over to me, and I'll deposit it and give you the funds."

Eve sighed in relief. "Great. Good. Thank you. With that money, we can buy our train tickets."

Maggie stared at Eve, as if seeing her for the first time. "Why are you risking your life for me, Eve? I don't understand. Why?"

Eve shuddered at the thought of Big Jim chasing after them. "Because Patrick wanted me to, and because I see the hope and fear in your eyes. You want to run away from Big Jim and this life as fast as you can, don't you?"

Maggie nodded. "Yes. I want to get away from here and start a new life. I want to be better than I am. Maybe I want to leave the theatre and meet a good man—a man who truly loves me. Who knows, maybe I even want to have children. I suddenly want to feel as if it's all possible."

Maggie went to Eve and drew her into a hug. "Thank you, Eve, for coming." She held Eve at arm's length. "But I warn you, you may need courage for the both of us."

Neither Eve nor Maggie could see Biddy hovering in the next room, her anxious ear cocked toward the startling conversation she was hearing. Big Jim paid her well for information about Maggie's friends, moods and behavior. She was to let him know, swiftly, if anything unusual or revealing went on in the apartment. Biddy liked Maggie, but she also liked shoes and hats, and she helped pay the rent on the Lower East Side tenement where she lived with her sick mother and 10-year old, pipe-smoking, bicycle messenger brother, who worked twelve-hour days for the telegraph company.

Yes, Big Jim would pay her well for this information.

CHAPTER 20

Eve returned to the Casterbury Mansion just before 6 p.m. on Thursday evening. Irene met her as soon as Charles opened the front door. She was all fluster and airy chatter.

"Where have you been, Eve? I have been worried sick."

"Didn't you receive my note?"

"Yes, of course, but you didn't say where you were going or when you'd be back. You were gone all day."

Irene gave Charles a knowing look, and he gently bowed and glided away.

"Let's go into the parlor."

Eve followed Irene into the parlor, and they sat on the couch near the crackling fire.

Irene lowered her voice. "I want to return to the hospital to see poor Duncan. I have been worried sick about him. What if he has taken a turn for the worst and I am not there to support him?"

Eve had thought about dropping by to see him, but she and Maggie had been busy all day, first going to Maggie's bank so Eve could cash her check, and then to The Biltmore Hotel, where Eve took a room for a week. Maggie had insisted on giving Eve a short tour of the impressive hotel, relating that it had opened on New Year's Day 1913. She said she would have moved there herself, but Big Jim said no, giving no reason.

After seeing Eve's large and elegant room, the two ladies went up to the 22nd floor to see the grand ballroom, and then the Italian Garden, situated between the north and south towers and overlooking Vanderbilt Avenue and Grand Central Terminal.

"You will love it here, and I will visit you," Maggie said with a broad, enthusiastic smile. "I am told that this garden will soon become an ice-skating rink."

Eve gave Maggie a cool glance as she lowered her voice. "Maggie, I won't be staying here long. We are leaving New York, remember?"

Maggie's smile vanished, and fear returned to her eyes. "I don't know... The more I think about it the more I'm having doubts."

Eve gently took her elbow and led her toward a row of exotic white and yellow flowers.

"Maggie, we have to leave. You know we have to."

Maggie nodded, head down.

After leaving the hotel, they walked to Grand Central Terminal, with Maggie frequently glancing back over her shoulder.

"Do you see anyone following us?" Eve asked.

"No... I don't think so."

Eve had wanted to travel to San Francisco by ship, through the newly built Panama Canal, which opened in

August 1914, but she was afraid they might be followed and then trapped, with nowhere to go except into the sea. At least on a train, if they were spotted, there was the possibility of escape.

At the Grand Central Terminal ticket office, Eve learned that the New York Central 20th Century Limited ran from Grand Central Terminal to LaSalle Street Station in Chicago. The first-class ticket price for both would be $130.00 plus $20.00 for two Pullman berths. For safety reasons, Eve's plan was to change trains in Chicago for the leg to Kansas City, and then change trains again for the final leg to San Francisco. They planned to leave early Monday morning, December 7th, after Big Jim left Maggie's hotel for work.

"Eve, you look so far away," Irene said. "Are you listening to me?"

Eve snapped out of her thoughts. "Yes, Irene. I'm sorry. I was going to go to the hospital today, but I ran out of time. I'll go tonight."

"Tonight?"

"Yes, Irene. I am leaving Casterbury Mansion. I have a hotel room."

Irene's eyes widened. "Leaving? But how can you? How did you get the money? Did you meet Addison?"

"No. Look, you have been an angel and I will be eternally grateful to you, but I must get on with my life now. I have much to do."

Irene's eyes suddenly welled up with tears. "But how can you leave me like this? How can you? Where is the gratitude?"

Eve reached to take Irene's hand, but Irene withdrew it, pouting.

"I told you I was going to leave as soon as I could."

"You are behaving very badly, Eve. Very badly indeed. First Addison, my beast of a brother, has forbidden me to ever see Duncan again, and now you are leaving me alone in this dreadful house. It's a ghastly thing to do. Please stay. I thought perhaps you and Addison would get to be... well, friends."

"Irene, I am married."

Irene looked doubtful, adjusting herself and looking away toward the fireplace, folding her arms tightly against her.

"Addison told me that you are not being entirely forthright about your husband. Of course, you must pretend to be married. I understand that as a woman alone in New York with no friends and no resources, you must pretend to be married. But my dearest Eve, you don't have to pretend with me. You can always be honest with me. In this short time that we have been acquainted, I feel like we have become sisters, and sisters confide in each other, don't they?"

Eve straightened and stood up. "Irene, I don't particularly care what your brother thinks about me. I am married. I do have a husband and his name is Patrick Gantly."

Irene's voice gathered force. "Then where is he, Eve? Why is there so much mystery about you? You seem to live in shadows—in some mysterious world that, frankly, I find quite strange and disturbing. I don't know why you will not confide in me."

Eve's gaze was stubbornly direct. "I have no more to say about this, Irene. I will return to the hospital tonight and check on Duncan, and then send you an update via telegram. Please give my regards and my gratitude to both your mother and brother. I will have your clothes cleaned and returned to you in a couple of days."

As Eve started for the front door, she heard Irene's footsteps coming after her. Eve turned to see Irene's face filled with conviction.

"I don't care what my brother says. I am going with you to the hospital to see Duncan."

Eve felt herself sink a little. Would she ever be rid of this family?

"All right, but I have to stop off at my hotel on the way. You must stay in the taxi and wait for me."

Irene stared. Her eyes held questions, but she didn't speak.

CHAPTER 21

The orange sun was sliding behind the cityscape when Eve and Irene arrived at Gouverneur Hospital. Before entering, a jumpy Eve threw a quick glance back over her shoulder. She had the uncomfortable feeling that they were being followed, probably because she'd been with Maggie earlier and had watched her darting, nervous eyes search the sidewalks and streets as they conducted their business.

Irene too was on edge, afraid her brother and mother would find out what she was doing and cut off her funds.

Luckily, the receptionist was a friendlier woman than the hag of a nurse Eve had met on Tuesday night. She informed them that Duncan had been moved to a room in another part of the hospital because his condition had worsened.

Before the receptionist could complete her information, Irene gasped and darted away in a blind panic, Eve hurrying off behind her.

With the help of an orderly, they found Duncan in a square, dimly lighted room with five other patients, all suffering from life-threatening illnesses. Three beds were against the wall under the windows and the other two pushed into separate corners, with privacy curtains drawn.

A concerned nurse came over, her lined face suggesting she was perhaps in her 50s. "Can I help you? You shouldn't be in here. These patients are contagious."

Irene stepped back, horrified, fear seizing her, her face contorted in anxiety and confusion.

Eve approached the nurse. "We're looking for Mr. Duncan Beaumont. Is he here?"

The nurse pointed to a bed with privacy curtains drawn. "Mr. Beaumont is there. In one of his more lucid moments, he asked us to call his father. We did, and he is on his way from Boston, but unfortunately, there was a train accident. We just received a telegram that the elder Mr. Beaumont's visit would be delayed."

Irene broke into tears.

The nurse turned to her with slight irritation. "Why don't you step outside, Miss?"

Irene retreated through the door into the hallway. Eve was relieved.

Eve put her full attention on the nurse. "She is very fond of the boy."

The nurse nodded, and her eyes filled with compassion. She wore an ankle-length, light gray dress with short sleeves, a long white apron, and a heavily starched nursing cap.

"May I ask your name, nurse?" Eve asked.

"I'm Nurse Collins, Miss…?"

"I am Mrs. Eve Gantly. I'm a friend of the family. Has Mr. Beaumont improved?"

Nurse Collins shook her head in sorrow. "No, and I'm afraid the pneumonia has progressed. His lack of proper nutrition and the excessive consumption of unfortunate, so-called medicines have left him in a weakened state."

As in 1885, Eve thought, if this time only had antibiotics, how many lives could be saved?

Eve lowered her voice. "I'm a nurse. May I see him?"

The nurse stared frankly. "If you wish. I would also take the time to pray for his soul. I am sorry to say that I believe the good Lord will be coming for him very soon."

Eve nodded.

Eve approached Duncan's bed reverently. She quietly slid back the curtain, angling herself so that Nurse Collins couldn't see her, and lowered her sad eyes on Duncan. He lay under a sheet, asleep. He was pale and drawn, his eyes twitching, face damp with sweat from fever. He looked so very frail. *What a waste it would be if this young, talented man died so young*, Eve thought. The longer she stared at Duncan, the more a firm decision took hold of her. Once again, she was going to challenge the fates. She was a healer, after all, and she had the means to do just that—to heal Duncan.

It was the reason she'd stopped at her hotel room at the Biltmore. Throwing one more careful glance toward Nurse Collins, Eve slid the curtain closed behind her. She swiftly unfastened her dress and found the black security belt around her waist.

The belt had been her idea when she and Patrick were planning their time travel. Instead of storing money from 1885, which of course wasn't available, Eve had filled the narrow channel with Zithromax Z-Pak tablets and painkillers. In 1885, after Patrick had been shot and developed blood poisoning, he had almost died because there were no antibiotics. She decided that this time she'd have antibiotics at the ready just in case.

She had enough for two courses, one for her and one for Patrick. She would give Duncan one course. Letting Duncan die was not an option when she had the means to save him.

The next problem was administering the pills to Duncan. He was delirious and unconscious. Ideally, the antibiotic would be given intravenously, but that was not possible. All she had were the pink tablets. Eve knew that crushing the oral tablet would disrupt the dosage and destroy the extended-release properties. It would also increase the risk of adverse effects or drug toxicity. So, Eve would have to find a way to get Duncan to swallow the pills.

There was a full glass of water on his side table. Glancing around to make sure she wasn't being watched, Eve removed six pills from her brown pillbox. Each pill was 250mg. She needed a loading dose of 500mg in Duncan's system right away. Then one 250mg pill for the next four days. Duncan was young. That should do it.

She put the pills in a small red velvet bag, replaced the box in her belt, and then refastened the belt and her dress. She reached for the glass of water and one pill. She touched Duncan's burning cheek and he moaned out unintelligible words. He jerked his head away from her. She placed her hand on the back of the pillow and gently lifted it, raising his head a little. Next, she whispered comforting words. She'd learned from years of practice that even if the patient wasn't conscious, kind and encouraging words often helped calm them. With two fingers, she gently touched his lips, opening his mouth. With her other hand, she placed a pill on his tongue and dribbled a small amount of water into his mouth.

"Swallow the pill, Duncan," Eve said sweetly. "Go ahead. It's all right. Swallow the pill."

She prayed he wouldn't choke on the thing and draw attention to what she was doing.

To Eve's delight, Duncan obeyed and swallowed the pill, mumbling irritably. Eve tipped more water into his mouth. He swallowed, then his head swam from side to side.

"Did you swallow the pill, Duncan?" she asked at a whisper, her voice close to his ear.

He grumbled, "Who? I can't find her... Where?"

Eve whispered. "It's all right, Duncan. Just rest now. Everything is going to be fine. Just sleep."

Thankfully, Eve managed to get Duncan to swallow the second pill. He was a good patient. He had actually responded to her soft, cajoling voice.

Eve slowly drew back the curtains and saw Nurse Collins with a clipboard looking her way. Eve silently recited a prayer of thanks.

Eve was preparing for the next part of her plan when Duncan began coughing violently. Nurse Collins hurried over and Eve faded back, out of the way, as Nurse Collins took a clean, white cloth and blotted Duncan's forehead, also wiping saliva from his mouth. Then she fussed with the sheet, adjusting it and then rearranging it again around Duncan's chin. Eve was touched by the act. All the fussing was unnecessary, but it was an act of compassion, as if Nurse Collins wanted to say, *I just want to do something to help this poor, dying boy.*

After Duncan had relaxed and fallen to sleep, Nurse Collins slid the curtain closed and lifted her eyes with a slow shake of her sorrowful head.

Eve approached her in a tranquil, whispering voice. "Nurse Collins…"

Eve opened her hand, displaying the small bag containing the pills. "In this bag are four pink tablets."

Nurse Collins' eyes lowered on the bag, then lifted to Eve as she waited for an explanation. Eve was about to lie.

"These tablets were developed by a doctor who used to work at the old Gouverneur Hospital, Dr. Ann Long."

Nurse Collins' eyes awakened. "Dr. Long? I know Dr. Long."

Eve was surprised. "You know Dr. Long?"

"Yes, I worked with Dr. Long at the old hospital many years ago, when I first became a nurse."

"What year was that?" Eve asked, wondering if they might have crossed paths back in 1885.

"Well, let me see… it was 1888. Did you know that Dr. Long was the first female ambulance surgeon in New York?"

"Yes, I did."

Nurse Collins continued. "In those days, when the hospital first opened, it was exclusively for treating accident cases. When I arrived, it had expanded to include a ward for patients with tuberculosis. How do you know Dr. Long?"

Eve couldn't tell Nurse Collins she had worked with Dr. Long in 1885. Eve had not aged. Twenty-eight years later, she would have been 58 years old. Once again, Eve would have to lie.

"My mother knew her. I'm not quite sure how they met, but for a time they were good friends. Do you happened to know where Dr. Long is now?" Eve asked. "We haven't communicated in a while."

Nurse Collins' attention was diverted as she glanced around the room to see if she was needed. When she saw all was in order, she focused again on Eve.

"Yes, she moved to Chicago in 1909 and is working at Augustana Hospital there. I received a Christmas card from her last year."

Eve made a mental note of that, while Nurse Collins' attention returned to the velvet bag that held four Z-Pak tablets.

"What were you saying about the tablets?"

Eve told her the pills were a natural remedy Dr. Long had developed and used on patients with infections. "Although they're not always successful, many times they are," Eve said.

Eve handed Nurse Collins the bag.

"I have to leave town. Could you please administer Mr. Beaumont one tablet per day for four days?" Eve whispered. "You know how doctors are. You probably shouldn't let Mr. Beaumont's doctor know."

Nurse Collin's eyes became bold. "Mrs. Gantly... the doctor has not been to see Mr. Beaumont for two days. I would only say this to another nurse, but I believe they have already given up on him. If these tablets were created by Dr. Long, then I will see that Mr. Beaumont receives them."

Eve thanked her, passed one last look toward Duncan's bed and left.

Back in reception, Eve found Irene hunched in a chair, weeping. Eve went to her, laying a tender hand on her shoulder. Irene lifted her head, pain in her eyes.

"I loved him, Eve. Duncan was such a kind boy. So good. So much better than me. He's going to die, isn't he?"

"The nurse said he's improving."

She sniffed back tears. "Is he? Truly? Has he improved?"

"Did you hear that his father is coming?"

"Yes, his father... He will no doubt take him away and I will never see him again."

"Perhaps, but I firmly believe that Duncan will make a full recovery."

Irene stood, hopeful. "Do you think so?"

"As a nurse, I've seen many surprising things happen. Sometimes people make miraculous recoveries. You just never know. Now, why don't you go and see him? If you love him, why don't you tell him you love him? I'm sure he'd want to see you."

Irene blinked, her thoughts scrambling. "But he is a carrier of disease, is he not, Eve? He's been sick for a long time. I do not want to sound like a frightened child, but perhaps I should not be in the same room with him."

Eve looked at Irene pointedly. "Go see him, Irene. You'll be fine. Go see him now and tell him how you feel, even if you're not certain he can hear you. It will do you both a world of good."

Irene hesitated, considering Eve's words. Finally, she gathered herself, adjusted her shoulders and started off down the hallway.

Darkness had descended when Eve and Irene shouldered into their coats, arranged their hats, and left the hospital.

They'd come in a taxi because Irene wanted to avoid using the limousine, knowing William would undoubtedly tell Addison where he'd taken them. He told Addison everything.

And now, outside, the ladies were alone on the deserted street. There was a wet chill in the air, as if more rain were on the way, and Eve turned up the collar of her coat, glancing warily about.

A misty glow shrouded the streetlights, casting eerie shadows on the cobbles and on the tenements, mostly obscured by a smoky fog. There was a disquieting melancholy hovering, as if all the despair and hopelessness of this unfortunate neighborhood had coalesced in that noxious, foul-smelling haze.

Suddenly, a big man loomed out of the fog like a ghost from the underworld. Eve's breath stopped. Irene made a little sound of fear.

"Oh, my, Eve," Irene said, fear tightening her voice. "We should have never come."

CHAPTER 22

The man crept toward them from the dark street and stepped into the dim, cruel light. He wore a stubby, flat-topped plug hat, low over his brow. He was on the fat side, with a heavy sagging face, his throat spilling out over his collar. His aggressive big stomach strained the buttons on his vest, and with his greatcoat swept back, it allowed that prodigious stomach to bulge like a weapon.

Eve and Irene were about to pivot and run back to the safety of the hospital when a tall, lean man jutted out behind them, blocking their escape. His lanky, loose-jointed build suggested quick reflexes and fast feet. His dark expression was sardonic and mean, his crooked gash of a grin calculated to intimidate. His bowler was cocked smartly left, and his greatcoat was open, flapping mischievously in the stirring wind.

"Good evening, ladies," the fat man said, in an arid, heavy voice. "Are you out strolling for gentlemen?"

He gave a fierce grin as he spread his hands, and in a mocking tone, he said, "Well, my good ladies of the night, here we are. You have found your gentlemen and we like what we see."

Eve detected a slight Irish accent, similar to Patrick's. But unlike Patrick's soothing, warm sound, this one was disturbing and frightening. Panic surged up in her. A deep, naked fear crawled up her spine and froze her, as if she'd just plunged into an icy river. She threw darting glances about, frantically searching the area for an escape route. There was no escape, and the street was utterly deserted. They were trapped.

"Will you please let us pass?" Eve asked, her voice trembling.

Irene followed Eve's lead, striving for calm. She managed to squeeze out, "Could you two gentlemen please find us a cab? We would be ever so grateful."

Both men laughed, but there was no mirth in it. It was a coarse, animal sound, as if coming from the depths of hell.

The tall one spoke up, pointing left into a foggy darkness. "Walk left, ladies, and do not scream out. If you make as much as a bird sound, I will cut your pretty little faces, and they will not be so pretty tomorrow."

He reached into his inside coat pocket and brandished a knife. He angled it toward the light, so the ladies could see the bright, five-inch steel blade glint and glitter.

Eve's heart thundered in her chest. She glanced at Irene, utter terror swelling her eyes.

"Walk. Now!" the tall man barked.

Eve calmly took Irene's elbow and willed her trembling body forward. Irene walked mechanically beside her while Eve led her out of the light and into the gray darkness of the dirty fog.

They moved slowly, hearing the scratching sound of the men's footsteps behind them. Forcing away burning fear, Eve forced her mind to calculate options. Did these men have guns? Didn't know. Were they only going to scare them, or kill them? Didn't know. Were these men sent by Big Jim Clancy? No doubt. Could she and Irene outrun them? Again, doubtful. These men were obviously professionals, and they knew these streets like a rat knows its sewer.

Should she scream? She saw flickering lights in windows above, but in this neighborhood, yelling for help probably wouldn't produce any results. Who would come to their rescue? This was a poor, depressed, overcrowded part of town, and the last thing anyone in this area needed was more suffering and threats.

So, what was left?

"Turn left!" the fat one ordered.

Eve stopped. She looked left into the narrow dark tunnel of the alley, flanked on both sides by tall, sooty, brick structures. There was but one leaning streetlamp near the middle of the alley, illuminating the damp cobblestones, a pile of discarded wood, two wooden barrels and a scattering of trash. Eve saw the skittering shadows of rats darting along the curbs and vanishing under scattered, stacked crates.

"Move!" the tall one bellowed.

Eve summoned every bit of courage she had, inhaled a breath and ventured left into the alley, with Irene in tow. Eve was afraid that Irene might faint. She was making little whimpering sounds, nearly hyperventilating.

"Keep walking!" the fat one said, his voice all rough gravel.

About midway, they heard "Stop!"

The ladies were standing near a wooden barrel with the faded black lettering ATLANTIC GARDEN printed on it. Eve had a view down the alley and, looking up in the gray light, she could see rows and rows of hanging laundry stretched across the alley from tenement windows.

"Turn around," the tall one demanded.

The ladies slowly complied.

They were now in a place of shadows—a foul-smelling hellhole, only fit for rats, feral cats, down-and-out drunks, and the scum of the Earth—these two men.

The fat one shoved his stubby hands into his vest pockets like a proud banker, lifted his double chin and strolled forward within about five feet of Eve. His bulging round eyes viewed her with a blatant, pleasurable lust.

"Well... aren't you a nice bit of stuff? Maybe you and me will have a go before Donny and me toss you two strumpets into the East River for a little swim to the bottom."

Irene groaned, a glassy shock filling her eyes. She whimpered, weaved and wilted like a rag doll, crumpling to the cobblestones, her lovely plumed hat rolling into a filthy puddle.

The tall one laughed. "Silly birdie. Lookie there, Alfie. She's all power puff birdie with no brains or guts."

Alfie looked down at her in disgust. "Daft floozie."

Eve instinctively turned to help Irene.

"Leave her!" Alfie, the fat one, bellowed.

"What do you want?" Eve shot back.

Alfie stepped up smartly, raised a fat hand and backhanded Eve violently across the face. Her head jerked right, and she stumbled, nearly falling. She fought to stay on her feet as the world swam around her. Her cheek burned, and she tasted blood.

The fat man jabbed a threatening finger in her face. "You keep your lips shut, you bloody harlot! I do the talkin' here, you see? Do you see that? Do you hear me?"

Breathing hard, Eve managed to straighten, glaring back at him.

He kept jabbing his finger. "You should have left Maggie Gantly alone, you daft harlot. You've been sticking your pretty sharp nose into other people's business, and that just ain't smart."

Eve fought to think, to come up with any options for attack or escape. During their nearly one year of marriage, Patrick had taught Eve some street fighting techniques, and now they flitted across her mind. She could spring on the fat man and claw at his eyes—dig her fingernails into his face. She would surely die for it, but it would be worth it.

"Now, you are gonna answer some questions for me. First, who are you?" the fat man asked. "And do not lie to me, cherry girl, or you will die slowly, with my hard fists and Donny's sharp knife cutting little pieces from your hair and face."

Eve felt her legs weaken. Fear was pounding away in her and she couldn't stop it.

"Who are you!?" the fat one shouted, spit exploding from his lips.

Suddenly, from somewhere out in the darkness, Eve heard a strong, booming voice.

"She's my wife, you dirt-dumb bootlicks."

CHAPTER 23

Startled, the two thugs whirled toward the sound.

Eve jolted to attention, hearing the rushing of her breath. She knew that voice. It was Patrick's! Her body surged with new life, and before she could stop herself, she shouted, "Patrick!"

And then Patrick Gantly emerged from the darkness, standing tall and resolute in the single pool of lamplight. He was hatless, wearing a dark suit, his face grim and hard, his dark hair gleaming, his hands hidden behind his back.

The goons stiffened, and their menacing eyes narrowed on him. They shuffled in front of the ladies, knives raised in a threat.

"And a good wife she is, gentlemen," Patrick continued. "But I warn you, she is not one to be trifled with, and from the looks of it, you two beard splitters did just that. Ah, yes, and now I'm afraid there will be hell to pay."

Eve's heart jumped. She stood stunned, thrilled and shaking with relief and joy, despite the knife that was pointed at her throat. She wanted to slap the thing away, run to Patrick and have him catch her up in his arms.

"Are you all right, Eve?" Patrick asked in a smooth, even voice.

"Yes… Yes… I'm fine, Patrick."

"You don't look so fine right now, Eve. You've attracted the wrong sort to you. Two clueless cowards, I think."

"Who are you?" the fat one shouted, snarling out the words.

"I'm Patrick, and I am assuming you work for Big Jim Clancy."

"I have a knife to her throat. You don't assume anything, or she dies."

"Ah, yes… the coward's way," Patrick said, coolly. "Don't fight the man, threaten the lady with a big knife. You disappoint me, bootlicks. Yes, you do. Little boys and cowards, with knives. I thought I had come to fight men, not a string bean and a big bloated potato with the courage of a mouse."

The fat man gave a broad, unctuous smile but revealed a savage expression. "I will kill her, friend. You walk away now or, so help me, I'll do it."

"Of course you will, you fat cowardly potato. Anybody ever tell you, you've a head like a bag of spuds?"

"Who the balls are you?" Donny barked out in a thick, raspy voice. He turned to Alfie. "Who is he, Alfie?"

"I told you, you thick blockhead. I'm Patrick, and I think you boys and me is gonna have a donnybrook.

You need to let the girls go now, so the men can go to work."

The fat one barked a laugh. "You're a pig, Patrick, and I'm going to cut you up into little pieces and make a good and crispy pork pie out of you."

Patrick grinned darkly, with a little shake of his head. "Why are all the fat and ugly lads always such braggarts? The last thing you need, piggy boy, is a pork pie. Hey, tell me true, boys: do the two of you bootlicks fancy each other? I've heard Big Jim's bully boys are all sweeties. Is it true, bootlicks?"

The two men looked at each other, rage building in them.

Patrick continued taunting them. "I have been checking up on you two blockheads and I learned that Big Jim always sends you two cowards out on the easy jobs. You go after old men and ladies because, hey, they can't fight you back, can they? Did you know that it's all over town that you two are Big Jimmy's favorite sweetie boys? Yeah, you can't fight the men, but you're so brave with the helpless ladies. Too scared to fight the lads who can give you a taste of the devil's own. Is that true, bootlicks?"

Alfie turned to Donny, his teeth clenched in rage. "Go get him, Donny. Cut him up and send him to hell."

Donny stared back at Alfie, his forehead pinched, eyes conflicted and shifting. He didn't move.

"Go, Donny! Take him."

Donny scratched his cheek, licked his lips and squared his shoulders, his right eye twitching.

"That's a good boy," Patrick said, beckoning Donny with a lift of his chin and wiggling fingers. "Come over here and send old Patrick to hell. Why don't you fight a man instead of the helpless, who can't fight back?"

Eve felt a furnace of fear. She'd just found Patrick again, and she couldn't bear the thought of losing him like this. Her breath stuck in her throat.

Donny advanced slowly, knife tight and visible in his big hand. He crouched, readying himself for battle. Patrick didn't stir. He waited and watched, his hands still hidden behind his back.

Donny paused about five feet away, glancing about to ensure Patrick was alone.

"Finish him!" Alfie shouted.

"You heard your fat yellow boss, Donny. Finish me."

"You shut up!" Donny thundered. "Just shut your mouth."

Donny lunged forward, the knife swinging at Patrick's belly. Patrick arched back and leaped away and, for the first time, Patrick released his hands from behind his back, revealing a three-foot-long 2x4. He gripped it threateningly in his right hand.

Donny stumbled backward in surprise as Patrick advanced on him, face hard, eyes afire. Patrick knew from his days growing up on the Lower East Side streets, and from working as a detective sergeant for the police, that the best defense against a knife was a chair or a barstool. He had neither. Even though he and Donny were about the same height, Patrick had at least twenty pounds on him. That was good and bad. Donny looked spry and quick, his arms long, with a good reach.

Patrick would have to watch him, bob and weave and skip. In a street fight, Patrick knew you didn't wait. You attacked, and you kept on attacking until one or the other was down.

"Get him, Donny," Alfie roared. "Now!"

Donny rushed Patrick again, the knife flashing in the light. Patrick danced away, spun around, found his balance and charged Donny, club poised. Flat footed, Donny stood frozen, eyes wide in shock. At the last minute, Donny tried to duck, but Patrick had him dead center.

Patrick came around swinging, bringing all his muscled 220 pounds to bear on the left side of Donny's head. Donny threw up a hand to protect himself, but it was too late. The 2x4 club caught him hard, the impact spinning him, his hat flying away. He went sprawling, a clumsy dancer all arms and fumbling legs. The knife flew off into darkness, and an angry, barking dog shattered the quiet.

Donny splashed to the ground, bouncing and rolling, crashing into a wooden barrel and toppling it. A rat broke from the shadows and fled up the alley, his bloated body waddling away into darkness.

On a furious impulse, Alfie broke away from Eve, springing into action, hurling himself forward toward Patrick, his knife poised to rip and cut.

Eve screamed, "Look out, Patrick!"

Patrick just managed to rotate and find his footing as Alfie lunged, swinging his long angry knife. It whispered past Patrick's face. Patrick backpedaled as Alfie attacked again, charging, swinging, growling. With a straining effort, he lashed at Patrick's body.

As Patrick arched back, the tip of the blade slashed an ugly gash into his coat, ripping off buttons. Patrick fought to anchor himself. He danced, spun and righted himself and returned the attack, swinging the club. Alfie ducked and faltered, breath puffing from his mouth. Patrick swung again, just missing, hearing the wind whoosh by Alfie's big head.

Off balance now, the fat man huffed out air, struggling to stay on his feet. Patrick didn't wait. He attacked, wheeling the club like a bat. It slammed into Alfie's right temple.

Eve heard the dull thud of impact. She winced as Alfie's plug hat flew from his head, hit the cobbles, skipped and rolled. Alfie screamed out in pain, angry and wounded. Patrick moved in fast, clubbing the knife from Alfie's hand. It dropped to the cobblestones, the steel blade looking up, shining and sinister.

Wasting no time before Alfie recovered his strength, Patrick dropped the club and charged. With a raised, heavy fist, he punched the fat man hard in his right jaw. Alfie's eyes popped open in shock. Blood gushed from the side of his head, pouring over his right eye. Still, he stayed on his feet, shouting obscenities, stumbling about like a drunken man, swinging his granite fists widely as if fighting off a gang of hostile ghosts.

"I'll kill you," he shouted. "I'll cut you, you bastard!"

Patrick darted in and threw a solid right fist into Alfie's Adam's apple. Stunned, Alfie jerked back, clawing at his throat, coughing and gagging. Disoriented and blunted, he staggered left and right, finally falling to his knees, his tormented face toward the sky, gasping for air.

As breath thundered in and out of his lungs, Patrick dropped down. He placed one of his palms over Alfie's chin and the other around the backside of his head. He twisted violently. There was a crack.

Eve hid her eyes and turned away.

Alfie toppled over in a heap to the damp cobbles, and the lamplight caught his open, vacant eyes. Patrick had broken his neck.

Patrick raised to his knees, glancing about, expecting another attack. When none came, he pushed up, shaken, his broad chest heaving, gulping in air. Seconds later, he crept toward Donny. He stood over his silent, still body, waiting, watchful. He crouched to one knee and stuck a finger in the side of Donny's neck. No pulse. He was dead. Both men were dead.

Patrick got to his feet, his breath stilted and ragged as he cast glances up and down the alley with a tense animal awareness. He tore a hand through his thick tousled hair, heaved out a sigh, and gathered up the two knives and the 2x4. He dropped the knives into his coat pocket and held on to the club. He'd toss them into the East River later.

When he started over to Eve, she rushed into his arms and buried her face in his broad shoulder. Feeling his thumping pulse and smelling the masculine scent of him, she wrapped him tightly in her arms. He wrapped his free arm around her.

"Are you okay, Eve?" he said softly, his breath still coming fast.

"…Yes. Now that you're here. Yes. Where have you been?"

"It's a long story, Eve. We've no time to talk now. Let's get your friend up and get out of here before the police come. It won't be pleasant if they find us."

CHAPTER 24

Later that night, in a room at the Hotel Bartholdi at Broadway and 23rd Street, Eve sat on the lumpy green couch next to Patrick. It was an old hotel, built in 1876, but Patrick had known about it in 1885 and he was happy to see it was still standing.

"It's cheap enough," Patrick said, "And it was the first place I thought of when I arrived here. I was so disoriented and exhausted that despite my determination to find you and Maggie, I dropped into the bed and slept for hours."

Eve appraised the room—the worn Victorian furniture, sagging bed, frayed carpet, heavy blue velvet drapes and faded rose wallpaper.

"Well, I like the wallpaper," Eve said, as she sipped brandy from a water glass. She leaned her head back as Patrick gently blotted her red cheek with a cool cloth.

"You can stop that now. I'm okay. Really."

"Humor me, okay, Mrs. Gantly? You're still shaking like a leaf and your face is all swollen up where that fat man hit you."

Eve shut her eyes for a moment. "I've seen people die, but never like that. It's going to take time to erase those awful images from my mind. I guess there was no other way? I mean, you had to kill them?"

"Those two lads were going to kill you and your friend, Irene, and toss you both into the East River. In case you didn't notice, they were also out to kill me. No, there was no other way. With men like that you kill or be killed. I learned that long ago, Eve. They are lost souls in this world, and they taunt and kill for fun and money."

Eve opened her eyes fully on him, exploring his handsome face with new pleasure. "God, I am so glad to see you, Patrick. If you hadn't shown up when you did, those men would have raped and killed us."

He took her hand and kissed it. "Sorry you had to see the violence of it. I know it wasn't pretty."

"When you were a detective sergeant back in 1885, did you have to do much of that kind of fighting? Did you have to kill like that?"

"Not so much. We had guns, you know. Thank the good Lord those lads didn't carry guns. Theirs was meant to be a silent killing, and it was meant to be easy. They didn't want noise or the cops coming down on them."

"Where did you learn to fight like that?" Eve asked.

"I grew up on the Lower East Side. My Da was out of work often, and times were hard, and times were rough. It was a bleak and fierce neighborhood, where fighting was the sport of the day. You had to learn to fight or you'd soon die. It's not like the coppers cared who we fought or who died, or how they died. I've fought lads like those two flat-footed duffers since I was ten years old. I didn't always have to kill, but it was often a fight to the death, with broken bottles, knives and clubs and plenty of broken noses and bones."

Eve was silent as she thought about it. "I'm not sure you ever told me that before."

"Well, there was no need, was there? And, like any new husband, I wanted you to think the best of me."

Eve shuddered. "Thank God you showed up."

He stroked her hair. "I will always show up. Anyway, now we're even."

"What do you mean, even?"

"You saved my life in 1885 when I was shot, and now I've saved yours. Do you know what that means, Mrs. Gantly? It means we will be together for all time."

Eve reached for his hand and kissed it. "And that's another reason I love you, Detective Sergeant Patrick Gantly. You're a true nineteenth-century romantic."

He rested his eyes on her warmly. "Drink the brandy, my love. It will help calm you."

Eve tipped back the glass and swallowed the last of the brandy. She winced, feeling the sharpness and the heat. "It's not the best brandy I've ever had, Patrick. I don't even want to know where you got this."

"Well, don't you worry about that. It will do the job, Mrs. Gantly."

He reached for the square brown bottle to pour her another. She held up a hand. "No, Patrick, I'm already light-headed."

"It's after midnight, Eve. You need to sleep, and I think that lump on your cheek is going to keep you up."

"Not to worry about that. Besides the antibiotics, I brought some extra strength *Tylenol*. I took two while you were out making sure we weren't followed. I'll be asleep in twenty minutes. But before I do drop off, when are you going to tell me what happened to you when we got separated, and how long you've been here?"

"I'll tell you everything in the morning."

"Come on. Tell me. I was worried sick."

Patrick stood up, set the brandy bottle on a side table and went into the small bathroom to drop the wet cloth in the sink.

When he returned, Eve was awake and waiting. "I will tell you, I promise, but right now we have got to make some plans and make them quick. Big Jim Clancy is going to be looking for you. He's going to be mad as the dickens and he's going to want to know who killed his two lads. He will be rabid, like a wild animal."

Eve looked down at her soiled dress. She hadn't taken the time to change when she'd arrived at the hotel. She'd just flopped down, shaken and exhausted.

After the fight, Patrick had swept the still unconscious Irene up in his arms and, with Eve at his side and still wobbly on her feet, they'd fled the alley, eventually finding a taxi a block away, near a spooky-looking all-night café and a shady-looking tavern.

Fortunately, Irene had returned to consciousness just as the taxi came into view, and Patrick lowered her to her feet, allowing her time to find balance as she staggered for a time on rubbery legs. Patrick did not want a suspicious hack driver asking a lot of questions, so he and Eve each took an arm and helped Irene into the taxi. For all Patrick knew, the driver could be on Big Jim's payroll.

Eve told the driver to drop them a block away from the Casterbury mansion. When they arrived, Patrick left the front seat for the back, and remained in the cab, while Eve escorted a still badly shaken Irene down the sidewalk to the mansion's walkway and front door.

Once Charles, the butler, had Irene safely inside, Eve turned away without explanation and hurried back to the taxi.

The car motored away into the night, leaving Charles to speculate and grow suspicious. No doubt, he'd promptly contacted Addison.

In the taxi, Patrick was on high alert. "How is she?" Patrick whispered.

"Traumatized."

"She kept staring at me," Patrick said.

"I told her you lived in that neighborhood, and you came to our rescue."

"Did she believe you?"

Eve shrugged. "She didn't say anything. Do you think Big Jim will go looking for her?"

"I don't think so… No one but those two lads saw her with you."

Patrick told the grizzled, gray-haired driver to take them to 22nd Street, near the East River. When they arrived, with Patrick still clutching the 2x4 at his side, he paid the driver, took Eve's arm and ushered her out. The taxi lingered for a time. Patrick didn't like that, so he waited until the red tail lights were swallowed by the hazy night and then he and Eve moved off into shadows. They passed gray, seven-story tenements, taking quick steps down a curved, feebly lighted walkway that led to the East River.

Standing behind a wrought iron railing, Patrick scanned the area for anything that looked suspicious. All was still and quiet. Patrick cocked an arm and flung the 2x4 away, watching it twirl, sail and splash into the dark, moving river. Next, he pulled the knives and tossed those. Eve saw a silver splash as they hit the water.

Patrick turned to her. She was trembling, and her teeth were chattering. He wrapped an arm around her shoulder and pulled her close.

"All right, Eve, let's get you someplace warm."

They walked briskly to Patrick's hotel, Eve being grateful for the movement to build body heat and shake off the jitters.

Back in the present, Eve watched Patrick pace the room, the smoke of worry on his face.

"Eve, I'm very concerned that we may have, inadvertently, hurt Maggie by what happened tonight."

Eve touched her sore cheek. "Yes, I thought about that on the way home."

"Just being here, in this time, means we are changing history."

"Well, that was a given, if we time traveled. How could we not?"

"Yes, of course, but my biggest worry is about Big Jim. He will respond. What will he do? What if he flies into a rage over Maggie's planned escape and he kills her now, and not on Christmas Eve? We may have set something into motion that can't be undone. Even if he doesn't kill her, what if he hides her or sends her off to some other city or small town, as a prisoner, and we'll never know where she is?"

Eve lowered her sorrowful head. "I'm sorry. I was just trying to help. I thought she and I could get away before Big Jim found out."

Patrick stopped, tenderness in his tone. "It's not your fault. You did what you thought was best. You were very brave. You risked your life."

"But now I've probably made it worse for us, and worse for Maggie."

Patrick's eyes held a curious glitter. "By the way, how is she? How is Maggie?"

"Have you seen her?"

"Only on the stage. I was... well, a bit nervous to approach her. I wanted to, but...well, I was afraid, for many reasons. But she's a lovely girl, isn't she, Eve? And a fine actress, too. A fine, fine actress and lady, I think, despite her messing with Big Jim."

"Yes, and she's smart, and she's scared. She desperately wants to get away from Big Jim."

Frustrated, Patrick punched a fist into his other hand. "Blast it! Obviously, Big Jim has eyes and ears all over this town. As much as I want to charge headlong to try to save her, I'm afraid we're going to have to let things settle for a time. You're going to have to hide out, for at least a week."

"A week? Patrick, we're running out of time as it is. We can't afford for me to hide for a week. That would make it December tenth."

"I know that, but you must hide. Big Jim will be combing the city looking for you. I will not risk your life any further."

Eve shut her eyes, suddenly exhausted.

Patrick began pacing again. "We must move from here, and you must cut and dye your hair black, and change your name. I have registered here as Patrick O'Hearn. We'll move tomorrow to the Hoffman House on Broadway at Madison Square, just in case we were followed."

Eve's eyes opened. "I paid for a room at the Biltmore for a week."

"You can't go back there, Eve. That will be the first place Big Jim will look. We'll register as Mr. and Mrs. O'Hearn. You can come up with a first name."

Eve rubbed her tired eyes and sighed. "What have we got ourselves into, Patrick? We thought this was going to be so easy."

Patrick drilled her with his eyes. "I never thought it would be easy, and that's why I didn't want you to come."

"Let's not start that again. I'm here, and we'll just have to work together and figure out a way."

Patrick stopped again, and they locked eyes.

Eve sat up straight, jaw set. "Okay, now, I'd like to know, finally, what happened to you and how we got separated after I lit the lantern?"

Patrick ran a hand over his shadow of a beard. "When I arrived here, I wondered the same thing. I was nearly out of my mind when I realized you were nowhere to be found. For a time, I was frantic. I searched everywhere for you. I thought I had lost you forever, and it was all my fault. I wanted to shoot myself."

Eve arose and went to him with a sweet, worried smile. She took both his hands.

"When did you arrive?" Eve asked.

"On Monday, November 30th."

"But that was two days after me," Eve said. "Where did you land? What time of day? What happened to you for an entire day?"

Patrick sighed. "We were together for a while. I could see you clearly, and then you just vanished into some blue, misty fog. I called to you—I kept calling out to you—but you were gone. And then I just felt disconnected from everything. I seemed to tumble in and out of water-like waves for what seemed like hours, until I was exhausted. I think I slept for a time. When I awoke, I moved about in a confused, cloudy atmosphere, in a smoky damp forest, with towering trees and darting colorful birds.

"Several times, I heard your voice and I called to you, but your voice soon faded, and I was alone again. Finally, I blundered about and then fell into a kind of deep well. I thought I was falling to my death. Next thing I knew, I was sitting on a park bench in Central Park.

"When I finally shook off my sleepy confusion, I asked a man who was walking by what day it was. He told me. That's when I went looking for you."

"How did you know that Irene and I were at the hospital?"

"After I pawned my ring for money and found this hotel room, I bought several newspapers and read them back to back. I saw that Maggie was in a play. I went to see her, and then I followed her. I saw you this morning come out of the hotel with her."

"Why didn't you say something? Why didn't you come to me?"

"I wanted to. Believe me, I wanted to. I almost screamed out to you, but then I thought, no, wait. See if you and Maggie were being followed. I didn't want to bring Big Jim down on you both, and me."

"And were we being followed?"

"Yes... You were. That's when I decided to stay in the background. I wanted to try to get the big picture. Forgive me, it's the detective in me. But from that time on, I followed you to make sure you wouldn't be harmed."

Eve touched Patrick's cheek and felt the familiar flair of desire for him. "I love you, Patrick. I love you very much, and I'm glad we both made it and we're both here and safe, at least for the time being."

Patrick's eyes changed, losing their worry. He stepped back a little, taking in Eve's thin, lush figure, her long lashes, her waiting lips.

"And there it is, Eve."

"There what is?"

"The miracle of you that always takes me by surprise. Here I am talking like a looney when I should be kissing you. I thought I'd lost you forever. I thought I'd never see you again. Who was the man who said, 'Remember why you fell in love?' Well, I do remember, Eve."

Patrick's expression was tender and eager. He placed a finger on her lips and traced them.

"How's the bed?" Eve asked.

Patrick leaned, kissing her, deep and warm. When they finally broke the opulent kiss, Patrick glanced over at the bed.

"It squeaks."

Eve grinned naughtily. "Good... Let's give it a long squeaky workout and bother the neighbors."

CHAPTER 25

As one day looped into the next and then faded, Eve remained sequestered in their room at the Hoffman House while Patrick spent each day wandering the City, seeking information about Daniel Fallow, Jacob Jackson, and Maggie. He'd come up empty on all three, and his mood was darkening.

The first snowfall of winter hit the city on Thursday, December 10th, dropping five inches of snow.

According to the newspapers, Maggie had left the Broadway show *Rose Pepper* because of an unspecified illness, and she would be out for an undetermined amount of time. The theatre owner was understandably concerned and worried. Maggie's understudy had taken over the role, and the reviews had not been entirely favorable. It was rumored that unless Maggie returned to the show soon, *Rose Pepper* would close.

Eve also read a newspaper account of the deaths of the two men Patrick had been forced to kill. It was reported that they were street thugs who had gotten into a back-alley argument and killed each other. All well and good. That meant Patrick had left no evidence behind, except for a couple of buttons ripped off his coat in the knife fight.

Patrick learned that Maggie had left the St. Regis, but he was unable to discover where Big Jim had hidden her. Big Jim obviously knew that somebody wanted to take Maggie away from him. Being a selfish and vicious man, he would kill anyone who had the guts to try to take her. Patrick prayed and hoped that his daughter was still alive.

Day after day Patrick had tirelessly meandered the City, talking to theatre stage managers, taxi drivers, tavern owners, bootblacks and newsie boys, but no one knew anything about Maggie, or, if they did, they were too scared to tell. Even money didn't loosen their tongues. Maggie had just simply vanished.

And as to Daniel Fallow and Jacob Jackson, the last two people to have seen the lantern? He had also made little headway. Perhaps Dr. Long knew something about them. They had sent her a telegram the morning they moved to Hoffman House.

On Thursday, December 10th, Eve couldn't take being inside the hotel's three rooms any longer. She had to get outside, even if it was just to take a walk around the block in the snow.

She put on a navy wool dress and looked in the mirror, nodding her approval. It was one of five dresses Patrick had had tailored for her, based on the dress Irene had loaned her. He'd also purchased undergarments, gloves, two hats, two pairs of shoes and two winter coats, following Eve's instructions as to color, style and fit. Patrick grinned after his excursion, saying he'd flirted with the shop girls and received a few discounts, to which Eve quipped, "I think you enjoy buying women's clothes."

"They're certainly more fun to buy than men's clothes. I especially enjoy exploring the lingerie that women wear in this time," he said, winking. "There are so many sizes and colors. And they feel so very good."

Eve had cut her hair to just below the ear, dyed it black and styled it into tight curls. She'd used Aureole, a hair color product Patrick found at Miller's, a pharmacy just two blocks away. It lent a rich, bitter-chocolate sheen to her hair. Patrick joked that he felt as though he was having an affair with another woman. It had been one of the few times they'd played and laughed. Patrick mostly arrived home looking weary and beaten, and it was a challenge to keep their spirits up.

At a little after noon, Eve was fully dressed and ready for her first foray out into New York as her new self, Mrs. Colleen O'Hearn. She paused one last time to examine her new self in the mirror, stepping back, turning left then right, patting her hair. The dark color gave her a more severe, no-nonsense look—perhaps she looked Russian. Eve wondered if Irene would recognize her.

Eve often thought of Duncan. A few days before, Patrick had dropped by the hospital to inquire about him and was told that Duncan had indeed improved, so much that he was soon to be released. Eve was relieved and pleased that the antibiotic had saved the young man's life. She ached to know if he and Irene had reunited or if he had returned to Boston.

Just as Eve reached for the doorknob to open the door and leave the room, it turned on the other end. She backed off, and when the door swung open, Patrick stood staring at her, curiously. He stepped in and closed the door behind them.

"Where are you going?" he asked, a little troubled.

"I have to get out of here, Patrick. I'm going stark raving mad. I'm sure it's safe now, and no one is going to recognize me—not that there are many people who know me in this time anyway."

Patrick stared, conflicted. "I don't know, Eve. It's chancy. Big Jim has long arms in this City."

"I can't hide in here forever. Let's go out together. Let's go to lunch somewhere. I have got to get out of here."

With a deep sigh, Patrick relented.

Outside, a light snow was still falling, creating a holiday spirit. Eve opened her navy-blue parasol against the snow, feeling quite fashionable, and held out her hand to catch the cold flakes. Meanwhile, Patrick waved down a hansom cab, not a motor taxi.

"You don't mind, do you, Eve?"

"Not at all."

Inside the cab, Eve thought it was fun to ride in a hansom again, pulled by a single horse, even though there were a lot of autos about. It was so unlike 1885, when no one had even heard about an automobile, much less ridden in one.

A car passed with an African American man behind the wheel, wearing a cap and white coat, chauffeuring a man with a bushy, white mustache. He was seated next to a stoic woman seated upright, wearing a green feather hat. She glanced over at Eve, her impressive heavy chin jutted out in a challenge.

The hansom plodded alongside the curb, passing pushcarts, letting the streetcars and faster cars chug by.

A stout policeman, dressed in a knee-length blue coat with brass buttons and tall felt helmet, waved his baton at the passing vehicles, his steely eyes watching three young boys darting in and out of the aggressive foot traffic.

Patrick sighed.

Eve turned to him. "What's that sigh about? I know all your sighs, Patrick, and that one sounds like despair."

He stared into her eyes with a serious expression. "I have to admit that I miss not having a cell phone, so I can *Google* facts and places. It would have made this searching a whole lot easier."

"Okay, Patrick, your expression tells me you're about to tell me something profound."

Patrick scratched the side of his nose. "I finally tracked down Daniel Fallow and Jacob Jackson."

Eve sat up, all ears. "And…?"

"Daniel Fallow died about ten years ago from tuberculosis. Jacob Jackson drank himself to death and died in 1908."

"Did you talk to their families? Did you mention the lantern?"

"I found Daniel's only daughter. She lives in Brooklyn. Not a pleasant woman, to say the least. After she called me several colorful names, she said everything her father owned she had tossed either into the garbage or into the river."

Now Eve sighed, resigned. "Okay, and what about Jacob Jackson?"

Patrick sat back, crossing his arms across his chest. "Jacob died at Gouverneur Hospital."

Eve's interest sharpened. "Really? How did you find that out?"

"I was a detective, Eve. I flattered a nurse, slipped her some money and was taken to a record room, down below, in a dank and dusty basement file room. Did you know that your friend Dr. Ann Long kept meticulous records?"

"I'm not surprised," Eve said. "She was an excellent doctor and administrator."

"Anyway, our friend Mr. Jackson died of cirrhosis of the liver and cholemia in 1908. Dr. Long signed his death certificate. It seems that Mr. Jackson had continued working for the hospital until only six months before his death. By the way, what is cholemia?"

Eve looked away, lost in thought. "Excess bile in the blood. It usually leads to coma."

"Well, that's it then," Eve said, her voice low and despairing. "Without that lantern, we have no way of getting back to our own time. We're stuck here."

Patrick gazed out into the traffic. "Yes, it would seem so. We're going to have to change our plans. We'll have to find Maggie and then escape to some other state or country where Big Jim will never find us. Which reminds me…"

Patrick dug around into his side coat pocket and drew out two passports. He handed one to Eve. "Finally got these. The pictures aren't the best, but they'll do."

Eve opened hers and grimaced at her photo. "I don't look so good in dark hair. How did you get them?"

"The son of a guy I knew back in 1885. He works out of the same storefront down on Delancey Street. I think the son's work is not as good as the father's. Anyway, at least we have identification if we have to leave the U.S."

Both sat in silence as the cab persisted uptown until it came to 58 West 36th Street, Henkel's Chop House. Located at the center of the Herald Square theater district, it was just a few steps from the Garrick Theatre's back entrance, a theatre Maggie had often performed in.

Eve and Patrick left the cab cautiously, Patrick's quick eyes swiftly scanning the streets as he led Eve into the restaurant. Inside, it was all dark wood and leather. Eve smelled roasting lamb, steak, whiskey and the ever-present-in-this-time tobacco smoke, which clouded the room.

A short, balding, white-aproned man led them through a maze of small tables, winding past well-dressed men and young secretaries, and loud, whiskey-drinking reporters slouched around a center table.

Eve and Patrick sat at a two-top, covered by a white linen tablecloth and a center candle. As Eve coughed and longed to wave away the cloud of cigar and cigarette smoke hanging in the air, she understood why the life expectancy of these people was lower than in her time. If she remembered correctly from her nursing school days, in the early 1900s, most men lived to about 45 or 50.

Patrick continued to study the room, looking for anyone suspicious.

"Relax, Patrick. We don't know anybody here."

"It's a small town, Eve…"

"Colleen," Eve whispered.

"All right, then. Colleen, you can't be too careful."

Patrick ordered grilled mutton chops and Eve chose roast beef.

Eve leaned in toward Patrick, trying to speak above the reporters' shouts and laughter. "What is it about this time that so many people eat grilled mutton chops?"

Patrick shrugged. "Because they're good. I've missed them. Didn't you have them in 1885?"

"No, I passed on them. I just couldn't get my head around it."

"Head around it? I'll never get used to your expressions."

"And I'll never get used to mutton chops."

"There's no restaurant in your time that knows how to cook mutton chops properly."

"My time?" Eve asked with an arched eyebrow. "Isn't my time your time?"

"You know what I mean…"

Eve surveyed the room, her mind still circling around the lantern. What could have happened to it?

"I can't help but be depressed, Patrick. I knew it was a slim possibility, but I had hoped we'd be able to find that lantern. I really did."

Patrick looked at his wife earnestly. "We're going to have to make the best of it here. We've done all we can, at least for now."

Then Patrick flinched, and he sat up straight, as a thought struck. "Oh, wait a minute. I almost forgot. What a blockhead I am."

"What?" Eve asked.

"A letter for you—from Chicago, addressed to Eve Kennedy, your old 1885 name."

He reached into his inside coat pocket, drew out the letter and read the return address. "It's from Dr. Long, special delivery. I picked it up in our post office box this morning."

Excited, Eve snatched the letter from Patrick's hand, focusing on Ann's name. "Yes, Chicago."

"We sent her the telegram just last week, right?" Patrick asked.

Eve brightened. "Yes. I can't believe she responded so quickly, and special delivery."

Eve aggressively slid her thumb under the sealed flap and with a little intake of breath, she removed the creamy bond letter from the envelope. She smoothed out the two folds and quickly skimmed the letter. Patrick leaned in, anxious.

"What's it say?"

Eve made a little sound of surprise. "Oh, wow."

"Wow, what? Tell me what the wow means."

She lifted her eyes on him. "You are not going to believe this."

CHAPTER 26

Eve lowered her voice and began to read Dr. Long's letter.

Dear Miss Kennedy:
I was surprised to hear from you. Well, yes and no. You were always a bit of a mystery to me, you know. I often had the impression that you were a person out of time and place: your mode of speech, your manner, your wisdom beyond your years. It was as though you were forcing yourself into a role that was not entirely comfortable for you. But I was delighted to have you as a friend and as part of my staff.

After you left, many patients were disappointed, and they communicated that to me and to other nurses. I dare say, some of the nurses seemed put off by it and jealous. No matter.

And when you vanished that night so long ago—December 1885, wasn't it? Well, the mystery grew and *became the stuff of legend, didn't it? Even poor Dr. Eckland, that dear man, was perplexed and disturbed by your vanishing act. You know how he loved Shakespeare. I recall him saying, "Dr. Long, how is it possible for Eve to simply disappear, just as the Fool in <u>King Lear</u> did, and no one can explain where she has gone? I find the entire thing quite extraordinary."*

And, Miss Kennedy, whatever happened to our hero, the very handsome and close-to-death Detective Sergeant Patrick Gantly? He vanished too, didn't he, never to be seen or heard from again.

Yes, I did have a conversation with Jacob Jackson and Daniel Fallow, when I learned you had fled in the hospital ambulance. (Strictly against the rules, mind you.) Both men were rather mum at the time, and both seemed truly frightened and agitated. They would only say that you had left town quite mysteriously.

Two days later, I visited Evelyn Sharland's room and found John Harringshaw there. He would not leave her bedside for any length of time. I asked them if either had heard from you.

In Mr. Harringshaw's guarded manner, I suspected an intrigue, and at that time, I believed he was instrumental in your and Mr. Gantly's escape from the City. I believed that for a long time—for many years in fact—until one night in 1908 when I heard a timid knock on my office door. Who walked in, but a rail thin and sickly Jacob Jackson.

I knew of his alcoholism and of his deteriorating medical condition. He stood before my desk, very contrite, head down, hat brim held tightly in both hands.

Mr. Jackson then proceeded to tell me your incredible story. He told me everything in great detail, as if it had happened only yesterday. He was still disturbed by it. His hands shook as the words came sputtering out.

He said, "I know I'm about to meet my maker, Dr. Long, and I must get this devil of a thing off my chest."

To my surprise, he excused himself, returning a few short minutes later with a lantern. He carefully and fearfully placed it on my desk and then quickly backed away as if it might leap out and attack him.

Mr. Jackson told me that on that dark night in Central Park when you lit the lantern, you and Detective Gantly slowly faded into a kind of blue mist and then completely vanished into thin air. Both he and Mr. Fallow stood quaking in their boots, staring, petrified at what they had seen. For a time, they searched the area but found nothing.

When it was clear that you and Detective Gantly were gone, they snatched up the lantern and ran for the hospital wagon. On the way back to the hospital they made a vow never to tell anyone what they had seen, fearing they'd be locked away in Blackwell Island's Asylum.

As I stared at the lantern sitting there on my desk, Jacob Jackson told me that he had hidden the thing in his tool shed behind his house since 1885, afraid to destroy the thing and afraid to light it. He told me he wanted to be free of it. With that, he left my office and we never discussed it again.

Eve raised her eyes to see Patrick staring back at her, his eyes burning with interest.

Their waiter drifted by to ask if everything was all right. Patrick ordered a whiskey.

After the waiter retreated, Patrick stared hard, then inclined again toward Eve.

"Why did you stop reading?"

"I need a minute. It's a bit overwhelming. Do you know what this means?"

"No, not yet. Does Dr. Long have the lantern?"

Eve adjusted herself in the chair, cleared her throat and continued reading the letter.

I'm a scientist, Miss Kennedy, and I have worked very hard to be a good doctor, and a respected doctor in a man's world of doctors, many of whom still consider me to be a foolish woman and an impediment to be circumvented. Fine, all well and good. As you know, I accepted all that long ago when I obtained the job as the first female ambulance surgeon in New York at the Gouverneur Hospital.

I do not believe in ghosts or mediums or fairies. I do not believe that people time travel, despite the entertaining story **The Time Machine** *by H. G. Wells, which I read sometime before the turn of the century. However, something told me that there was a possibility I might see or hear from you again at some point in the future. So what was that belief? Intuition?*

You said in your telegram that you wanted to know if either Jacob Jackson or Daniel Fallow had spoken to me about the rather extraordinary event that happened in 1885. I suspect, Miss Kennedy, that you want to know if I have the lantern. I'll not beat about the bush. In short, yes, Miss Kennedy, I have it. I kept it. I also suspect that you are in some sort of trouble, although for the life of me I cannot imagine what that trouble might be.

Miss Kennedy, I will only tell you where the lantern is if you come to Chicago and meet me. Frankly, I want to see you and speak with you. There are many things I wish to learn. Perhaps you'll think that unfair of me. Perhaps it is, but I am getting on in years and, I must admit, I care much less about what people think of me now than I did many years ago. I am sixty-nine years old, Miss Kennedy. My eyesight has diminished, and my knees are starting to fail me. I shall not mention my heart, other than to say it is getting a little weary.

My entire life has been dedicated to medicine, and there are times, on holidays and on cold nights here in Chicago, when I think about what the great beyond holds for me. I have no family, at least none I will speak about here. My mother and sister have passed. I am quite alone in this world, except for some cherished friends and maybe a secret or two which perhaps I might share with you when you come.

Don't misunderstand. These are not complaints, and I have no regrets. Let me just say that I long to see an old friend, or perhaps, Miss Kennedy, I want to see your face. Perhaps you will have aged as I have; perhaps not. Perhaps you will impart knowledge of events I know nothing about and cannot even imagine.

When I was a young woman, I would have scoffed and had no time for such fanciful notions as time travel. But now, I wonder. Wasn't it Socrates who said, "Wonder is the beginning of wisdom?"

Will you come to Chicago to see me, Miss Kennedy? I have listed my address below and you can always reach me at Augustana Hospital, telephone number also enclosed.

From your telegram, I suspect there is some urgency in the matter. Perhaps you'll want to send a telegram to the hospital.

And yes, as I said, I do have the lantern, and I will be happy to return it to you. I will be waiting to hear about your fascinating life with great anticipation.

With fond regards,
Ann Long

Eve lowered the letter just as the waiter arrived with Patrick's whiskey. Patrick tossed it back in a gulp, replacing the shot glass gently on the table, his mind spinning out new plans and possibilities.

"Well, isn't the world just filled with surprises?" Patrick said.

Eve pondered the letter. "This scares me."

"Why? I would think you'd be thrilled."

"A part of me is thrilled and relieved. A part of me wonders if Dr. Long wants more than just to see me."

"You mean, she might want to return with us to the future?"

"Her future, our present."

Patrick shrugged. "I wouldn't worry about it. She sounds more like a woman who is seeking answers. I'd send her a telegram today. Once you hear back from her, take the first train to Chicago."

"And what will you do while I'm gone?"

"Search for Maggie. What else?"

"And if you find her?"

"I *will* find her, Eve. Make no mistake about that. I will surely find her and get her away from Big Jim one way or the other."

And then Patrick's thoughts stalled.

Eve saw alarm on his face. "What is it?"

"Don't turn around. Don't move."

"What?"

"Guess who just came in."

"Who?"

"Big Jim and a friend, a gentleman. Don't turn around, Eve."

Patrick glanced away as Big Jim and Addison Casterbury, led by the portly owner, passed the table and were seated at a private table near the back of the room.

Eve recognized the man with Big Jim and felt a knot of fear lodge in her gut. She whispered, "That's Addison Casterbury."

"Irene's brother?"

"Yes... What are they doing here together?"

Eve's shoulders tensed, her mouth twitched, and she and Patrick wrestled with thoughts and emotions.

"We should leave," she said.

"Not yet. They won't recognize you."

Addison casually glimpsed the room, checking out the women. Eventually, his eyes settled on Eve and her breath stopped. She snatched her glass of water, trying not to look self-conscious as she drank. To her relief, Addison's gaze offered no recognition, just an obvious attraction. Big Jim said something, and Addison's attention was diverted. Eve let out an inaudible sigh. Her Colleen disguise had worked.

"I can't believe those two are together," Eve said, speaking under her breath. "Why? Why would Big Jim be with a rich and influential guy like Addison?"

Patrick crossed his hands on the tabletop. "I have no idea."

Patrick had seen Big Jim mostly at a distance as he'd followed him. Here he got a good look at him. He'd known men like Big Jim when he was growing up on the Lower East Side. They were sullen bullies, and they were mean. Patrick could see that Big Jim had good wads of muscles on his shoulders and a powerful barrel chest, despite the paunch.

His essence, his posture, was one of seedy, indolent brutality. He was a born antagonist, a natural bad boy, a primitive animal that women might be attracted to when they leveled their sultry eyes on him. Maggie had surely been one of those women, and now she was trapped.

It made Patrick angry, and it sharpened his resolve.

"What do we do, Patrick?" Eve asked.

"You go on to Chicago and get that lantern. I'm going to follow up on Addison Casterbury and find out why he and Big Jim are pals. Something doesn't smell right."

"Do you think Irene's in danger because she was with me?"

"I don't know. Maybe."

"I should go see Duncan. Maybe I can warn him. By now, he'll be out of the hospital and back in his apartment."

"Warn him about what?"

"That Irene may be in danger."

"No. Too risky. No one can know who you are. I don't want any more of Big Jim's roughscuffs coming after you. Let me follow up with him. Give me his address and I'll learn what I can about Irene and Addison."

Eve took Patrick's hand. "You'll be careful, won't you, Patrick? I don't want any more of Big Jim's roughscuffs coming after you either."

"Don't worry. My advantage is that Big Jim doesn't know who I am. I'm going to keep it that way. You go get that lantern and hurry back to New York. By then, I hope to know where Maggie is. We'll grab her and then run for it. Since we can't text, we'll have to use telegrams and the phone."

Eve kept her face in tight control, but she felt a storm brewing in her chest.

CHAPTER 27

Two days later, on Saturday, December 12th, Eve and Patrick left the Hoffman House in a cold, misty rain and taxied to Grand Central Terminal. Eve purchased a first-class ticket and a private Pullman berth on the New York Central 20th Century Limited to LaSalle Street Station in Chicago. The journey would take a little over 20 hours. Eve and Dr. Long had communicated by telegram, arranging to meet at a popular Chicago restaurant for dinner on Sunday evening.

Standing on the platform, Patrick tried not to appear worried as the train left the station and he waved goodbye to his beloved wife. Eve pressed her nose to the window, waving back, her heart sinking. Why were they always parting?

He mouthed the words, "Don't worry. I love you."

She blew him a kiss as the train hissed clouds of steam and the whistle moaned out its departure.

After Eve was gone, Patrick left the terminal and headed to the 30th Street station of the elevated railroad to catch the downtown train to Greenwich Village. As he walked, Patrick had a flashback to when he was eighteen, when the Village was home to both the first streetcar and the first elevated rail line. The Ninth Avenue Elevated Railway, or El, began operation in 1868 and originally ran from Battery Place to 30th Street on a single steel track, with cables powered by steam engines.

The El became known as "the One-Legged Railroad," and as it expanded, it allowed New York City to expand as well. During the thriving years of the industrial revolution and the mass immigration in the decades following the Civil War, the City swiftly grew northward and its people were carried there by the El. The El also allowed quicker transit above the congested Lower Manhattan streets, which were filled with horses, carts, streetcars, and people.

Patrick boarded the elevated El and clung to a pole as the train rumbled down to the Village. The car was crowded with well-dressed men in dark suits and derbies, shabby men with wide-brimmed hats, stylish women who worked in the ladies' shops, and workmen in dusty laborer's clothes. The cigar smoke was stringy and the air moist with humidity. The sweet and sour body smells twitched his nose. He noticed that the ladies' low-hemmed dresses were damp from the rainy streets, and their eyes were shut or focused ahead, ignoring the wandering eyes of men.

Patrick took it all in with great pleasure. There was a visceral familiarity here, in this early twentieth-century city. The smells, the sounds, the air, all awakened in him old memories, being closer to his life in 1885. He felt more attached to them, more alive. He breathed them in with relish.

He'd been living in the modern world for almost two years, and he was still having trouble adjusting. He had difficulty with the language, the food, the culture, and the people. They all seemed to have come from another world, and indeed they were from another world.

Patrick didn't often mention his homesickness to Eve; he didn't want to whine or be a burden. But there were times, deep in the night, when he wished he could return to his world, to his people, and to his culture, as flawed as they were. He sometimes wondered if his body, mind and emotions would ever adjust to the world of the 21st century.

In fact, he was frequently exhibiting signs of stress. He sometimes had spotty recall about facts and places, probably caused by stress. He had started clenching his jaw and grinding his teeth. Eve suggested relaxation techniques and wearing a mouth guard when he slept. He practiced her relaxation techniques but dodged the sleep guard. He'd also developed hyperhidrosis, excessive perspiration due to stress. He often took three showers a day.

Time travel was jarring, disorienting and, often, just plain terrifying. Here, now, in 1914, his breathing came more easily. His body was more relaxed. He did not clench his teeth or sweat excessively, despite anxiety about finding, and then possibly losing, Eve.

And he had to admit that even though his plan to steal Maggie away from Big Jim was a very dangerous game, at least he was back doing work he had always loved—being a detective. He was living as the man he had been, using his skill and instincts, his intelligence and his wits to survive and achieve goals. Yes, if he and Eve were forced to live in this time, it might not be so bad.

The El arrived at the corner of Greenwich Street. Patrick glanced out to see a stone marker between the third and fourth floors of a brick building abutting the intersection. **Charles Street and Greenwich Street** were carved into it. The sign would be difficult to see and read at street level, but for the passenger on the Ninth Avenue El, it was a welcome indicator of the train's location and progress.

Patrick left the train, descended the platform stairs and made his way toward Christopher Street. Another thought arose. If he had remained in 1885 and not time traveled to 2016, he would be sixty-four years old. What would his life have been like?

Patrick found the address, a four-story narrow red brick, with a zig-zagging fire escape and tall windows, with most curtains drawn. One window was wide open, on the fourth floor. As soon as Patrick entered the building, he sensed danger. It was a learned, experienced sensation he'd felt many times in his police career. It was a rubbing, gnawing thing that put his system on high alert.

The hall lighting was dim, the staircase narrow. He heard the muted cry of a baby. He smelled bacon and coffee. From two flights up, a lilting melody danced from a violin.

Patrick edged toward the stairs, gazing up into the murky distances of the upper floors. He laid a hand on the wooden banister and started up, stairs creaking beneath his boots. Beads of sweat popped out on his forehead. He nudged back the bill of his bowler hat and ascended, every sense awake.

Reaching the fourth floor, he heard something shatter. He heard a thump. He looked right at apartment 43, Duncan Beaumont's apartment. He heard a low, muffled voice. It was not a friendly voice. He heard another thump, as if someone had fallen.

Patrick eased his way toward the apartment door, casting glances about to see if curious heads were poking out of other apartment doors. He saw no one.

Patrick gently pressed an ear against the door. He heard the low, gruff voice again. He could just make out the words.

"Are you going to tell me where she is, you goosecap, or do you want more of the same?"

No response.

"You are a dumb boy, aren't you?"

Patrick heard a slap, a cry and a whimper.

Patrick decided to act. He pulled himself to his full height and rapped on the door.

Silence.

Patrick knocked harder.

"Who is it?" came a harsh voice.

Patrick went into a thick Irish brogue. "It is Father O'Neil, from the hospital, come to see how Mr. Beaumont is feeling. Will ya let me in now?"

"Go away. He doesn't want to see you."

Patrick knocked again, waiting, body tensing.

"I said, go away!"

Patrick persisted. He knocked again.

When the door swung open, Patrick cocked a fist. The face he saw before him was tough, bony and narrow. Patrick punched that face hard in the nose.

The man stumbled backward, hands to his nose, falling on his ass.

Patrick swiftly entered, shook out his sore hand and shut the door behind him. He quickly scanned the room. Duncan was cowering in the back corner, near a radiator, his nose trickling blood, eyes darting about, frightened, like a cornered mouse.

Duncan's downed attacker was a pro and he responded quickly. While holding his bleeding nose with one hand, he pulled a knife from his coat pocket and then grabbed hold of a chair and pulled himself up, knife poised and threatening.

Patrick offered an ingratiating smile. "And a good day to ya, son. May the good Lord be with ya."

"I told you to get out of here, you daft priest, if you are a priest. And what priest thuds a man in his nose for nothin'?"

"Ah, but you just frightened me for a second with that face of yours. Please forgive me, Lord," Patrick said, folding his hands and looking heavenward.

"I told you to get out of here."

"So ya did, my son, so ya did. But the Lord has his work to do and I have mine. Yes, I do. So here I am to check on this poor lad, and from the looks of it, it seems you two are having a bit of a scuffle."

"I will cut you, priest, so help me God, if you don't leave, and leave now."

"Now why would ya do such a thing, son? Have you no respect for…"

The man cut him off. "No! I have no respect for you, priest. Now get out. Now!"

Patrick saw the chair. As the bad man stepped to his left, as if to block Duncan, Patrick made his move. He surged forward, snatched the top rail of the wooden chair, lifted it, and swung its four legs, jabbing them at the attacker.

The man was startled by the aggressive, unexpected move and stepped back. Again, he recovered, with a dark, sinister grin.

"Priest, do not play with me. I will cut you, make no mistake, and I will leave you bleeding in the gutter with the rest of the trash."

Patrick stared into the man's narrow snake eyes and saw pure evil intent.

"Well, my son, I believe you have the blackest of hearts, don't ya? Well, I'm a forgiving man, just like the good Lord himself, and I will give you but one more chance. You drop the knife here and now, my son, and I promise not to drive you back toward the open window and shove your sinning soul out into the cool morning air to smash on the street below. Now, when you fall to your death and splatter on the street, I guarantee the devil will be a-waitin' for ya."

The man must have seen the hard glare of truth in Patrick's eyes. He wavered, but only for a few seconds. He laughed, but it was a nervous laugh, and he threw nervous glances toward the open window.

"I don't see a collar on you, priest."

"Of course you don't, my son. Your black soul blinds you to the goodness of things. Now, what will it be? Will you drop the knife, or will you go straight to the devil?"

The man's eyes shifted toward Duncan. "I will stab the boy first."

Patrick knew not to wait. Always attack first. Fast and sure, he did attack, surging forward, thrusting the four wooden legs at the man. He backstepped, eyes shocked round circles.

The man broke for Duncan, but Patrick blocked him with the chair. The man skipped right, but Patrick was there, the four sharp legs spoiling his move. Patrick drove forward, enclosing the sweating man, pinning him. Before the agile man could free himself, Patrick launched ahead, shoving him toward the open window. The man backstepped, struggling for balance. He was only inches from the window ledge, cool air rushing in.

Below, came traffic sounds: a car horn, the hollow moan of a boat whistle. The violin below playing a lively waltz.

The man still gripped the knife, his eyes now stung with fear. He glanced behind, faced Patrick again, and measured his expression.

"Will you drop the knife, son, or will ya fly off to meet the devil?"

The man made one last attempt to break free, but Patrick caged him firmly, wedging him against the window ledge with the chair legs.

"I'll say a prayer for ya, son."

Patrick did not want to kill this man. Patrick didn't want to kill any man, and shoving this wicked man out the window was not practical. It was a last resort. Although it was a gray misty day, it was broad daylight. Neighbors would appear, look up and speculate about which floor and which window. The police would be called. Patrick and Duncan would have to run for it, and Patrick didn't know if Duncan was up to it, and Patrick didn't know the neighborhood. Was there a back door? Was there an alleyway? He didn't know, but he should have looked. He should have checked the place out before he mounted the stairs and went blundering into Duncan's apartment. The old Patrick would have investigated the area. The new one was rusty. He'd rushed in too fast without a plan. He was too emotional because Maggie was involved; because Eve was involved.

Patrick and the bad man hovered in a tense silence, waiting.

Finally, to Patrick's relief, the man dropped the knife.

Patrick grinned. "You did the wise thing, my son."

"You go to the devil, priest."

Patrick slowly lowered the chair. "Will you leave us in peace now, my son?"

The man grinned, darkly. "Sure I will, priest."

"Perhaps I'll see you in the confessional soon?"

"You can count on that, priest. You and me will meet again, that I can promise you."

Patrick swung the chair to the floor. Just then, the bad man reached into his left coat pocket and Patrick knew what he was going for. Patrick launched himself at the man, connecting to the man's face with a hard right. The blow drove him back, smashing him into the wall, just inches from the open window.

Patrick pressed the attack, lunging forward, hooking the man in the belly. The impact doubled him over. Patrick slammed a left into his jaw and a right under his chin. The bad man slammed into the wall again, his eyes bulging. As he slid down to the floor, the air left his lungs and his eyes grew glassy and blank. His body sagged and slumped to the right.

Duncan struggled to his feet, face pale, body trembling. "Who are these animals? These horrible sick animals?" Duncan asked, voice quivering.

"I'd wager he's one of Big Jim's bully boys. I'd also wager he has a second weapon. They always do."

Patrick kicked the knife away, crouched over the man and padded him down. Sure enough, in the left coat pocket, Patrick found a chrome-plated derringer with a pearl grip.

Patrick pocketed the derringer and tossed the knife aside. He looked up at Duncan.

"Are you a priest?"

"No, Duncan."

"How do you know my name?"

"I'm Eve Gantly's husband."

Duncan stared, processing the words. "A nurse at the hospital said she brought pills that saved my life."

"Yes, Duncan. Let's talk about it later. Do you have rope, wire?"

"No…"

"A tie? A long string tie?"

"Yes."

"Get it. Hurry."

Minutes later, Patrick had the bad man's hands tied securely behind his back.

Duncan stood over Patrick, spots of blood on his cream-colored shirt. His eyes were still spooked, his hands shaking.

Patrick arose, wiping the perspiration from his forehead.

"Once he wakes up, this won't hold him for long. We've got to go."

"Go?"

"Yes, go. Take whatever you need. You can't come back here."

"I can't leave."

"Duncan, don't be stupid. When this guy wakes up, he'll kill you. If he doesn't, somebody else will. Now let's go."

Duncan glared down at the man. "I wish you would have killed him. They beat her up, you know."

"Beat who?" Patrick asked.

"You should have killed him."

"Who did they beat up, Duncan?"

"Poor Irene. That big man beat her up and her brother did nothing to stop it. They should all die for that."

Patrick was stunned. "Irene Casterbury? Did Big Jim beat up Irene Casterbury?"

Now Duncan could hardly contain his rage, as he squeezed his hands into fists. "Yes! Yes... she was taken to the hospital. I saw her there."

"Why, Duncan?"

Duncan's red-rimmed eyes held Patrick. "They wanted to know where that woman is. Where your wife is. She was Irene's friend."

Patrick sighed. "Of course..."

And Patrick was glad Eve had left town.

The man on the floor groaned. To Patrick's surprise, Duncan kicked him in the gut.

CHAPTER 28

At eight in the morning on Sunday, December 13th, Eve checked into her room at the Morrison Hotel on Clark and Madison Streets, a hotel that had been suggested to her by Ann. Ann had also suggested two respectable lady's boarding houses, but Eve had decided on the hotel. It had 519 rooms, and the one item that had sold Eve was the private bath, an amenity which had not yet become commonplace in the hotel industry.

Eve found some bubble bath packets in a rose porcelain soap dish. She turned on the gold faucet, sprinkled half a package into the full stream and undressed while the water churned and foamed. The train trip had not been difficult, but she was still not used to people smoking in the dining car and in the lounge, and she'd developed a persistent cough because of the smoke. She'd also had to fend off an obnoxious and irritating salesman who had repeatedly invited her to dinner and "a libation" in the lounge.

Ten minutes later, Eve was inside the warm tub, contented and engulfed in bubbles. As she closed her eyes, an image of Patrick slid into her inner vision. She would be glad when this whole adventure was over, and they were safely back in their own time in their own place and in their own bed.

And then thoughts of the lantern intruded. What would she say to Ann about the time travel adventures? How much could she say? Would Ann want to time travel to the future?

And then Eve's body took over. The water felt luxurious and relaxing and it lulled her into a peaceful trance. She sank further into the tub and fell asleep.

At six o'clock that evening, Eve emerged from a taxi at State and Randolph Streets, wearing a long tapered woolen coat, black embroidered shoes, and an elegant plum dress and hat. She took in the tower clocks, awnings, trolleys, cars, wagons and crowds of people. Eve had never been to Chicago in her own time, and she was charmed by the 1914 architecture, shops and restaurants. She liked the good energy of the people.

She entered Angelo's, an Italian restaurant with a Pompeian theme of Roman columns, colorful frescos of nymphs and shepherds, white table cloths and gold-tinted chairs.

The fastidious, thin-mustached Maître d' led her to a cozy table on the right side of the already bustling restaurant. There, for the first time since her last time travel journey to 1885, Eve caught a glimpse of her dear friend, Dr. Ann Long.

Ann stood as Eve approached, and Eve saw the expanding surprise in her eyes. Of course, Eve had not aged at all. Ann Long, on the other hand, was a thin, gray-haired woman with a pocked face mapped with lines, the pockmarks a result of smallpox Ann had contracted when she was a teenager.

In her dark, conservative dress, with a bit of lace around the neck, Dr. Long appeared like a woman from a past age. If Eve was honest, she'd say that Ann Long appeared older than her 69 years. To her experienced nurse's eyes, Dr. Long did not look healthy and she did not appear to be physically strong.

But Ann's smile was warm and welcoming, and her blueberry eyes twinkled with pleasure. She did not hug Eve, but simply offered a thin hand and a cordial "Hello, Miss Kennedy. It is so pleasant to see you again."

Eve handed Ann a gift box, artistically wrapped in evergreen paper with a lavish red bow. She'd purchased it that afternoon at Rothchild's Store on South State Street.

"It's a 'hello again' and a Christmas present," Eve said.

Ann took the gift with a pleased, small smile. "Well... how nice of you. I'm afraid I have nothing to offer you."

"Not to worry. Forgive the sentiment, but seeing you again is gift enough," Eve said.

After they sat and menus arrived, Ann gently unwrapped the gift, lifted the lid, and parted the white tissue paper. Inside was a floral, rose-colored silk scarf. Ann's face opened in extravagant pleasure as she removed it from the box and held it up.

"Oh, my, how lovely it is, Miss Kennedy. How wonderfully beautiful. Oh, I'm so sorry I have nothing for you in return."

As Ann returned the scarf to the box, she said, "This dinner will be my gift, Miss Kennedy. It will be my Christmas present to you."

And then they fell into easy conversation about Eve's train journey and about the New York weather. Eve relaxed, enjoying Dr. Long's clear, creamy speech and warm, formal voice.

Ann ordered veal chops sauté with pizzaiola, and Eve chose spaghetti with Romana sauce and meatballs. A carafe of dry red wine was on its way.

After the waiter glided off into the crowded room, Ann leaned back and studied her old staff member. She smiled wistfully.

"It appears you have found the fountain of youth, Miss Kennedy."

"You can call me Eve, Dr. Long."

"All right, then you must call me Ann. Shall we jump right into it, or should we dance around it a bit?"

"Well first, I'd love to know how you like Chicago, Ann."

Ann surveyed the room as the hum of conversation hovered and the lighting suddenly dimmed, adding a romantic atmosphere. Table candles began to glow and flicker, and the smell of the Italian food was ubiquitous.

"I like the people of Chicago," Ann said. "I like this town, I think, even more than I liked New York. Do you know that I have even taken an interest in baseball? I actually attended a game at Weeghman Park. The game was between the Chicago Federals, or Chi-Feds, as they say, and the Kansas City Packers. I admit to having a wonderful time, especially since the Chi-Feds won."

"I never thought of you as a baseball fan."

"And that is not all," Ann said with enthusiasm. "Last summer, a younger colleague told me that I should go to 63rd Street and King Drive and fly over the city in a dirigible. She said it was the most thrilling experience she'd ever had. Well, at first, I was terrified at the thought. But then, as the days passed, I gathered up my courage and I did it. Yes, I did. I flew in a dirigible over Chicago, from the South Shore to the mouth of the Chicago River. It was so exhilarating. It lasted for 25 minutes, and it was not inexpensive, of course. It cost $25 per person. Well, the price almost changed my mind for me. But I swallowed my parsimony and my fear, and I did it."

"I am impressed. Again, that doesn't sound like the woman I knew in 1885."

Ann shifted in her chair, suddenly serious.

"Eve... as I said in my letter, my heart will not last much longer. As such, I decided I wanted to do some things I'd never even thought about doing before, and you know what? I wish I had done them sooner. I wish I hadn't been so absorbed in my work for so much of my life. I wish I had discovered baseball sooner, and dirigibles, and the beach at 58th Street. I believe I would have been a better woman, a better doctor and a happier person. Yes, I do believe that."

Eve saw the earnest glint in Ann's now sad eyes.

Ann made a vague gesture with her hand. "And then again, maybe it also had to do with this awful and terrible war that is spreading around Europe like a firestorm. There have been pro-Germany marches here, and there are some who want us to get involved in the war. Thankfully, President Wilson is against it. But, oh, how I wish that little Bosnian Serb had not assassinated Archduke Ferdinand and his dear wife, Sophie, in June. I fear the worst. I fear that it won't be long before the entire world will be engulfed in some devastating war."

The wine arrived. The very upright waiter, with a bushy black mustache, filled their glasses and then hurried away.

Eve sipped her wine, looking at Ann over the rim. Ann stared back, strangely.

"Perhaps you know what will happen, Eve. Perhaps you know things that no one else in this world knows. Do you know if the entire world is about to go to war? Perhaps you know many other things, as well. I suspect so. I have thought much about it since Jacob Jackson set that lantern on my desk and told me his incredible and unbelievable story. But now, here you are. Here you sit opposite me, and you have not aged since I saw you last, some twenty-eight years ago."

"Why did you want to see me, Ann?"

Ann's left eyebrow arched. "Why? To confirm Mr. Jackson's story, of course. Because part of me—no most of me—could not and did not believe it. But how can I doubt my own eyes? Although your hair has changed, you are exactly the same. Tell me, Eve, will this war in Europe spread, and will we get involved? Will it last for a long time?"

Eve considered her answer. When Patrick was adjusting to his new life in 2018, he had become obsessed by the Great War or World War I, and he had spent hours online learning about it. He could not believe the scope, the brutality and the devastation that would have occurred in his lifetime.

Eve could have told Ann that the war would be one of unprecedented destruction and loss of life, resulting in the deaths of some 20 million soldiers and civilians, and the physical devastation of much of the European continent. But she didn't.

Eve sat in silence for minutes, while Ann waited, not stirring or moving her eyes away from Eve's face. When Eve finally spoke, her voice was low, just loud enough for Ann to hear.

"The world does improve, Ann. We do make progress. Women do receive the right to own property and the right to vote, and they do obtain meaningful and important jobs. Women will be elected to public office, and many will thrive and help to enlighten the world. There will be struggles, of course, but the world does improve, little by little."

Ann lowered her eyes just as their food arrived. The silence lengthened as they ate. Eve saw a gradual awkwardness, as Ann glanced up at Eve several times, nearly speaking, but then holding back.

After Ann had finished her meal, she laid her fork aside and looked Eve directly in the eye.

"Will you tell me, Eve, everything that has happened to you? Part of me is frightened by what you might say, but most of me would like to know if such things truly do happen in this world."

Eve's eyes came to Ann. She saw nervous anticipation and tender sadness.

Eve began the story slowly, giving Ann a condensed description of her life in 2016, how she found the lantern in the antique shop, and her subsequent travel to 1885. As she continued, Ann's uncertain eyes slowly drifted away, staring out into remoteness, as the long and extraordinary story began to unravel.

When Eve told of her marriage to Patrick, Ann perked up eagerly as she listened to Eve's description of married life in 2018. She also described some current events and cultural advances in the modern world. When Eve said there were still few women in government and that there had never been a woman president, Ann slumped a little in her chair.

Ann also saddened when Eve shared the reason she and Patrick had returned to the past, and their utter shock and surprise at arriving in 1914 and not 1885.

While Eve told the story, coffee had arrived, along with some colorful Italian cookies and two cannoli. Neither had touched the dessert or drunk the coffee.

An accordion player began playing Neapolitan songs, and a guest stood at his table and sang in a bright tenor voice. That snapped the solemn mood, and Ann sat up to listen while sipping her coffee.

When the song ended, Ann peered at Eve with new eyes, probing her, replaying the story, her mind still struggling with belief.

"Well, Eve, that is quite a story, isn't it, and it seems to be a story without a finish. Quite honestly, it's a story that seems contrived by someone with a highly imaginative and fantastical mind. One who is simply not anchored in any kind of reality."

Eve heard the edge of anxiety in Ann's voice. Her response wasn't what Eve had expected.

"Then you don't believe me, Ann. You don't believe the story?"

Ann's smile was strange and vivid. "Oh, yes, Eve. I do believe the story. I don't want to, but I do. I see the authenticity in your eyes and I hear it in your voice. Now the question for me is, what do I do with it? Perhaps I will have to broaden my thinking, abandon my scientific worldview, my entire belief system."

Ann tried to read Eve's face. "How do you live with it? How can you reconcile it all?"

"It hasn't been easy, Ann. But, on the other hand, if I hadn't time traveled to 1885, I would never have met Patrick."

Ann smiled. "Yes, of course. Speaking of 1885, have you contacted the Harringshaws or anyone else from 1885?"

"No... Patrick and I decided not to disturb the past any more than we had to. We have already made more ripples than we had intended. You're the only one we've contacted, and only then because of the lantern."

Eve leaned forward, a glimmer of hope in her eyes. "Now that you know everything, Ann; now that you understand why Patrick and I have come to this time, will you tell me where the lantern is?"

Ann's forehead wrinkled in thought. "There is something I don't understand. When you lit the candle in your time, 2018, why didn't the lantern go with you?"

Eve sighed. "I don't know. Each lantern, even though it is the same lantern, exists only in its time. It does not travel into the future or into the past. That's why Patrick and I need the lantern that Jacob Jackson gave you. That is the same lantern that sent us to 2016. We must have it to return to 2018. You said in your letter that you have it."

Ann glanced away and listened to the accordion player dedicate the beloved Christmas carol *O Come,*

All Ye Faithful to the men fighting in the European war. Many patrons joined in the singing, including Ann. Eve remembered most of the words and, as she sang, she thought of Patrick and wished he were here, rattling off one of his old Irish sayings.

When the carol ended, peace hovered in the room while the two women sat quietly in the afterglow of song and candlelight. But Eve was growing anxious, and she broke the mood. "You do have it, don't you, Ann? The lantern?"

Ann's eyes narrowed. "Yes, and no."

Eve's shoulders sagged. "What does that mean?"

Ann looked at Eve pointedly. "Let us find a taxi and take a little tour of this fascinating city while I tell you a little secret that I have never told anyone. It concerns where the lantern is."

CHAPTER 29

Late Sunday morning, Patrick was relieved when he received a telegram from Eve saying she'd arrived safely, and she was off to meet Dr. Long for dinner that evening. He shot off a return telegram simply saying,

PLEASE LET ME KNOW WHEN YOU GET THE ITEM

Eve didn't need to know that Irene had been badly beaten by Big Jim himself, and that the newspapers stated that she'd been struck by a carriage and was convalescing in the Woman's Hospital at 110th Street and Amsterdam Avenue. Her brother, Addison, told reporters that she was "improving splendidly" and would be returning home any day.

Eve also didn't need to know that Patrick had moved Duncan to another apartment on the edge of the Village. There, he'd forced him to take a 1904 Colt police 32 revolver, six shot, and directed him to a shooting range on the lower East Side where the kid could learn how to shoot the thing.

Patrick's mind was flaming with anger, and he was struggling to contain his rising violent emotions. Why had Addison allowed his own sister to be beaten to near death by an animal like Big Jim? What kind of a man was he? Was he scared of Big Jim? Were they both working together in some business that Eve and Irene had inadvertently threatened? Patrick wanted to meet Addison in person and find out for himself why he'd allow his beautiful and innocent sister to be beaten up by a perverted jackal like Big Jim. Patrick vowed to get the truth out of Addison, even if he had to beat him the same way Big Jim had beaten Irene. Was Irene beaten because Big Jim was trying to find Eve—to try to stop her from helping Maggie get out of town?

Patrick had slept little as he worked to shove aside his hot feelings for revenge. He had to stay focused on finding Maggie before it was too late. An obvious thought kept striking his brain like a loud gong, reverberating and keeping him from restful sleep.

Why didn't he just track Big Jim down on a dark street and shoot him? That would take care of everything. Or would it? First, could he really kill a man in cold blood, even if he was an animal like Big Jim? No, he couldn't. He knew himself that well. If all else failed, could Patrick burst into Maggie's St. Regis hotel suite and then shoot Big Jim before he killed Maggie? Yes, he could and would.

But there was a problem with that last-ditch strategy now. Eve had altered the future, trying to help Maggie escape from Big Jim. According to history, that should not have happened—at least not in the past that Patrick had read about on that laptop in 2018. So, Eve had changed the course of history, making it entirely possible that Big Jim would not kill Maggie on Christmas Eve, or at least not at the St. Regis. Maggie had been moved. But where?

Would Big Jim kill her at another hotel or apartment? A bad thought. And then there was an even worse thought. Had Big Jim already killed Maggie for betraying him and trying to escape? Again, Patrick didn't think so. There was the awful and terrible thought that Big Jim had also beaten Maggie. But if he had killed her, then why would he have bothered to find Irene, beating her senseless, trying to learn where Eve was? Why did his man also go after Duncan?

Patrick had to face it: history had been changed, and that meant his tactics had to change. He no longer had the convenience—if he could call it that—of knowing where Maggie was going to be on Christmas Eve 1914. Most certainly, Big Jim would not return Maggie to the St. Regis until he found Eve to learn who she was, what she was up to, and who she was working with.

Now, not only did Patrick have to find Maggie, and find her fast, he also had to make sure Big Jim never learned who or where Eve was. The one tortured thought that kept haunting him was an obvious one: perhaps Eve should have thrown that lantern in the Hudson after all, and then there would have been no possibility of his going back in time to try to save Maggie. And what if he couldn't save her? What if she was already dead? What then? How would he live with himself? Could he face Eve, knowing he had failed to save his daughter after he had put both their lives in great danger?

On Monday morning, December 14th, as Patrick stopped by the Hoffman House lobby desk to see if he had any messages, the clerk handed him another telegram from Eve. Patrick stepped away toward the front window that looked out onto the street and opened the telegram.

TRIED TO CALL. YOU WERE NOT THERE. DO NOT HAVE ITEM.

LEAVING HERE MON 1PM. TRAVELING TO CANADA.

Patrick let out a breath of surprise. Canada? Why was she going to Canada? He cursed under his breath, wishing again that this time of 1914 had cell phones. He stood for a time in the lobby, his forehead knotted into a frown, as he gazed out the plate glass window to see snow flurries drift and glide. If Eve didn't have the lantern, then obviously it had to be somewhere in Canada. How? Why?

Patrick felt urgency build in his chest. He had to find Maggie, and he had to find her fast. That morning he had formed a short-term plan, although he had no idea where it might lead. He walked aggressively out of Hoffman House and headed downtown.

At the City Register Office, Patrick entered through two heavy wooden doors into a busy, bright cavernous lobby, filled with echoing voices and businessmen clumped in conversation.

He descended two flights of white marble stairs to the Hall of Records to search property deeds and land title records.

A crickety, dour clerk, about fifty, sat behind a scuffed mahogany desk. He wore a green visor, a dark suit, a tie, and a practiced smirk. He raised his droopy eyes from his ledger, regarding Patrick with little interest.

Patrick flashed a phony police badge he had bought two days before from a crook on Bleeker Street and asked to see land deeds and titles for lower Manhattan. The clerk's eyes widened only slightly. It never hurt to have a police badge. You just got better, faster service, and people like this bored and territorial bureaucrat would often deign to answer your questions.

Patrick was directed down a long, dimly lit narrow aisle with tall shelves on either side, stacked with volumes. He wandered, searched, wandered some more and stopped short when he saw what he was looking for. He reached up on a third shelf, hauled down the thick heavy volume and dropped it on a tall pedestal mahogany table. He swung it open and began thumbing through the pages until he found the name he was looking for. And it wasn't difficult to find. There it was, written in a clear meticulous script–Addison Reed Casterbury.

Patrick ran a finger down the page, examining the Tract, Lot and Parcel. Addison Casterbury owned tenements all over the Lower East Side, some on Orchard Street, as well as storefronts and buildings on Mulberry Street and Mott Street, and several apartment buildings in Greenwich Village, including the one Duncan Beaumont had lived in, but not the one he was currently holed up in. Good.

Patrick felt the burn of anticipation as he flipped the page, his eyes darting along the yellow page with blue lines, his forefinger sliding up and down the page. When he found it, he nearly yelled out in excitement.

Addison Reed Casterbury and James Faolan Clancy.

Patrick jabbed a forefinger on the blue line, his eyes expanding on what he read. Together, Addison and Big Jim owned The Gibson Hotel at 28 E. 30th St, constructed in 1892. They also owned several saloons and two warehouses along the East River.

Patrick looked up from the page, the light of triumph glowing in his eyes. Only a few days ago, he'd followed Big Jim to O'Casey's, an Irish Pub located near The Gibson Hotel.

An hour later, Patrick stood across the street from the twelve-story Gibson Hotel, in a sharp wind and dancing snowflakes. The hotel was typically Victorian, with a heavy bracketed cornice, attractive bay windows, soaring turrets, and a mansard-roof with patterned shingles. In his research, Patrick had learned that it was frequented mostly by tourists and middle-class tenants.

Patrick lingered outside for a time, getting familiar with the area, then he crossed the street and entered through two double glass doors.

Inside, the breath of heat felt good on his cold bare hands and ears. The gracious marble lobby with brass railings was adorned with murals recalling New York Central Park scenes, the graceful Brooklyn Bridge, and the impressive City Hall Post Office, built in 1878, in an architectural style that was not well received in its day.

Patrick noticed a bank of golden elevators, with attentive elevator operators standing by, dressed in chocolate brown uniforms and gold caps. Bellhops glided by hauling luggage, and at the back newsstand, two attractive women lingered, flipping through fashion magazines in giggling whispers.

Patrick roamed the space, angling toward the brown marble fireplace, standing for a time by a six-foot Christmas tree trimmed in tinsel and holly but no lights. His vigilant eyes studied the lobby desk staff. They worked with formal efficiency and courtesy, answering the questions of the many guests who approached them.

In the center lobby, tourists were seated in burgundy, hand-tufted chairs and couches, the men engrossed in newspapers or smoking a pipe or a cigar. Some women in elegant attire were busy with children, while others read magazines or examined the bagged items they'd purchased.

Patrick noticed, with satisfaction, that the loud, omnipresent music so prevalent in the modern world was missing. There were also no TV screens blaring out sports or news, and there were no cell phones, laptops or computers. Patrick found the entire experience quite pleasant. The lobby was a quiet place except for the comfortable gurgle of a fountain in the lobby's center.

But Patrick was on edge. Was Maggie in this hotel somewhere and, if she was, where was she and how would he get to her? Of course, when the time was right, he would rent a room and then reconnoiter the upper floors until he found the one that was being guarded, but then what? For now, he'd have to wait and watch. He wouldn't do anything until he heard from Eve.

Patrick decided to hang around the lobby for a time, just to see who came and went. If the Gibson was owned by Addison and Big Jim, who among their crowd might be living there, or having meetings there? Maybe nothing would turn up, but it was worth a wait.

Patrick spent time at the newsstand, scanning the headlines. The war in Europe predominated. While Patrick kept one eye alert to the traffic of the lobby, he bought a copy of the *New York World*, just in case the house detective might be watching him. He strolled lazily, appearing to read the paper, but he was checking out the exits. He wandered past the lobby desk into a back-lounge area, where guests sat around marble-topped tables and sipped coffee, nibbled tea sandwiches, and engaged in friendly conversation.

Patrick observed another exit. He explored it, leisurely. It led outside on the north side of 32nd Street.

Returning to the lobby, he took an easy stroll to one of the elevator operators, who was standing at attention.

"Good afternoon, sir. Going up?"

"Actually, I was wondering if there are exits in the basement…in case of fire, of course."

The operator touched his hat with two fingers. "Yes, sir, there are two. One leading out to 32nd Street and the opposite to 31st. Do not worry about fire, sir, we have plenty of exits. This hotel is very safe."

"Good man," Patrick said, with authority. "You can't be too sure these days."

Patrick thanked him and moved off toward an empty chair near the fountain and sat. He snapped out the newspaper and superficially perused some articles until one caught his attention, LETTERS IN SANTA'S BOX. Patrick smiled and decided to read a few.

Bronx New York—Dear Santa Claus: Will you please send me a doll, if you have one to spare? I want one eighteen inches long, kid body, bisque head, light hair or dark will do. Yours truly, Bessie Hanks.

Brooklyn, New York—Dear Santa Claus: Please send me a toy cannon, train, magic lantern and a small boat, some candy, nuts of all kinds, apples, oranges and some fireworks. I am a little boy 6 years old. Your little friend, Tommy Webber.

Patrick thought the request for a magic lantern particularly coincidental and poignant since he and Eve wanted one as well. Enjoying himself, Patrick read on.

29 East 23rd Street—Dearest Santa: Though I look older, I am only 5 years old. I don't want a doll, but I want a watering pot and a carpet sweeper, and some ginger-snaps and jaw-breakers. My Mommy said you may not come this year because your reindeer are sick. If they get better, my sister Almira also wishes for a coat, hair ribbon, dress, cap, shoes, fruit and nuts, and some other items, including a little piano. Is that too much? Please help your reindeer get better.
Yours lovingly, Brooksie T. Penn.

Patrick smiled, touched by the letters and eagerly read on.

West Sixtieth Street
Dear Santa,
Would you please give me something for Christmas, as we are very poor and have no papa? My mamma works downtown in offices and sometimes she takes in washing and does the best she can. You see, Santa, it is very hard for me also, for I get up very early and have to send my sister and brothers to school. I don't care for much so long as my mamma and sister and brothers have a happy Christmas. Thank you, Santa.
Your true friend, Lizzie Parsons

Patrick was noting the name and address where he could mail a financial contribution when something caught his eye. It was Addison Casterbury himself walking purposefully, head held arrogantly high, as he drew up to the lobby desk. The front desk clerk crisply and efficiently handed Addison a key. Without a word or applying his signature, Addison started for the elevator.

As Patrick arose from his chair, he noted a broad, blunt-faced man following Addison. This would be the house detective, Patrick thought as he sauntered toward the elevators, newspaper at his side, his nonchalant expression pleasant.

Addison stood at Elevator One. Patrick stood leisurely behind, about five feet back, the house detective measuring him and the couple beside him, as well as the very tailored man behind them, nervously fingering his waxed mustache.

As the elevator's black dial descended to four, three, two and one, Patrick stepped back behind the waiting guests.

When the elevator slid open, Addison stepped in, turning about, facing the waiting guests with the lift of an arrogant nose. The house detective held up a meaty hand and spoke in a blunt, raspy voice, "Take Elevator Two. This one's private."

The couple voiced disapproval, and the waxed mustache was annoyed. But they obeyed and moved away.

The detective stepped in next to Addison, the elevator operator pressed the button, and the doors whispered closed.

Patrick watched the elevator dial climb clockwise until it stopped at the twelfth floor. When a second elevator arrived at the lobby, all but Patrick climbed aboard. He faded back and returned to his chair and to the Santa Claus letters.

Minutes later, Patrick glanced over the top of his newspaper to see a very striking woman of about thirty years old walk aggressively through the lobby and approach the lobby desk. She wore a slim, fashionable coat, complete with hat, fur muffs and a stole. Having a near photographic memory for faces, Patrick appraised her from head to toe, her full breasts, pink lips, and mass of honey blonde hair, crowned with a purple hat. She possessed a proud, severe, wealthy countenance. She smelled of money and privileged. She looked angry.

A quick and well-dressed front desk manager appeared from around the desk, all silent bowing and gestures, indicating toward the elevators. Again, Patrick arose and positioned himself behind, keeping at a safe distance.

When the next elevator doors opened, the lady was ushered inside by the effusive manager, who kindly instructed the other waiting guests to take the next elevator. They voiced displeasure.

The doors closed, and Patrick watched the dial ascend to the twelfth floor and stop. Considering his next move, Patrick turned back toward the lobby and noticed a man standing near the Christmas tree. Only minutes before, Patrick hadn't seen him there. He was staring at Patrick with mild curiosity.

He wore a gray overcoat, scuffed boots, and a bowler hat pushed back from his broad forehead. He held a pipe in one hand, his other hand stuffed easily into his pants pocket, his dark handlebar mustache needing a trim. He stood relaxed, with a sinister smile. His eyes narrowed on Patrick as he puffed on his pipe and blew a feather of smoke toward the ceiling.

Patrick's pulse quickened. From his dress and manner, Patrick was almost positive that this man was a reporter. But why was he staring at him? Normally, Patrick would have ignored the man, but time was running out and so were his options. Perhaps this staring fellow had information Patrick needed, so he hesitated for only a moment before venturing over.

CHAPTER 30

In Chicago, Eve had caught the Montreal Express, her destination being the village of Coldwater, Ontario. As the train went thundering along the tracks, the haunting moan of a whistle echoed across the vast snowy landscape, where deer emerged from evergreen forests, their heads alert, their noses sniffing at the cold air.

Eve settled back in her seat and tried to read a novel, but her mind wandered and then stalled and then raced.

She glanced at her watch. She'd left Chicago on Monday at 1:30 p.m., and if the Grand Trunk Western Railroad schedule was correct, she'd arrive in Toronto in about eighteen hours, around seven o'clock on Tuesday morning. She wasn't sure about the distance from there to Coldwater.

Her thoughts circled around Patrick. She hadn't been able to reach him by phone. In Detroit, she'd tried to call, but once again, he wasn't in his room. She needed to know what was going on, and she needed to tell him why she was traveling to Canada.

Now that she was only hours from her destination, she was second-guessing her decision. Should she have returned to New York instead? Did Patrick need her help? Was he okay? Had he found Maggie? In Detroit, she'd sent Patrick yet another telegram.

WILL CALL WHEN ARRIVE IN CANADA

Eve sat opposite an elderly woman and her daughter. To Eve's relief, both women seemed to be introverts and were not interested in communication. That was fine with Eve.

She rested her head back against the headrest and closed her eyes. An image of Ann Long's gloomy face cut into her inner vision, and Eve played back the revealing conversation she'd had with her on Sunday night. After dinner, they'd climbed into a taxi and taken a tour of Chicago while Ann began her story. Eve was nearly sitting on the edge of her seat, wanting to know what had happened to the lantern, and why Ann didn't have it with her in Chicago.

"I was in love once, Eve," Ann began, as the taxi roamed through light traffic.

Ann folded her hands in her lap and struggled for words. Then her hands became fidgety. Then she folded them again. She turned her head away and, when she spoke, her voice was so soft that Eve had to lean in to hear her.

"He was a doctor, in his early forties, and he was married. Well... you see, I was a young doctor—and a female doctor, which meant that all the male doctors ignored me. They thought I was incompetent and presumptuous and, therefore, I was not considered a true or equal professional. I shouldn't say that all the male doctors ignored me. There was one doctor, a very gifted doctor, who did not ignore me. He genuinely wanted to help me be the best doctor I could be."

Ann paused as the memories came flooding back.

"Yes... Dr. Ogden Bennett did not ignore me. He was quiet, kind and patient. He allowed me to attend his surgeries. He instructed me on surgical technique and eventually allowed me to perform certain procedures along with him. In those days, that was unheard of, and he received several reprimands from his superiors for doing so. He ignored the gossip about me, and he ignored the other male doctors, some of whom worked in vain to try to get him removed from the hospital."

Ann finally turned to face Eve, her eyes solemn and sad. "You must understand that Dr. Bennett took all the criticism and the threats against him with grace. When he was forced to defend his decision to educate me, he did so with a firm conviction that it was not only good for the hospital and the education of all, but it was also good for his female patients, many of whom felt more comfortable with a female surgeon than a male one. Yes, Dr. Bennett defended me, and he educated me. Without his help and support, I would never have obtained the position of the first female ambulance surgeon at New York's Gouverneur Hospital."

Ann's head lowered. "I was 35 years old when I first met Dr. Bennett. I have never been an attractive woman, Eve. The smallpox took care of that. But beyond that, I was not blessed with the beauty that men are attracted to."

Eve spoke up. "Did you know, Ann, that there were men—attractive men at the Gouverneur Hospital back in 1885—who not only admired you but also found you attractive? Had they not been laborers or immigrants or poor, they would have invited you out."

Ann turned, smiling. "Thank you for that. You were always kind and strong. You were always confident and so very attractive. When you left me all those years ago, I was depressed for days. I missed your professionalism and friendship. But let us not travel into fantasy. I was never attractive to men—except to Mr. Bennett. Dare I say it? We fell in love—at least I fell in love with him, a man I admired for his dedication, skill and independence. I don't know why he loved me, but he did. He told me so several times, to my utter girlish delight."

The taxi was driving past the University of Chicago when Eve saw Ann's eyes mist over.

She heaved in a breath and seemed to hold it, as if she didn't want to release the words, those prisoned words she had kept locked up for so many years.

Ann let her breath out slowly. "We had a son, Eve. Mr. Bennett and I… yes, we had a son. We named him John Logan Bennett, although we finally just came to call him Logan."

Ann brightened and wiped away a tear. "Oh, he was the sun and the moon to me, Eve. So smart and so very handsome, like his father. Thank God he did not look like me, except maybe he had my eyes. My eyes are not so bad to look at, I think. Whenever I looked into Logan's bright little eyes, I felt the swelling of a love I had never thought possible. Where did it come from? As a scientist, I wanted to know. I wanted to see it under a microscope or cut open my chest and find it inside."

Ann laughed a little. "Oh, what a silly woman I was, but I loved our little Logan with such a pure and simple heart, Eve. I loved him more than my own life. But then, I suppose that is how love is supposed to be, is it not, because I loved Mr. Bennett just as deeply. Yes, just as much. We were a family, and I had always wanted a family."

Eve was deeply touched. She had the impulse to take Ann's hand to comfort her, but Ann was not the type. She was formal and guarded, so Eve respected that and simply listened.

Ann's head lowered by degrees. "As I said, Dr. Bennett was a married man, and it was not right what we did. It was not what I wanted for him. I wanted only happiness for him. Anyway, I gave birth to Logan at a private hospital that Dr. Bennett had arranged. I was 36 years old, and I lived alone in a New York apartment for a time. Money was not an issue, as Dr. Bennett had come from wealth and he was a respected doctor who had many wealthy patients in addition to the poor ones he often treated but did not charge."

The taxi driver stopped and twisted around, revealing a scar on his right cheek. Eve saw hardness in his old, wrinkled face.

"Do you want me to keep driving?" he asked, in an accent that Eve couldn't place. Ann nodded kindly. "Yes, driver, thank you. Perhaps my friend should see the Field Museum and the Ryerson Mansion. Would you mind driving by those?"

The driver shrugged, turned, and shifted the taxi into gear. It shuddered ahead and gathered speed.

"I will make this brief, Eve. It is still quite painful for me to recount. Dr. Bennett came to me one night, and I saw a heavy sorrow on his face. He looked so forlorn. He had aged so much in such a short time, with gray at his temples and new lines etched into his face. He told me that Logan would have to be sent away to a home in Canada. As you can imagine, at that moment my heart seemed to explode. For the first time, we argued. It was a terrible scene as I fought to keep our baby. I told Mr. Bennett I would never give up my baby... our baby. Mr. Bennett dropped into a chair and was silent for a long time."

Ann massaged her forehead while she spoke, as if she'd developed a headache.

"Dr. Bennett had a career and a family to protect. One of Dr. Bennett's enemies learned about Logan and me and he threatened to tell his wife, as well as the president and the chief surgeon of the hospital, if Dr. Bennett didn't agree to break off the relationship. This same doctor also threatened to go to the press. Dr. Bennett's career would not have survived the scandal. Not in those days. I dare say, not even in these."

Ann's gaze was direct for a moment, and then it drifted away.

"Dr. Bennett had a younger sister living in Ottawa, Canada, and she was married to a country doctor. They could not have children, for whatever the reason. Anyway, his sister agreed to take Logan, but only if she and her husband were given legal custody, and only if Logan was never told who his biological parents were. Logan was to grow up thinking that she and her husband were his birth parents."

Eve shut her eyes, feeling a wave of emotional pain. Ann sat up straighter, her chin lifted in a fragile pride, as if to bolster herself—to brace herself against the words to come.

"Yes, well, I lost my Logan, didn't I?" she said, her voice filling with emotion. "What could I do, Eve? I couldn't destroy one love to save another, could I? If I did that, I knew I would eventually destroy us all. I couldn't ruin Dr. Bennett's career, and yet a part of me didn't care about anything else except keeping my baby. But then, what kind of life would Logan have had? He would have been ostracized. He wouldn't have a father, and he would have been marked and called all sorts of unkind names by children and adults alike."

Ann's voice dropped into anger. "The day Logan was taken from me I went through every kind of madness. My father was a major in the Army. Did I ever tell you that?"

"No," Eve said. "You never talked about your family."

"When Dr. Bennett came to take Logan from me, I had planned to shoot Dr. Bennett, Logan and myself. Yes... I was that mad—a real crazy woman."

Ann paused, her eyes shifting down and away. "But then, when I held Logan for the last time and looked into his dear, twinkling eyes, something changed in me. Instead of wanting destruction and death, I felt a sudden burst of hope and love. I suddenly wanted Logan to have the best life he could have, and I knew that he would be loved and cared for in ways that I could never give him. So when Dr. Bennett reached for him, I offered Logan with a full and generous heart, even though my father's service revolver was lying on the kitchen table like a live thing."

Ann inhaled a bracing breath, struggling to go on. "Dr. Bennett took Logan away, and I never saw Dr. Bennett again."

Ann's head slowly dropped to her chest. "A year later, he died from a heart attack."

There was a long painful silence. Neither woman said a word until the car turned into the crowded Morrison Hotel parking lot and pulled up to the entrance.

Eve finally broke the silence. "Did you ever see Logan again?"

Ann smiled. "A few months after Dr. Bennett's death, a letter arrived from his attorney. It contained a brief note Dr. Bennett had written shortly after he'd taken Logan away from me. It revealed where Logan was living and that his full name was John Logan Tyler. It concluded with a tender apology for all that had happened to me, and a declaration of love that he said would never die. He wrote, 'I love you deeply, Ann, and I always will.'"

The driver waited. Eve waited.

Ann raised her head as a tear raced down her cheek. "Logan is a fine man, Eve. A handsome man, like his father. He works as a conductor on the Canadian Northern Railroad. He and I were united when he was 28 years old, after his adopted mother died. Logan's adopted father was a good and kind man. He sat Logan down one day and told him the truth about me and Dr. Bennett. To my great surprise and delight, Logan located me, and we finally had a tearful meeting in Canada in December of 1910. We have become close since then. I plan to visit him on Christmas Eve. We have spent every Christmas together since 1910."

Ann's eyes were now clear and direct. "Eve, I gave Logan the lantern."

Eve stared, trying to understand. "Why? Why did you give it to him?"

"Because I am his mother and I wanted to give him something extraordinary. I wanted to make up for all the hard, weeping years, Eve. I wanted to give him something that could potentially change his life, if that is what he wished. I told him everything about you, and what Jacob Jackson had told me. I told him he should light it and travel to a new and better world. I told him that perhaps he could travel to the past and we could play out our lives all over again and, this time, we'd get it right as rain."

"Why didn't *you* light it, Ann?"

Ann sat in a placid dignity. "Because I am a scientist, Eve, and I don't believe in that sort of superstition."

Eve questioned her with her eyes.

Ann smiled. "...And because I didn't have the courage."

Eve swallowed. "Did Logan light it?"

"Not as of his last letter, which I received three days ago."

Ann reached for Eve's hand and squeezed it. "Eve, go meet Logan. Go to Canada and meet my son. Tell him who you are and why you have come. Go get your lantern, Eve, so you can return to your own time."

CHAPTER 31

Patrick approached the presumed reporter with some caution. What if he wasn't a reporter? What if he worked for Big Jim or Addison?

"Hello, friend," the reporter said.

He was short and broad; his chin had a proud angle, and his teeth were crooked. He was probably in his late 30s.

"It's *my* story, you know," he continued.

"And what story would that be?" Patrick asked.

The reporter regarded Patrick with a frank curiosity. "Who are you working for, friend? Big Jim? Casterbury?"

Patrick was silent, hoping to learn more without revealing anything.

"You a gumshoe, friend?"

Patrick glanced about to see if they were being watched. He didn't see anyone.

Indicating with his head toward the elevators, Patrick asked, "Who was the highbrow lady in the fur, who just went to the twelfth floor?"

The reporter took another draw on his pipe, studying Patrick. "I'm Stuart T. Bates," he said with some pride. "*New York World*, since I assume you don't know who I am."

Patrick held up his *New York World* newspaper.

Stuart grinned. "Well, don't you have the good taste, friend."

Stuart looked past Patrick to the elevators. "Who is the fur dame? Friend, whoever you are and whatever you're up to, you can't be the fastest horse on the track if you don't know that is Mrs. Mary Daisey Crocker."

Patrick didn't have a clue who she was, not being of this time. Again, he stayed silent, hoping to appear all wise.

Stuart flashed a crooked grin. "They said they'd shoot me in the neck, you know, just like James J. Gallagher shot Mayor William Jay Gaynor in the neck in 1910 on board the SS Kaiser Wilhelm der Grosse, docked at Hoboken. Now I know you recall that one, friend."

Patrick nodded, but he was faking it.

"They know I covered that story in great detail. It was one of my best, if I can put on the fine coat of a braggart. Well, you know what happened to Mayor Gaynor, friend. He lived for three years with that bullet stuck in his throat, but he finally died in February last year. You recall all of that, don't you?"

"Yeah, sure," Patrick lied. "But who is 'they'?"

Stuart shrugged. "Big Jim, of course. You know Big Jim, don't you, friend?"

"Yes, I know *of* Big Jim."

"So why are you here, friend? I've been doing all the talking. Now it's your turn."

Patrick pulled something out of thin air. "My client wants something on Casterbury."

Stuart grinned again, and again it was the grin of a bad guy in an old cartoon.

"Then you've got it, don't you?"

Patrick's face didn't betray his ignorance. "You mean the lady in the fur?"

"Or are you working for the City and Comptroller Connolly?"

Patrick's eyes shifted. He wished he knew what this reporter was talking about.

Stuart nodded, taking his own meaning from Patrick's shifting eyes.

"Well, you know Connolly is trying to clean up the corruption of the Tammany years, which Big Jim and Casterbury are working very diligently to maintain."

Patrick nodded. "Yes."

"The City controls valuable water grants—rights to construction piers and storage facilities along the East River. You must know that members of some of the most prominent families in New York—families with names like Casterbury, Goelet, and Delano—received water grants at prices far below their market value. Addison Casterbury is into honest graft, isn't he? What is honest graft, you may ask, friend? Well, Addison Casterbury learns that a park or a bridge is going to be built. He travels there, and he buys up all the land he can in the neighborhood. Then, just like magic, the Board makes its plan public, and there is a rush to get Casterbury's land, which nobody seemed to care about before. So Casterbury thinks it is perfectly honest to charge a good price and make a profit on his investment and foresight."

"What about Big Jim?" Patrick asked.

Stuart was obviously a man who liked to talk about what he knew.

"Now Big Jim, on the other hand, makes most of his money in graft—blackmailing gamblers, politicians, saloon-keepers, disorderly people, and the like. He also owns a fair number of brothels and gambling joints. But then, I'm sure you know that."

"So that brings us back to the lady in the furs," Patrick said, venturing another look toward the elevators.

"And what do I get in return, friend? That's how business works, isn't it?"

Patrick knew but one sure thing about 1914. From his historical research in 2018, he'd learned a remarkable event happened on Christmas Eve and Christmas Day on the Western Front during World War I. There were movies and documentaries about a truce, a cease of hostilities in an otherwise brutal war.

Patrick decided to be bold. "On Christmas Eve of this year, on the Western Front, there will be a Christmas truce."

Stuart looked away, unimpressed. "Yeah, so Pope Benedict XV has already proposed a truce on Christmas Day, and all the leaders on both sides of the trenches have said no."

Patrick fixed Stuart with his eyes. "It *will* happen."

"And how do you know this, friend? Have you been to the gypsy card readers?"

Now Patrick grinned, his clear eyes meeting Stuart's. "I came to this time, 1914, from the future—over a hundred years in the future—and I can tell you for sure that it will happen."

Stuart stared hard into Patrick's eyes, trying to read him. And then he laughed, stopped and then laughed again at the absurd statement.

"You've got some kind of humor, friend. I like it."

"Even if I'm wrong, if you write articles supporting that truce, you can't go wrong. You know how much everyone in the world loves Christmas and the idea of peace on earth. And you know how much they really do want to believe in Christmas miracles. If you're wrong, and there is no truce, the public will love your positive effort. If there is a truce, you will be a hero. Maybe your boss will even give you a raise or a byline. How can you go wrong?"

Stuart took in Patrick's words carefully, scrutinizing them, turning them over in his cunning head. He twisted up his mouth in thought. "So, you're from the future, huh?"

"Yes…" Patrick said, with a wry grin. "I am. And there *will* be a Christmas truce."

Stuart shook his head, chuckling. "I don't know where you're from, friend, but with your size and manly looks, you should join the gypsies and go into prognosticating. You could make a fortune."

"Maybe I will," Patrick said.

"All right, friend. Mary Daisy Crocker has been married to J. W. Crocker for nearly two years. Of course, you know he's one of the richest men in New York, if not the entire country. He's thirty years older than she, and he is insanely jealous. He also hates Addison Casterbury, who he thinks is a corrupt upstart with visions of political grandeur."

Stuart paused for dramatic effect. "Mary Daisy Crocker is pregnant with Addison Casterbury's child and, so far, he has refused to own up to it. He, in fact, just wants her to go away. She is not happy about going away, and as you saw when she entered the hotel, she has not gone away. The scandal is about to explode, and I will be the one to expose it, with several articles already written and waiting for my editors. Well, why not me? Who else in this town wants to risk being shot in the neck by Big Jim's men? Addison Casterbury is Big Jim's clean and wealthy front man, you know. Big Jim doesn't like Casterbury, but he will fight to keep him alive and not let him get all caught up in any publicity scandal that could come back and bite Big Jim in his big wallet."

Patrick spoke up. "Speaking of Big Jim. Any idea where his girlfriend is, Maggie Lott Gantly?"

Stuart's eyes gleamed with pleasure. "Now there, my friend, is a woman. She's the best-looking woman on the stage today."

Patrick threw a glance toward the elevators. "Nobody seems to know where she is. I think she's upstairs, maybe in a suite on the twelfth floor. What do you think?"

Stuart placed the stem of the pipe between his teeth and worked it up and down, considering his answer. When he pulled it out, he licked his lips.

"And you'd be right again, friend, but you didn't hear it from me. Big Jim would have me sliced up and thrown into the river. No one, and I mean no one, messes with Maggie Lott Gantly. She is Big Jim's property, and she will continue to be his property until one of them dies."

Patrick hated the reporter's use of the word "property."

"So, friend, even if a newsie or bootblack knows where Maggie Gantly is, they won't say, nor will anybody else. So, you'd best leave it alone, friend, unless you want to wind up in the river floating to China. But, what the hell, yes, Maggie is upstairs on the twelfth floor."

Suddenly, both men heard a sharp sound. Patrick pivoted to see that the fastidious front desk manager, now alarmed, had slammed down the telephone. His face went white, filled with terror. He called for the house detective, but Patrick knew he was upstairs with Addison, so the house manager snatched up the phone, shouting at the cop on the other end.

"Shots have been fired!" he yelled.

An elevator returned from the upper floors and people scrambled out, women crying, men shouting at the free elevator operators to hurry up to the twelfth floor to offer assistance.

"What the hell just happened?" Stuart asked, as a man hurried by, heading for the street to call a cop.

"A man has been shot!" He shouted over his shoulder. "Call the police."

Both Patrick and Stuart broke for the elevators at the same time, shouldering in as the doors were sliding closed.

"Take us to the twelfth floor," Patrick ordered, pulling out his police badge.

Stunned, Stuart's eyes darted toward it. "Well, I'll be a dumb mug's mutt," he said. "I should have known."

Patrick stayed quiet. "Hurry," he told the nervous, bug-eyed operator.

"It was the dame," the young operator said. "The dame in the furs shot Casterbury in the chest two times. Right through the heart. He's cold, stone dead. What about that?"

Stuart yanked out his notepad and began to jot down notes, while Patrick ran through escape steps that he ticked off in his head. When the elevator doors slid open on the twelfth floor, Patrick burst out first, casting darting looks. Stuart charged out, turned right and loped down the burgundy-carpeted hallway.

Patrick faced the anxious elevator operator. "Do you know where Maggie Gantly is? Which suite?"

The elevator operator's startled face flushed. "I... I can't say, sir."

Patrick held up the badge. "Where? Tell me now!"

Hesitating for only a moment, the operator pointed left. "She is in Suite 1203."

Patrick hurried off, pausing when he came to the end of the corridor. 1203 was located left, around a corner. He slowed, listened and placed his back flush against the wall. Carefully, he peered around the corner. A man stood by a chair outside the door, his attention focused on the commotion down the hallway in Addison's suite.

Patrick inhaled a breath, pulled himself to his full height and turned the corner, striding fast toward the man, who straightened, ready to face the threat. Patrick didn't stop. He walked aggressively toward him and, for a second, the guard seemed confused. Patrick stopped two feet away, cocked a fist and punched the man in the stomach. He doubled over, his hands going to his stomach. Not waiting, Patrick hit him with a solid left in the jaw. The man slammed back against the wall and Patrick finished him with a good hammer blow to the back of his neck.

The guard slammed into the carpet, head first, and sagged out cold. Patrick glanced about for an exit. He didn't see one. Pulling in another good breath for strength and courage, he grabbed the doorknob, twisted it and swung it open wide, body poised for any attack.

There she stood, his daughter, Maggie Gantly, frozen in terror, dressed in an emerald green dress and flat shoes. Patrick took her in, his heart slamming into his chest. He had come a long way for this—to see her. To help her. To save her.

He melted for a minute, taken by her poise and beauty. The reality of the moment was almost too much for him to take, but he had no time to think about it.

"Who are you? What do you want?" she shouted.

"Is anyone else here?"

"Who are you?"

"Are you alone?" Patrick barked.

She stepped back, scared. "Yes... I'm alone. What are you doing?"

"I'm a friend of Eve Gantly. We have to go. Now. Do you have a passport?"

"What?"

"A passport. Get it, now."

Maggie threw up her hands, left the room and soon returned, holding up the passport.

"What is going on out there?"

"Never mind."

He reached out a hand. "Come on. We're getting out of here."

"Eve Gantly sent you?" Maggie said, as if the name was something she'd nearly forgotten.

"Yes. Come on, Maggie."

Maggie glanced about, as if trying to decide what to bring. "I should pack some things."

"There's no time for that. We must go now. Grab a coat with a hood and let's go. Hurry!"

CHAPTER 32

They rushed down the hallway to the elevator, hearing frantic voices. As Patrick had hoped, all the focus was on Suite 1201, Addison Casterbury's suite. It would provide the perfect cover for escape.

An elevator was standing open, the operator leaning out, staring down the hallway. When Patrick and a hooded Maggie approached and stepped inside, he snapped to attention.

"Hurry," Patrick demanded.

The elevator doors whispered shut, and Patrick felt beads of sweat run down his back.

"The basement," Patrick said.

"The basement, sir?"

"Yes, the basement."

"Yes, sir."

Maggie was staring at Patrick, intently. She whispered. "Who are you?"

Patrick ignored her. His every sense was on alert, his pulse high and drumming. As they descended, Patrick smelled Maggie's lilac scent, and, in the glow of golden elevator light, she appeared angelic. He observed that both her jawline and her mouth favored his; the color of her hair, the shape of her nose was from her mother. Patrick fought a chaotic mix of emotions: fear, pride, confusion, as the elevator seemed to take an eternity to reach the basement.

"Can you make this thing go faster?" Patrick said, impatiently.

"All most there, sir," the operator said, as the elevator finally came to rest at the basement level. Patrick handed the elevator operator a generous tip, seized Maggie's arm and ushered her out.

The elevator operator stared down at the bills in surprise and uttered, "Thank you, sir."

Patrick hoped the money would help compensate the man for the grilling and perhaps the beating he would get from Big Jim's men.

Patrick glanced around at a rustic gym area, sparsely in use, and spotted an exit door leading to 31st Street. Gripping Maggie's arm, he made for the door.

Outside, traffic was heavy, snow flurries drifted, and a gray and quilted sky rolled overhead.

"You're hurting my arm. Where are we going?" Maggie asked, feeling the vice grip of Patrick's fingers.

Searching the street, Patrick spotted a cab near the curb and yanked Maggie toward it. Once inside, he told the driver to take them to Broadway at Madison Square. As the taxi nudged into traffic, Maggie shoved the hood back and stared hard at Patrick, his face filled with a watchful anxiety.

"You said you're a friend of Eve Gantly?"

Patrick jerked a nod, glancing back over his shoulder to ensure they weren't being followed. "Yes."

"Are you her brother or something?"

"We can't talk now."

Maggie turned away, crossing her arms, frustrated. "I hope you know what you're doing, whoever you are, because if Big Jim catches us, he'll kill us both."

"Don't talk," Patrick scolded. "And put your hood back up."

Maggie huffed out a sigh, but she obeyed.

When the cab bounced to a stop, Patrick gently led Maggie out and away down the street to the Hoffman House. He hoped and prayed Eve had left a telegram or phone message telling him where she was, so he and Maggie could immediately flee the City.

They entered, Maggie still hooded, her face turned away from the lobby desk, and Patrick was handed a telegram. He eagerly took it.

Upstairs in the room with the door locked, the two stood for a time in strained formality, eyes not meeting. Neither spoke as Patrick anxiously tore open the envelope and read:

WILL CALL WHEN ARRIVE IN CANADA

Patrick blew out a frustrated breath, cursing. "Where in Canada, Eve? Where?"

Maggie looked on, concerned and nervous. "Was that from Eve Gantly? Is she in Canada?"

Patrick didn't look at Maggie. He hung his head, thinking. After it was discovered that Maggie was gone, it would take only an hour or so before Big Jim would have men combing Grand Central Terminal, the shipping piers and the exits out of the City. Big Jim had police connections. They'd try to lock down the City.

But Patrick couldn't leave until he knew where in Canada Eve was. Without an address or phone number, they'd have no way to connect. If they left, could he trust the front desk clerks to take a message? Could he call in later and learn where Eve was?

No, he couldn't take that chance. What if Big Jim's men somehow found out about the Hoffmann House and monitored the calls. A remote possibility, yes, but still too risky. For now, Patrick would have to sit tight and wait for Eve's call, or for another telegram from her.

What about Ann Long? Perhaps she would know where Eve had gone. He called the front desk and had them put a call into the Augustana Hospital. And then he stalked the room, waiting.

Maggie studied him, her face stern and rigid. "What is your name? And don't tell me any lies. I'm sick and tired of lies."

"Patrick..."

"How nice. You do know what you're doing, don't you, Patrick?"

Patrick tried to hide the storm that was raging inside. "Of course. We'll be leaving town soon and you'll be safe."

Patrick pointed to a rickety looking chest of drawers. "Meanwhile, in that drawer over there, you'll find a blonde wig. You'll need to put it on when we leave here."

Maggie lifted a surprised eyebrow. "Really? Blonde. I don't look particularly attractive as a blonde."

"All the better. And there are also some rather ugly-looking glasses in there, too. They should help change your looks."

"May I ask now where you plan to take me?"

"I'm waiting for a call."

"Waiting for a call? Well, now, that doesn't sound promising. So you just burst into my suite and snatched me away from Big Jim's clutches like some daft hero in a farce, without knowing where you're going to take me?"

Patrick removed his hat and ran a hand through his thick hair. "You're going to be okay. I'll get you out of here. You'll be safe."

"Why?"

"Why, what?"

"Why are you doing this? Why are you risking your life for me? Do you know how vicious and brutal Big Jim can be?"

Patrick held her stare. "Yes, I know all about Big Jim."

"Then why are you doing this? Big Jim knows everybody who is anybody in this town, people you can't even imagine are in his fat greenback pocket, and if you make even one little mistake, he will kill you, and then he will kill me. Forgive me for my blunt talk, but I suspect you and Eve are two well-meaning sods from Ohio, who think they can come to the big City and rescue poor, helpless, damsel in distress, Maggie Gantly, and become hometown heroes. Well, let me tell you, Patrick, I'm not ready to die just yet, so if you will just let me go, I will run back to Big Jim and tell him that some lunatic from the Willard Asylum for the Chronically Insane was a fan, and kidnapped me, but I managed to escape and run back to you, good and loving gent, Big Jim Clancy."

"No, don't go back to him. Don't ever go back to him," Patrick said forcefully. "You deserve better. You deserve the best, and if your father had been there for you like he should have been when you were a kid, you'd never be with Big Jim."

Maggie's starched features melted a little. "Did you know my father? His name was Patrick, you know."

Patrick ignored the question. "To answer your other question, I'm doing it because I owe you. I'm doing it because I want you to have a good life."

Maggie stood blinking at him, trying to grasp the words, trying to decipher their obviously veiled meaning, because she knew there was more to this business than she was being told.

Patrick shoved his hands into his pockets, softening his voice. "Can I get you anything? Do you want some tea or coffee? Are you hungry?"

"Do you have Champagne?"

"No."

"Nothing then."

"Brandy?"

"Why not?"

As Maggie slowly removed her coat and laid it across the back of the couch, she kept her wary eyes on him. Studying him more meticulously, she seemed to see him for the first time. There was a familiarity about him; his manner, the shape of his face, the expression in his eyes; the way he lowered his chin at times when he talked.

She had never met him before. Or had she? Perhaps he had worked in a theatre at some point during her career. Maybe he had been one of her many admirers. Maybe he had waited for her at the stage door after a show. Had he brought her flowers, like many men had done, wanting favors?

Perhaps she'd given him her autograph. He was certainly handsome enough. In fact, the longer she gazed at him, the more she realized that he was quite pleasant to look at. Yes, he was strikingly handsome, with that muscled body, good shoulders, masculine face and sharp blue eyes that seemed to take in everything, to see everything, and yet be hard and tender at the same time. What an absolute flipsy and intoxicating thing that was for a woman. Yes, he was like a new and very delectable cocktail. Something akin to a fine, tawny scotch.

Maggie was puzzled, unable to place him in her life. She would have remembered this man if she had previously seen him. She would have flirted with this gentleman because he was wonderfully attractive. He had that something that stirred the hidden passion—that inexplicable thing that some men have that lures women.

Maggie had seen enough leading men and famous men and rich men to know that Patrick was a magnetic marvel. In show business, you either had it or you didn't. Patrick had it, and Maggie began to relax and swell with an inexplicable attraction to him. She liked what she saw, and because she liked him, she began to feel as though she could trust him with all her girlish, pulsing passion, and trust him with her life.

Maggie fingered her hair in shape, smoothed out the dress along her willowy hips and focused a bright, flirtatious eye on Patrick.

"Did you know Eve's husband, Patrick?"

Eve had told Patrick about her conversation with Maggie. He knew Eve had told Maggie that her father had died recently, and in his sixties.

Patrick considered his response. As his eyes sharpened on her, he noticed that her entire demeanor had changed. It was as if she'd just stepped out from behind a velvet curtain into dazzling light, making a grand and majestic stage entrance. She was shining the bright light of her sexy appeal on him, like a spotlight. It was a bit unnerving.

Maggie moistened her lips, lowered her smoldering eyes on him and adjusted her manner to that of a beguiling coquette. She flashed him a warm, magnetic smile, showing off perfect white teeth.

"Are you and Eve friends, Patrick?"

Patrick's eyes flitted down and away, hoping to deflect her gaze. "Yes, we are friends."

"Are you more than just friends? I know that her husband, a much older man than she, passed away. Are you just good friends, Patrick, or is there something more going on?"

Patrick raised his eyes. "Maggie...Excuse me, Miss Gantly..."

She cut him off with a flick of her elegant, feminine hand. "Oh, call me Maggie, Patrick. If we're going to possibly die together, we might as well be on a first-name basis, don't you think? So, now... Are you and Eve more than just friends?"

Patrick decided to close the door on this escalating flirtation before it went any further.

"Yes, Maggie. Eve and I are to be married."

Maggie's smile didn't fade. Her glowing countenance wasn't diminished in the least. In fact, her seduction swelled. To Patrick's surprise, she laughed.

"Oh, well, I think that is just the sweetest thing, Patrick. Eve is a very pretty girl, you know. She could be in the theatre. And she has moxie, I'll give her that."

"Well… thank you, but to be in the theatre, I think she would have to be able to act, and Eve, at least from what I know of her, is much too practical, forthright and scientific to be a very good actress."

"She might surprise you, Patrick. You should have seen the performance she gave when she first came to see me. I was impressed. Speaking of Eve, will we be meeting her soon?"

The worry returned to Patrick's face. "Yes… Well, yes, that's the plan."

The telephone rang, and Patrick moved and snatched it up. It was the front desk.

"Mr. O'Hearn, this is Oscar at the front desk. I have a call for you from Chicago."

Patrick breathed in relief. "Yes, put it through."

The voice on the other end said that Dr. Ann Long was not at the hospital and wouldn't be for some days. She had taken time off for personal reasons.

Patrick hung up and lowered himself in the chair, placing his face in his hands, his mind churning, emotions throbbing. He shut his eyes, hoping for some inspiration. He did not want to stay in the City, but what else could he do?

When he felt Maggie's soft hands begin to massage his neck, he tensed up, dropping his hands from his face.

"Relax, Patrick, I'm not going to bite you. At least not right away. Did anyone ever tell you that you are a very attractive man?"

CHAPTER 33

Eve stepped off the train onto the Coldwater, Ontario platform on Tuesday, December 15th at 2:10 p.m. A cold, white sun slid in and out of gray moving clouds, as snow flurries caught the wind. Her sleepy, sticky eyes searched for John Logan Tyler, who was supposed to meet her. The air was frigid, and her breath smoked as she looked to her right toward an open meadowland with snow-heavy trees and blowing snow.

Eve lingered briefly on the platform, observing others met by loved ones, and then she finally decided to slip into the train station for warmth and search for a telephone or telegraph office. She had to get in touch with Patrick. Early that morning, she'd tried to call him at the Toronto station, but the telephone lines were long. She'd dashed off a note at the telegraph office, but she was afraid to say too much, not knowing what was going on in New York and if Patrick had had to move again.

Her telegram said,

ITEM IN COLDWATER ONTARIO

Inside the train station, Eve hurried to the ticket agent and asked where the nearest telephone was. Without speaking or looking up, the agent pointed left.

"The assistant engineer is at the control panel, but he may be busy," the agent said.

As she started over, she noticed a man of Logan's description looking around. He wore a heavy overcoat and gripped a Canadian Fur Trapper Hat. He fit Ann's description: not tall, but sturdy of build, with shortly cropped blonde hair and a strong face. His mouth was thin, complexion powder white, brown eyes clear and watchful, just like his mother's, and his lantern jaw distinct. Eve's first impression was of a practical man with a serious mind, solemn nature and shy manner.

Their eyes met at the same time. Eve offered a little wave and a quick smile, and Logan a quick nod. As they closed the distance, Eve offered a hand to shake.

"Logan?"

He nodded and shook her hand limply. "Yes... Mrs. Gantly?"

"Yes."

Eve was a bit taken aback by his withholding, cool manner.

"Do you have bags?" Logan asked flatly.

"Over there." Eve turned, pointing to a wooden bench where the porter had deposited them. "But I need to call my husband in New York. Are you in a hurry?"

His eyebrows raised in query. "He's still in New York?"

"Yes... I need to tell him to meet me here. He doesn't know where I am."

Logan nodded thoughtfully, and Eve had no idea what the man was thinking.

"Yes, I'll wait then."

At the station booth, Eve was handed a heavy rotary phone and the operator dialed the number. It was another five minutes before the call went through. Eve waited anxiously while the Hoffman House operator put the call through to Patrick's room. Eve prayed Patrick would pick up.

"Hello..." Patrick answered, his voice guarded.

Eve sighed audibly into the phone. "Thank God, Patrick, finally."

"How are you, Eve?" Patrick asked. "Are you all right?"

"I'm fine. Tired, but fine. Are you okay?"

"Good. Yes."

"Sorry I couldn't reach you before now."

"It has been an agony of a wait, my love. Listen, I have Maggie with me here."

Static scratched Patrick's voice. Eve switched the phone to her other ear, sure she'd heard wrong. "Maggie? Did you say Maggie is with you?"

"Yes, she is."

"How? What happened?"

His words were garbled, lost in another spray of static, and Eve felt a chaos of images and emotion. She couldn't even imagine what had happened.

"Patrick, how did you find Maggie? Where is Big Jim?"

"I'll tell you later, Eve. Now tell me where we should meet you. We must leave New York as soon as possible. We should have left yesterday. Big Jim surely has men everywhere looking for us. Your last telegram said the lantern is in Coldwater, Ontario. Is that right?"

"Yes. I just arrived. I haven't actually seen it yet."

"Are you sure it's there, Eve?"

"As sure as I can be. I'll know as soon as I get to Logan Tyler's house. I'll explain all of that when I see you, or when we can talk next. How is Maggie, Patrick?"

"Nervous and worried. We must leave for Coldwater before we're tracked here."

"Okay, yes, get out of there, now, and be careful."

"By the way, your old friend Duncan Beaumont is here as well, and he wants to come with us, and bring Irene."

More static crackled and Eve cursed. "Did you say Duncan and Irene are coming with you?"

"There is much to say, Eve, and no time to say it. Much has happened."

"Okay, okay…just be careful. How do you plan to travel?"

"First by car to Poughkeepsie. Big Jim will have men at the train station here and at the boat docks. From Poughkeepsie, we'll catch the train to Toronto, and then travel to Coldwater. But if things aren't complicated enough, I've heard a large snowstorm is coming. We might be delayed. Do you have a phone number where I can reach you there?"

Eve caught Logan's eye and waved him over. He arrived, his forehead pinched in a frown. She asked him if he had a phone. He nodded, gave her his number, and returned to Eve's bags. Eve watched Logan pace in front of the wooden bench holding her bags. There was something about him that was disturbing.

Eve read Patrick the number.

"Okay, Eve, I have it. It's almost three o'clock. We'll leave as soon as it gets dark."

"Please be careful, Patrick."

"Yes, my love."

"Patrick, did I do the right thing in coming here and not returning to New York?"

"You are spot on, as usual, Eve. We need that lantern to get you, me and Maggie back home. You're a smart lady."

"About Maggie... Does she want to go with us back home?"

He hesitated.

"Have you told her everything?"

"No. I'll tell her on the train journey. I must go now, my love. You take care of yourself as well. I love you, Eve. God's good love and protection go with you."

"And I love you, Detective Sergeant Gantly. Please be careful."

After Eve hung up, she felt the rise of nerves and a mounting anxiety. Could Patrick get four people out of New York without Big Jim catching them? She turned and refocused her anxious eyes on Logan. Something was wrong. She could feel it. Why was he being so cold and strange?

When Logan saw Eve had hung up, he swung on his fur hat and dutifully hefted her bags, starting for the back exit doors.

"Follow me..." he said blandly, and she made a couple of running steps to reach the door just in time to pass through after him. Outside, she braced against the cold and the desolate, snow-blanketed world. She wondered what Ann had said to her son. Logan knew about the lantern, so that couldn't have been a surprise. Ann didn't say what her son's response had been, just that he had never lighted the lantern. Or had he? Or did he still have it?

Eve was surprised when Logan crunched through the snow to a horse-drawn sleigh, the bay standing still, jets of vapor puffing from his nose. Logan heaved her bags into the rear seat of the two-seat sleigh and turned to her as she approached.

"You can sit in the back if you like. There's a wool lap robe to cover yourself."

He looked skyward. "Don't think we'll get much more snow today. The storm is heading south."

Eve decided to be bold. "May I sit up front with you, Logan?"

Logan hesitated, looking away toward the snowy trees. "As you please, Mrs. Gantly."

Minutes later they were gliding smoothly over the ground, the snow muffling the trot of horses' hooves, accenting the clinking bells. With her lap covered by a very thick plush woolen blanket, she eased back in her leather seat, watching the winter wonderland world pass, presenting her face to the fresh, cold breeze.

Logan offered no conversation, so she did. "How fast does this sleigh go?"

"It can trot two forty."

Eve nodded. She didn't have a clue how fast that was. She persisted.

"And how fast is that?"

"On this road, the sleigh can cover a kilometer in just a little under four minutes. We're not so far away from the house. We'll be there in about twenty minutes."

"Thank you for picking me up, Logan. Your mother and I had a delightful reunion on Sunday."

Silence.

"I hear she's coming to see you for Christmas."

"She can't come. I called her yesterday."

Eve turned to him. "Why? She was looking forward to it."

"There's a war on, Mrs. Gantly. It's time I left to do my bit."

Eve looked away, thinking that Ann must have been devastated by her son's news. Eve made a mental note to write to Ann as soon as she could.

"Then you've just recently joined?" Eve asked.

"Yes, the Army. I'll be leaving for Valcartier, Quebec in a few days. Things are really heating up over in Europe. They need every man they can get."

Eve stared ahead, struggling to tamp down her feeling of anguish. So many men were killed in that awful war, she thought. Would Logan be one of them? After all Ann had been through with Logan, if he was killed in Europe, would the burden be too much for her bad heart?

As the snowy road angled left and rounded a bend, Eve saw a two-story log cabin loom in the distance, framed in firs, oak and beech.

"That's my place," Logan said, pointing.

"It's lovely," Eve said, taking in the quaint-looking cabin with its wide porch and outer stone chimney, a thin trail of gray smoke curling up into the wind. A single-story log garage stood off to the right, near a cord of wood, neatly stacked and sprinkled with snow.

"I built it myself," Logan said, proudly.

He drew the sleigh up to the front stairs. "The door is open. Go on inside. I'll bring the bags."

Eve climbed down, mounted the cabin stairs and entered. It was a stunning rustic space, with wooden floors, throw rugs, a ceiling with heavy crossbeams and a long wooden table with artistically crafted chairs. She instinctively moved to the masonry fireplace, where red embers still glowed with heat, and sighed at the warming comfort. As she turned her back to the low, gleaming fire, she saw a heavy-looking wood stove, a comfortable couch and chair, a tall bookshelf filled with hardback books, and mahogany stairs spiraling up to the second floor. The next item that caught her was unexpected. It was a violin and bow, attached to the wall next to the bookshelf.

Logan was obviously a craftsman, a musician and a reader of books. Ann had said he had been married, but his wife had run off one day, never to be heard from again. Eve had followed up with a few questions, but Ann had been evasive and reluctant.

Ann said the police were called to investigate Logan's wife's disappearance, but they were never able to learn what had happened to her or where she'd gone. She had left no trace whatsoever.

Months later, with no clues or witnesses, the police gave up the investigation. Some had suspected Logan of foul play, but since nobody was ever found, nothing came of it. Ann had told Eve the strange story in the cab as they were parting. Her final words were,

"Goodbye and write when you can," and then she added, "Logan can, at times, be somewhat remote."

Eve had removed her coat and was sitting in the comfy chair near the fire when Logan entered, closing the door, immediately removing his fur hat and coat and hanging them on a wooden peg. He moved stiffly toward the fireplace to warm himself, his downcast eyes avoiding Eve.

"Thank you again, Logan, for picking me up and letting me stay."

"Only one night, Mrs. Gantly," he said abruptly. "You can only stay one night."

Startled by his bluntness but being naturally forthright, Eve sat up straight, spine erect.

"Logan, my husband and his companions may not arrive for a couple of days, depending on the snowstorm."

"It's not right that you, a married woman, should be staying here with me. I have a good job with the railroad and I don't want people to talk."

"You're going into the Army, Logan."

"Nonetheless, I don't want people talking. You can stay upstairs tonight, but tomorrow you have to leave."

Eve softened her voice, trying not to sound insulted. "All right. Fine. Is there someplace else I can stay while I wait for my husband?"

"There's a boarding house a few miles away. I can take you there."

Eve settled back down into the chair. She decided to be bolder. "Logan, did your mother tell you why I'm here?"

He nodded, not speaking, his eyes still avoiding her.

"Do you have the lantern, Logan?"

His eyes shifted nervously.

"Do you, Logan? It is very important. It literally could mean life or death for me and my companions."

Logan buttoned the top button on his red and black flannel shirt and then pocketed his hands in his brown work pants and looked down at his damp boots. He left the fireplace, roamed the room and then returned to the fireplace. He stared down at his boots again.

"Did my mother tell you that my wife left me? Just up and left one day and was never heard from again?"

"Yes... she did, but she didn't go into any detail about it."

When Logan raised his eyes, they burned with anger. "My wife, Kady, did not leave me—at least not that way. She found that damned lantern of yours and when I was standing only a few feet away from her, she lit the devil of a thing. Do you know what happened then, Mrs. Gantly? She vanished. She just vanished into a misty blue fog and I have never seen her since. I couldn't tell anyone what had really happened, could I? Not the police. Not my co-workers. Not my neighbors. They all would have thought I had gone stark raving mad. I couldn't even tell my mother. I couldn't tell anyone... until now."

Eve felt the cold rise in her. If Kady Tyler lit the lantern and vanished, then that meant the lantern possessed time travel power for somebody else—not just for Eve. Eve was too stunned to speak, so she just stared at nothing and saw nothing, and her mind reeled.

Finally, she swallowed hard and found her voice. "Logan, do you still have the lantern?"

CHAPTER 34

In the Hoffman House living room, Patrick stood tall and resolute, his hands on his hips, hoping to convey strength and courage to his band of three as they sat together on the couch: Maggie, Irene and Duncan. His fixed stare took them in individually. Maggie was smiling with a forced facade of calm, picking lint from the navy blue woolen dress Eve had left behind.

Irene's face still bore the bruising around her startled eyes from the beating, and Duncan, a frigid introvert, appeared thin and fragile, as if a puff of wind might blow him away.

Patrick thought, *How am I ever going to get these three safely out of New York?* Patrick did not show his nervous apprehension. He couldn't let them see his trepidation and the crushing sense of responsibility he felt weighing on his shoulders. Right now, his job was to project courage and confidence.

They all had passports. They all said they would take the risk. They were all trying so hard to be brave.

He had to take them all. Maggie was his daughter. Irene had been beaten nearly to death because she knew Eve. And Duncan? Well, if Duncan stayed in New York, Big Jim's men would eventually find him and kill him.

Patrick's soft eyes settled on Irene. "Irene, are you sure you want to leave your mother at a time like this? Pardon me for being frank, but it will be a difficult time for her."

"Addison was a beast," Irene said, coldly. "He has scandalized our name in this City. I will be ostracized by every club and charity. And Addison allowed that brute of a man to beat me unmercifully, and then he hid me away in that uptown hospital on West 110th Street. He might as well have sent me off to Alaska. If I stay in this town, Mr. Gantly, now that my brother is dead, no doubt those terrible men will come after me again, if they know you and Duncan have left. No, I must leave. I will contact mother when I'm in Canada. She blamed me for what happened, and all she does is weep for Addison, calling him her little angel boy. No, I must leave. I can't stay here, and I can't let Duncan leave without me."

"All right, Irene. I just want to make sure you're committed to this. The journey won't be easy," he said, calmly, "especially if we hit that snowstorm. Four hours could turn into seven or eight hours. You all must do everything I tell you, without any argument, without any hesitation. Is that understood?"

They nodded.

"All right. I've already described the car to you. It is waiting on the south side of Broadway. You can't miss it. It's a Cadillac Model 30. Duncan will be driving. I'll sit next to him in the front and ride shotgun, and you two ladies will sit in the back. You'll be better hidden back there. Irene and Duncan will take their bags and leave the hotel first, then Maggie and I a few minutes later. Walk leisurely, as if you are out for a Sunday stroll. Don't worry. I haven't seen anyone outside watching the hotel, and to the best of my knowledge, no one has been shadowing us. Is everything clear?"

They nodded.

Patrick glanced down at his watch. "All right, it's nearly seven o'clock. Let's hope the snowstorm doesn't hit until we're well out of the City. Ladies, put on your wigs and glasses. It may not help, but you never know."

Patrick took a deep breath and blew it out all at once. He smiled warmly. "All right, then, let's go."

When they were all seated in the car, snow flurries were already falling. Duncan engaged the electric starter and the copper water-jacketed engine came to life. Patrick sat alert, his eyes carefully scanning the sidewalks and streets. Everything appeared quiet and safe.

Duncan craned his neck, checked the traffic and nudged the car away from the curb. They moved into a steady traffic flow, passing horse carriages and pushcarts, bumping along streetcar tracks, working uptown toward the Bronx.

As they entered the Bronx, a sparsely populated place in 1914, Patrick began to feel uneasy. He had that same tickle he'd always felt whenever danger was close. Casually, he looked sideways and then twisted around to look out the back window. A hot electric shock jolted his spine and he sat up.

Duncan glanced in his rearview mirror. His nervous expression confirmed Patrick's fear.

"Are we being followed?" Duncan asked, his voice trembling.

Maggie and Irene glanced around, swiftly alarmed.

"Don't look," Patrick barked.

"Are we being followed?" Maggie asked, her voice tight with nerves.

"Listen to me, all of you," Patrick said. "Stay calm. Do not panic. If we are being followed, we'll know soon enough."

"Oh, my gracious God," Irene said, about to hyperventilate.

Maggie wrapped a comforting arm around her. "We'll be okay, Irene," she said, also fighting for calm.

Patrick lowered his window and ventured a backward look. He suppressed a curse. He saw two headlights looming out of the darkness, gaining on them. Yes, they were definitely being followed.

Patrick had planned for this. He reached into his coat pocket for the smooth cold metal of his .32 caliber Smith & Wesson. He gently wrapped a palm around the grip. If the car overtook them and came alongside, he'd fire at the driver and then at the tires. But they won't be that stupid, he thought. They'll creep up from behind and fire. And there was no way to know how many cars were back there, and whether Big Jim himself was in the car following them.

Patrick mentally flipped through his options. Maybe they could outrun the car. The Cadillac did have 40-50 horsepower, which is why he laid down most of the money he had left to buy the thing. It wasn't the 132 horsepower of Eve's 2017 Toyota Corolla in 2018, but it would do.

"They're closing in," Duncan said. "What should I do?"

Patrick saw a turnoff ahead. "Turn off right," he said, pointing. "There!"

Duncan whipped the wheel right and they skidded into the turn. They bounced along a rutted road, past some dark, abandoned cottages and a bleak, leaning shack.

"Stop the car, Duncan. It's quiet here. No one around."

"What? Here? Now?"

"Do it!"

Duncan hit the brakes and the car jolted to a stop, pitching the girls forward, their arms bracing against the front seat. Patrick whipped around to the frightened ladies. "Get out. Hide behind that first cottage. Stay out of sight and don't move."

Maggie didn't protest. She threw open the door, snatched Irene by the arm and climbed out, tugging a weeping Irene along after her. They stumbled over rocks and gravel and clambered off behind a single-story cottage with a flat roof and dark windows.

Patrick narrowed his eyes on the looming car head-lights approaching. He faced Duncan, the boy's face taut with fear.

"Listen to me, Duncan, and don't talk. Turn the car around and drive straight for those oncoming headlights. Understand?"

Duncan opened his mouth to speak but Patrick stopped him. "Don't think. Do it. Now. They will not be expecting us to attack. We're going to charge them. Now, let's go."

With a grimacing effort, Duncan muscled the big steering wheel and gunned the engine. As the tires fought for traction, Patrick braced himself and again felt in his pocket for his revolver.

"Charge them, Duncan. They'll turn away before we collide."

Duncan's face was set, his hands sweaty, trembling on the steering wheel.

The car gathered speed as the oncoming car's headlights appeared like two white moons. Patrick hoped that Big Jim was in the car. He was ready to have it out once and for all with the man.

The two cars drove in a collision course like two jousting knights, lances at the ready. Patrick gritted his teeth. Duncan's eyes grew small, his arms braced against the steering wheel as the two advancing headlights bathed him in light.

"They're going to ram us," Duncan shouted.

"Hold fast, Duncan. Hold it!"

At the last possible moment, the oncoming car swerved and shot away. It left the road, dropped, bounced into a ravine and crashed into the stump of a tree. The front hood buckled, releasing a geyser of steam. The Cadillac shot by and skidded to a stop.

"Turn it around, Duncan. Hurry! We want the headlights on them."

Duncan slammed the gear in reverse, backed up, rammed the shift forward and gunned the accelerator. The car jumped ahead before coming to a skidding stop.

The Cadillac's headlights framed three men, one stumbling out onto the road, limping, one holding a handkerchief to his forehead to stop the bleeding, and the third one, a big man, stood tall and angry, shading his eyes from the glare of the Cadillac's headlights.

Patrick turned to Duncan. "All right, Duncan, get out of here. Run for it. No matter what happens, keep out of sight. Got it?"

Duncan swallowed. "But what about you?"
"Go!"

Duncan shoved his door open, ducked and ran off into the darkness for a grove of trees.

Patrick licked his lips, drew his revolver from his pocket and pushed open the door. He swiftly leveled the revolver on the big man's body. It was Big Jim.

CHAPTER 35

Big Jim started to step away from the car's bright headlights, but Patrick stopped him.

"Don't move, Big Jim. Stay right there."

Big Jim froze. When he spoke, his voice was packed with venom.

"You could have killed all of us with a damned stunt like that. Are you daft?"

Patrick ignored him. "Now tell your bootlicks to slowly pull their guns and toss them out into the light where I can see them."

Big Jim kept his hard, burning eyes on Patrick, but he made a motion with his arm, and the two men standing beside the car complied.

"All the guns," Patrick said. "Even the leg holsters."

"Do it!" Big Jim growled.

The man with the handkerchief pressed to his wounded forehead glared hate at Patrick as he leaned over, rolled up his pant leg, withdrew the pistol from his leg holster and tossed it onto the road into the light.

"You too, Big Jim. Unload the blaster…very slowly." Then in sarcasm, Patrick said, "I'd hate to have to blow your head off."

Big Jim complied, dropping his revolver. "You fit the description," Big Jim, said. "Did you slay my two men down on the Lower East Side? Alfie and Donny?"

"They were going to kill two harmless young ladies, but then you know that, don't you, Big Jimmy?"

"Who the hell are you? Why did you take my Maggie?"

"She's not your Maggie anymore, Big Jim. She was never your Maggie to begin with. Anyway, that's over now."

"Oh, so she's yours now, is she? Who are you?"

"I'm going to give you a choice, Big Jim. You can take your men, get back into your car and drive away, or you can die. It's your choice."

Big Jim barked out a hoarse laugh. "You cheeky bastard. Who do you think you're talking to? I'm Big Jim Clancy and nobody talks to me like that. I'll kill you and rip your heart out."

Patrick stared coldly. "Threats are made by men who are afraid. Are you afraid, Big Jimmy?"

A menacing delight flickered in Big Jim's eyes. "I'm not afraid of the likes of you, whoever you are. Is that Eve woman your whore?"

"Big Jim, you really are a very small, disagreeable man, aren't you?"

Big Jim squared his shoulders. His forehead lifted as a sudden realization struck.

"Nah... I get you now," Big Jim said. "I know what's been going on now. You've been out with my Maggie, haven't you? So, it's just as I suspected. She has been out tramping around with you behind my back, hasn't she?"

"No, Big Jim. You've got it all wrong."

He shook his head, unconvinced. "Don't lie to a liar. For what you've done to my Maggie I will kill you, and then I will kill her."

"Big Jim, you're as stupid as you are ugly. My name's Patrick Gantly, and I came a long way to get Maggie away from you. So you need to let go, and let her go so she can get on with her life. It's all over."

"Gantly? Patrick Gantly? Are you her brother, then?"

"No, Big Jim. I'm her father."

Big Jim stared hard, as if trying to understand. Finally, he broke into harsh laughter.

"Her father?"

"Yes, that's right, Big Jim. I'm Maggie's father."

His laughter was cold and guttural, and there was no mirth in it. "Okay, Patrick, if that's what your name is. You're going to have to shoot me right here and now, because I'm coming after you, and I'm going to take you apart, piece by piece."

Patrick slowly lowered his revolver. "You toss your other pistol away, Big Jim, because I know you've got one. Then I'll toss mine. Then it will be just you and me. Whoever wins walks away."

An ugly smile creased Big Jim's lips. He slipped a hand into his greatcoat pocket, lifted the gun by the walnut grip and tossed it off to his left.

Patrick dropped his. Both men shouldered out of their greatcoats and dropped them. They stood tall, poised for battle, determined, their dueling eyes already speculating advantage and position.

Big Jim started forward. "This is going to be a real pleasure, Patrick Gantly," he said, biting off the words and flinging them like shards of glass.

Patrick set his chin, his breathing coming easy, the cold air already chilling his ears and his hands, now formed into ready fists.

The two men met on the edge of light, the night surrounding them, snow flurries drifting, a dog's growling bark echoing from across a field.

Patrick and Big Jim circled for a time, measuring, feet scratching at the dirt. When Big Jim lunged at Patrick, it was cat quick. He had two hard punches into Patrick's left stomach and jaw in the blink of an eye. Patrick stumbled back in surprise and pain. He had underestimated Big Jim's reflexes, skill and speed.

Big Jim glared at Patrick with an arrogant challenge. "You're a dead man, Patrick. Nobody crosses Big Jim and lives."

Big Jim screwed his heels into the ground and charged again, throwing big hooks with each fist. Patrick backpedaled as Big Jim hammered away at Patrick's arms, shoulders and elbows. He landed a good one over Patrick's ear and another over his ribs.

Big Jim blew out air as he worked, punching and swinging, clouds of white vapor puffing from his mouth. Patrick managed to take the blows without taking on too much injury, and soon Big Jim's punches began to lose their snap. He then went to jabs.

Half turning and crouching, Patrick retreated and slumped a little to let Big Jim think he had worn him down. Big Jim pulled back to gather some quick breaths and renew his strength. That was what Patrick was waiting for.

Patrick charged. He threw a blow that caught Big Jim in the side of his head. The blow startled him just enough for Patrick to come down hard on Big Jim's instep. Big Jim yelled in pain. With his hands locked, Patrick jammed his right elbow up under Big Jim's lower jaw. Stunned, Big Jim stumbled backward, his feet struggling to find the ground. Patrick pressed the attack, eyes blazing. He jabbed and punched, driving Big Jim back, attacking with all the rage, pain and fury he'd held in for days.

Patrick danced in and gave Big Jim a thunderclap slap on both ears and Big Jim growled, wounded and reeling. Patrick slammed a rock-hard fist into Big Jim's face, and a solid punch to his nose. Big Jim's head snapped back, and Patrick hooked him deeply under the belt buckle. Big Jim doubled over, the air exploding from his lips. As he bent, Patrick snatched Big Jim's wrist, turned it up between his shoulder blades and shoved him, four steps and head first, into the side of the Cadillac.

Big Jim bounced back, damaged. His wild eyes searched for reality, as he faltered and went loose. He turned to face Patrick, his face streaming blood. He tried to recover but wavered and stared with crazed, astonished eyes. Patrick glared as Big Jim strained to raise a defiant fist, but lost.

Big Jim wilted, dropping down to one knee. He wobbled, body swaying, and then like a great building, he tumbled over and hit the rocky ground, eyes closed, breathing labored.

Patrick bent over, the cold sapping his strength, his fists sore and throbbing. He gasped for breath, a pained exhaustion nearly overwhelming him. As he worked to recover, he saw Big Jim's two bootlicks emerge into the light, their greatcoats flapping, hands shoved into their pockets, hats pulled low, eyes threatening.

Patrick got a good, clear look at the taller of the two men. He was the same man Patrick had fought in Duncan's apartment when Patrick had posed as a priest.

Patrick frowned as he straightened, ready for another attack.

The taller man said, "You will die for what you did to Big Jim. You will die for what you did to me."

Big Jim suddenly stirred, managing to sit up, unsteadily. In a great bear of a growl, he yelled, "Kill him. Kill him and I'll rip his heart out!"

Patrick's strength was ebbing, but he readied himself, knowing he might die fighting. His only prayer was that somehow Duncan and the ladies had made a clean escape.

Just then a gunshot exploded, shattering the night. It froze the men in the headlights, their eyes wide, searching, scared.

From the outer edge of darkness, Duncan emerged into the light, his young face set in a rigid, deadly purpose. The revolver that Patrick had given him only days ago, a .32 caliber revolver was pointed directly at the two men.

Duncan's voice was shaky, but resolute. "I will shoot you men," he said, the revolver steady and sure.

"Run away now, or so help me God, I will shoot you dead."

"Kill him!" Big Jim shouted. "Kill them both!"

Big Jim's men stood rigid, uncertain.

Duncan leveled the .32 at the tall man, the one who had beaten him in his Greenwich Village apartment. As the man lunged to attack, Duncan squeezed off a shot. A bullet rang out and struck the man just above the kneecap. He flinched, whirled, and screamed out in pain, crumbling to the ground.

Duncan fired another shot. The bullet whizzed over the stockier man's head. In a full panic, the shorter man turned and galloped away, ignoring his injured buddy.

The man Duncan had shot raised a helpless hand. "Don't shoot! Don't shoot me. Please."

"Run!" Duncan shouted as he squeezed off another explosive shot.

Terrified, the man struggled to his feet and went limping off into the darkness, grunting out curses.

Undaunted, Big Jim jabbed a hand into his tweed jacket pocket and whipped out a two-shot derringer. In a huffing effort, he swung it toward Patrick and fired. Two shots blasted.

Patrick ducked and felt the breath of a bullet whizz by his left ear. At the same moment, he heard another pistol blast to his left. Duncan had fired.

Patrick whirled to see a bloody mist splatter Big Jim's face as Duncan's bullet struck Big Jim between the eyes. Big Jim jolted back and slammed into the ground, his dead eyes blank and staring.

The world went silent for a time, and then gusts of wind whistled by, sending snowflakes into a scattering panic, making the world seem blurry and confused.

Patrick turned to Duncan. The boy was shaking from head to toe, the gun still poised at Big Jim.

"Is he dead?" Duncan said. "Is that terrible, devil of a man dead?"

Patrick swallowed. "Yes," he said, staggering over to him. "Yes, Big Jim is dead. You can lower the gun now, Duncan."

Duncan didn't move or respond. His eyes were wide, spooked. "Are you sure he's dead?"

"Yes, Duncan. It's over. He's dead. I'm going to take the gun from you now, all right? Relax."

Patrick gently and carefully reached and removed the revolver from Duncan's shivering hand. Patrick looked softly at the thin, fragile kid, who maybe wasn't so fragile anymore. Duncan kept his wide eyes fixed on Big Jim's dead body, his mouth firm and tight.

"It's all over, Duncan. Thank you for saving my life."

Duncan seemed lost in a dream. "What? What did you say?" he asked, his eyes twitching.

"I said, thank you for saving my life. Big Jim's next shot would have hit me."

Duncan still couldn't move. "I'm glad I did it. God forgive me, but I'm glad I shot him dead. He deserved it, didn't he, for what he did to poor Irene? He beat her up so badly, and she said he laughed while he punched her about that hotel room where they took her. He just laughed and kept hitting her. He deserved it, didn't he?" he said, turning to Patrick, his eyes pleading, filling with tears.

Patrick nodded. "Yes, Duncan. He was an evil man."

The emotion took over and Duncan doubled over and wept, his shoulders rolling.

"It's all right, Duncan. It's going to be all right."

Patrick gazed out into the darkness to see Maggie and Irene standing by, neither moving. They were two quiet silhouettes.

"We have to go," he said, loud enough for all to hear.

Patrick placed a soft hand on Duncan's shoulders. "We have to get out of here. Duncan, can you drive?"

Duncan slowly straightened, eyes wet with tears. He nodded. "Yes… I can drive. I have to get the ladies away from here. Yes… let's go."

CHAPTER 36

Eve and Logan sat at the wooden table opposite each other, bowls of moose stew, plates filled with sliced bread and butter, and hot mugs of tea between them. Eve could hear the groaning wind circle the house and was grateful for the comforting warmth of the cozy room.

But she felt a heaviness of heart, and her mind was absorbed in thoughts about Patrick and Maggie. She was worried they wouldn't escape New York alive; worried about the snowstorm they would run into; worried about Patrick telling Maggie the truth of who he was and where they had come from. She was also uneasy about what she and Patrick had done in this time—they had no doubt changed the past and, at this very moment, the future was surely rearranging itself.

How would the changes affect their world in 2018? How would it affect the world at large? And if they did return home, would it be the same home? Previously, when she'd time traveled back from 1885 to 2016, there had been subtle changes. Would Georgy Boy be changed again? Would Eve's parents be her parents? Would she still be a nurse practitioner? Would Joni still be there, waiting for them?

Logan's voice snapped Eve out of her misty dream and forced her back to the moment.

"I had to face the truth after Kady was gone," he said. "I suppose she wasn't so happy with me. I thought she was, but after a lot of thought and reflection, I don't think she liked her life here with me. I guess she felt too confined."

Eve shifted her focus. "What did your mother say when she first brought you the lantern?"

Logan lowered his spoon, staring down at the table. "She told me the story… your story. Everything she'd learned from some old man who'd brought her the lantern just before he died. She told me about you, and about the hospital where you both worked. She said that from the first time she'd met you, she felt there was something about you that was different; something she couldn't quite grasp."

"Did Kady hear your mother's story?"

"No… at least I didn't think she had. Mother told me the story late one night after Kady had gone off to bed. But she must have heard the story, right?"

"Did you believe your mother?"

Logan looked up. "No, of course not. I thought she was going a bit batty or something. I mean the whole thing sounded like some storybook fable or fairy tale. Who could believe such a thing? Magic lanterns? Time travel? No, I didn't believe her, but I didn't tell her I didn't believe her. She was my mother. My birth mother. We had grown close, and I didn't want to jeopardize that, so I just indulged her little fantasy."

"Did Kady ever talk to you about the lantern?"

"No. Never. I just assumed she hadn't heard and didn't know anything about it. Mother asked me never to tell anyone. So, she pulled this old lantern from her canvas bag and set it here on the table. And then she said a strange thing. She stared at me somberly and said that perhaps one night, when I was alone, I should light it and see what happened."

"And did you ever light it?" Eve asked eagerly.

"No, of course not. It looked old and dinged up. I told Mother I wouldn't light the thing, and she just shrugged and asked me to put it in a safe place. She said the woman who owned it might come looking for it someday. Of course, I thought that was crazy too. I mean, what person in their right mind would travel here from America looking for an old lantern, when new ones are in every general store and catalog in the world? So, I took the lantern outside, placed it on a lower shelf in my tool shed and forgot about it."

Logan stared ahead, his gaze more inner than outer. "I thought Kady was happy with me and our way of life. But after she vanished, I went through her private trunks. I found travel magazines and letters from her friends and sister. I could tell that she'd wanted to run off to some exotic island, or to Europe or New York. She felt like a prisoner in this place."

Logan looked away. "And I guess she said some other things about me…well, I don't think she really loved me."

Eve sipped her tea, thoughtfully.

Logan's eyes held questions. "Do you know where Kady is, Mrs. Gantly?"

"No, Logan. Of course not. I have no idea."

He lowered his sad eyes and his voice. He stirred his stew absently, staring as if defeated. "I believe in that lantern now, don't I? I have to, because I've seen its power."

He slumped in his chair and pushed his bowl of stew away, his appetite gone. His somber eyes took Eve in.

"What time in the future do you come from, Mrs. Gantly?"

Eve set her mug of tea down. "My husband, Patrick, and I live in 2018, in New York City."

It was a long moment before he spoke. "Do you think Kady went there, to that time and place? To 2018?"

"I don't know, Logan."

He pounded the table with his fist. "Well, you must know, if you use a lantern and you time travel to different places. You've got to know how it all works, and why it works, and why these things happen. You've got to know where my Kady is."

Eve was startled by his unexpected outburst. "I don't know how it all works, Logan. I found the lantern in an antique shop in 2016. There was a letter inside it, written by a man who had deep regrets about a woman with whom he was in love. She was lost to him and he'd learned that she was dying. When I lit the lantern, I found myself back in 1885. Through a series of difficult events, I was able to help bring the couple together. While there, I fell in love with my husband, Patrick."

Logan squinted at her as if he was trying to understand.

Eve sat back in the chair. "Logan, there seems to be an intelligent energy contained in the lantern and in its light. I don't know how or why it does what it does, but it seems to respond to an intention. It seems to support a person to do some good—to improve the world or save a life or, as romantic as it may sound, to bring two ill-fated lovers together."

Logan kept his attention firmly fixed on Eve, waiting for more.

Eve continued. "After I returned to my time, I made a vow never to use the lantern again. I vowed to toss it into the river because I didn't understand its power, and it scared me. I barely made it out of 1885 alive. I was nearly trapped."

Eve pointed to the lantern. "But it was *that* lantern that sent me back to 2016."

"But it didn't travel with you?"

"No, Logan, that lantern remains fixed in its time. I don't know why. The lantern in 2018 that brought me to 1914 is the same lantern that brought me to 1885, but it stays in the 21st century. Again, I don't understand why or how it does what it does."

Logan stared uncertainly. "So why didn't you toss the lantern in the river?"

Eve let out a long breath. "I don't know. Something stopped me."

Logan stood up, abruptly. "Well, I don't understand any of it. I'm a simple man who just wanted a home, a wife and some children. I just wanted to live a good, clean and happy family life. I curse the day my mother brought me that lantern. I curse it and, God forgive me, I curse everyone connected with it."

Eve turned away from his anger. She was so very tired, feeling a weary, dragging fatigue. She had not slept well in days.

Logan paced to the fireplace, stared into it for a time and then returned to the table, his face softening.

"I didn't mean that, Mrs. Gantly. I'm sorry. I do not curse you. That was not a good Christian thing to say. Please forgive me."

"I understand, Logan, and I am truly sorry for what happened."

His restless eyes moved. "Well, you know what? Kady probably would have left me anyway, one way or the other, wouldn't she? It was just a matter of time."

"You will find another wife. You're young, Logan."

"Not now. No. There's a war on. I must go and fight."

He ran a hand along his jaw, thinking, and stood by his chair, his hands resting on the top rail.

"Logan..." Eve said in a soft tone. "You haven't said if you still have the lantern. Do you have it?"

Logan stared down. "When I saw Kady vanish right before my eyes, as she stood over there by the fireplace, I screamed. I was so confused and scared that all I could do was just scream, and then go on screaming. I was helpless, you see, and I went a little mad for a time. I ran around the house searching for her, calling for her. I picked through closets, tossed her clothes aside, yanked out drawers and fell to my knees looking under the bed. And then still in a hot madness, I stumbled outside and circled the cabin, sure she was hiding from me. But she was nowhere to be found. Then I staggered out into the newly fallen snow, screaming up into the sky. I bolted for the trees and ran until my strength left me, and I fell into cold blowing snow. I don't know how long I stayed there. I think I nearly froze to death."

Logan slowly lowered himself back into the chair. "When I finally came to my senses, I staggered back inside the house, dropped before the fire and just stared at that lantern. I stared until my eyes burned and watered. I stared until late into the night and the fire went out, and I shivered from cold and exhaustion."

Logan continued, in a low, husky voice. "Finally, I gathered up the last of my dignity and stormed over to the damned thing. I grabbed it up, went to the back door, pushed it open and, with all my strength, I slung that lantern out into the darkness. I left it there for many days. I don't know how long…maybe weeks."

Logan pushed up again, turned and walked purposefully across the living room floor to the back door. He exited.

Eve waited, feeling a desperate anticipation.

Minutes later, Logan entered. He closed the door and stood for a time in a ringing silence. Only the fire crackled orange.

Eve rose to her feet, her eyes enlarging on the lantern that Logan held up by the wire handle. He held it cautiously and away from his body as if it were a bomb about to go off.

Eve started toward Logan, taking small steps.

"This is it," Logan said. "Like I said, its pretty beat up."

Eve stopped, first staring at Logan, and then at the lantern. It was not in the best of shape. Two of the four glass window panes were gone. One was cracked, the other intact. The wire guards were bent, but the anchor design on each side of the roof was still visible.

Eve felt a crashing relief. It was the lantern—the same lantern that had sent her home from 1885.

Logan handed it to Eve and she took it, reverently, lovingly, with a smile. Again, an odd and haunting feeling washed over her: how did this lantern finally find itself in Granny Gilbert's *The Time Past Antique Shop* in Pennsylvania in 2016?

"Do you think it will work, Mrs. Gantly? Do you think it will light?"

And then the telephone rang, and they both pivoted toward the sound.

CHAPTER 37

The Cadillac battled on into the grinding teeth of the snowstorm. The miles flew by in a hazy vision of splattering snow, slapping wipers and the ghosts of towering trees.

Angry winds punched the car as it bucketed and ramped its way toward the Poughkeepsie train station. As a shuddering Irene and tense Maggie peered out of their back windows, they saw only blinding snow. Still in the front seat, Patrick watched snowflakes play across the headlights like fleeing insects.

Duncan's head was jutted out over the steering wheel, his eyes straining to find the road and keep the car on it.

"We're almost there," Patrick said. "How are you doing, Duncan?"

"I'm all right," he said, the strain of the night showing on his face.

"We'd better catch that train," Maggie said. "We won't be able to find a hotel in this mess."

"We'll make it all right," Patrick said.

They pressed on until muted lights beckoned in the distance, like a saving grace.

"That's it," Patrick said, excitedly pointing. "That's the town, and the train station is about two miles from there."

"Thank God," Irene said.

Patrick glanced at his watch. "We've got fifteen minutes."

At that moment, the car skidded and lurched left. Irene screamed as Duncan wrestled for control. The back tires lost traction, gliding helplessly across the snow-covered road. They all braced for impact as the dark trunk of a tree raced in to meet them.

At the last second, Duncan wrenched the steering wheel in a hard right, but he lost the battle and the car slammed into the tree, tossing the passengers about.

As the wind whistled all about them, Patrick shook off the impact. He looked first at Duncan, who was holding a bleeding nose, and then he swiveled around to check on the women.

"Are you ladies all right?"

Irene was crying, holding her head. "I hit my head. It hurts."

"Are you bleeding?" Patrick asked.

She was nearly hysterical. "We are all going to freeze to death. We'll never get out of here."

Patrick ignored her. "Maggie?"

"I'm fine," she said, calmly. "Thank God for good solid Cadillacs. Good thinking, Patrick."

Patrick jerked a nod. "We could have used seatbelts."

"Seatbelts?" Maggie asked.

"Never mind. Maggie, help Irene."

Patrick turned back to Duncan. "Are you all right, Duncan?"

He nodded, throwing his head back. "Bumped my nose on the steering wheel."

Patrick pulled a handkerchief from his pocket and handed it to him. "Use this."

Duncan took it, nodding.

"Bye-bye, train," Maggie said.

Patrick rubbed the knee he had jammed into the dashboard and forced his mind to work.

"Okay, look. I'm going out to try to push us out. Duncan, can you still drive this thing?"

"Yes... I'm all right."

Without another word, Patrick shoved the door and it flew open. He tumbled outside into the mad tempest, shielding his face from the attacking snow. As he stamped through the snowy mounds, his hair instantly caked with icy flakes, he kept a hand on the side of the car to steady his uncertain feet until he came to the tree. He assessed the damage. The engine was still purring; that was good. The headlights were on, also good. There was hope. It was the left back tire that seemed buried. If he could free that, there was a good chance the heavy car could find purchase and fight its way back to the road.

Using the car's headlights, Patrick searched the area for a sturdy, fallen limb he could use as leverage. He tramped about searching, raking through the snow until, minutes later, he was lucky enough to find one. It wasn't as thick as he'd hoped, but it would have to do. He grasped it with his already numb, gloveless fingers—he'd misplaced his gloves sometime after his fight with Big Jim—and he carried the heavy limb to the back tire.

He worked and jiggled until he wedged one end of the limb under the tire just enough so that he could bounce it, as Duncan hit the gas.

Duncan stuck his head out, one hand still holding the handkerchief to his nose.

"Ready?" he shouted.

"Yes," Patrick called, with a thumbs up.

Duncan gunned the engine and Patrick wrapped the branch with both arms. With a straining effort, he bounced, pushed and heaved as the icy wind bit into his face. The back tire spun and squealed but refused to budge. Patrick tried again, putting all his weight into it, as a driving snow struck his face and white clouds of smoke puffed from his mouth. Again, the tire whirled, making a high-pitched whine like a dentist's drill, but refused to budge.

Now looking like a snowman, Patrick straightened, wiped his face and took in gulps of cold air, his pulse racing, arms aching.

It didn't look good, he thought.

When the back door flew open and Maggie emerged, a hat pulled tightly over her head, Patrick looked on, curious.

He called to her, his voice nearly swallowed by the wind. "What are you doing?"

"Well, obviously you can't do this by yourself. Let's see if I can help get us out of here before Big Jim's men show up."

"Do you really believe Big Jim's men would chase after us in this storm?"

"Yes, Patrick, I do. They're animals. Come on, let's get this thing free and back on the road. I don't want to miss the train."

Patrick put her to work on the limb, pushing and rocking it up and down, while he crouched at the left bumper and put his shoulder to it. They labored and rocked and grunted and cursed as the car bounced, but the tire refused to catch. Patrick could feel slick sweat on his back as he soldiered on.

Finally, he stopped, his shoulders aching, back sore. Filled with frustration, he yelled out. "Okay, okay, Maggie, take a break. I need to catch my breath."

Maggie's hat and coat were now white. She shoved her hands into her coat pockets, stood up straight and tall as if she were about to recite some lines, and looked skyward, gasping, her heart pounding.

"All right, it's time for a Christmas song."

"A what?" Patrick shouted, incredulous.

"Singing gives me strength and, anyway, I haven't sung a Christmas song yet this season, so I'm going to sing."

Patrick stared in disbelief as Maggie lifted her chin high and began to sing *Jingle Bells*.

Dashing through the snow
In a one-horse open sleigh,
Over the fields we go,
Laughing all the way,
Bells on bob-tail ring,
Making spirits bright,
What fun it is to ride and sing
A sleighing song tonight,

Jingle bells, jingle bells,
Jingle all the way!
O' what fun it is to ride
In a one-horse open sleigh.

"Come on, Patrick," Maggie shouted over the moaning wind. "Join in."

Duncan stuck his head out the window, looking back, bug-eyed. "What's going on back there?"

Patrick shook his head, put fists on his hips and hollered. "We're singing *Jingle Bells*."

"*Jingle Bells*? At a time like this?"

"Apparently so…"

And then Patrick joined in on the next chorus, having learned the lyrics only last Christmas, in 2017.

Jingle bells, jingle bells,
Jingle all the way!
O' what fun it is to ride
In a one-horse open sleigh.

Patrick looked at her. "You have a beautiful voice."

"Thank you. You know, Patrick, you can't carry a tune worth a spit. You just missed every note."

Patrick ignored her insult, his mind on other things. "So how did you end up with Big Jim?"

Maggie threw her hands to her hips, as snow pelted them both.

"What do you care?"

"I just want to know."

"This is not the time nor the place to discuss this."

"So, of all the men in New York City, you hook up with Big Jim. How? Why? I don't understand it, a girl like you who is so pretty and smart. Tell me. Why?"

"It's none of your damn business, Patrick. You sound like my father, although I never had a father."

Duncan's head was out of the window again. "What's wrong back there? Irene is having a breakdown. Please, get us out of here."

With a shake of his head, Patrick lowered himself to the bumper and Maggie, now angry at Patrick for his critical remarks, felt as strong as an Amazon.

They went back to work, both filled with new power. Patrick dug in his heels and shoved and heaved, while Maggie put all her weight on the stick, bouncing it and cursing it. Slowly, grudgingly, the tire began to grind a hole in the snow, finding the hard rocky earth. The tires clawed at the ground, as Duncan flattened the accelerator and the engine roared. Finally, grudgingly, the car grabbed the hard dirt and broke free, shooting ahead, fishtailing up and onto the road. Exhausted and freezing, Patrick fell to his knees, his chest heaving, his breath smoking.

Maggie placed her hands at her sides and bent at the waist, gulping in air.

Patrick looked at her. "Thanks, Maggie. I couldn't have done it without you."

Maggie's face was still tight with fury. "So, is that why you spurned my advances the other day? Because of Big Jim? Because I'm not good enough for you?"

"What? No... of course not. That wasn't it at all."

"Most men find me very attractive, you know."

Patrick jerked a nod. "Yes, well, I know that, don't I? And you should be a little more careful and discerning about the men you run around with."

Maggie glared at him. "You can just go to hell!"

CHAPTER 38

The Poughkeepsie train platform was covered by a slate roof that protected passengers from the snow. Two resolute men were shoveling snow into piles, while a big northern wind blew sharply through the open spaces, reddening cheeks and whipping up coattails. Hands were clamped down on hats to keep them from sailing away, and a scruffy old brown dog shuffled about like a watchman, his leery gaze taking it all in.

Patrick, Maggie, Duncan, and Irene all stood on the train platform next to the luggage cart that held their bags. The young porter would load them as soon as the train arrived.

All four passengers were leaning anxiously forward, peering ahead as the approaching locomotive's headlight pierced the haze, shining like a spotlight, the train's forlorn whistle announcing its arrival. The passengers stepped back as the train rumbled into the station, braking in a hiss of steam as it screeched to a stop.

Maggie and Patrick were still damp and shivering from their ordeal, their muscles tight and throbbing. Duncan had a gentle arm resting around Irene's shoulders, as she mumbled complaints and fears.

"Thank God this thing was late," Maggie said.

"We were lucky. Let's hope there aren't more delays," Patrick said.

Maggie turned to him. "How did Eve sound on the telephone? You were lucky to reach her in this storm."

"She's fine."

"Did she give you directions?"

Patrick pulled the paper from his pocket and read it: "Eve said we're going to the original Coldwater station, at Coldwater Junction. It's a few miles outside the village of Coldwater, Ontario. She and the man she went to see, Logan Tyler, will be there with a horse and sleigh."

"How quaint," Maggie said.

Their attention was suddenly diverted by Irene's brittle sounding voice. "I want to go home," she whimpered.

Her face was colorless and drawn. "I want my Mummy. I want to go home. I'm so cold and hungry. I'm so tired."

Duncan's soft voice tried to soothe her. "It will be okay, Irene. Once we get on the train, everything will be all right. You'll be warm and safe. They have a café car. I'll get you something to eat and you can sleep."

She shook her head as new tears glistened her eyes. "I want to go home." She continued to repeat it like a mantra.

Maggie rolled her eyes and looked away.

Patrick stepped over, keeping his voice low but firm. "Irene, is that what you really want? Do you really want to go back to New York?"

She averted her eyes. "Yes... I'll be safe now that that scoundrel of a man is dead. My Mummy will take away my money if I leave her now. I'll be a pauper."

Duncan spoke up. "I'll support us, Irene. I'll get a job. You'll never go hungry, I promise. I'll take care of you."

Irene sniffled as she spoke to him with pleading eyes. "But you'll always be poor, Duncan, don't you see? You're a painter and they don't make any money. I don't want to be poor, Duncan. You are such a good boy, but I don't want to be poor for the rest of my life. I'll be safe now in New York, don't you see? I can go back home and be with my Mummy, and I'll be warm and safe."

Duncan looked away, helpless.

Patrick nodded. "All right, Irene, if that's what you want. I'd suggest you take the Cadillac, but can you drive?"

"I can't drive that big thing, Mr. Gantly. Anyway, it's not proper for a woman to drive."

"Of course," Patrick said. "According to the schedule, the next train to New York doesn't arrive until morning. Are you going to be okay here alone?"

"She won't be alone," Duncan said, disheartened. "I'll stay with her. I'll go back to New York with her."

Irene pulled away from Duncan, facing him fully. "No, Duncan. You must go on. That awful man has so many connections in New York. They know you shot Big Jim. They will find you and kill you. No, you must go with Patrick and Maggie. You must go to Canada and make a brand-new life for yourself. Don't you see?"

It was obvious that Duncan did not see. With his thinking eyes in motion, his features gradually fell apart in degrees of disbelief and sadness. He lifted a weak, shaking hand and opened his mouth to speak, but nothing came out. He gently touched her cheek and gave her a tender, loving smile. Then he turned from her and started walking toward the train, just as the conductor bellowed, "All aboard!"

Patrick looked at her with compassion. "Goodbye, Irene, and I'm sorry for all that happened to you because of me."

Irene's face turned sour. "It wasn't you, Mr. Gantly," she said harshly. "It was Eve. I wish I had never met her. She has brought me nothing but bad luck ever since I first saw her on that Central Park bench."

Patrick ignored that. "Do you have money, Irene? Do you have enough to buy something to eat and to buy a ticket back home?"

"Yes, I think so."

Patrick pulled a wallet from his pocket, drew out some bills and pressed them into her hand. "Take this, just in case."

She sniffled again, touched by his concern. "Thank you, Mr. Gantly, for being so brave. We would have all died if you hadn't been there for us."

"Take care of yourself, Irene," Patrick said. "I hope everything works out for you."

Her sad eyes came to his, and they swam in tears. "They've just got to, don't they?"

As Patrick turned to follow the others onto the train, Irene's voice stopped him, and he glanced back.

"Duncan was brave too, wasn't he?"

"Yes, Irene, he was. Very brave."

"I'm glad he killed that man. I will always love Duncan for that, and for so many other things. He is a great artist, you know, and he is such a good boy."

Patrick nodded.

As the train lurched ahead and pulled away from the station, Duncan sat heavily into a seat by a window. Gloomy and lost, he waved goodbye to Irene.

She grew animated, taking quick little steps toward the departing train, waving back and flashing him a sweet, girlish smile as she wiped her tears with an embroidered hanky.

An hour later, Patrick and Maggie sat in the café car, having finished their beef sandwiches and boiled eggs. Each lingered quietly over a cup of black tea.

They had left Duncan forward in his seat, his shoulders hunched, looking lost and dejected. He had refused to join them, saying he wasn't hungry.

Maggie ordered tea and had it sent to him.

"I'm sorry for the kid," Maggie said.

"I don't think he's a kid any longer, Maggie. We wouldn't have made it without his courage and strength. Thank God Eve saved his life."

Maggie lifted her tired eyes on Patrick. "I wouldn't have made it without you. I'm sorry for what I said back there in the snowstorm... you know, about my flirty come on, and Big Jim."

Patrick lifted his cup and sipped. "You're right. It is none of my business."

Maggie slid her teacup and saucer aside. "I heard you, you know."

"Heard me what?"

"Irene and I crept forward just as you and Big Jim were about to fight."

Patrick stayed mute.

"When he asked who you were, you said Patrick Gantly. When he asked if you were my brother, you said, no, you were my father. Why did you say that?"

Patrick shrugged. "I don't know. It seemed like something that would throw Big Jim off a bit. I needed him off balance."

"Really? So, your name is Patrick Gantly?"

"Yes…"

"And Eve was married to my father?"

Patrick shifted uncomfortably. "Yes…"

"So, who are you then, Mr. Gantly? A cousin? What?"

Patrick just stared at her, feeling so exhausted from the day and the warmth of the food and heat that he didn't think he had the strength or will to have this conversation. At least not now.

"Did you know my father, Patrick? And don't lie to me."

"Yes, Maggie, I knew your father."

Maggie sat back, digesting his answer. "And you're from Ohio, as Eve is?"

"No, I'm not."

Maggie leaned forward, irritated. "Who the hell are you, Patrick? Tell me. No more games. You and Eve went to a lot of trouble to get me away from Big Jim—risking your lives for me—and I want to know why. So tell me."

Patrick saw that Maggie was not going to back down. He would have to tell her everything—all the truth—and risk never seeing her again.

Patrick took a long, pleasurable look at his daughter, her lovely face and natural lush hair, mussed a bit and tangled from their hard travel. How he wished he could have seen her as a baby; helped to raise her; teach her, care for her, love her. How he regretted not knowing her all these years. Would they have many years ahead? Hopefully. After he told her the truth, would she want to time travel to 2018 and be with him?

"Maggie…I want you to listen and not talk. Please don't say a word until after I have told you the whole story, the entire truth from beginning to end. I'll explain everything, but you must promise me that you will not utter a word. Do you promise?"

Maggie sat up rigid, her eyes filled with apprehension. "You and Eve are married, aren't you?"

"Yes, Maggie, but you must promise me now that you will sit still and silent while I tell you my story. Will you do that?"

Maggie stared at him long and hard. "Yes…"

"All right, then. I'll start from the beginning. I'll start from 1885."

About forty-five minutes later, Patrick had his hands crossed on the table, gazing into his daughter's fathomless eyes.

"So you see, Maggie, I am truly your father. And that's why I had to come back and save your life."

Maggie stared at him for long, awkward minutes with a troubled, entranced expression.

Patrick waited, patiently, pulse racing.

Maggie felt displaced, dizzy and a little crazy. Inside her soul was a frayed wire, loose and dangerous. She struggled to settle the thoughts and emotions that swarmed in her, threatening to detonate a wild outburst of rage and laughter. To her surprise, she contained them—held them in—trapped and squeezed the madness tightly, as within a fist. But with that fist, she wanted to strike something or somebody. She wanted to punch this man who sat before her in the gut, and call him ugly names, and pretty names and aching names—names that had no letters, only stinging, tearing emotion.

Finally, without a word, she shot up. After a long, somber and painful silence, her eyes boring a hole into Patrick, she pivoted and left the club car, leaving him alone to hear the echo of his impossible words hanging in the air.

CHAPTER 39

On Wednesday morning, December 16th, the train huffed into the Coldwater Junction station and squealed to a stop in clouds of steam. Eve paced the narrow platform, anxious to catch a glimpse of Patrick, while Logan stood by, nervous and watchful.

The sky was a sea of rich blue, the sun glistening on snow-heavy green pines.

Maggie emerged first, stepping down to the platform, then Duncan and finally Patrick, all three looking weary and worn.

Eve went to Patrick in a rush. His eyes sparkled when he saw her, and he gathered her up into his arms with a broad grin and a bear hug. Maggie, Duncan and Logan looked on, Maggie sullen, Duncan remote, and Logan curious.

When they broke the embrace, Eve turned to Maggie with a spirited smile and warm greeting, noticing her cool welcome and blank stare. Eve ignored it and turned to Duncan, beaming.

"I'm so happy to see you again, Duncan. I'm so glad you're safe."

To her surprise, he took her hand in a noble manner, bowed and kissed it.

"Thank you, Mrs. Gantly, for saving my life."

Patrick spoke up. "And *he* saved mine, Eve," Patrick said, laying a gentle hand on Duncan's shoulder.

Eve stepped back. "Well, I am looking forward to hearing this story."

"There is a lot to tell," Patrick said, looking toward Maggie, who refused to meet his eyes.

Logan drifted over, and Eve introduced them all. Logan was comfortably outgoing, much more so than when Eve had first met him. She believed it had to do with Logan opening up to her about his wife and the lantern. It had helped to change and soften him; it had allowed them to bond in a small way. And although he didn't verbalize it, Eve sensed that Logan held out some meager hope that when she returned to the future, she might try to find his wife Kady.

Once everyone was inside the sleigh, and the bags were tied up behind the back seat, Logan climbed in, shook the reins, and they were off, Logan driving, Eve and Patrick in the front, and Maggie and Duncan in back.

The snowy landscape stretched out in smooth, undulating blankets of white, broken by tall groves of pine and hardwood trees. Thick, gray clouds were piling up on the horizon, revealing patches of blue sky. Eve spotted three deer loping off into the trees.

As Maggie took it all in, she fell in love with the quiet, spiritual land, with its bleak sublimity. The power of its desolate beauty helped soothe the storm that was still raging in her soul. It seemed a promised land to her, a place of peace and refuge. A place to renew herself, her body and spirit.

Now that Big Jim was dead, and she'd left New York and her theatrical career behind, what awaited her in this grandeur of land, where everything seemed magnified and blessed? What would she do here? Where would she go? And what about this man who claimed to be her father? How ridiculous, absurd, and yet exciting.

As Patrick had told his remarkable story, she'd watched him closely and seen the truth, the pain and the regret in his eyes. She'd also felt the goodness in his heart, and a warm and timeless connection to him—something she now realized she'd felt at their very first meeting.

Whoever Patrick was, and whatever time and place he'd come from, Maggie couldn't deny that he had saved her life. Patrick had saved her from Big Jim, whose rage and jealousy would one day have been ignited by a word, a rumor, a flirtation, or by her attempting another escape. When Patrick told her that unless she fled New York, Big Jim would kill her on Christmas Eve, she didn't doubt him. But what was she going to do now?

Duncan sat slumped, lost in his own miserable thoughts. He could not understand most of what had had happened to him. He had shot a man and killed another. They were bad men, yes, but as he reran the whole nightmare, it seemed as though it had been an imagined thing; an article he'd read in the newspaper; a dark play he'd seen in a New York theatre.

Surely, he didn't pull the trigger and shoot Big Jim in the head? And it had been the luckiest of shots. Duncan had only fired the revolver a few times at a shooting range on the Lower East Side. He was not a good shot, or an accurate one.

But if killing Big Jim seemed only a wild theatrical dream, then losing Irene was a real ache that cut him like a knife. Irene was not a dream. She was his own true love, and he had thought he was hers. She had told him many times, hadn't she? Hadn't she said they'd run off together and be the happiest of couples on this Earth?

Was she really so childish, materialistic and vacuous that she would leave him over money? Didn't love exalt all things, beareth all things, believeth all things, hopeth all things, endureth all things?

He had believed in their love with his whole heart, and he had believed Irene's true nature was mature, lofty and spiritual, not so tethered to the silly and mundane fear of losing all her family money. Duncan lowered his head and shut his eyes against the start of hot tears. How would he ever understand any woman, if he couldn't begin to comprehend his one true love, Irene Casterbury?

In the front seat, Eve leaned toward Patrick's ear and whispered.

"Did you tell Maggie everything?"

He nodded.

"She doesn't look happy."

"No. She's hardly said more than two words to me since then. She wouldn't join me in the café car for breakfast."

Eve wrapped her arm in his and pulled him close. "Detective Gantly, I have missed you. I don't like sleeping alone."

He patted her hand and, as his warm eyes came to hers, he whispered, "As my old Da used to say, 'A man without a spirited woman in his bed will never know the blessing of a good night's sleep.'"

Eve looked at him doubtfully. "Did your Da say that or did you just make it up?"

Patrick stared coyly. "Who cares who said it, Mrs. Gantly, if the verse is true?"

A slow, naughty smile creased Eve's lips and she whispered, "I'm feeling rather spirited right now."

Patrick winked. "We'll soon be home, my love. That is, if you have the lantern."

Eve turned from his gaze.

"Eve? *Do* you have the lantern?"

"…That would be a yes and a no."

Patrick scratched his head, blinking from sudden anxiety. "Well, all I can say, Mrs. Gantly, is that I hope the long road out will be the shortest road home."

"I'll explain everything when we have some privacy," Eve said. "And then I want to hear what happened to all of you back in New York."

Inside the cabin, Logan graciously offered Eve and Patrick his upstairs bedroom, Maggie the downstairs bedroom, and Duncan the bed in the garage, complete with a small stone fireplace. Logan insisted that he would be comfortable on the couch near the fire.

After everyone had settled in, Patrick and Eve closed themselves in their room. While Eve sat on the bed, Patrick paced and brought her up to date on everything that had happened. He reenacted the fight and flight from New York, as well describing his, and Maggie's, herculean effort to free the car from its snow trap.

Eve listened silently, her eyes fastened to him, turning sad when he told her Irene had returned to New York. He concluded his debriefing with an account of his talk with Maggie in the café car. Afterward, Patrick stopped pacing and Eve stood up. A moan of wind rounded the house.

Eve wrapped Patrick with her arms, pulling him in close. They rocked gently for a time, and Patrick dropped a kiss on her hair, as he often did. The gesture warmed and comforted her, making her very homesick for their sweet life way out there somewhere in 2018.

"I want to go home now, Patrick. Can we?"

He eased her back to face him, and she smiled up into his lovely eyes.

"What about the lantern, Eve? You said something about yes and no."

Eve's smiled faded. "It's been damaged. The glass panes are broken, and the burner is all bashed up."

"How? What happened?"

"It's a long story. I'll condense it. Ann is Logan's mother. Ann got the lantern from Jacob Jackson, and she gave it to Logan. His wife lit the lantern one night."

Patrick stiffened, cocking his head to the right, eyes widening. "And…?"

"She disappeared and has never been heard from again. When Ann told Logan about the lantern, they thought it would be their secret, but Logan's wife must have overheard the story."

Patrick's face dropped into deep concern. "A secret is not a secret if it is known by three people. The lantern can be fixed, can't it? I'm sure I can get it to work."

"Logan took it to his tool shed. He said he'd repair it."

"Logan? Do you trust him?"

"Yes…" she said, and then her voice dropped into doubt. "Yes, I think so."

"Eve, do you think he wants to use the thing to go find his wife?"

"No, we talked about that, and I told him there is no way to know where or to what time she landed in. Besides, he's joined the Canadian army. He's leaving in a few days."

"To fight in that terrible first world war?"

"Yes…"

"Did you try to talk him out of it? He won't survive it, Eve. You know how many men died in that hell of a war."

"No, I didn't try to talk him out of it. I didn't know what to say. I simply said that I know the war will last a long time. He said he didn't care. He just kept saying that he was going to do his bit. That he had to, for his own self-respect."

"Should I go talk to him then?" Patrick asked.

"I think you should talk to Maggie. I assume you have asked her to return to 2018 with us?"

Patrick's eyes dropped to the floor. "Not yet."

"You want her to return with us, don't you?"

He looked up. "Of course, Eve, but she has a strong will and I can't read her—what she thinks or how she feels."

"Okay then, so you two need to go off together and talk it all out. Get to know each other, Patrick. We've got to know what she wants to do."

Minutes later, Patrick descended the stairs, went to Maggie's room and knocked on the door.

"Who is it?" she called.

"It's Patrick."

The door opened, and Maggie appeared, wearing a woman's bathrobe Logan had left in the closet. She stood barefoot, with a defiant lift of her chin, staring at Patrick in a challenge. "What do you want?"

"Logan said I can borrow the sleigh and go for a ride. Will you come with me?"

"Why? Are you going to give me more fatherly advice? Anyway, I was about to take a bath. Do you know there is an honest-to-goodness bathtub in this bathroom? Logan told me his wife refused to marry him unless she had a bathtub. What do you think about that, father?"

Patrick ignored the snide comment. "I just want to talk to you, Maggie. I want us to spend some time together, get to know each other. Will you please take a ride with me?"

Her eyes held him for a time, as if seeking answers, and then they drifted away toward the knotty pine walls. She unconsciously touched the nape of her neck as she composed the right words.

"How old are you?"

"Thirty-six."

"Tell me about my mother, Pauline. How did you meet her? Did you love her?"

"Not here, Maggie. Not now. Let's take that ride. I will tell you everything you want to know."

Maggie hesitated, tapping a foot. "You know, Big Jim's men could show up at any minute."

"I don't think so, Maggie, and if they do, I'll deal with it. Now, will you please take that sleigh ride with me? Please?"

Maggie massaged the back of her neck while she regarded him. "All right...father," she said, sarcastically. "Why not?"

CHAPTER 40

Maggie was wrapped in a warm blanket seated next to her father. As they glided through the snow, the sounds of tingling sleigh bells comforted her, despite her edgy mood. She inhaled several breaths, gradually feeling joyfully alive in the spectacular scenery, her senses arrested by the natural beauty and crisp, clean air.

It had taken Patrick nearly a half hour to answer all of Maggie's questions: how he and Pauline had met; why they parted; why he never appeared. He tried to tie up all the loose ends and he watched, pained, as Maggie wept silent tears. He repeated how sick he'd felt when he'd read her obituary, and how she'd been murdered.

"I had to come back, Maggie. I couldn't have lived with myself if I hadn't taken the chance to come back and save your life."

Maggie had sat in silence for long minutes, allowing the sun to warm her face. Patrick often shielded his eyes from the glare of the snow as they trotted through a canopy of snow-heavy trees, passing open land and frozen ponds.

When Maggie finally spoke, her voice was soft, her expression calm. The accusation and bitterness were gone.

"What I find hard to believe is that Eve risked her life to come back with you."

"Yes, well Eve is a unique and special woman. She is a rare gem. I tried to leave her behind, but she wouldn't hear of it. She said we are married, and we will stick together no matter what happens."

Maggie smiled at him. "How lovely that is, Patrick. So, you are a romantic man, aren't you?"

Patrick shook the reigns to coax the horse up a slight hill. "I'm not innately so. I think Eve has made me so."

"You're lucky, you know. Everyone wants to find that blessed kind of love you and Eve have."

"In the future they call us soulmates," Patrick said.

Maggie pondered that. "Soulmates? Oh, I like that. Yes, I like that very much. I must use it if I'm ever lucky enough to find my soulmate."

Patrick glanced over with a loving smile. "You will, Maggie. I'm sure of it. Now that your dark past is behind you, you are free to cast your life in an entirely different and happier direction."

Maggie nodded. Her gaze was direct and speculative. "What I find utterly fascinating is that you wouldn't have met Eve if she hadn't time traveled to 1885."

"Yes, we often talk about that, but the conversation becomes a dead-end street, usually ending with the realization that the world is a much more mysterious and complex place than either of us could have ever imagined."

"What is it really like in the future, in 2018? Are people happier? Healthier? Prettier? Richer? They must be."

"Just like in any time, Maggie, some people are all those things, but many are not. There are so many fast things in the future, Maggie. So many little gadgets, or electronic devices they call them, and they constantly try to lure you away from yourself, distracting you and, frankly, at times irritating you."

Patrick indicated toward the quiet winter scene unraveling before them. "It is difficult to find this kind of peaceful silence in the future, Maggie. Everything in that time is so fast and impatient. Air machines zip through the skies at incredible speeds and cars whiz by faster than you can imagine, and nearly every place of business you enter has this loud and thumping music playing. I feel like those people are at war with silence. They want noise and distraction every minute of every day."

"Then you don't like it?"

"Like with most things, Maggie, the answer is a yes and a no. I will be honest with you, but please don't tell Eve. I sometimes long for my own time, back in 1885. Sometimes, I feel a bit lost and out of place. Well, let's face it. I am, at heart, body and soul, a 19th-century man who finds himself on an entirely new planet. But don't misunderstand me. There are many good and kind people in the future—people who work courageously and unselfishly to improve the world, and I believe they are doing so. But let me tell you one remarkable thing: they have the most amazing medicine. They have pills that cure almost everything... any infection or disease."

Maggie's head slipped to one side. "And what of New York, Patrick? What is it like in the future? Do you think I would like it?"

"Yes, Maggie, you would love it. Despite all the clang and crush of the traffic and the rushing of the crowds, there is a tempting magic to the City, even in the boisterous and flashy Times Square, a Times Square you cannot even imagine." Patrick became more assertive. "Yes, Maggie, I am sure you will like it. I think you might even take to all of it much more than I and be quite at home there."

Patrick waited for Maggie to comment, but she stayed silent.

As Logan's cabin gradually came into view and a flock of birds sailed over the distant trees, Maggie turned to her father. Many questions were still bursting inside her.

"Patrick...I need to think about all this. I feel as though I'm on a carnival ride, with bright lights and bells and strange contorted faces whirling by. I feel both breathlessly free and hopelessly scared and confused."

"Of course, Maggie. Of course, you need time. I understand. Even after living in the future for nearly two years, I still find myself disoriented and misplaced. Without Eve's love and understanding, I fear I might not make it. But I think you will adjust better than I, faster and more easily than I, Maggie. You're an actress, and even in 2018, New York City is filled with theatres, and there are things called television and movies that you cannot even conceive of but will offer you endless possibilities to display your looks and talent. Yes, I think you will fit in just fine there."

In the late afternoon, Eve napped, giving the others the opportunity to prepare for a secret birthday celebration for her. Patrick had quietly spread the word earlier in the day and encouraged her to rest for a few hours. Maggie immediately went to work in the kitchen, helping Logan prepare smoked meat, beans cooked in maple syrup, peameal bacon, and a butter tart. Neither Maggie, Duncan nor Patrick had ever heard of peameal bacon, so Logan explained.

"It used to be my father's favorite breakfast food," he said while he cut thin slices and placed them in a hot pan. "It's made from lean boneless pork loin cured in maple brine, then it's rolled in cornmeal."

While Patrick helped Maggie finish up in the kitchen, Logan led Duncan outside, where they cut down a six-foot spruce tree and gathered bright red-orange winterberry fruit, evergreen branches and pinecones.

After the Christmas tree was up and Duncan was working on making a wreath and a centerpiece, Logan went to the garage and came back carrying several four-inch red tissue bells, a foot-high glass figurine of Santa Claus that didn't resemble the modern image of Santa, and a box containing several Victorian Christmas ornaments that would adorn the spruce tree.

After the sun had settled over the snowy trees, a sleepy-eyed Eve descended the stairs, having been awakened by the heavenly kitchen aromas. The living room glowed with a fresh fire that colored the walls yellow and orange, and a table centerpiece made of winterberry and evergreen scented the room with the smells of Christmas.

Patrick and Logan had just finished hanging a burlap Happy Birthday banner above the hearth, and just as Eve left the last step, Patrick burst into *Happy Birthday*. The others joined in, all off key except Maggie, whose voice rose smooth and mellow, ending with a high, dramatic flourish.

In bright surprise and delight, Eve clapped enthusiastically as she took in the decorations and the festive table setting. Patrick mounted the first step to stand tall and make an announcement.

"Mrs. Eve Gantly, even though your birthday is technically tomorrow, December 17th, we have decided to celebrate tonight, since we will be leaving tomorrow."

And then they surrounded her with kisses and congratulations.

As they arranged themselves around the table, Maggie and Duncan insisted on being waitress and waiter. They started by filling everyone's wine glass with Logan's homemade blackberry wine.

Everyone ate voraciously, laughed easily and recapped their escape stories. Only Duncan remained largely quiet, although even he laughed when Maggie recounted how she had jumped up and down and cursed at that stubborn back tire.

They toasted Logan for his great food, wine and hospitality, and he blushed, although he seemed genuinely touched by their tributes.

For his part, he was enjoying himself more than he had in many months, forgetting, for a time, about his wife's disappearance and the war in Europe. He toasted his guests, generously announcing that they could stay as long as they wished.

The butter tart was served with strong black tea and a jug of homemade apple cider, and after another round of *Happy Birthday*, Eve got up and thanked everyone for one of the most fun and memorable birthdays she'd ever had. And then her eyes strayed toward Logan's hanging violin. She turned to Logan and pointed.

"Do you play, Logan?"

He lowered his eyes. "Not so well, Mrs. Gantly. I haven't' played in a long time."

"Would you mind playing a little waltz so that I can have a birthday dance with my husband?"

Without another word, Logan arose and went for his violin.

"Well, you will get what you pay for," he said, carefully removing the violin from the secure brackets. All waited and watched as Logan handled the instrument lovingly, tuning it, plucking the strings with a close ear and running the bow across the strings until he was satisfied it was tuned.

He stood tall and straight as he announced his selection, the golden glow of the fire bathing him. "All right, then, it just so happens that I do know a waltz. I shall play *Destiny Waltz* by Sydney Baynes."

Poised and ready, Logan began, the bow sweeping down and dancing gently upon the strings.

Eve reached a hand to Patrick and, with a tender smile, he took her hand and led her to the middle of the room. They swayed easily, finding the rhythm and soon falling into a slow, easy turn, circling the room, dipping and whirling as the melody lifted spirits and brought smiles. From the table where Maggie and Duncan still sat, they tapped their feet and fingers.

Within a few moments, Maggie had Duncan on the floor joining the dance, their technique and style polished and lilting, bringing a bright smile to everyone's lips.

When Logan started a second waltz, a cheerful melody called *Hearts Longing*, Maggie touched Eve on the shoulder. "Do you mind, Mrs. Gantly, if I dance with my young and handsome father?"

Eve bowed and retreated. Maggie and Patrick stood silently for a time, looking long and steady at each other before Patrick finally took her hand. She placed her other hand on his shoulder and soon they were off, waltzing about the room, Patrick all grins and pleasure. Maggie's head was arched back in sophistication, her lithe body moving in grace, her face serene, her burgundy dress swaying.

Eve and Duncan joined in, and the night was filled with the perfect pitch of romance, enjoyment, dancing and good hearts.

At some point, as exhaustion was settling in, Logan took another swig of cider and got a second wind. He grabbed his violin and struck up a lively song. The fiddle sprang to life with an Irish jig in 6/8 time.

To Eve's great surprise, Patrick leaped to his feet and began to dance in a series of hops, steps and turns. He was absolutely magnificent. She'd never seen him dance so expertly or with such energy and enthusiasm. Maggie soon joined him, skipping along, hair bouncing, her agile feet rarely leaving the ground for long. Eve watched the two of them dance and her heart opened. Patrick and Maggie had finally joined as father and daughter, and Eve had never seen her husband so happy.

Logan caught the fever, and his fiddle exploded to life, the bow a blur of movement, his face filled with delight.

Eve grabbed Duncan and soon they were flying off in quick breaths, caught with elation, hands clapping loud and sharp. The room was riotous with the spirit of the dance as they hopped, arched and swayed and, for a time, the world was a good and loving place, where good hearts joined and would always be joined.

After the clean-up, though all were fatigued and sleepy, they finished the night seated around the fire, with Logan again playing his violin. They joined in singing Christmas carols, ending with the reverent *Silent Night*.

Near dawn, Eve awoke with a start, having felt Patrick leave the bed. She lifted on elbows. "Can't sleep?"

"Eve... the last time we used that lantern, it set us down in two different places and in two different times. There's no guarantee the thing will take us back home."

"No, Patrick, there is no guarantee. But we must try to get back home."

"It's just that I'm afraid for you and Maggie."

"Are you sure she wants to come with us?"

"Of course, I'm sure. Her life as she knows it has ended in this time. She'll get a brand-new start in our time, and I know she'll fit right in."

Eve sat up and leaned back against the headboard, wanting to change the subject.

"Thank you for my beautiful birthday necklace. I'm going to pack it in my security belt just in case."

"Do you like it? I found it in an old shop in the Village."

"Of course, I like it. I love the amethyst opal."

"I've been thinking. If for whatever reason the lantern doesn't return us, we could make a good life in this country. It's a vast and good country, I think."

Eve crossed her arms. "Logan said he'd have the lantern ready for us in the morning. He said he'd get up early and work on it."

"He's a good man, Eve. I like him. I wish he would come with us as well, instead of going off to fight in that terrible war."

Eve fell into silent thoughts, as worried as Patrick about the lantern, if it would work and where it would leave them if it did.

CHAPTER 41

Logan sat slumped at the kitchen table, the lantern and a mug of coffee before him. Eve approached in an olive day dress, her hand covering a yawn. Patrick had gone back to sleep, but she couldn't, so she got up.

"Good morning, Logan," she said. "Thanks again for letting us invade your place. I had such a good time last night."

Logan was quiet. He didn't respond or stir. Her eyes were stuck to the lantern. It had been completely repaired. The glass panes had been replaced, the wire guards straightened, the burner repaired, the wick new and visible. It had been buffed and polished to its original rich green/brown patina. The anchor design on each side of the roof was as sharp and clear as Eve had ever seen it.

In a wonder, Eve sat to Logan's right and reached to touch it. "It's remarkable, Logan. It looks new."

Logan's eyes were red-rimmed, and they had a vacant, weary look.

"Are you feeling okay, Logan?"

His stare remained fixed on the lantern. When he spoke, his tone was rusty and breathy, with a faraway quality. "What is the origin of this lantern?"

"I don't really know, Logan. It was taken from the rear axil of a wagon in 1885 during a snowstorm. A woman took it to help a man out of an overturned carriage. I found it in an antique store in 2016. That's all I know about it."

Logan kept boring into it with his eyes. "I almost destroyed the lantern last night. I had the hammer in my hand, and I was going to bash it into pieces and bury them out in the trees where no one would ever find them."

Eve folded her hands on the table. "Why didn't you, Logan? What stopped you?"

"Who can understand it? How can I understand how it is that this worthless old lantern took my wife from me? It makes no sense. Is it an evil thing or a good thing?"

He finally pulled his eyes from it and looked at her. "Mrs. Gantly, Eve, can you explain it to me?"

"I can't, Logan. I don't know."

"When you return to your own time, will you promise me that you'll try to find my Kady?"

Eve saw the painful force of his gaze.

"Will you please try to find her?"

Eve had decided that when they returned home, she would toss the lantern in the Hudson River and be done with it. She wanted no more time travel.

Eve squirmed.

"Will you please, Eve?"

"Logan, we have no way of knowing where Kady went. You asked me if the lantern is evil. I don't think so. It seems to have some kind of strange otherworldly intelligence. It seems to take a person where they need to go, and not always where they want or wish to go. Chances are, your wife landed in some other time and place that has some personal meaning for her. I doubt if she would have ever thought about traveling to New York City in 2018."

Logan turned thoughtful, his face haunted. He turned left and reached for a magazine cover that had been carefully cut from the body of the magazine. He handed it to Eve.

"I found this placed on top of Kady's private trunk. She had always talked about how much she wanted to travel to New York."

Eve took the cover, apprehensively. It was the 1914 popular magazine, *New York Illustrated*, featuring a colorful panorama of lower Manhattan taken from the Brooklyn Bridge tower. On the left was the tallest building in the world, The Woolworth Building. To the right was the 40 story Municipal Building. It also showed the waterfront, South Street with its docks and shipping activity that was the hub of maritime New York.

Logan waited for Eve to lift her eyes. "You see... Well, I thought that maybe Kady was thinking about New York just before she'd vanished, and since that lantern had taken you to 2016, maybe it took her as well."

Eve laid the cover aside. "All right, Logan, when we return—if we return—I will do some searching and, if by some chance Kady did travel to our time, I'll try to contact her."

That seemed to satisfy him, and he managed a tight smile. "Thank you, Eve. Thank you for that. You see, I keep thinking that maybe she got into some trouble and she needs my help. She wouldn't have any money or friends—no one to help her if things went wrong. Maybe she wants to come back home, but she has no way of accomplishing it."

"Okay, Logan. I'll do what I can."

His eyes came to hers and he smiled gratefully. "Thank you. I am truly grateful to you."

As the fire hissed and crackled, Logan's smile fell away. "According to what you told me yesterday, after you and the others have, well, gone into the future, the lantern will remain with me, will it not?"

He seemed to steal the thought from her brain. "Yes, Logan. You know how important it is that it doesn't fall into the wrong hands. If the wrong person got the lantern, they could use it in the wrong way... Well, you understand."

"Yes, I have thought about that. I thought about what might happen if I were to give it to our military. Perhaps it would help end this war before it grows worse."

Eve shot to her feet. "Logan, you can't do that. It could change history and the entire balance of the world."

"Haven't you and your husband already changed history?"

Eve stared at him. "Yes... but we can only hope it won't change things too dramatically. If the military got ahold of it..."

Her voice trailed off. "You know what could happen."

Logan pulled the lantern closer to him. "So maybe I should destroy it then."

They heard a voice behind them. "No, don't do that."

Eve and Logan turned to Maggie. She approached the table, wearing a long white gown, her creamy skin glowing, her hair piled high on her head, looking very much like a sleepy goddess.

Maggie's complete attention was focused on the lantern. "Logan, the lantern is yours, given to you by your mother. It is yours to keep, yours to give and yours to destroy. If you don't wish to keep it, then I ask that you give it to me."

Eve didn't stir.

Maggie rested her soft almond eyes on Eve. "Eve, I'm not going with you and Patrick."

Eve noticed Patrick standing at the top of the stairs. She could tell by his worried expression that he had heard Maggie's decision.

"I don't understand," Patrick said.

Maggie pivoted. Their eyes met. "I'm not of your time, Patrick. I don't want to jump into the future. My life is already topsy-turvy, and my head is reeling from the last weeks. I have to find a new home, a new career and a new way to live, but I want to do it in this time. In my time. It's a time and a world I know. I want the natural progression of my life in this time, and not in yours."

Patrick struggled to hide his anguish. Not only was he disappointed at the thought of losing Maggie but, Eve knew, in many ways he felt the same way. Had he been given the choice, he certainly would have stayed in 1885. But he'd been denied that opportunity. If Eve had not brought him to 2016 New York, where he could receive antibiotics, he would have died.

Maggie started for her father, pausing at the base of the stairs. "Patrick, you understand, don't you?"

Patrick stood still and tall, hands on his hips. "So after finding you, I'm going to lose you again?"

"No. You saved my life. You freed me to choose my own way. Isn't that what you intended to do?"

Patrick didn't speak.

"Patrick…I made a mess of my life in the past, but I'll be better and wiser in the future."

Under Patrick's thoughtful gaze, she smiled coquettishly. "And how would I ever explain you to my friends in the future? Yes, this is my father. Yes, I know, he is very young to be my father; he is only seven years older than I. How do I explain it? I can't, can I? I'm 29 years old and you are 36."

Maggie looked at him lovingly. "You have given me life twice, father. You and Eve risked your lives to save me from certain death. Thank you. I will be grateful to you forever. But now I must live that newly-given life in my own way."

Maggie turned to Logan. "About the lantern. Logan, I know you're about to leave for war. If I can be so bold, and if you can be so generous, I would like to have the lantern. I mean, what if I change my mind and decide to travel to see my father in the future?"

Logan slowly pushed up. "I understand your implication, Maggie. If I am killed, there is no way of knowing who might take possession of the lantern. Yes, I've thought about that."

Maggie took steps toward him. "I hope and pray you will not be killed, Logan. And I hope we stay in touch and that we will correspond and stay the best of friends."

"I would like that, Maggie. I would like that very much."

Eve got up, glancing back toward the garage. "What should we do about Duncan? He doesn't know anything about the lantern."

Patrick descended the stairs. "I don't think he *should* know. The fewer who know, the better."

"I'll send him to the General Store for supplies," Logan said.

"When he comes back, won't he be curious as to where we've gone?" Eve asked.

Maggie spoke up. "We'll tell him friends came for you. Don't worry. I'm an actress, I'll convince him. Anyway, we're all going to be leaving today, right? Duncan and I talked about it last night. We've decided to travel together."

"To where?" Patrick asked.

"Somewhere west. Perhaps to Winnipeg or Saskatchewan, or even Alberta. Just like all of you are about to do, Duncan and I will be off on a journey to begin our new lives. Isn't it exciting?"

Duncan joined them for a breakfast of bread and butter, tea and oatmeal. The conversation was muted. Duncan noticed and asked why everyone had lost their good cheer from the previous night.

Eve answered, "Maybe we all had a little too much spirit, Duncan."

After breakfast, Logan and Duncan prepared the horse for the ride to the General Store, and as Duncan was about to jump into the sleigh, Eve rushed out, gave him a hug and kissed him on the cheek. "Goodbye, Duncan," she whispered. "Be careful."

Duncan was surprised by her gesture. "No need to worry about me," he said. "I'll be back in a couple of hours. I've driven many a sleigh in our Massachusetts winters."

Eve stood outside on the porch, watching the sleigh dwindle in size and slowly disappear into the glare of snow. When she returned inside, Patrick and Maggie were in a father/daughter embrace.

An hour later, Eve and Patrick were ready to go. Maggie and Logan were waiting, tentative and nervous. Logan lifted the lantern by its wire handle and turned to face the others.

"We should proceed before Duncan returns. Of course, I don't know where you will arrive in 2018, but I suggest we walk back into the trees and light the lantern there. Chances are, in a hundred years or so, the trees will still be there."

Eve wore a woolen dress and a trim winter coat, Patrick a dark suit, minus the tie, with his greatcoat. They hoped their wardrobes would not be conspicuous in 2018.

The four left the cabin and tramped off through virgin snow to a level area just outside a grove of trees. It overlooked a meadow and a distant lake skimmed with ice, flashing under the bright morning sun.

Logan handed the lantern to Patrick.

"This is as good a place as any."

"Give it to Eve, Logan. I trust her luck better than mine."

Logan nodded, and Maggie came forward, crunching through the eight inches of snow to bid her father farewell.

"Safe journey," she said.

"And you, my dear Maggie. I will wait for you in the future."

She stood on tiptoes and kissed him on the cheek. Then she embraced Eve and thanked her.

Maggie and Logan backed away thirty feet, according to Eve's instructions.

Eve turned to Patrick. "All right, Detective Sargent Gantly. After I light this thing, we are going to embrace, and hold that embrace. This time, we're not going to be separated."

Patrick grinned. "Yes, Miss Kennedy. Whatever you say."

The first match fizzled. The second was blown out in the fast wind. The third reached the lantern's wick and caught. Patrick pulled Eve into his arms and they embraced in the lantern's swelling radiance.

There was a whirring sound, like a small motor. Golden light expanded into a cone of brilliance, and Maggie and Logan looked on in amazed wonder. Logan stepped back further. Maggie took a step forward, hypnotized by the rich, buttery light.

Her eyes widened in shock as the light engulfed Eve and Patrick, swirling around them in a storm of rainbow colors. Enthralled, Maggie moved closer as the couple, still in an embrace, dissolved into a towering blaze of blue and gold that shot high into the sky.

And then they were gone, and the light extinguished as if snuffed out, golden smoke curling, rising high up into the trees, vanishing into the rich blue sky.

Logan was frozen, trapped in disbelief and utter terror.

Hypnotized, Maggie started toward the lantern, now dark and silent. She hovered over it for a time, staring in rapt wonder. Finally, she gathered the courage to reach for it. She touched it and drew back. She reached again, took the handle and lifted it. It was heavy in her hand and she could still feel the warmth.

She turned back to Logan, who trembled.

"I hope they made it back home, Logan."

CHAPTER 42

Eve awoke with a start, her eyes flipping open when she heard the female flight attendant's voice over the intercom, announcing the final approach into New York's LaGuardia Airport. Was Eve dreaming?

She blinked around in dazed astonishment. The seat next to her was empty. Where was Patrick? What time was she in? She was about to spring out of her seat in panic when Patrick appeared, dropped into the seat beside her and refastened his seatbelt, looking at her.

"Are you all right?"

"Where were you?"

"The bathroom. You sure you're okay?"

Eve swallowed, readjusted herself in the chair and slowly eased back into her seat.

She took Patrick's hand. "Yes… I'm okay."

She gazed outside the window to see the magnificent Manhattan skyline slide by.

"Bad dream?" Patrick asked.

"Yeah... I was back in 1914, and we were being chased by four very ugly men down dark alleys."

"It's going to take a while for our bodies to adjust, just like the last time. I'm feeling a bit shaky myself, like part of me is still lingering somewhere in 1914."

They held hands as the airplane descended and Eve closed her eyes, replaying yet again the events of the day before—her birthday—December 17, 2018.

After she'd lit the lantern, they were seized and then flung into tunnels of blue light. They sailed and tumbled through currents of cold and heat and streams of golden light. Through all the turbulence, they'd clung to each other, holding tight and never letting go.

Eventually, they'd burst through a flash of white light to find themselves standing in snow on the edge of a grove of trees. As they recovered, Patrick pointed toward a three-bedroom bungalow about 40 feet away.

Disoriented and weak, they'd stumbled down an incline to a car that sat in the driveway. They needed confirmation about time and place. The license plate told them they were back in 2018. Relieved, Eve turned away, while Patrick gave cover. She unfastened her dress, reached into her security belt and retrieved her credit card and bank card. After placing them in her small leather purse, Patrick took her hand and led her to the bungalow's front door.

The doorbell "bonged." A minute later, a heavyset man in his 30s cautiously opened the door and peered out, looking them up and down, his eyes wary.

Patrick smiled and said, "Sorry to bother you. Would you mind calling us a taxi? We seem to have lost our way and our cellphones."

Although the man pulled his cell phone out and placed the call, he didn't converse or invite them in. Eve and Patrick waited at the end of the walkway until the taxi arrived, aware that the man was watching from behind his brown living room curtains.

The taxi driver recommended the Quality Inn, and he drove them there through a dancing snowfall. Eve and Patrick spent the rest of the day buying clothes, a suitcase and toiletries at the local mall, and then burrowing themselves in their hotel room, resting and making travel plans to fly from Toronto to New York.

When Eve called Joni from the hotel phone, it jumped into voicemail. Eve left a message, relieved that Joni's number was the same and that she was still around.

That night they hardly slept, both feeling loopy, weak and worried about what they might find when they returned to their New York apartment.

The hydraulic sound of the landing gear lowering brought Eve back to the present. The airplane descended from low clouds and drifted over the flat gray East River, hovering for seconds above the runway before touching down.

Eve and Patrick exchanged relieved glances.

"We made it, Eve. We're home."

As the taxi drove along West 125th Street, Eve noticed holiday flavor was in the air, from Christmas decorations on street lamps to blinking lights in store windows, to sidewalk Christmas tree stands.

"Let's get a Christmas tree tonight," she said to Patrick.

As they approached West 107th Street, Eve could feel her muscles tense up. Patrick's jaw was set, and she knew that meant he too was nervous.

The taxi drew up to the curb and Eve stared out apprehensively. The last time she had arrived home from time travel, the location of her apartment had disturbingly been altered from the second floor to the third floor. Her dog, Georgy Boy, had changed from being white with black spots to being white with large brown spots, and his ears were totally brown. Had anything changed this time?

After the taxi drove away, the couple stared up at the brownstone to the bay windows of their third-floor apartment.

"Ready?" Eve asked, inhaling a breath.

Patrick lifted the carry-on bag and they started up the cement stairs. Inside, they mounted the stairs to the third floor. Eve took in another quick breath before she inserted the key and turned the knob. The door swung open into an apartment that was just as they had left it.

They wandered the rooms, searching for any clues of change. There were none. Everything was exactly as they'd left it.

Eve met Patrick's eyes. "Nothing has changed."

"Except us," Patrick said.

"Now all we need is Georgy Boy, and everything will be back to normal. Joni will probably bring him over in a couple of hours."

And then they fell into each other's arms and stayed there for a long time, just happy to be safe and home again.

Two hours later, when Eve opened the door to see Georgy Boy and Joni, she was shaken to her very core.

Georgy Boy burst into the room, charging into Patrick's arms. He barked and leaped and circled, his tongue wild and wagging. He swam about Eve's legs, the same dog as when they'd left.

But there was something that had changed—and changed dramatically.

Eve stared hard at Joni, who stared back, perplexed. When Joni entered the room and shut the door behind her, Patrick slowly rose from his crouched position rubbing Georgy Boy's head. His big eyes were riveted on Joni. He tried to swallow, but he couldn't.

"What's the matter with you two?" she asked. "You're looking at me as if I'd just dropped in from another planet."

Patrick and Eve exchanged worried glances.

Joni had always been tall, with jet-black hair, snow-white skin, and dark blue eyes. Her voice had always been rather low and resonate.

This Joni—the one she and Patrick were looking at now—was changed. She was shorter, with wide hips and long, shockingly beautiful red hair, styled in a flip. She had sharp green eyes and cute freckles. This Joni's voice was rather high in pitch, definitely a soprano, and not the contralto she'd always been. Eve had heard the difference on the phone, but she hadn't given it any thought.

Eve couldn't find her voice. Joni was a different person: her expression, the set of her mouth, and yet, there was also something familiar. It was weird and disconcerting.

Joni lifted her hands and then dropped them. "So, what's going on? Why are you both looking at me like that? I'm the one who should be looking at you. Patrick has lost weight and you, Eve, have cut your hair and dyed it. Not the best color for you. It washes you out. Anyway, don't just stand there gawking at me, give me a hug."

Eve staggered forward mechanically and hugged her old and now-new friend.

After Joni hugged Patrick, she slipped out of her coat and surveyed the apartment. "Well, has anything changed like the last time? Is Georgy Boy a different color? Is the apartment the same?"

Joni draped her coat on the back of the couch and waited. Eve managed a nod.

"Everything is... well, basically the same," Eve said, woodenly.

Patrick struggled for words. "So how is the acting business, Joni?"

Joni folded her arms, cocked her head left and studied him. "Acting? What acting?"

"You know, acting? Auditions. Any new shows coming up?" Patrick asked.

Joni shrugged. "Patrick, I haven't been to an audition in four years."

Eve controlled the urge to scream. What was going on? She forced herself to stay calm. "Well, then, Joni, what are you doing?"

Joni dropped her arms. "Okay, you two are really starting to freak me out here. I'm a massage therapist, and I have been a massage therapist for three years, okay? I gave you both massages before you left, remember? You were both all stressed out about the time travel thing. What's happened to you two? You look, I don't know, different somehow."

Eve absorbed a wave of dread. "Joni... Something has happened. I don't know how to say this but...you're not the same as when we left. You look different. Your voice is different, and you were never a massage therapist. You were an actress who worked part-time at some camera rental house that rented cameras and lenses to Indie filmmakers."

All three stood as still as statues. Georgy Boy, feeling the stress, barked.

Long, painful minutes later, Joni gathered up her coat and slipped it on. At the door she turned back to them, her expression sad.

"I don't know what's happened to you both but call me when you wake up from whatever weird freakin' dream you're having. I'll be around."

Eve spoke up. "Joni... do you have the lantern?"

Joni stared at her old friend, estimating the scene. "Yes, I have it. I assume you want it back?"

"Yes, Joni...And I want us to meet to talk about all this."

Joni stared at them defiantly. "Hey, maybe I'll go home and light the lantern and return to the world we were all living in before you left—before you got all crazy. I haven't changed, okay? You two have. Well, whatever. I'm outta here."

After she was gone, Eve slowly and reluctantly went to the window and parted the curtains. As a light snow fell, she watched Joni march off down the street. Her energetic walk was the same walk as before; her shoulders back, her self-assured head held high. But it was not the same Joni. Eve shut her eyes, feeling nauseous. What else had changed?

EPILOGUE

On Christmas Eve morning, Eve and Patrick slept in until 10 a.m. Patrick had been up late doing additional research about Duncan Beaumont. It had been an ongoing project for days.

Still in the pink silk pajamas that Patrick had bought her for her birthday, Eve padded off to the kitchen to make coffee. Patrick soon followed, in sweatpants and a red T-shirt. He sat on a counter stool and booted up the laptop, clearly an aspect of technology that he'd grown attached to.

"So, did you find more info on Duncan last night?" Eve asked.

"Yes, I wanted to fit all the pieces together before I told you."

Eve leaned back against the counter. "But in all your research, you still haven't been able to find out anything about what happened to Maggie or Logan?"

Patrick shook his head. "No… I may have to go to Canada for that. I can't find anything on the internet. I've searched everywhere."

"So what have you found on Duncan?"

Patrick clicked through the links until he came to the one he was looking for.

"Okay, here it is," he said, eagerly. "Do you want me to read or just sum it up for you?"

"A little of both. Just don't leave out anything important."

"All right," Patrick said, pointing at the screen. "Duncan Beaumont ended up in Chicago, working as an illustrator, creating a vast portfolio of work for magazines and advertisers. He was also a landscape artist who, in later years, produced large canvasses revealing the changing face of Chicago, from the stockyards and the Southside to the dawn of the skyscrapers. In 1962, he was commissioned to paint 'Murals of Western Progress' for the Los Angeles Public Library. As of 2015, his paintings were being sold for more than $500,000 each."

"Well, what do you know? Impressive."

"There's more. His work was championed by none other than Irene Wilkes Casterbury Morgan."

Eve pushed away from the counter, leaning in toward the laptop screen.

"Irene?"

"Yes, *our* Irene. Irene was responsible for putting Duncan in contact with the influential art crowd in Chicago. She helped support him financially and through commissions until he made a name for himself."

Eve nosed in. "Irene married Morgan?"

Patrick pointed. "Yes, Winston Capshaw Morgan, the man her mother wanted her to marry."

"Wow… So Irene did love Duncan."

"That was easy to see, wasn't it?"

"I wonder if they ever met in Chicago?"

"I would assume so, since her husband had business interests in Chicago. Surely Irene traveled there from time to time."

"What did he do?"

"He was a banker and land speculator. He was worth millions."

"So Irene married the money."

"Yes, but it seems her heart was always with Duncan."

"How long did she live, Patrick?"

Patrick searched. "Yes, here it is. Irene Wilkes Casterbury Morgan died of cancer in 1943."

"She was so young."

"Yes, only 57."

"How sad. And what about Duncan? How long did he live?"

"Duncan married, had two children, a girl and a boy, and lived to the ripe old age of 76, passing away peacefully in his sleep in 1967."

Eve stared thoughtfully. "He had a good long life then."

After the kettle whistled and hissed, Eve hurried over, switched off the gas flame and poured the steaming water into the red coffee filter cone.

"Patrick, has anyone responded to our query about Kady Tyler?"

"No. And I've checked *Facebook*, *Linked*, *Instagram*. On *Facebook*, I found a photographer with the name, but she is not our Kady Tyler. There are a few others, but none have responded except one who spelled her name with a T. She wanted to know if I was married."

Eve turned, playfully annoyed. "And?"

"I told her I was quite single, and she should contact me as soon as possible."

Eve shook her head. "If I wasn't so far away, I'd slap you."

As they ate scrambled eggs and toast, Eve noticed the faraway look in Patrick's eyes.

"You'll find Maggie, Patrick. If we need to go to Canada, we will. I'm sure we'll be able to find out what happened to her there."

Patrick set his admiring eyes on her. "A lucky man I am, Eve, to have found you. You are quite the adventuress, my darling lass."

"Don't you have some kind of saying for this moment, Patrick? Something your old Da used to say?"

Patrick sipped at his coffee. "Just this. Home is where the heart is, Eve, so my home will always be wherever you are."

Eve melted a little, feeling the sincere warmth of his love. She smiled. "You are a real charmer, Detective Sergeant Gantly, and a sentimentalist. Who would have thought—a superhero sentimentalist."

Patrick grinned. "Well, I will admit that I often shed a tear or two whenever I hear the song *Molly Malone*."

That evening, as snow fell outside, and Christmas music played from the living room speakers, Patrick and Eve were layering up to go sledding in Riverside Park.

"I still haven't heard back from Joni," Eve said. "I've called and texted. I'm getting worried. And she still has the lantern."

"You should go see her. We need to get that lantern back."

"How could she have changed like that, Patrick? I know I keep talking about it, but it just weirds me out. I mean, she sort of looks like the old Joni, but then again, she doesn't. And what is this about her being a massage therapist?"

Patrick tugged on his winter boots and laced them up. "Let's face it, Eve, we changed the world back there, in small ways, and maybe in ways we'll never know. Perhaps we altered Joni's ancestors' destiny in some way. Maybe an ancestor lived who would have died, and vice versa—one died who would have lived. We just can't know."

"Then what world have we returned to, Patrick? It can't be the same world we left."

Patrick sat back with a sigh. "No, Eve, but it's the only world we've got."

Just then, the doorbell rang.

Eve turned to Patrick. "Who's that?"

Patrick shrugged.

Eve left the couch, went to the hall speaker and pressed the call/answer button. "Who is it?"

"It's Maggie."

Eve froze. "What? Who?"

"Maggie Kering. I'm here to see Eve and Patrick Gantly…"

"Who is it?" Patrick asked, now standing, seeing Eve's startled expression.

Eve shrugged and pushed the button. "She said her name is Maggie Kering."

Eve and Patrick were standing by the open door, looking out, when a woman in her fifties climbed the stairs to the third floor, turned left and saw the couple waiting for her, their faces filled with strained curiosity.

"Hello, I'm Maggie Kering," the woman said, breathless. "I guess the stairs are good for exercise."

"I'm sorry," Eve said. "The elevator is out of order. It seems to go out of order a lot."

Eve received the woman with a tentative smile, and Patrick stepped aside to let her in.

Patrick closed the door, and then Eve and Patrick stood patiently, awaiting an explanation.

Maggie studied the couple. "You are Eve and Patrick Gantly, are you not?"

"Yes," Patrick said.

Maggie smiled with some relief. "Well, I'm glad of that."

"Can I take your coat?" Eve asked, suddenly all nerves.

Eve helped Maggie out of her coat and hung it in the nearby closet.

"Please have a seat," Patrick said, indicating toward the couch. Maggie walked to the couch and eased down with an audible sigh. She wore a gray top with dark pants, a white sweater, and low black boots. She was a bit thick around the waist and had stylishly cut salt-and-pepper hair, a friendly manner and lively, intelligent eyes.

Georgy Boy, ever the friendly animal who loved company, was instantly at Maggie's side with a panting tongue, warm brown eyes and a head lifted, ready to be patted.

"Do you mind the dog?" Patrick asked.

"No, not at all. I have three of my own," Maggie said.

"Can I get you anything?" Eve asked.

"No, thank you. It is Christmas Eve, and I promise I won't stay long."

After everyone was seated, Patrick in the chair and Eve next to Maggie, Eve looked at Maggie with an eager restlessness.

Maggie took in a little breath. "I am Maggie Lott Gantly Fitzwilliam's great-granddaughter."

On reflex, Patrick shot up. "Maggie's great-granddaughter?"

"Yes. I know it must be a surprise, especially for me to show up on Christmas Eve, but I'm here because I was instructed to come by Maggie Fitzwilliam. Of course, I was named after her."

Patrick and Eve could only stare.

Maggie reached into her purse and drew out an old yellow envelope. She handed it to Patrick. "This is addressed to you, Patrick."

Patrick and Eve gawked at it.

Maggie continued. "This letter has been passed down from daughter to daughter since my great grandmother's death at 81 years old in 1966. My great grandmother stated very clearly that whichever daughter was alive on December 24th, 2018, she was to bring this letter to you, Patrick, and to your wife, Eve. Of course, over the years, we all wondered who you two were, and what you would be like. We invented so many stories and we couldn't imagine how Maggie could possibly know anyone in 2018. It was a great mystery to us."

Patrick and Eve exchanged another glance. And then Patrick's hesitant eyes rested on the old letter. He took it, reading the handwritten names and address on the face.

Slowly Patrick turned the envelope over, examining it, imagining Maggie's elegant old hand sealing it. He opened it with care, sliding his thumb along the stubborn old seam. He glanced up at Eve once more. "Should I read it aloud, Eve?"

Eve gave Maggie a side-glance. Patrick noticed Maggie's eager expression.

Eve said, "Perhaps you should read it first, to yourself."

He nodded, lowering himself in the chair. He felt a catch in his throat as he began.

My Dearest Father and Dear Friend Eve:
Well, the years have melted away and I have become an old woman of 80 years. This is Christmas Eve, and it is my birthday. Don't imagine me old and decrepit, stumbling about with a cane and granny glasses. No! I can still dance a waltz or two, if it isn't too lively, and take a couple glasses of Champagne at dinner. I still sing, if only to myself.

So it is 1965 and, speaking of music, I'm quite taken by the new basso nova sound and, of course, I love Elvis Presley. I would love to meet him.

But I must not ramble on. My doctor tells me that my heart is not as strong as it used to be. Well, I told him, "I have lived, Doctor, and so my heart has simply grown tired of all my shenanigans."

The long and the short of it, my dear ones, is that I will not be in this world much longer, which is why I am writing you this letter. I will instruct my daughter, Denise (or Dena as I call her), to ensure that this letter is passed down from daughter to daughter until it is delivered to you on December 24, 2018. I have left them some money in my will with the understanding that if my wishes are not carried out, they will receive nothing. So, my darlings, I am sure you will read this at the right and proper time.

You will recall that you gave me your address just in case I decided to use the lantern and come to you in your time. Well, I never did, did I?

Father, I want you and Eve to know that I had the best of lives, perhaps not one fit for the telling to priests, the pious and young children, but a grand life all the same.

After you both vanished—and what an astounding scene that was—Duncan and I trudged off to Edmonton. We lived together for a time, but just as friends and not as lovers. When I met the sensational and life-grabbing Noah Fitzwilliam, a man a few years older than me but at least 20 years younger in heart, I fell in love. Can you believe it? Yes, I fell head-over-heels in love with that crazy man. He was not the masculine, handsome man you are, Father. Fitz was a rather short, a rather portly and a rather rich man, and he always treated me like a queen. In 1929 when the market crashed, my good husband had shorted the market. He made over one million dollars.

We traveled the world, gambling, tasting the finest wines of Europe, living for a time in Paris, London and

Rome during the roaring 20s, as they became known, and then we finally settled down in Edmonton.

But allow me to back up just a bit because I have always been known for getting ahead of myself. I am, as you know, Father, an impatient woman.

Fitz and I had Dena in 1918, just after the war. We took her with us across the world, but she didn't like any of it. She wanted a settled life, so we left her with one of Fitz's sisters for a time. That seemed to work for a while, although I missed Dena terribly, so we finally returned to Canada. Dena grew up to be a practical woman and eventually found a good man who worked for the government, and they settled down in Washington, DC and had one lovely daughter.

I stayed in touch with Logan Tyler until 1916 when, unfortunately, he was killed in France at the Battle of the Somme. When his letters stopped coming, I persisted in writing to the Canadian government for two years, until I finally received a letter from the War Department confirming that Logan had been killed in action. I was sad and low for many days. I even went to the local cathedral and lit a candle for him. He was a kind man, who only wanted a simple and good life. Do you know what? I still pray for him. Imagine me praying for anyone. But I recall with warm smiles the evening he played his violin and we danced late into the night. I will cherish that memory to my last breath.

But let me move on. After we finally settled in Edmonton, my great love, Fitz, enthusiastically produced many shows for me in and around Edmonton and in other cities in Canada. I was a local star for a time, and that suited me just fine.

I had a son in 1921. We named him Patrick. He was much like you, Father. Not as tall, but broad and handsome. He flew fighter planes during World War II and was seriously wounded in 1944 when his P 51 was shot down over Germany. He spent the rest of the war in a German prison camp. He survived that, but I am sorry to say, he died of war injuries in 1959, when he was only 38 years old. It nearly killed me, Patrick. I'm afraid I spent many nights crying and drinking Champagne.

So, as you see, I have had a full and rich life thanks to you and Eve. Fitz died in 1950 at the age of only 73, and I have missed him daily. His great bear of a laugh and the endless joy he brought to my life are sorely missed, and I am looking forward to seeing him again in the great beyond.

Patrick, Father, please know that I have carried you and Eve in my thoughts and my heart constantly, and I have daily blessed your names. If you hadn't had the courage and the fortitude and the will to return to 1914 to save my life, I would have surely perished by the hand of Big Jim Clancy.

Do you know that after his and Addison Casterbury's deaths, their corrupt organization soon disintegrated? New York City was much the better for it. So, you see, your good works did more than just save me. I dare say, you saved many others.

Now, my dear ones, I must go. I do get fatigued rather easily. My hope is that the two of you also have the best of lives together. Perhaps, just perhaps, we shall meet again in some time past. One never knows.

Finally, please forgive me for what I am about to tell you. I did take possession of that lantern. Logan was happy to be rid of it. Unfortunately, I lost it.

In 1924, at a rather wild party at some vast and spectacular bootlegger's mansion in St. Paul, Minnesota, it was taken from me. I met a famous actress at the time, Lilly Hart, who had come from Los Angeles for the party. We became fast friends and she returned to Edmonton with us.

A few days after our return, we had a bash at our place and, in a Champagne stupor, I retrieved the lantern and told Lilly all about it. We even tried to light it, but something was wrong, and it wouldn't light.

Unfortunately, Lilly must have taken the lantern, because the next morning I discovered that both she and the lantern were missing. I frantically tried to contact her, but I couldn't track her down. And then, tragically, six months later, as I was reading the morning paper, I saw that she had been killed in an auto crash near Santa Monica, California.

I apologize for being so frivolous and irresponsible. I tried several times to find the lantern, but I never did. I am dreadfully sorry for losing it. Perhaps it will show up on your doorstep someday? Who knows, perhaps you and Eve will have to travel back to find it. I'll be here waiting for you if you do.

I send all my love to you both, and I vow that we shall see each other again, here in this world, in a past time, or in some other future world. After all, isn't this world a truly wonderful and mysterious place?

All my love,
Maggie Lott Ganley Fitzwilliam
Edmonton, Canada
December 24, 1965

Patrick lowered the letter and sat for a time in silence. Finally, he got up and presented it to Eve.

As she read it, Patrick stared off into distances—into old worlds and new worlds.

Maggie Kering sat quiet and still, wishing the letter had been read aloud. There was so much she wanted to know about the past.

Eve asked Maggie Kering if she would join them for a Christmas Eve dinner with friends, but she declined, saying she had plans of her own and didn't want to intrude.

"Perhaps then you'll be able to join us for Christmas dinner tomorrow afternoon?" Patrick asked. "Eve and I will be the chefs."

"We would love to have you," Eve said, secretly wondering how she would ever be able to explain Maggie and the letter to her parents.

Maggie offered a sweet smile. "Would my husband be an intrusion?"

"Of course not," Patrick said. "As long as you don't mind being with Eve's parents. They're flying in tomorrow morning."

"Then we would be delighted to join you," Maggie said.

At the front door, as Maggie slipped on her brown leather gloves, she hesitated.

"If I may be so bold... How did my great grandmother know you two would be here at this address when she wrote her letter in 1965? And, as a Gantly, what was your relationship to her?"

Patrick looked at Eve, who looked at Patrick.

Patrick finally spoke up. "We are distantly related, Maggie. As to your great-grandmother knowing we'd be here, some things just can't be explained, and I'm afraid this is one of them."

Maggie smiled. "Well, perhaps in time, as we get to know each other better, everything will come to light."

When she was gone, Patrick sat on the couch reading over parts of the letter repeatedly, his eyes glazed with tears.

"Why didn't Maggie come with us, Eve? We could have had so many good years together."

Eve sat down next to him, taking his hand. "It was her choice, Patrick, and from her letter, it sounds like she had a wonderful life. And think of all the ancestors and the great-grandkids you have now in Minnesota and Canada. We'll go visit them all."

Patrick turned to Eve and his eyes slowly yielded. "Yes, you're right of course. Maggie needed to choose for herself."

"We did good, didn't we, Patrick? Going back in time, I mean. You were right. It was good that we went back and saved Maggie."

As the white winter sun slid behind the hills of New Jersey, a steady snow was falling when Eve, Patrick and Georgy Boy reached the glistening white sledding hill at Riverside Park. Patrick had found an antique Flexible Flyer sled on *eBay,* insisting that they needed to have the true experience of sledding.

Eve sat perched on the front and Patrick behind, his arms wrapped about her.

"You guide it with your feet," Patrick said.

"I know, I know, Patrick. I had one like this when I was a girl. I had the fastest sled in the neighborhood."

"Okay then, Mrs. Gantly, let's go."

Patrick kicked them off and they gathered speed, plunging down the sugary hill, bouncing and rocking off into the snowy night, with Georgy Boy galloping behind. As they ramped and sailed, their laughter rose and blended with the whistling wind, barking dogs, the shouting glee of children, and somebody's wireless speaker playing *Jingle Bells*.

Thank you for taking the time to read *The Christmas Eve Daughter*. If you enjoyed it, please consider telling your friends or posting a short review. Word of mouth is an author's best friend and it is much appreciated.

Thank you,
Elyse Douglas

Other novels by Elyse Douglas that you might enjoy:

The Christmas Diary
The Christmas Eve Letter Book 1
The Lost Mata Hari Ring – A Time Travel Novel
The Christmas Women
The Christmas Town – A Time Travel Novel
Christmas for Juliet
Christmas Ever After
The Summer Letters
The Summer Diary
The Other Side of Summer
www.elysedouglas.com

Printed in Germany
by Amazon Distribution
GmbH, Leipzig